You Me Everything

YOU ME EVERYTHING

CATHERINE ISAAC

THORNDIKE PRESS

A part of Gale, a Cengage Company

GALE
A Cengage Company

Farmington Hills, Mich • San Francisco • New York • Waterville, Maine
Meriden, Conn • Mason, Ohio • Chicago

Copyright © 2018 by Catherine Isaac.
Thorndike Press, a part of Gale, a Cengage Company.

ALL RIGHTS RESERVED
This is a work of fiction. Names, characters, places, and incidents are either the product of the author's imagination or are used fictitiously, and any resemblance to actual persons, living or dead, businesses, companies, events, or locales is entirely coincidental.
Thorndike Press® Large Print Basic.
The text of this Large Print edition is unabridged.
Other aspects of the book may vary from the original edition.
Set in 16 pt. Plantin.

LIBRARY OF CONGRESS CIP DATA ON FILE.
CATALOGUING IN PUBLICATION FOR THIS BOOK
IS AVAILABLE FROM THE LIBRARY OF CONGRESS.

ISBN-13: 978-1-4328-5067-8 (hardcover)

Published in 2018 by arrangement with Penguin Books, an imprint of Penguin Publishing Group, a division of Penguin Random House LLC

Printed in Mexico
1 2 3 4 5 6 7 22 21 20 19 18

For my family

PROLOGUE

*Manchester, England,
2006*

Sometimes life takes the best and worst it has to offer and throws the whole lot at you on the same day.

This probably isn't an uncommon conclusion to reach during childbirth, but in my case, it wasn't the usual cocktail of pain and joy that led me to it. It was that, although I was finally about to meet the tiny human who'd shared my body for nine months, those eight agonizing hours were also spent trying to reach his father on my mobile — to drag him away from whatever bar, club or other woman he was in.

"Did you remember to bring your notes, Jessica?" the midwife asked after I'd arrived at the hospital alone.

"I've got my notes. It's my boyfriend I've mislaid," I said, through an apologetic smile.

7

She glanced up at me from under her eyelashes as I leaned on the reception desk of the delivery suite, waiting for the searing pain in my belly to pass.

"I'm sure he'll be on his way soon." Sweat gathered on the back of my neck. "I've left him a couple of messages." Twelve, to be exact. "He's at a work event. He probably can't get a signal."

At this stage, part of me was still hoping this was true. I always was determined to see the good in Adam, even in the face of clear evidence to the contrary.

"We never used to have men here," she reminded me. "So if we need to do it without Dad, we'll be just fine." *Dad.* I couldn't deny the biological facts, but the title sounded wrong when it was applied to Adam.

The midwife looked reassuringly matronly, with stout legs, a bosom you could stand a potted plant on and the kind of hair that had been in foam curlers overnight. The name on her badge was Mary. I'd known Mary for about three minutes, and already I liked her, which was good given that she was about to examine my cervix.

"Come on, lovely, let's get you to a room."

I went to pick up the overnight bag that the taxi driver had helped me with, but she swooped in and took the handle, staggering under its weight.

"How long are you hoping to stay?" she hooted, and I did my best to laugh until I realized another contraction was on its way. I stood in mute agony, screwing up my eyes but determined not to be the woman who terrified everyone else by screaming the place down.

When the pain subsided, I slowly followed Mary down the overlit corridor, pulling out my phone to check again for messages. There were a dozen texts from my mum and Becky, my closest friend, but still none from Adam.

It wasn't meant to be happening like this.

I didn't want to be on my own.

No matter how worried I'd been about our relationship in recent months, right then I'd have done anything to have him with me, holding my hand and telling me everything was going to be all right.

I'd discovered I was pregnant the day after my twenty-second birthday. Even though it wasn't planned, I'd convinced myself in the nine months that followed that I'd be a confident mum. That suddenly felt like fragile bravado.

"All right, dear?" Mary asked, as we arrived at the door of the labor room.

I nodded silently, despite the real truth: even in her capable hands, I felt alone, terrified and certain that this feeling would continue until Adam arrived to do his brow-patting, hand-clutching duty.

The room was small and functional, with thin patterned curtains that gave it the air of a dated Travelodge. The sky outside was the color of treacle, black and impenetrable, a pearlescent moon reclining into the shadows.

"Hop on," said Mary, patting the bed.

I followed her directions to lie back and open my legs. She then coolly declared, "Going in," before maneuvering her hand up my unmentionables as my eyes popped and I lost the ability to breathe.

"Four centimeters dilated." She straightened up, smiled and snapped off her latex glove as the contraction started building. "You're in labor, Jessica."

"Exciting," I replied, too polite to mention that this didn't feel like a revelation; I'd already christened my kitchen floor with amniotic fluid hours earlier.

"The best thing to do is get on the birthing ball and let gravity help us out. I'm going to check on the lady next door, but don't hesitate to use your call button. Is there anyone else who could join you? A

10

friend? Or your mother?"

Becky didn't live far, but Mum was always the only choice, as humiliating as it had been to call and explain that Adam was AWOL.

"I've got my mum on standby. If I haven't heard from my boyfriend by 2:00 a.m., she's going to drive over."

"Excellent," she said, before leaving me alone with an iPod full of Jack Johnson songs and a gas and air machine that I'd forgotten to ask how to use.

I called Mum on the dot of two. She arrived at six minutes past, in slim-legged jeans and a soft linen blouse, the whisper of Estée Lauder Beautiful clinging to her neck. She was carrying a massive gym bag, which contained her last-minute "birthing kit." This consisted of a compact video camera, a goose down pillow, a tube of toothpaste, a copy of *Woman and Home,* some Neal's Yard hand cream, a bunch of grapes, two large Tupperware boxes containing a selection of recently baked cakes, some pink towels and — I kid you not — a cuddly toy.

"How are you?" she asked anxiously, dragging up a chair as she tucked a wisp of short blond hair behind her ear. She wore the softest hint of makeup; she had good skin so never needed much, and her brilliant blue eyes were luminous.

"Okay. How are you?"

"I'm great. Over the moon to be here, in fact."

Her foot was tapping against the bed as she spoke, the metallic sound clanking through the room. Mum always kept her head in a crisis, but I'd noticed her nervous tics lately; that night her leg had a life of its own.

"It can't have taken you six minutes to drive from home?" I said, trying a suck of the gas and air for the first time, before coughing as it caught at the back of my throat.

"I've been in the car park since midnight. I didn't want to get stuck in traffic."

"If only Adam had been so thoughtful," I muttered.

Her smile faltered. "Have you tried texting him again?"

I nodded and attempted to hide how upset I was. "Yes, but clearly, something was more important than being here."

She reached over and squeezed my fingers. She wasn't used to hearing me sound resentful. I hardly ever got *really* angry with anyone or anything, with the possible exception of our crappy broadband connection.

But you wouldn't have known it that night.

"I hate him," I sniffed.

She shook her head as the pads of her fingertips stroked my knuckles. "No, you don't."

"Mum, you don't know the half of what's been going on lately." I dreaded filling her in, because that would've burst the bubble, the idea that my family life with Adam could ever compare with the one she and Dad had given me. I looked back on my childhood as largely blessed — secure and happy, even accounting for some difficult periods that were by now all in the past.

She exhaled. "Okay. Well, don't get yourself worked up about that now. You're never going to get this moment back. Are you hungry?" She opened up one of the Tupperware boxes.

I managed to smile. "Are you serious?"

"No?" she said, surprised. "I was starving when I had you. I got through half a lemon drizzle cake before my waters had even gone."

My mum was a brilliant birth partner. She made me smile between contractions, kept me calm until everything felt so out of control that I couldn't stop myself from screaming.

"Why haven't they given you something for the pain?" she said under her breath.

"I told them I didn't want an epidural. I did a natural birth plan. And . . . I've done yoga."

"Jess, you're trying to push another human being out of your vagina; I think you need more than breathing exercises and a candle."

She turned out to be right. By the point at which I'd vomited for the umpteenth time, I was in the grip of such incomprehensible agony that I'd have sucked on a crack pipe if it'd been available. A muted sun began to blur through the window, and a different midwife — who'd probably introduced herself earlier, when my mind was on other things — stooped to examine me.

"Sorry, my love, you're too far along for an epidural. You can have a pethidine injection if you want, but this baby is going to be born very soon."

My legs started shaking uncontrollably, the pain catching my breath, robbing my ability to speak properly, or think rationally.

"I just want Adam here. Mum . . . *please.*"

She frantically fumbled with her phone to try to call his number. But she dropped the handset, cursing her clumsiness as she scrambled on the floor, chasing it around like a bar of soap in the bath.

Events after that are vague, because I

wasn't concentrating on phone calls or the needle in my thigh; I was delirious with the terrible and miraculous force of my own body.

It was about a minute and three pushes after the pethidine was administered that my baby made his entrance into the world.

He was a thing of wonder, my boy, with chubby limbs and a perplexed expression as he blinked his eyes and unscrunched his little face when the midwife placed him in my arms.

"Oh my God," gasped Mum. "He's . . ."

"Gorgeous," I whispered.

"Massive," she replied.

I'd always thought of newborn babies as delicate and helpless, but William was a nine-pound, four-ounce bruiser. And he didn't cry, not in those first moments; he just curled into the warm curve of my breast and made everything all right.

Well, almost everything.

As I pressed my lips against his forehead and breathed in his sweet, new scent, the door crashed open. There was Adam, entirely disproving the theory that it's better late than never.

I don't know what was more overpowering as he approached us, the smell of another woman's perfume, or the bitter reek of stale booze. He was still wearing last night's clothes. He'd failed in an attempt to wipe the lipstick off his neck, leaving a violent, slut-pink smudge that started by his ear and ended on his shirt.

I suddenly didn't want him anywhere near me or our baby — no amount of antibacterial hand gel would've changed the fact that he was a complete mess. In more ways than one. I wondered desolately how long ago I'd come to that conclusion.

"Can I . . . can I hold her?" he said, extending his arms.

Mum winced as I drew a sharp breath. "It's a *boy,* Adam."

He looked up, surprised, and withdrew his arms. He sat looking at us, apparently unable to say anything, let alone the right thing.

"You missed it," I said, brushing away the sting of new tears. "I can't believe you missed it, Adam."

"Jess, listen . . . I can explain."

CHAPTER 1

Ten years later,
summer 2016

I don't know when I became so bad at packing. I was good at it once, in the days when I had the time and headspace to stock up on inflatable travel pillows and mini toiletries. It's not volume that's lacking; my old Citroën is bursting. But I have an unshakable feeling that I've forgotten something, or several somethings.

The problem lies in the fact that I didn't make a list. Women of my generation are led to believe that lists are the solution to everything, even if the world around them is falling apart. Right now, I'm beyond lists — there comes a point where there's so much to do that stopping for something as indulgent as *list making* feels like pure folly. Besides, if I've forgotten anything, I can just buy it when we get there — we're only going to rural France, not the Amazon basin.

If my packing has been haphazard, I'm not sure what you'd call William's. The contents of his bag largely involve Haribos found under his bed after a recent sleepover, books with names like *Venomous Snakes of the World,* several water pistols and a selection of heavily spiced toiletries.

He's only recently begun taking an interest in the latter after his friend Cameron decided turning ten was the time to start wearing deodorant to school. I had to gently point out to my son that walking round in a mushroom cloud of Lynx Africa wouldn't get him very far in France without any actual trousers.

I jump into the driver's seat, turn the key and experience the usual flicker of surprise when the engine starts. "Are you sure you've got everything?" I ask.

"Think so." The flare of excitement on his face makes my heart twist a little. He's been like this ever since I told him we'd be spending the summer with his dad. I lean over to give him a quick kiss on the side of his head. He tolerates it, but the days of him flinging his arms round me to declare, "You're the best mum I've ever had," are long gone.

William is tall for his age, gangly almost, despite an enormous appetite and the recent

18

obsession he's developed with Domino's. He got his height from his father, as well as those liquid brown eyes, skin that tans easily and dark hair that curls at the nape of his neck.

As I'm five feet four, it won't be long before he towers above me, at which point he'll probably look even less like he belongs to me. My skin is pale, freckled and prone to turning pink in the slightest heat. The blond hair that skims my shoulders doesn't curl like my son's, but it's not straight either; it has a kink that used to annoy me in the days when that was all I had to worry about.

"Who's going to look after the house while we're away?" he asks.

"It doesn't really need looking after, sweetheart. Just someone to pick up the post."

"What if someone burgles it?"

"They won't."

"How do you know?" he asks.

"If anyone was going to break into a house on this street, ours would be the last one they'd choose."

I bought our tiny terrace in south Manchester thanks to a financial leg up from my dad shortly after I'd had William and before the neighborhood became fortuitously trendy.

I've never joined in the ironic bingo nights in the falafel bar at the end of the road and must've only bought one quinoa-laced sourdough since the artisan bakery opened. But I'm all for these kind of places, as they've made house prices soar.

It does mean, however, that I am probably the only thirty-three-year-old single parent on a salary like mine who lives round here. I teach creative writing at our local sixth form college, which has always offered more in the way of job satisfaction than financial rewards.

"Jake Milton was burgled," William tells me somberly as we turn down the street. "They took all his mum's jewelry, his dad's car and Jake's Xbox."

"Really? That's awful."

"I know. He'd got to the final level on *Garden Warfare,*" he sighs, shaking his head. "He'll just *never* get that back."

It will take four or five hours to reach the south coast to catch our ferry, but we're leaving earlier than we otherwise would, so we can make a stop-off, not far from our house.

We arrive at Willow Bank Lodge ten minutes later and pull into the small car park at the front. The building looks like an oversize Lego house from outside — with uniform mud brown bricks and a grey tiled roof. But then, nobody chooses a care home for the architecture.

I key in the code for the two doors and sign us in as we're hit by the smell of over-roasted meat and mushy vegetables. Inside, the place is clean, bright and well maintained, even if its interior designer must've been color-blind. The swirly wallpaper is a thick avocado green, the floor covered in patterned navy and red carpet tiles, and the skirting boards tinted with a marmalade varnish that someone misguidedly must've thought looked natural.

The sounds of lunchtime drift out from beyond a set of double doors and the television area, so we head in that direction, instead of turning down the corridor towards Mum's room.

"Are you all right there, Arthur?" I ask gently, as one of the long-term residents wanders out of the bathroom with an expression like he's just stepped into Narnia. He straightens his back defensively.

"I'm looking for my pans. Have you taken my pans?"

"Not us, Arthur. Why don't you come and try the dining room?" I'm about to rescue him before he steps into the broom cupboard, when the double doors open and one of the nursing staff, Raheem, appears to offer him a reassuring arm and guide him away.

"Hiya," says William. In his midtwenties and of Somalian descent, Raheem also owns an Xbox, so they always have plenty to discuss.

"Hey, William. Your grandma's about to have lunch. There might be some pineapple turnover left if you fancy it?"

"Yeah, okay." My son never declines an offer of food, unless it's something I've gone to enormous effort to make, when he invariably looks at it like I've presented him with a plate of steaming industrial waste.

As Arthur shuffles through the door, followed by Raheem, the figure of a man appears in their place. The skin around his temples is etched with years of spiraling pressure, which has surely had a more potent effect on his health than the fact that he's a reformed alcoholic.

"Granddad!" William's face erupts into a smile, and my dad's pale grey eyes sparkle into life.

CHAPTER 2

It's one of the small miracles of my world that, even in the face of unimaginable strain, every bit of my dad smiles when his grandson is around. "Are you all set, William?"

"Yep. Packed and on our way, Granddad."

Dad ruffles his thick, curly hair and steps back to examine him. "I could've taken you for a cut before you left."

"But I like it long."

"You look like a burst cushion." William chuckles, even though he's heard this quip more times than he could count.

"How many minutes in four and a half hours?" Dad challenges him.

"Hmm. Two hundred and . . . seventy."

"Good lad." He pulls him in briefly for a hug.

That my son is on a gifted and talented register for maths is not something for which I can take credit. Arithmetic is definitely not my forte, and the only figures

23

at which Adam excels are of the hourglass variety.

But then my dad, an accountant, was always more of a father to William than Adam ever was. My parents' semi is only ten minutes away from where we live, and it was a second home to William before he started school; the place he'd puzzle over jigsaws with my dad and bake fairy cakes with Mum.

Even later on, it was Dad who'd wait at the school gates and take William back to their place to supervise homework or ferry him to karate club, while I finished up at work.

Everything's changed in the last couple of years.

My mum is no longer the grandma she once was, someone who, seven or eight years ago, would be the first in line to shoot down the big, wavy slide in our local soft play center with William on her knee. She was never concerned about looking like a big kid; she just kicked off her shoes and got stuck in, as William shrieked with delight and other women her age remained at the sidelines, sipping their lattes.

"Let me give you something to spend," Dad says, rooting in his trouser pocket.

"You don't need to do that," William

murmurs unconvincingly as my father thrusts a twenty-pound note in his hand.

"Buy yourself a comic on the ferry."

"Could I get some Coke?"

"Of course," Dad replies, before I can say definitely not.

"Thanks, Granddad. I really appreciate it." William skips into the dining room to find his grandma, while I hold back to talk to Dad.

"You should've gone straight off for your ferry, love," he tells me. "You didn't need to stop here on the way."

"Of course I did. I wanted to give Mum lunch before I go."

"I'll do that. I was only popping out to buy a paper."

"No, I'd like to do it, if you don't mind."

He nods, inhaling slowly. "Well, listen. Try and relax in France. You need a holiday."

I smile dubiously. "Is that what you're calling it?"

"You'll enjoy it if you *let* yourself. And make sure you do. For your mum's sake, if it makes you feel any better. She really wants this, you know."

"I still think it's too long to be away."

"We've lived with this for a decade, Jess. Absolutely nothing is going to happen in five weeks."

25

Mum is on the far side of the dining room, next to the open patio window, with William sitting next to her, chatting away. It's the plum spot at this time of day, when the sun is high and she can feel a cool summer breeze against her skin.

She is in her wheelchair, wearing the turquoise dress I bought her from Boden a few months ago, and in a position you could call sitting, although that implies keeping still.

In reality, Mum is rarely still these days. Thanks to her hefty medication though, she no longer jerks as violently as she used to.

Still, the drugs do not work miracles, as I am painfully aware.

So she squirms and twists, her facial features and bony limbs contorting into improbable shapes. She is thin these days, joints protruding from her elbows and knees, her cheekbones so pronounced that I sometimes look at her and think her eyes seem too big for her face. Her hands are gnarled too, twisted beyond her years. She looked young for her age once. Now, you'd never know she was only fifty-three.

"Hi, Mum." I bend down to give her a

hug, squeezing her a little longer than usual.

When I pull back, I look at her drooping mouth to see if she can return the smile. It takes a long time for her to respond to me, but eventually she manages a disjointed: "Eh . . . sweetheart."

I can still understand Mum most of the time, though I'm one of the few who can. She only speaks in three- or four-word sentences, and they're always slurred, her voice hoarse and quiet.

"I see you've managed to get the best spot. Everyone will be jealous."

A long interval follows, during which Mum visibly searches for words. "Bribed them," she says eventually, and I laugh.

A new member of staff appears and places Mum's lunch on the table, before unfolding a large plastic bib and tying it gently round her neck. I reach across to smooth it down, but her left arm continues to flick it upwards. It floats downwards momentarily, before flying off again.

I consider picking up the baby spoon at the side of her plate but decide to leave it in case Mum wants to have a go at feeding herself. She hardly ever does these days, though she was full of indignation when anything else was first suggested.

It's been nearly a year since she moved

into Willow Bank Lodge. We all wanted her to stay at home for as long as she possibly could, but it became too difficult, even when Dad set up a bed for her downstairs. Dad still works, which kind of gets in the way of being a twenty-four-hour carer — it had become obvious to everyone she was going to need more than only him, ideally in a place where just getting to the bath didn't represent a life-threatening journey. And she's never short of visitors here. In fact, she has a small circle of friends who've helped her through every dark moment of the last ten years. Her best friend Gemma comes every weekend, usually with a new audiobook or a batch of the deformed cherry scones she calls her "signature dish."

"Excited?" Mum asks William.

"I can't wait!" he replies. "Dad's planning loads for us, Grandma. We're having the best cottage, aren't we, Mum? We're going kayaking and rock climbing, and he's going to let me help him do some DIY jobs."

I seriously worry about my mum's expectations of this trip, which was all her idea. Not that I was surprised when she suggested it, adding rather dramatically that it was her "dying wish." She openly admits this is a surefire guarantee she'll get her own way.

After Adam and I split up, Mum was as

furious with him as I was and understood why I wanted to keep him at arm's length. But while she never had any aspirations about us getting back together again, she did assume, or at least hope, that William would have some kind of relationship with his father.

Then Adam moved to France, and it became apparent that wasn't going to happen.

Adam is not a neglectful father, strictly speaking. He pays his maintenance on time, remembers William's birthday and Skypes when he says he will. But our son is no more than a small piece in the jigsaw of Adam's colorful life. They see each other twice or three times a year, if that. And I'm not even sure Adam would protest any longer at the accusation that he was uninterested.

Mum has always had a bee in her bonnet, not only about this lack of contact, but about the fact that I've never said or done anything about it. I willingly let Adam drift away. If I'm honest, I welcomed it. I had enough love for William for both of us.

I'm fairly sure she never envisaged Adam and me sitting round the dinner table every Sunday for William's sake, hating each other's guts as we passed the gravy, but she has banged on for years that he needs a "real" relationship with his dad. Perhaps it's because she was adopted, so never knew her own mother and father. Either way, these days Adam lives a luxurious lifestyle in the Dordogne, while we live in a two-up two-down terrace in Manchester, and the fact that there's a fancy bread shop on the corner of the road doesn't bring our circumstances any closer. Still, I hear what she's saying. I don't agree, but I hear it. And every time I look at her these days and think about what she has to contend with, I'm reminded that I am hardly in a position to dig my heels in. So I emailed Adam and suggested we pay him a visit. I suspect he nearly keeled over in shock.

Anyway, if I could at least get them, I don't know, *bonding,* then I'd feel as though I'd achieved something that would give my mum a sliver of comfort. Plus, I've got backup, at least for some of the time when we're there. My friend Natasha is joining us for a few weeks, then Becky and her husband and kids will arrive.

"I . . . love France," Mum pipes up, as her eyes land falteringly on William. "Take pictures."

We had a handful of French holidays when I was William's age. We stayed in a mobile home on the same campsite year after year

— it was heaven, a new world of endlessly sunny days and breakfasts that involved pastry with *actual chocolate* inside.

"Try a pedalo," Mum says. "Your mum . . . loved them."

I feel my throat tighten at the memory of Mum and me pedaling round the lake at the edge of the campsite, giggling together in the sunshine.

As William starts babbling on, something about a bunk bed, I have to look away to stop either of them seeing the film of tears on my eyes. I swallow hard and remind myself that we'll only be gone for a few weeks. It'll do nobody any favors if I start crying now, no matter how much this is making my chest ache.

I look down and realize Mum hasn't touched the baby spoon. So I pick it up and tentatively scoop some of the mush, raising it to her mouth.

"Silver service," she mumbles, and I let out a snort.

CHAPTER 3

We begin our 825-mile, 28-hour journey in
high spirits, singing along tunelessly to a
playlist that includes everything from the
Beatles to Avicii. We chat about what France
was like when I was little — the soft, sandy
beaches, the dreamy ice creams, how Mum
taught me to master a mean game of black-
jack for francs and centimes.

William plays on my iPad for a while,
hunched over the screen until I become
concerned he'll get stuck like that and
finally pry it off him. Instead, we put on the
audiobook of *Billionaire Boy* by David Wal-
liams and are soon laughing so much that
my cheeks hurt. Then a particular story line
crops up involving a character who dates a
glamour model. I'm not even sure he knows
what one is. All I know is that I have a
similar feeling to when he asked me to
explain where babies came from earlier this
year. I rushed out and bought a book ad-

dressing this and other related issues, suggesting he read it by himself, before asking me any questions. That way we'd avoid any embarrassment. "Why would I be embarrassed?" he asked innocently, forcing me to try to sound cheerfully relaxed when reading out phrases like, "and that's what some people call *wanking.*"

By the time we get onto the ferry, William is feeling significantly less inclined to talk. His cheeks are pale as we park in the vaults of the ship and make our way upstairs to sit by the window.

"We'll get a good view from here," I remark brightly, to which his response is: "I'm going to puke." He chucks up seven times over the course of the six-hour overnight trip — the one we're supposed to be sleeping on — and emerges from the ferry looking like that child in *The Exorcist*. We stop at the first picnic area we encounter on French soil and wait for his nausea to pass, sipping water as we watch the stream of British families attempting to drive the wrong way at a roundabout.

William sleeps for the rest of the journey, waking only for pee breaks as we speed along the motorway. This leaves me alone with my thoughts until we reach the Dordogne, crisscrossed with woodland and fields, and we slice through the countryside, brief visitors to dozens of sleepy hamlets dotted with pots of fiery geraniums and creamy stone houses with shuttered windows.

Despite the beauty of the landscape, I can't stop dwelling on Mum, haunted by the same thoughts that have left me so anxious that — for the first time in my life — I started taking antidepressants earlier this year. I've never thought of myself as the kind of person who'd need medicinal help for her mood. I'd always thought of myself as *fun*. The first to put on a silly hat at Christmas, or leap up and butcher a song on karaoke, or join in one of William's water pistol fights. The most I'd ever need to get over a bad day was a Magnum ice cream, with an occasional pinot grigio chaser, while work appraisals highlighted my "boundless energy and popularity with the students" — and I never even had to pay anyone to say that.

But since Mum was admitted to Willow Bank, as great as I think the place is, there's been a creeping change in me. Six months ago it went off the scale. Not that most people can tell. I put on a good show of being the same old Jess. But inside, things are different.

What started out as an understandable level of worry took on a life of its own as Mum's deterioration accelerated. Depression was the wrong word for it. It was a crushing anxiety, an inability to think about anything other than a future that seemed bleaker the harder life became for my poor mum.

The pills have helped, even though I still don't like the idea of being on them. They haven't changed the fundamental fact that kicked it all off: that my mum is in a home, slowly losing her grip on the person she is. And there's not a thing anyone can do about it.

CHAPTER 4

As we're surrounded by serried rows of walnut trees and swirls of lush foliage, our GPS finally announces that we have reached our destination. Given that we're miles from anywhere, our GPS is very clearly talking crap.

I root in the glove compartment for the map I'd hoped I wouldn't have to use and, after several wrong turns, find my way to a junction pointing to Château de Roussignol. I crunch onto a sandy driveway, as the flutter of my heart makes me wonder for a moment whether I'm actually pleased at the idea of being on holiday. I suppose it is allowed, even if it does mean being around Adam.

There was a point when I hated him, but that's not an emotion that comes naturally to me. I found it exhausting.

So I've been the definition of civilized for a long time — smiling, for William's sake,

36

when he'd arrive to pick him up; exclaiming "how fantastic!" when our son would return extolling the gastronomic virtues of the McDonald's Happy Meal to which he'd been treated.

Even if I did want to waste time and energy resenting Adam, I don't have it in me with everything else going on. These days, I'm numb to him. I go along with the pretense that he's in France because that's where work has taken him, not because he never wanted to bother with anything as mundane as monogamy and fatherhood. My son stirs and sits up, rubbing his eyes as we are rewarded with our first glimpse of Château de Roussignol. I've only seen it in pictures, in every state of renovation, right from the beginning when it was a neglected wreck.

That was in the days before William was old enough to talk, when Adam would email me intermittently, attaching pictures of the château. Everyone thought he was mad when he first bought it.

You could tell there was a grand building somewhere beyond the thickets of overgrown bushes and unkempt gardens. But it had no electricity, mice under the floorboards and a sanitation system from the Dark Ages. But Adam, for all his faults, was always single-minded enough to make it work.

As the emails dropped into my inbox each month for three years, I got an insight I never asked for and never wanted into his new life: his hours of physical toil, his obsessive approach to planning, the ludicrously ambitious vision he had for the place. I worried endlessly about the financial risk he was taking and how it would affect his ability to contribute to the cost of raising William, without which we wouldn't have survived in the early days.

I read the emails with a mixture of intrigue, jealousy, anger and despair. But with hindsight I think his main motivation for sending them was merely an almost childlike need to prove that he was really making something of himself.

When the château was nearing completion and our son approached his third birthday, it was apparent Adam had managed to pull it off.

I refused to let myself be bitter, at least not about his success, which he's worked hard for. Though I'll admit I could never *quite* believe how quickly he started dating someone else after our split — while I was adjusting to life with sore nipples, no sleep and the idea that a successful day meant brushing my teeth before 3:00 p.m.

"Are we here?" William asks, brightening. "Wow, it's amazing, isn't it?"

"Sure is. Your dad's done a great job."

The château is disarmingly beautiful, more of a French manor house than my idea of a castle, but with all of the grandeur and neoclassical glamour you could wish for.

It's three stories high, with a silvery grey roof that slopes towards the biscuit hues of its walls and huge windows, flanked by elaborate shutters painted the color of seashells. Two ancient stone steps with an intricate wrought iron bannister lead to an oversize arched doorway. A high ivy-strewn balcony overlooks the graveled driveway and feathered cypress trees. Pots of brightly colored flowers line the outside of the building.

We bump along in silence, the scent of thyme and bellflowers hanging in the air as the only sounds to be heard are the chirrup of nightingales and soft rustle of the breeze.

"I can't wait to see Dad," William says. "Is he coming to meet us?"

"He's going to try. He told us to head to reception as soon as we arrived."

Adam swore that he would rush out and throw his arms round William the second we appeared, but I'm playing this down. Given that this is Adam we're talking about — and that he hasn't responded to the text I sent an hour ago when we stopped for petrol — I'm not prepared to risk it. I turn off the engine and open the door.

"Let's go and see if we can find him," I suggest, swinging my legs out of the car. "He won't recognize you. You must've grown two inches since he last saw you."

We've only seen Adam in the flesh once since Christmas, when he was staying in London at his new girlfriend Elsa's place. Like many of the women Adam has dated since me, Elsa is several years younger than he is and is positively breathless in his presence, at the mercy of a twinkly look from those brown eyes.

Most of the time, I find it hard to remember feeling that way about him myself, but logic tells me I must have, because we were together for more than three years, in love for at least some of that time, and managed to make a baby together, albeit by accident.

That was before I realized that when Adam had said he'd never wanted to be a father, he really meant it.

He was the first to admit he wasn't cut out to be the kind of father I had. My dad was far from perfect, but his love still shone through in every hour he spent playing with my dollhouse with me or, when I grew up, teaching me to drive. That kind of thing didn't appeal to Adam, even after fatherhood had become not a lifestyle decision but an unavoidable reality.

All of which is why I had to end our relationship. It was one of the hardest things I've ever done. But I had no choice.

CHAPTER 5

Stone steps lead us up to the heavy set of doors and into a cool reception hall tiled in weathered stone.

We approach a long, ancient-looking desk upon which sits a glass bowl of billowing, heavily scented white blooms and a snowy blotting pad. The chair behind it is empty, which William takes as his cue to ping the silver bell several times.

We're greeted by a young woman wearing a short black skirt, semisheer white blouse and ballet pumps. She has plump, dewy skin, gleaming teeth and long blond hair scraped back like the tail on a dressage pony.

"Can I help you?" She's English, with a high, confident voice that suggests privilege and breeding. I'd put her in her mid-twenties. She's not skinny by any means, but not a bit of her wobbles, except the bits that are meant to. They wobble quite a bit.

"We're booked into one of the cottages.

The name's Pendleton. Jessica."

Her face breaks into the sort of smile you'd expect on hearing the news that there are no calories in chocolate Easter eggs. "Jess! I'm Simone."

She puts down her pen, marches round the desk and throws her arms round me. This strikes me as quite an approach to customer service, particularly given that I'm getting this holiday for free.

"And you must be William!"

William shuffles in his spot. "Yes."

She keeps grinning. "You *really* look like your dad."

He looks pleased. "Oh."

"Honestly, you're the spitting image. Just gorgeous." William's cheeks are now crimson. "Well, I'm over the moon to meet you both. And William, I'm sure I'll get to know you better, because I've managed to persuade Adam that we should start some children's activities this summer, and *I'll* be organizing them."

William grins again. In fact, you could put a pencil in the dimples in his cheeks and it'd stay put. "If you like soccer, you're in the right place. Would you like me to sign you up?"

William is the only child in his class, and probably in the entire eighty-nine-year history of his school, who is not even vaguely interested in the game. The closest he's ever come to a sporting achievement is joining the school debate team.

"Um . . . yes," he replies. I do a double take.

"What team do you support?"

He swallows. "Manchester."

"City or United?" she asks.

"Um . . . both."

She giggles, and so does he. She returns to the desk and clicks on her computer. "Right, let's get you checked into your cottage." As luxurious as the château is, I'm glad not to be staying there, where I know Adam has his office. It feels too close for comfort.

"There's a third person booked in with you too, is that right?"

"That's my friend Natasha, but she's not joining us for another week or so."

"Ah, of course. Well, the rooms are all ready. I can take you over there now."

She disappears into an office to grab a key, then tells us to follow her outside, back into incandescent sunshine. There, she leaps into a golf cart as William and I slip into my car to follow her.

"Well, she was friendly, wasn't she?" I say.

"Yes, and she smelled lovely," William

replies enthusiastically, to which I can't think of an appropriate answer.

The road snakes around the château to a beautiful pool, dotted with sunflower yellow loungers and matching umbrellas. There are a handful of young families there, toddlers in Breton stripe surf suits and kids who look William's age, splashing in the deep end.

It is overlooked by a terraced bar area, with a handful of tables and chairs, shaded by a canopy of climbing honeysuckle in full, scented bloom. On the far side, I can see a tennis court, a sports pitch and a Crayola-colored play area, all flanked by well-kept gardens and romantic beds of rambling roses and daisies.

I spot a signpost to "Les Écuries" — The Stables — as I follow Simone's cart towards a wooded area. The temperature drops in the shade of the trees, and after a short drive we reach a small car park next to a clutch of stone buildings with pale blue shutters and individual patios full of white geraniums arranged around an attractive courtyard.

"It's gorgeous," I tell Simone as we cross the dusty courtyard to the door right at the end. "How many cottages are there?"

"Twenty-one. Some of them are two bedroom, others three. They're not all in the stable block though — the old servants' quarters on the other side of the grounds have been renovated too." She leans in and whispers: "These are the nicest though. And they're only a few minutes' walk to the château if you take the path through the woods."

She slides a cast iron key into a heavy wooden door and pushes it open. Inside, the cottage is simple and rustic, with a pale tiled floor throughout and an open-plan living room and kitchen. The dominant feature is a big, old-fashioned fireplace in front of which two small blue sofas are arranged. There's a big dining table and a functional but sweet-looking kitchen, with a deep ceramic sink, cast iron pots hanging on the wall and worktops made of thick slabs of oak. The bedrooms are whitewashed and beamed, with pretty patterned bedspreads and enamel vases.

"It's lovely. Thank you," I say as William lays claim to his bedroom.

"Adam will be so glad you like it," she replies.

"So . . . where is he?"

"Oh! I was meant to say: he had something on this afternoon," she replies vaguely. "He wanted to be here when you arrived, but it was unavoidable." I bite the inside of my mouth and nod politely. Somehow, it always is.

CHAPTER 6

"This car isn't going to unpack itself," I say to William, after Simone has gone. "If I drive it to the door, will you help me?"

"Just let me finish this," he murmurs, his forehead poised three inches from the iPad.

"What are you watching?" I ask, peering over his shoulder.

"The Woman in Black."

"When did you download that? Surely that's too scary for you?"

"Mum, it's only a 12A," he sighs.

"Is it?"

"Yes."

Age ten is a strange milestone. William is very much a child but showing alarming glimmers of his future as a teenager. On the one hand, I've explained the facts of life to him. On the other, he still goes along with the idea of Santa (though I'm pretty sure he's humoring me).

"Just don't come running to me when you

get nightmares," I tell him.

"Mum. I'm *not* going to have nightmares."

"One minute, okay? Then I need you." He doesn't answer. "William?"

"Yep. No problem."

I head outside, feeling mildly dizzy from heat and tiredness as I pull the car up next to the cottage, then jump out and open the boot. I gaze inside, wondering how I managed to get all that stuff in there. I'm not even sure how legal it is to have this much clogging up the back windscreen. I gently click the lock and, quickly realizing my error, throw my body against the boot door in order to prevent the whole lot from falling out. As sweat beads on my brow, I tentatively begin to pull out the contents, until I'm surrounded by detritus and aware that I've still got a picnic basket, twelve paperbacks and my four-pound dumbbells to go.

"William?" I call out, not entirely expecting him to rush to my aid. *"WILLIAAAM?"*

"I'd recognize those dulcet tones anywhere."

I spin around and feel my neck prickle at the sight of Adam walking towards me. "Oh. Hello," I mumble.

"Let me help." He flings a bouquet of pretty blue flowers on the patio table, followed by a brown paper bag.

"I'm fine, honestly," I insist, but he dives in anyway and takes the strain.

"I'll hold it, you pull out some stuff and we'll see if we can manage this without a forklift."

By the time we have an enormous pile on the ground and there's no longer a danger of anything tumbling out, I register the turned-up corner of Adam's mouth.

"Have you brought *everything* you own?" He picks up one of my mini dumbbells and starts pumping it. They're the only thing between me and bingo wings, but I'm not going to explain that, so I simply snatch it out of his hand.

"There's not *that* much. It's deceptive because my car is really small. And there *are* two of us — for five weeks. We *needed* stuff."

He lifts up William's popcorn maker. "Is this for emergencies?"

"That isn't mine."

You only have to look at him to see that Adam eats the kind of fresh, ripe food that makes your eyes gleam, enjoys a good red wine, gets lots of exercise and likes the warmth of the sun on his skin. It takes only the faintest prompt for him to smile widely, and there are no signs of stress on his brow. His dark hair is half an inch longer than in the days when he had an office job and now curls loosely onto his tanned forehead.

"You're looking well," I say, politely.

He seems slightly taken aback, before casting his eye over me. "You too, Jess." I turn away before he can see the heat in my cheeks.

Adam peers into the boot and picks up the facts-of-life book. I'm baffled about how this ended up in the car; surely no ten-year-old needs to know any more detail about the sprouting of pubic hairs than he's already read.

"You should've told me if you needed anything explained, Jess," Adam continues, flicking through it. "I'd have been happy to offer some insight."

"Ho ho."

He continues to flick. "I take it this is for William?"

"Good guess."

He sighs. "It only feels like I was pushing him on the swings five minutes ago. Anyway, sorry I wasn't here when you arrived. I was sidetracked."

I feel my jaw tighten but remind myself what I'm here for. "That's okay. Thanks for putting us in such a nice cottage. I know they're in demand in the summer."

"I'm glad you like it. Oh . . . I got him a

couple of things." He walks to the table and picks up the paper bag, before returning and handing it to me. "Some sweets and a few tops."

I pull out a T-shirt. It's so small it would be snug on a garden gnome.

"That's lovely. Have you kept the receipt, in case it doesn't fit?"

"Oh. Not sure." For a brief moment he looks so much like his twenty-one-year-old self, all contradictions and charisma.

"Why don't you go and surprise William so you can give them to him yourself?" I suggest. "He's in the bedroom."

A heartbeat passes before he nods and says, "I will." He goes to head to the door, then stops and picks up the bouquet from the table, before thrusting it towards me, straightening out the stems. I take it from him uncomfortably.

"That's very thoughtful of you. Thanks," I mutter, realizing how unsettling it is when he tries to be nice to me. "Go on," I add, nodding to the cottage. "He's dying to see you."

CHAPTER 7

I'm not sure how I imagined my son's reunion with his father as this trip approached. Given how excited William is and how long they've been apart, a bit of me pictured them in a field bounding towards each other in slow motion, like the stars of a bad 1970s perfume advert.

In the event, the reality falls some way short, which I realize when I spot Adam creeping round the side of the stable block.

"What are you doing?" I ask, following him.

"Shhhhh," he says, finger to his lips before he peeks through the bedroom window. "BOO!"

"ARGGGHHHH! MUM!"

I look through the window in time to see William crashing off the top bunk and onto the floorboards. I head to the front door as he scrambles out.

"Something crept up on me through the

53

window!" he blathers, clearly convinced supernatural forces are at work.

"William, calm down. It was your dad." Being an arse.

His shoulders deflate as Adam appears from around the corner. "Oh, William. I'm *sorry,*" he says, suppressing his amusement as our son stands in mute mortification.

I nudge him. "Go and give your dad a hug."

He steps forward, and Adam launches himself at him, grabbing his skinny torso and pulling him into his chest. "Hello, you."

William looks up and blinks. "I didn't realize it was you, Dad. I wasn't *actually* scared though." You can still almost see his heart pounding out from his bony chest.

"Don't worry about it," Adam says, failing to realize that this was his cue to apologize. "So how was your journey? Your mum texted and said you were puking the whole way."

William scowls at me. "Not the *whole* way. Just a bit."

"Well, you're here now. What do you think of the place?"

"It's brilliant," he says, suddenly animated. "I love the bunk bed. My friend Jack has got one."

"Lucky him."

Then they stand there awkwardly, three feet apart, and it becomes painfully obvious that this *might* be the singular thing they have in common to talk about all holiday.

"So," Adam says, clapping his hands.

"So," William repeats.

"Glad to be off school?"

"Definitely."

"You like school," I point out.

"I know, but I'd prefer to be here."

"Is maths still your favorite subject?" Adam asks.

William thinks for a moment. "Hmm. I think I like history better. We've been learning about Queen Victoria this term. It's quite sad actually. When her husband, Albert, died, she missed him so much that she had a plaster cast made of his hand so she could hold it." He doesn't pause for breath. "And that's not the only fascinating thing about the Victorians," William continues earnestly, before proceeding to give Adam a five-minute lecture covering everything from medical advances at the end of the nineteenth century to the subjugation of women.

"Wow. I never realized I knew so little about diphtheria," Adam concludes flatly.

"I can tell you some more if you like," William offers.

I glare at Adam, making it clear he needs to respond carefully. "Yeah. I'd like that."

William smiles. "I'm going to go and get my iPad," he says, returning to the cottage.

"I think you'll find it's *my* iPad," I call after him.

Adam picks up a holdall and heads inside with it. "So I thought we could have dinner tonight with some of the team who work here. I can't wait for everyone to meet William. And you, of course."

I follow him in as he puts the bag down and then doesn't move. "I'm fine with the rest of the stuff. Thanks for helping," I say.

"No problem." He still doesn't move. "It's good to have you here, Jess."

I nod briskly. "Well, William can't wait to spend some time with you."

He looks as though he's suddenly remembered something he should already have asked about. "How's your mum?"

I feel my ribs tense. "She's not brilliant." I unzip the bag and start to unpack it onto the table. "You probably wouldn't recognize her these days."

"I'm really sorry. It must be hard for you."

"It is, Adam," I say, deciding to change the subject. "So, I met Simone."

"Oh, did you?"

"When did you stop seeing Elsa?"

He freezes. "How did you know I'd stopped seeing Elsa?"

I look up. "I presume Simone *is* your new girlfriend?"

"Is it that obvious?"

"I can read you like a book. And not a very complicated one."

"It's a good thing I'm not the sensitive type," he laughs, waving as he heads towards the door.

I watch the way the contours of his back move through his T-shirt, as he puts his hands in his pockets and walks away with what can only be described as a swagger.

"Don't worry, Adam. Nobody could ever accuse you of that."

CHAPTER 8

Dinner takes place round a long communal dining table on the terrace behind the château.

William and I arrive as its old walls are bathed in the rose gold light of a setting sun, the air heavy with the scent of herbs and citronella.

The surface of the pool is silky and silent, and the loungers have been arranged into neat rows. There are a handful of families on the other side of the terrace sharing large plates of green bean salads and duck breasts, as wineglasses clink and the ringing laughter of young children drifts into the sky. I take my place at a long table dotted with twinkling tea lights and accept a glass of pastis so cold it beads with condensation.

Among those gathered this evening are several older French staff members, including the groundsman Jean-Luc and an elderly couple called Monsieur and Madame Blanchard, from whom Adam bought the château all those years ago. It had been in their family for generations, but for the last decade they'd struggled to maintain it, meaning their hopes to open it as a hotel never materialized, until it was bought by Adam. Although largely retired, they are both excellent cooks so return once or twice a week to apply their skills in the kitchen and give lessons to guests, even if Adam jokes that he insisted they hang around to make sure he doesn't make a mess of the place.

There are also four young Brits and their French counterparts who have the air of a group of gap year students, all ankle tattoos and travel anecdotes. Adam slots in with them unfeasibly well. At his age, my dad had a mortgage, family and the sort of accountancy job from which you don't come up for air until you hit sixty-five.

But here, Adam can be twenty-one forever, with the sun always shining, the girls young and eager to please. Not that it's just the girls who are taken by him. He's treated like a cross between a cool older brother and a benign dictator, holding court as the booze flows. Before long, the searing heat of the day gives way to a balmy night, and we're illuminated by an orange moon, candlelight and the blue glow from beneath the water.

The food is served in a relaxed French style, starting with crisp mixed salad leaves and a charcuterie platter with dry cured meats, mousses and sliced, smoked duck breast, all served on a slate board.

"What are they?" asks William, examining the salad. He's wearing one of the T-shirts Adam bought him, and it's so tight under the armpits it's almost cutting off his circulation.

"*Gésiers.* Try some — they're delicious," Adam says, spooning some on his son's plate.

William scrunches up his nose. "But what are *gésiers*?"

"Gizzards. Part of a goose's digestive tract, if you want specifics, but I'll admit they don't sound appetizing when you put it like that." He grins. William grimaces, and I point him in the direction of the salami instead, assuring him that it's just like the stuff he eats on a pizza, only better.

"Adam tells me you're a lecturer," Simone says, lifting a glass to her lips.

"Yes, I teach creative writing at a sixth form college."

"How fascinating. Do you enjoy it?"

"I love it," I reply, which is a default position. It's too complicated to explain that I was once passionate about my work, until the start of this year when I was feeling so low that I wondered if I'd actually enjoy *anything* again.

"You must have to juggle, being a *single mother.*" She puts a peculiar emphasis on the two final words.

"Yeah, life's busy," I agree. "Plus my mum's not well, so she can't help out like she used to."

"Oh dear. Fingers crossed she'll be on the mend soon," she says breezily.

I smile and nod, wondering afterwards if this might be the most British thing I've ever done: not wanting to blight small talk with something as inconvenient as an incurable disease.

"You know, you really remind me of my mum," Simone says all of a sudden.

I look up, surprised. "Oh. I hope your mum's Angelina Jolie." I grin, but she looks at me blankly.

"She's got lots going on too. When women reach a certain age, they have loads of commitments, don't they? My mum's rushed off her feet. That's why I'm determined to make the most of my twenties before I get tied down with responsibilities and stretch marks." She smiles, then catches herself.

61

"Not that I'm suggesting you've got stretch marks. Oh, that sounded *terrible,* didn't it?"

"Not at all," I reassure her. "And anyway: guilty as charged."

Later, when Simone excuses herself to go to the ladies,' there is a moment of silence between Adam and me.

"She's sweet," I tell him.

"Thanks."

"And William likes her." He looks like it's never occurred to him to consider what William might think of her. "Have you met her parents yet?"

He splutters into his wine and turns to look at me, filling my head with an unexpected burst of whatever scented shower gel he's using these days. "Is that your way of saying she's too young for me?"

"How old is she?"

He hesitates. "Twenty-two."

"Far be it from me to judge." I smile into my glass, then feel his eyes on me. "No, she's nice. Seriously," I insist, deciding that's enough of this conversation. "Oh, William: let me take a photo of you to send to Granddad."

William pauses to smile for the picture, before Adam offers to take one of the two of us as well. I choose an image and compose a text.

Arrived safely, and William's having fun already after a long journey! How's Mum?

x

I press "send" and watch the little line on my phone screen trundle along, struggling.

"The Wi-Fi isn't exactly supersonic around here, I'm afraid. We're too rural," Adam tells me. "It should get there eventually, but if you need to Skype your parents or send something urgently, come into the office to do it."

"Thanks." Adam removes a pack of papers and some tobacco from his back pocket. I lower my phone. "I thought you'd given up."

"I'm just a social smoker these days." I watch him begin to roll up his cigarette, as I glance at William. I know he's smart, but I still don't want him getting any ideas. "We've all got our vices," Adam says with a shrug.

"Yes, but mine's cake and Netflix, neither of which is fatal."

He flashes me a dismissive glance. "Give me a break, Jess."

And while there are two dozen responses to that whizzing round my head, I take a deep breath, followed by a mouthful of wine, and look for someone else to talk to.

"How's your cottage, Jess?" The young

guy sitting next to William has sleepy brown eyes and the softest of Welsh accents, but hair like a surfer, blond and salty.

"It's lovely, thank you."

"Did you hear that, boss?" He smiles at Adam.

"Top marks." Adam turns to me. "Ben cleaned it before you got here. He's unstoppable with his Marigolds on."

Ben laughs. "These are the pitfalls of coming to work in a gorgeous place like this. You might have sunshine and beautiful scenery, but you also have to roll your sleeves up and scrub toilets when the cleaner phones in sick."

"Well, it sparkled," I assure him. "You have my compliments."

"Cheers to that," he says, lifting his glass.

By the time William and I crash into our respective beds a couple of hours later, I lie on my back and check my phone, realizing a text from Dad has made it through.

Glad William's having a nice time. What about you? Mum's had a good day. I spent the afternoon at Willow Bank, and the weather was lovely, so we sat in the garden and looked at her cake books. Dad x

I close my eyes and picture them sitting among the roses as he turned the thick, glossy pages, giving her eyes a chance to settle on each photograph. There can't be many of the sugarcraft designs she hadn't attempted at some point — to Mum, this wasn't just a pastime; it was her passion.

And although the elaborate creations in those books are now beyond her capabilities, she likes to look at them and remind herself of the magic she once made with a cupboard full of ingredients, a little patience and her natural artistic flair.

CHAPTER 9

The best cake my mum ever baked for me was for my sixth birthday, and to this day my heart still leaps every time I think of it.

"Are you sure it'll be ready in time?" I had asked, as she finished sandwiching together three Victoria sponges with a mountain of pale, fluffy buttercream.

Our kitchen was small in those days — it was before my parents had it knocked through to the dining room — with immaculate white Shaker cupboards, beige patterned floor tiles and a microwave that nobody entirely trusted.

"You haven't got much faith in me, have you?" she laughed, handing me the spatula to lick, which was obviously the best bit of the whole process.

"Does that mean yes, it *will* be ready?" I asked.

She leaned down and kissed me on the head. "Jess, I promise that by the time fourteen girls descend on this house tomorrow, your cake will be complete, even if I'm up until midnight."

She wouldn't have minded if she had been.

She never needed to be asked before she got to work on those cakes for every family birthday, christening or wedding: a ladybug for my third birthday, a four-tiered wedding cake for my cousin Charlotte and another masterpiece that featured my dad as Superman.

I wandered through to the dining room and found Dad hanging decorations.

"Have you come to supervise?" he asked from on top of a ladder. He'd attached blue, green and white balloons to the picture rails along with a huge "Happy Birthday" banner. Streamers swept down from the bookshelves that dominated three of the four walls.

There must've been hundreds of novels in that room, if you'd bothered counting them. Mum had a section reserved for her cake books, but most of the paperbacks were fiction. Crime was her favorite genre, everything from Ruth Rendell to *Murder on the Orient Express*, which she read over and over again.

"I'm so excited!" I said again.

"Yes, I was getting that impression." Dad

grinned, stepping down from his ladder. "So remind me . . . what's the present you want more than anything else in the world?"

"A bike," I lied.

He smiled uncertainly. "Really? I thought there was something else, but . . . you're sure a bike would be okay?"

I didn't know if I should say anything.

I'd seen a grown-up princess-style dressing table in the window of a department store in London when we'd been visiting my uncle Alan in the summer, and it was the first time I'd longed for something that wasn't a toy. It was a thing of beauty in my eyes, with a kidney-shaped surface, an ornate three-piece mirror and a tapestry curtain that swept around the bottom, concealing a labyrinth of wooden drawers.

"No, really, I'd love a bike." I felt my cheeks warm up.

His eyes grew serious. "You know why you couldn't have the dressing table, don't you?"

I nodded. "It'd be silly to buy something that cost that much, wouldn't it, Daddy?"

"Really silly," he agreed and went back to the balloons.

The following morning, I opened the bike and was delighted with it. I made sure to show it too, because I'd recently watched *Willy Wonka and the Chocolate Factory* on

TV and didn't want to turn out to be a brat like Veruca Salt.

The morning passed painfully slowly, as Mum finished the sandwiches and Dad got the music and cushions ready for pass the parcel, before slipping out for a lunchtime pint while he had the chance. Then Grandma Jill arrived and helped me into my red party dress, white tights and black patent leather shoes.

"What are belly buttons for?" I asked, as Grandma Jill pulled me into the gusset. I'd been reading my *Children's Encyclopedia of the Human Body* a lot at the time, and while I had an extensive knowledge of the functioning of the lower intestine, I couldn't recall reading anything about why there was a hole in my stomach.

Grandma Jill twisted my tights into place. "Because after God puts your ears on and chooses your hair, he sticks his finger into your tummy and says, 'You're done.' Then you're ready for the stork to take you to the mum and dad he had in mind for you."

I scrunched up my nose. "That *can't* be true."

"Course it is." The bell rang. "There's your first guest!"

I was too busy enjoying myself to notice right away that Dad hadn't arrived back for the party. I was too busy twirling round musical chairs, ripping open presents and — mainly — reveling in the gasps of admiration when my mum brought out the cake.

It was spectacular: a seashell white fairy-tale castle, with a trellis of yellow fondant roses and turrets covered in sprinkles.

As I blew out the candles and the girls around me erupted into applause, I noticed Grandma Jill touching Mum's arm. "Probably better that he's *not* here."

Mum nodded and looked like she was going to cry.

"Are there any more sausages on sticks?" Sarah Hems asked.

Mum snapped out of it. "Yes, there's plenty more. Then, how about we do another party game?"

I remembered then that organizing the party games wasn't meant to have been Mum's job. "Why isn't Daddy here?" I asked.

"He'll be here later," Mum said vaguely.

"Has he forgotten about the party?" She didn't answer. "Perhaps he thought it'd be better to leave us girls to it, like when we watched *The Sound of Music*?" I offered.

"Yes, that'll be it," she said.

But I didn't believe that was it. And I felt a wave of sadness that Dad was missing my

big day. He could be forgetful at times —
he was always turning up late for things,
and Mum would hit the roof. But I knew
he'd be upset once he realized where he was
meant to be.

I tried to forget about it and enjoy the rest
of the party, but I couldn't help worrying.
For all we knew, he could've been run over
by a bus. That idea grew in probability as
the minutes ticked by, especially given how
often I'd heard Mum say that very thing.

As parents started arriving to collect their
daughters, I tugged at Grandma Jill's arm.
"Do you think we should call the police and
see if they know where Dad is?"

"Why, where do you think he is?"

"Flattened on the road by the Number
86."

Her eyes creased up, as if she was really
sad but annoyed at the same time.

"Afternoon, folks!"

My head snapped up to the parents mingling at the door, and there, pushing his way
through, was my dad, looking really happy
and with his hair fluffed up at the front like
a feather duster. I ran up to give him a hug
and got an overwhelming waft of the sour
smell that always clung to his coat after he'd
been in the pub.

"Right, birthday girl. You need to go in

71

the living room for a moment. I've got a surprise for you."

His voice was fuzzy and loud, and I glanced at Mum, wondering how annoyed she was with him, but this time she just looked surprised and a bit nervous, the same as everyone else.

"Here, mate, give me a hand with this?" Dad said, sounding uncharacteristically macho as he grabbed Vicky Jones's father by the arm and dragged him, staggering, towards the door. "Go on, scoot, Jess!"

Grandma Jill stiffly led me into the living room and shut the door. A minute and lots of kerfuffle later, someone yanked the handle down, it sprang open again and Daddy shouted: "Surprise!"

There, in front of me, was the princess dressing table, all the way from London.

Sarah Hems's jaw dropped. "You are SO lucky."

As I stepped forward to touch it, I felt as though there was a little bird flying around in my chest. "I know," I whispered, promising myself I'd pray to God that night, to thank him for sending my stork to the best mum and dad in the world. And perhaps to also ask if he'd keep Daddy out of trouble from now on.

CHAPTER 10

The morning view from the kitchen window is hazy and unpromising, with a low sun obscured by mist. I make myself a coffee before taking it outside.

As I take a seat, a door on the other side of the courtyard opens, and a man steps out with a girl who appears to be his daughter. He looks about my age, possibly older, and is wearing shorts that reveal a pair of muscular, tanned legs. His shirt is smart and cleanly pressed. The girl has long black hair, a nose ring and so much makeup she could be twelve or twenty-five.

"Morning, Mum!"

I look up to find William stretching in the doorway, his eyes still sleepy and his pajama bottoms inside out.

"Morning, sweetheart, how are you?"

"Starving." I hear this refrain at least twelve times a day lately, except, apparently, when gizzards are on the menu. "Can we

73

go and get some *pains au chocolat*?"

"Okay, we'll walk over to the château," I reply. "It'll give me a chance to practice my French."

I studied the language when I was at secondary school. This has stood me in great stead over the years, for all the occasions when I've had to explain that I'm fourteen years old and my hobbies include netball and reading Judy Blume books. I recently downloaded an audio language course, however, which I hope has at least updated my repertoire of phrases.

Once William and I are dressed, we step outside to find the haze quickly burning away. It feels fresher than yesterday afternoon, with powdery clouds high in a sharp blue sky. We emerge from the dappled light beneath the trees to find a handful of couples are on the terrace, relaxing over the papers and breakfast. It bursts with the dreamy scent of sweet, freshly baked pastries and strong coffee, while pots of damp, just-watered flowers provide a riot of glistening color.

Double doors lead us to a cool drawing room, with a polished antique table and a bowl of large, ripe figs in its center. A tall glass vase filled with agapanthus sits across from it in the corner. The whole place smells of designer soap, freshly cut flowers and luxury.

"*Bonjour, madame.*" The lady who greets us is several decades older than some of the staff, but she has a bright smile and skin that glows with vitality. "*Je peux vous aider? Vous avez l'air un peu perdu tous les deux.*"

She speaks in the soft tones of a lullaby, gently laughing at the final part of her sentence. I join in too, despite not having a clue what she's saying.

"*Vous désirez quelque chose?*" she continues, significantly faster than anyone on my audio download.

I clear my throat and decide to keep things simple by starting with a drink. "*Vous avez EAU?*"

A quizzical line etches itself above her nose.

"*Eauuuu,*" I repeat.

I say the word as clear as day, but she looks at me as if I'm demanding something so obscure she'll need to Google it first, then place an order to a small specialist store on the outskirts of Siberia.

"OOOhhhhww?" She frowns slowly.

"*Oui!*" I grin, triumphantly.

"*Je ne comprends pas. Vous pouvez répéter? Si nous n'en avons pas, je peux en commander.*"

75

I redden around the gills. "Are you okay, Mum?" William asks.

"Yes, absolutely," I say, deciding to show her what I mean. I proceed to mimic unscrewing a bottle and pouring myself a glass of water, before glugging it down my neck enthusiastically.

"Ahh!" she says at last, inviting us to take a seat outside, before she disappears back into the château and returns with a wine list.

"Can I help?" Adam steps out of the doorway dressed in cool grey trousers and a soft blue shirt that falls open at the neck.

"All under control," I insist, before she addresses him in rapid-fire French, he proceeds to *reply* in rapid-fire French and I sit nodding, to convey the impression that I'm following the entire exchange.

"What are you trying to order?" Adam asks. "Claudine seems to think you want some antifreeze for your car, but I didn't think that could be right."

"I just want some water," I mutter. "That's all."

"AHHH, *water*!" Claudine exclaims.

"Yes, water." I smile helplessly. "*Eau*. Just *eau*. Oh, and two *pains au chocolat* and a café au lait, if you don't mind."

"*Bien sûr,*" she replies and disappears

76

through the double doors. Adam and William look at me and exchange an amused look.

Not quite the type of bonding I had in mind.

CHAPTER 11

Adam returns to the office to make a phone
call as a little girl in a yellow swimming
costume and matching sun hat arrives,
clutching her father's hand, the other of
which is laden with plastic buckets and
spades.

I delve into my bag for some sun cream
and when I look up realize that the teenager
staying in the cottage opposite ours is at the
next table. She is wearing a pair of dark
sunglasses, a black T-shirt and cutoff jeans
that skim her pale, slim thighs. She is
engrossed in Kafka's *The Metamorphosis,*
which has never struck me as a holiday read.
She glances up and catches me looking.

"Hi." I smile, but her nose crumples into
a suspicious frown. "Excellent book. Are
you enjoying it?"

"I think it's overrated."

"Oh?"

"I preferred *The Trial.* It was funnier. I'm

78

more of an existentialism fan, to be honest."

She doesn't expect a reply, instead placing her head firmly back in her book. I open the sun cream, when she glances up. "You're opposite us in the Stables, aren't you?"

"That's right. We arrived yesterday," I tell her.

"Us too. Thirteen more days to go." She sighs theatrically.

"Where are you from?"

"Devon," she replies. "At least I am — I live there with my mum. Dad's in Cheshire."

"Oh — that's near us. We're from Manchester."

For a moment I think she's going to go back to her book, but she looks up again. "Have you heard of Hampson Browne?"

"Aren't they solicitors?" The company has an advert that comes on during the commercial breaks after the local news.

"Yeah. That's my dad's company."

"He works there?"

"He's the Hampson." If she's proud of this, she doesn't look it.

My phone rings, and I excuse myself, registering Becky's number as I press "answer."

"Hello there, stranger. How are things?" I ask.

79

"Well, it's 10:30 a.m., and I'm contemplating opening the sauvignon blanc, if that answers your question. More importantly, *how are you*?"

That used to be such a straightforward thing to ask. But it takes a second for me to locate the cheerful note in my voice. "I'm okay."

"Really?"

"Yes, the weather's great here. Sunny but not too hot. And there are things for the kids to do — they've got a little five-a-side pitch and a playground, plus the pool's great —"

Two high-pitched voices burst out of my handset. I immediately recognize them as Becky's two eldest children, seven-year-old James and five-year-old Rufus.

"BOYS, STOP FIGHTING!" Becky shrieks. "BOYYYS!"

This is followed by a clatter of shoes, doors slamming and the din quietening. When she finally returns, she's out of breath. "Sorry about that."

"Have you locked your children in a wardrobe?"

"No, I've locked *me* in one, or at least the shoe cupboard."

I burst out laughing, and she joins in. "I was only improvising, but this is a pretty good office. A bit smelly, admittedly, but I can at least hear what you're saying — and Poppy likes it because she thinks we're playing hide-and-seek." Poppy is Becky's two-and-a-half-year-old daughter.

"Listen," she continues, "I'm just phoning to ask if the cottages have a hair dryer — or do I need to pack one?"

"Ours has two. I'm sure yours will be the same."

"Great. So how are things with Adam?"

"Oh. Fine."

"Is he still annoyingly fit?" she asks.

"Oh please."

"Sorry. Is he still a wanker then?"

I snort and glance at William, hoping he hasn't heard. "You'll have to judge for yourself."

"Well, I'll forgive him anything if we manage to get a minute's peace on this holiday. Oh . . . no."

"What's up?"

She sighs. "The boys have spilled a two-liter bottle of milk, the window cleaner's at the door and Poppy's done a poo. It's nonstop fun around here."

CHAPTER 12

The flaky croissant on my plate smells so
heavenly that it makes my mouth water. In
the last ten minutes, however, we've become
surrounded by soft-skinned women in their
late teens and early twenties, wearing the
kind of shorts that I last had the guts to
wear at age nine. I push away my plate with
my forefinger. "Don't you want it?" William
asks, his cheeks full of chocolate.

"Of course I want it. I *want* ten of them."

William's eyebrows rise, as if he'd never
thought about asking for ten, but now this
opens up a whole wealth of possibility. I
look at the *pain au chocolat* again and
wonder why I'm bothering to restrain
myself. I pick it up and take a bite.

"Why don't you go and explore?" I suggest, when William's finished eating.

"Okay," he says with a shrug, pushing out
his chair.

"Don't go too far, will you?" He rolls his

eyes as Adam steps out of the château holding a coffee cup and heads towards me.

"Oh, I can't wait until he's a teenager," I mutter as Adam sits down.

"He's a good kid. I'm sure he won't give you too hard a time." I feel like saying: *How would you know?*

"You've done an amazing job on this place," I manage instead.

His eyes flicker with pride. "Well, it's taken a long time to get it to this point."

"I know. You must be incredibly pleased with it."

"Yeah. I am." He reaches for his coffee, and I notice how different his thick, tanned fingers look since the days when he was office bound. He always had masculine hands, but his nails were naturally neat, his skin soft and supple. These days, they're darker, with a honey-colored hue that's scuffed around the knuckles.

"Someone made me an offer to buy the business last month."

"Really?" I say, looking up.

"I'd never sell it, but it was flattering."

I look at William, picking up stones and examining them like he used to when he was a toddler.

"Listen, about the smoking," Adam says suddenly. "I'll try to remember not to do it in front of William."

I'm slightly taken aback by this softening of standpoint but don't want to push the issue. "Okay."

"I'm not giving up, but I get why you wouldn't want him watching his dad doing it."

"Thank you."

"I think you vastly overestimate how much influence I have over him though."

"You might be surprised," I say under my breath, as William appears at the table again.

"Is there anywhere to buy sweets?" he asks Adam.

"You've just had two *pains au chocolat*!" I protest. "We're going to the supermarket soon to stock up, so we'll get some. And plenty of fruit. So, what have you got lined up for us for the next few weeks, Adam?"

He freezes midsip, then lowers his cup slowly, his eyes glued to the saucer. This protracted movement is clearly designed to buy time while he thinks about how to answer.

"Well, there's lots to do around here," he says eventually.

"So I've read. What have you organized?"

"I thought it'd be better to wait until you got here to discuss what you fancy."

I narrow my eyes cynically. "That's . . .

considerate of you."

He ignores my tone and turns to William. "There's loads for you and your mum to do. There are walks I can show you, or you could go canoeing. If you're both feeling adventurous, I could put you in touch with a company that could take you scrambling."

"I've read the guidebooks," I tell him. "I just wondered what *you* want to do with William."

He pauses. "Me?"

"Yes."

Judging by the way he straightens his back, he realizes his mistake. "Right. Well, it's peak season, so it's impossible for me to take a lot of time off. I can do the odd afternoon, but there's Simone to consider." Coffee catches the back of my throat.

"But clearly *you're* my priority while you're here, William," he adds hastily. "Tell you what, how about one day we go and do some gorge walking or easy canyoning?"

"What does that involve?" I ask. "It sounds dangerous." Adam's judgment about the sort of activity that's suitable for a kid William's age is woefully underdeveloped. For his fifth birthday, he bought him an enormous Thomas the Tank Engine set, despite the fact that he'd last shown an interest in the character when he was three. When he

85

was eight, he bought him a bike big enough for a fifteen-year-old, one so enormous that it took three goes and my best cocker spaniel impression to get my *own* leg over it.

"The canyoning will be fine," he says dismissively, in a way that doesn't sound fine.

"But what does it *involve*?"

"A bit of rock climbing, jumping into pools, sliding down waterfalls. It's great. I've got a mate who can take us." A cold sweat beads on my spine.

"How about you stick to something along the lines of . . . a bike ride," I suggest. "Or is there somewhere they have pedalos?"

"I'll do the canyoning," William decides.

I close my mouth. "Um . . . okay." I turn to Adam. "I'll need to chat through a few things with you before you go anywhere with him. Like his allergies. And he's got a phobia of wasps."

"I have not!"

"You were hysterical for most of last summer every time one came near you."

"That was last summer. I was only *nine* then," he says, as if this was decades ago.

I glance at Adam and realize his dark eyes have wandered listlessly across to the other side of the pool, where there's an elegant

86

woman in tennis shorts and a chic wide-brimmed hat. She must be about fifty but has the hard, slender body of someone who maintains herself with religious levels of commitment.

I turn back, and Adam eventually realizes I'm looking at him. "Sorry — I thought I recognized someone. What's up?"

"Nothing," I reply, wondering how I ever got involved with someone like him. Especially as I can't claim I wasn't warned.

Chapter 13

Adam had a reputation even before he and I got together, but it made no difference — because there's no logic behind falling in love. When your heart is singing, your head is completely at its mercy.

We met in Edinburgh, where we both studied English literature at university. I first became aware of him at a lecture on the Enlightenment, about a week into the course. It wasn't some thunderbolt moment, when I was so dazzled by him that he took my breath away. But, as the weeks went on, every time I caught a glimpse of his face, even from the other side of the room, my entire body would soften.

He had acquired some standing as heart-throb of our course, someone who made otherwise intelligent girls lose their heads. I was one of them. Yet, for the whole first year, I sat tight at the side of the lecture theatre, invisible.

I ended up confessing my feelings for him to Becky on our summer break, while we were traveling round Thailand. It was a trip in which she'd swum naked in the sea at midnight, had a threesome with two Swedish bartenders and smoked pot from the minute she woke up every morning at eleven. Personally, I preferred to stick to my coffee at that hour, or roll up my skirt for a paddle and chat with a really nice woman we met from Dunstable who'd always wanted to come after watching *The King and I*.

"I have no idea why you don't just go and talk to him," she'd said, as if it would be as simple for me as it was for her.

Instead, when we returned for the second university year, I embarked on a low-maintenance relationship with a very nice guy called Carl, who these days is something big in insurance. I only know this because he popped up on daytime TV a few years ago commenting on a woman whose ingrown toenail cost her a fortune on holiday because she hadn't read the small print on her travel policy documents. We didn't last long and split up just after Christmas. Neither of us was especially devastated.

A few weeks later, in the dying hours of one January night, I found myself on the sticky dance floor of a nightclub with music thrumming through my sternum and darkness and light blinking in my brain. Becky's tongue was mostly latched onto a bloke in a Sex Pistols T-shirt as I hovered awkwardly on the sidelines, wondering if I should try to drag her away.

When I became aware of someone next to me, I looked up and felt my chest erupt. Adam was not a showy dancer, but he moved with instinctive rhythm and a lack of self-awareness. Heat radiated from him as I held my breath, trying not to look at his sleepy eyes, full mouth, the outline of those broad shoulders as they moved underneath his T-shirt. Becky pushed me towards Adam as the opening bars of "Common People" by Pulp pumped out of the speakers.

He always said afterwards that that was the first moment he saw me — I mean, *really* saw me: hurtling straight at him while Jarvis Cocker pounded out a line about dancing and drinking and screwing. All three of which suddenly felt like the greatest inventions on earth.

We didn't say a thing to each other. Not a single word. He simply took me in his arms as my body throbbed with the music and something else far more potent. For the rest of the night, we danced and we kissed. We

90

did try to talk but couldn't really hear a word over the sound system, until after the club closed and we walked hand in hand looking for a taxi. It was a bitter, black evening, and I was on fire.

"I'm doing English lit," he told me, clearly convinced this was news to me.

I was embarrassed that I had to spell this out. "Yes, I know. Me too. I'm in a couple of your classes."

He was surprised, but I thought I also detected a touch of concern that he was going to have to see me again. I always have been a catastrophist when it comes to Adam.

But when I walked into our lecture theatre the following Monday, I felt a tap on the shoulder and turned to find him smiling at me. "Hi. Can I sit next to you?" he asked.

And that was the start of everything.

In the first three years we were together, I really was happy. Broke, but definitely happy. We both were.

With no real family ties of his own, Adam followed me home to Manchester after we graduated, before we moved into a small, sparsely furnished flat in Salford. It overlooked the spot where MediaCityUK now sits, the buzzing state-of-the-art metropolis that houses the BBC, ITV and a host of glittering bars and restaurants. At the time, it was a car park. But we didn't need a view. We had each other, and that was more than enough.

I embarked on a yearlong course to qualify as a lecturer, while Adam, who'd strolled away from university with one of the highest marks in the course, became a graduate trainee at an energy company. We had a great social circle. As well as reigniting old friendships from my childhood, I met new people at my program. Meanwhile, Becky and her boyfriend Seb, who I'd assumed would stay in Edinburgh, were instead offered jobs in Manchester and relocated.

Unfortunately, it wasn't long before Adam's enthusiasm for his work began to wane. I only recognize this with hindsight; at the time I barely noticed it. I'm not even sure he did. Life in those days was all about the two of us. It was a heady time, when I'd wake every day to a freshly made cup of tea and the warmth of his mouth on my neck.

"Why don't you come back to bed?" I murmured one morning from underneath the sheets. He was clean-shaven and ready for work, looking sharp and tasting sublime.

"Because I'm meant to be in at 8:45 a.m. for a staff meeting."

"Okay," I said, forcing my arms to my side.

"I could be persuaded to be late though," he whispered, kissing me on the lips.

"I don't want you to get in trouble."

"Well, the trains *are* terrible these days." He grinned as he took off his jacket and crawled back onto the bed and into my arms.

He didn't even rush away afterwards, refusing to dart off and miss the dreamy postcoital chat we would always steal between kisses. The one in which Adam would always want to talk about the future. Hardly ever the present, and certainly not the past, for reasons that only became apparent later.

"Where shall we go and live after you've finished your course?"

"Oh, somewhere glamorous . . . Burnley?" I suggested.

He laughed. "I can't wait."

"Though . . . New York could be good too," I offered.

"God, it would. What about France? Or Italy?"

"They're all expensive."

"Yes, but we could buy a wreck of a house together and do it up. Somewhere that had been neglected for centuries and just needed a bit of TLC. I'd love that, wouldn't you?"

"I would, Adam," I told him, truthfully.

"Though I'd miss our friends."

"Oh, we'd be all right anywhere as long as we had each other," he said dismissively.

"You old romantic," I murmured sarcastically, but actually, I'd thought he meant it.

CHAPTER 14

The labyrinthine streets of Sarlat hold a timeless fascination that, in the height of the summer, everyone seems to want to discover. The medieval town buzzes with activity, its caramel courtyards and elegant central square filled with the scent of freshly baked bread, potent cheeses and thick black coffee.

William and I find ourselves there on our third day of sightseeing, threading through the throngs, past mansions and café terraces.

"This is a little market, apparently. At certain times of year they sell nothing but truffles," I say, looking up from my guidebook as we stumble across a covered corner of the town trading in gourmet fare, arranged in endless small baskets on large trestles. William throws me a skeptical look, and I must admit, of all the things in my life I've ever felt the need to purchase,

95

truffles aren't high on the list.

Yet somehow, it's surprisingly easy to sleepwalk into spending the equivalent of twenty-two pounds on a piece of fungus, before stepping out and realizing you might as well have bought half a tennis ball for all the culinary use you're likely to make of it.

This becomes immaterial anyway when we stop for a coffee and two gooey *gâteaux aux noix* in one of the pretty street cafés, where I manage to leave my purchase under the table in its little brown paper bag. I realize my error ten minutes after we've left, but when I drag William back, the table has been taken by two debonair-looking gentlemen, whose dog is merrily lunching on my tuber.

Given that *nowhere* on my audio download did they teach you how to say, *Your poodle is eating my truffle,* I decide not to make an issue of it and instead slip away.

There are several other attractive towns we could visit afterwards, but it is painfully obvious that even William — whose earliest party trick was reciting the wives of Henry VIII in order — has little appetite for another medieval church.

"Have you got my iPad in your bag?" he asks idly.

"You mean *my* iPad. Yes, it's here."

He perks up. "Shall we go and get lunch?"

"You mean shall we go somewhere with a Wi-Fi connection so you can play Clash of Clans?"

"Well, can we?"

"Come on," I concede, resting my arm on his skinny shoulder blade as we meander down the cobbled street.

"What about this place?" William says, clearly desperate to get to his game. But the café does look nice — they all do — with huge umbrellas the color of double cream, shading rows of little tables from the sun.

I can't deny that Adam's absence from these day trips has started to bother me. His vaguely promised activities have yet to materialize and are showing no signs of doing so. Instead, he's been permanently dashing from one part of the estate to the other, picking up supplies or attending meetings with unspecified but *very important* people.

William hasn't complained about this, which worries me in itself. He's become too used to low-level disappointment and lack of effort from his father. And while I understand that it's peak season, after driving 825 miles I don't think it's too much to have hoped for. This is particularly the case when I've left my mother back home, with Dad doing everything he can, as she loses grasp of her old self little by little.

None of this gives me comfort for the future. I keep trying to imagine scenarios that involve Adam stepping in to do the things other dads would do as their sons grow up. Driving William to university, or helping him move into his first flat. Somehow, I just can't see it.

I already feel like I'm letting Mum down, to the extent that I actually found myself fibbing when I spoke to Dad on the phone last night.

It was the first phone call I'd made home since we arrived, though Dad and I have exchanged innumerable texts. He keeps asking if I'm "relaxing," to which I reply: "Yes, absolutely!" It's easier for both of us to keep up the charade, I think. But last night I needed to hear the sound of his voice, even if I've heard him tell me a dozen times that nothing will change dramatically just because I'm here. He's probably right — my mum's body and brain have been ravaged over years, not weeks.

By the time William and I return to Château de Roussignol, it's gone three o'clock and Adam is nowhere to be seen. I bump into Simone, who tells me that he's been called to a meeting in Salignac but should be back later. "Would you like me to give

98

him a message?"

I think carefully before answering. "It'd just be good if he could let us know when he can do the activities he's promised William." Her smile flickers as my son looks up expectantly.

"I'm sure I heard him say earlier that he had something good planned," she says brightly, and I can almost see her nose growing several centimeters longer. "In the meantime, I've organized a soccer match for the older children that starts soon — William, why don't you join in? And Jess: there's aqua aerobics in the pool if you fancy that? It'd be right up your street."

"William's not really into soccer, are you, sweetheart?" I turn to look at him and realize the color of his cheeks has deepened slightly.

"I'll give it a go," he mumbles. "You go to the aquathingy, Mum. I know you like that kind of stuff." And I know when someone wants to get rid of me.

Not long afterwards, I am standing in the pool waiting for the aqua aerobics session, and I'd estimate that I am approximately half a century younger than the average participant.

There are only five others, but they're in

their seventies and eighties, except for the sweet lady directly in front of me with a humpback, who could possibly have seen the Boer War. Once the class starts, the most athletic move we undertake involves bouncing gently up and down on the spot to a French cover version of "Eye of the Tiger." This is all done while a woman, who is positively juvenile at about sixty, stands at the side of the pool in a retina-burning pink combo, sweating profusely and looking as though she might keel over at any moment.

I quickly decide I'm going to slink out of the pool. But when I'm halfway out, the teacher presses pause on her music system and starts shouting at me in French.

"Pardon?!" I offer.

"She wants her float back."

I spin round to see the guy from the cottage opposite ours, the *one half of Hampson Browne*. He points to the blue polystyrene in my hand. "Oh, sorry. *Pardon!*" I repeat, placing it on the side of the pool, before skulking away.

"I'm not sure you quite looked at home with that group."

I sit down on the lounger next to him, where I'd left my towel. He's surrounded by papers but has lost his office pallor after a couple of days in the sun, and it's had a dramatic effect. He looks almost outdoorsy.

"I'll stick to running in the future," I say, pulling the towel up my chest self-consciously.

"There's a good trail if you head around the lake. It's about three miles, so not too much."

I wonder exactly how unfit I look. "Great. I'll go round twice then." He laughs. I feel like an idiot. I *am* an idiot.

"Well, I need to go and see if my son has finished his soccer match," I say, standing up. "It's nice when they lift their heads up out of a computer game, so I'm making the most of it."

"Let me guess: teenager?"

"Not yet — he's ten."

"Well, you've got lots of fun to come. I say this as the father of a fourteen-year-old girl."

"I feel your pain. Though I met your daughter yesterday, and she was absolutely charming."

A hint of fatherly pride appears at the side of his mouth. "She's not bad, Chloe, is she? Especially when she smiles or has an actual conversation, which happens every couple of weeks or so."

"I'm Jess." I offer him my hand, and he reaches out to shake it.

"Charlie. Very nice to meet you. So I can tell you're British, but where is it you're from?"

"Manchester," I say, which leads to ten minutes of small talk about how much development is currently happening in the city and which gigs we've been to at the Etihad Stadium . . . before we manage to work out that his office is very close to where I live.

"That's a lovely area," he says. "Good for families."

"Yes, William and I like it."

A beat passes. "You're not married?"

I shake my head.

"Me neither," he replies. And my stomach flips. Partly because of the way he looks at me. Partly with surprise that I've still got it in me to like it.

CHAPTER 15

On Saturday morning, it's raining. I curl up on the sofa in my pajamas, clutching my knees to my chest and nursing a coffee as trails of water snake down the glass. It echoes my mood, the things I can't just forget despite being in a pretty place, surrounded by glorious flowers, food and wine.

There is a sharp bang on the window, and I look up to see Adam. Before I have a chance to move, William is out of his bedroom and inviting him in.

"Fancy a dip?" he asks William.

"Okay!"

"Right, you'll need trainers, shorts and a towel."

"Trainers?" I ask, bewildered. "Why does he need shoes in the swimming pool?"

Adam turns and grins at me. "Who mentioned a swimming pool?"

Two hours later, the rain gives way to what

must count as the coldest Dordogne day since records began. Under the dubious care of a guide called Enzo, we plod a short distance up a mountain pathway and find ourselves in front of a waterfall that's flowing fast enough to cover our faces in a mist of white spray. We're wearing wet suits, shin pads and helmets, none of which belongs on a holiday as far as I'm concerned.

"Did you remember William has a history of asthma?" I say to Adam.

"He'll be fine," he replies, dismissively.

I frown. "How do you *know* he'll be fine?"

He beckons William over. "How long is it since he's needed an inhaler? He was in nappies, wasn't he?"

I decide not to answer, watching as Adam checks the fastening on William's helmet. "But, look at it. Seriously, Adam. This can't be suitable for a ten-year-old."

He turns to Enzo, who's shorter than I am, with darkly tanned skin and shoulders like a Lego figure. They have a conversation in French that I completely fail to follow. "Enzo confirms that it's fine," Adam tells me.

"Enzo can't be trusted," I mutter under my breath.

Enzo grins at me. "You trust me, no worry. I look after your son."

I nod and bite the knuckle on my thumb.

"Mum, I'm not scared," William pipes up. "Besides, you're coming with us, aren't you? You'll be able to keep an eye on me if you're worried."

This is the other issue. I don't want to be coming with them. I'd rather be doing virtually anything than this: filling in a tax return, paying off a parking ticket, having a Pap smear. Any of those would be tremendous fun by comparison. Because while I know that scrambling up rocks and sliding on your back down waterfalls is some people's idea of heaven — the kind of activity you see people doing in muesli adverts — it really isn't my sort of thing.

I glance at William, who doesn't look at all unsettled by the prospect of full-body plunges into icy water, or the potential for injury or — as the disclaimer form I've just signed highlighted cheerily — DEATH. Judging by the way his cheeks are flushed with quivering excitement, the likelihood of my persuading him to drop everything to come and do a nice brass rubbing at the nearest fourteenth-century cathedral seems remote.

"*La première chose à faire, c'est d'entrer dans l'eau comme ça, tout doucement, pour éviter une crise cardiaque,*" Enzo says.

Adam bursts out laughing.

"What's he saying?" I grimace, tapping Adam on the shoulder as Enzo sinks into the first pool.

"He said get in. But it might be cold." Adam sits down in the water, up to his waist, and doesn't flinch. I follow suit, subjecting my lady bits to an experience so horribly freezing and deeply unpleasant that I'm convinced it'll be days before I thaw out.

"Vous me remercierez de vous avoir avertis," Enzo declares, as I look at Adam for a translation.

"He says you'll thank him for this."

Before I get a chance to ask *for what,* Enzo starts swinging his leg backwards and forward like a psychopath, kicking icy water in my face — sending it up my nose, into my eyes, taking my breath away. When he finally stops, I realize that if I wasn't in such shock I'd be weeping. William and Adam, who've also been drenched, are both squealing with laughter.

"You okay?" Adam asks, putting his hand on my arm. Reflexively, I shake him off and try to stop my jaw from chattering.

"Of course," I reply, removing a thick clump of wet hair from the recesses of my nasal passages. "Just look after your son."

He looks at me again and frowns. "Jess, I promise you. He will be *fine.*"

Over the next hour and a half, we experience nature at its most raw, wild and raggedly beautiful. It is one of the worst experiences of my adult life.

It's not even that I am on the verge of hypothermia that bothers me. It's that, contrary to everything Adam and Enzo have said, this pastime is obviously dangerous, and clearly unsuitable for a child. Or at least *my* child. Who is so oblivious to all these facts that he appears to be having a whale of a time.

As we slide down waterfalls, into deep pools of water, I can think of nothing but broken bones, submerged lungs, gaping wounds and the lot of us getting stranded out here and with little more than a packet of roast chicken crisps between us.

"Mum, this is AMAZING!" William declares.

"Oh . . . good," I whimper.

As I'm vaguely hopeful that we're nearing the end, Enzo turns and flashes me his teeth. "This is the bravery test. Just for you." He winks. It takes a lot for me to dislike someone, but I think Enzo might have managed it.

"Voici comment il faut faire. Si vous ne faites

pas comme moi, vous vous ferez mal, donc écoutez moi bien."

"He says you have to do it *exactly* like him or you'll get hurt," Adam tells me.

Enzo stands at the edge of the rock, a vast rush of water skimming his shins.

Then he leaps.

A heartbeat passes before I hear a crash in the water below. I peer over the edge to see Enzo finally appear and give us the thumbs-up before climbing onto the bank.

"My son is not doing that," I tell Adam.

Adam assesses the rock edge and his jaw twitches. "Okay."

"I'm serious, Adam. That's ridiculous. He's ten years old."

"I agree," he says. "I think you're right on this —"

The echoing splash that interrupts us sends adrenaline blistering through me. I look up and I realize that there is an empty space where William was standing. Adam and I race to the edge, and I peer down at the water, to the shadow underneath it, bubbles raging at the top where the force of my son has plummeted under.

My legs go weak.

I know there's no point relying on these two to save him, so I race down the side of the bank, my feet sliding and tripping over themselves in the mud, until I find an opening. It's then that I do the only thing maternal instinct will allow: scramble down on my backside, grasping handfuls of grass and mud and rocks to steady myself. I plunge into the water arse-first and cannot fully describe the blinding white rush that engulfs me for the five seconds I'm submerged and my mouth is bulging with ice-cold water. Except to say that I feel like a hamster being flushed down a toilet.

I pedal my arms frantically until I grab something that seems to be William's leg. I'm contemplating my next move, face scrunched up and ears full of sound, when I become aware that my son is actually alive and kicking. Kicking ME, to be precise.

Against the tide of raging water and thrusting limbs, I pull myself up onto the bank, spluttering as I wipe my eyes and see him sitting on the side, shaking his head.

"You could've waited until I was out, Mum," he mutters. "It wasn't even your turn."

Afterwards, we change in a tall pop-up tent, which is all you get in the way of facilities when you're this far out in the countryside. Having spent the morning behaving like a miniature marine — capable, solid, someone who can negotiate anything nature throws at him — William is suddenly unable to get his sock off by himself.

"It's really wet though," he complains. "It's stuck. I can't get it off."

I spend the next three minutes attempting to remove his footwear, my teeth chattering wildly, before sending him out to his father so I've got space to undress. This involves contorting into a variety of unlikely positions, with the tent billowing around me as I nearly dislocate my elbow when attempting to get my bra back on. By the time I emerge, the sun is pushing through the clouds and Enzo is piling equipment into his van. I hand over the wet suit.

"Thank you," I say, forcing out a smile.

"Your son was good. Brave," he tells me.

I feel a strange sense of pride. "He was, wasn't he?" He slams shut the door. "Where is he now?"

He gestures to the other side of the road, to Adam and William sitting next to each other by the lake. With shards of light searing through the grey recesses of the sky, I walk towards them, slowing my steps as I approach.

I can't hear what they're saying, but it's making both of them laugh, loud, unselfconscious guffaws. Adam puts his arm around William and squeezes him into his side.

I stop and quickly pull out my phone, stealing a picture of them.

The relationship between my son and his father is far more fragile and complicated than the photo implies, even with an Instagram filter for added gloss. But it's still a beautiful image. One I hope my mum will keep in her heart for as long as it's still beating.

CHAPTER 16

The problem with Adam is this: he's easy to fall in love with. If you don't really know him, I mean, *really* know him, his terrible characteristics are obscured by the good ones: the fact that he's clever and funny, charismatic and handsome. He has an ability to make you feel like you're the center of his world — at least for a moment — which is how William feels this afternoon.

But I worry about him getting hurt and let down, being sucked in by Adam at his most wonderful, before his young soul is wounded by Adam at his most neglectful, and selfish. I've known that version of Adam firsthand, even if I can't claim to have seen the demise of our relationship coming until it was too late.

The first real hurdle we faced was when the job Adam had initially tolerated became something he actively despised.

I knew he'd reached this point because

I'd hear his key in the door as he returned from work and ask, "How was your day?" with tension clutching my throat. Because I knew that his day would have involved stress, petty office politics and a vacuum of fulfillment. The effect of which would leave a bitter aftertaste on most of our evenings.

"How can I put this?" he said, emerging into the living room one night and slumping onto the sofa, where I sat with my laptop, television on low in the background. "The highlight of my day was winning bullshit bingo three times in one meeting."

I put the laptop on the cushion next to me and slid my arms round his neck, briefly pressing my lips against his five-o'clock shadow. "Sorry it's so shitty at the moment."

"I don't mean to moan. I just hate the place."

I don't know if the issue was simply that Adam was trapped in a bad relationship with a soulless company and a "career" that was as mundane as they got. Or that some people just aren't built to be constrained by corporate life. My boyfriend, a dreamer and an adventurer at heart, was one of them.

"It won't be long before my course is over, then we can do all the things we've talked about," I said. "I want you to know how grateful I am though, Adam."

"For what?"

"The fact that you're having to subsidize me while I finish studying. That *I'm* the reason we're eating baked beans every night. That all I can contribute to this flat is the pennies from my student loan."

"Yeah, when you put it like that, you're not much of a catch, are you?" He smiled.

"Ho ho."

"I don't mind any of that, Jess. It's not going to last forever. Shall we have another look at that Jobs Abroad website tonight?"

"You know how to live it up, don't you?"

He leaned in and sank into a brief, tender kiss before pulling away. "Oh, by the way, do you mind if I go out with Georgina on Thursday? She's in town for the night."

Adam had dated Georgina for a few months when he was only seventeen. They'd split amicably when he'd left home for university, but had stayed in touch, as good friends.

"Of course not."

"Why don't you come with us?"

"I've got too much work, Adam. And I'm broke."

"I'll pay. Oh, come on, I'd prefer it if you were there too."

"Adam, I can't. Just go by yourself," I

insisted. "Have a great night, and give her my love."

I felt none of the unease many girlfriends would with the idea of them going out for drinks; Georgina might technically have been an old flame, but I knew there was nothing between them these days. Besides, the first time I'd met her, I remember thinking she wasn't as gorgeous as I'd imagined, despite the long legs and voluptuous cleavage. Her face was striking, rather than pretty, with thick lips that she slicked with bright pink lipstick and porcelain skin, framed by a curtain of black hair.

She was witty and spoke like a freight train: too fast and loud, like she was permanently racing to get to the end of her sentence. I liked her. At least I did until I realized she'd spent the night with Adam when he was meant to be with me for the birth of our baby. But I'm getting ahead of myself.

The point is, they'd always been close, and I was completely okay with that. And I promised myself that one day I'd make up for all the sacrifices he'd made for me and we'd do the traveling he longed for.

Then something happened that wasn't part of the plan.

I got pregnant.

It's difficult to know how you'll feel about an unplanned pregnancy until it happens. And my reaction was the polar opposite of Adam's. It wasn't simply that he wasn't ready, that he had a life to live, the world to travel and a head full of ideas.

It was that he'd never be ready.

That was obvious not just from his horrified expression when I showed him the pregnancy test, confirming the news that the nausea I'd had for the previous few days could not be attributed to a dodgy chicken Madras, but from the fact that, a full week afterwards, when he'd had plenty of time to let the idea sink in, he was no less horrified.

"Look, I know this isn't what either of us would've planned, but we can make this work," I argued, hearing my voice rise several octaves as he sat rooted to the sofa, staring at an episode of *Fawlty Towers* that he hadn't laughed at once.

I was scared and didn't have a clue what I was doing.

I knew the timing was all wrong and that there were a million reasons why we were supposed to think this was a disaster.

But, as the days had passed, there was also

a lightness in my veins, a bloom on my cheeks, a fluttering in my pulse every time I thought about the idea that I was going to be *a mother.* I didn't just feel physically different; something had changed inside me already, and even if I'd wanted to, I couldn't stop my heart from lifting in my chest every time I thought about it.

Adam did not share these sentiments.

"I understand why you didn't want this to happen. But it has," I continued, desperate for him to say something. "We can't make it *un-happen.*"

He slowly lifted up his head, his eyes flat. "Well . . . we *could.*"

A bolt of adrenaline shot through me as I decoded what he was saying. "You mean have an abortion?"

"Jess . . . at this stage, it's just a pill. Then this whole problem would be solved. That's all it would take, one visit to a clinic and —"

"And the line on the pregnancy test would disappear and we could go back to how things were," I finished for him.

His eyes burned with defiance. "Is that such a terrible thing to want?"

I walked out of the room, but he leapt up and followed me. "Don't make me feel like some bastard here, Jess, just for having the

117

discussion."

I spun around. "But we're not *just having the discussion,* are we? You've made your mind up, and you want me to get rid of a baby that's growing inside me right now."

"This does affect me too, you know, Jess." Indignation billowed up in my stomach, but I didn't answer. "Anyway, I thought you were pro-choice," he muttered.

"*Choice* is the operative word, Adam. And my choice couldn't feel clearer. I wouldn't have gone out of my way to conceive, but the fact is, I have. And . . . I'm keeping this baby." I was shouting at this point, because I knew if I stopped I'd burst into tears.

"Right. End of story then," he snapped, before announcing he was going for a walk to clear his head, something that apparently took three hours.

What followed was not an ideal start to our countdown to parenthood. We bickered and fought for weeks. I'd never experienced anything like it — with him or anyone else. Every night there was a conflagration of varying degrees; every night my feelings for the man I'd been crazy about were being chipped away. His response felt so unreasonable, so petulant.

Yes, I know William wasn't William back then — Adam could not think of him as anything other than a blue line on a stick and the unraveling of all his ambitions. But to me, my baby was a beating heartbeat inside me. I loved him, and the idea of him, from the first moment I knew he existed. So, no, sorry, I wasn't going to have an abortion. Not for Adam, not for anyone. I could not have been gladder that the baby, the womb, the decision, were all ultimately mine by sheer fluke of biology.

After four weeks, he said he accepted it. I suppose he had to. He was trapped. And it became very clear that men like Adam do not like to feel trapped.

In the months that followed, he blamed me for everything. He didn't need to say it; you could see it in his eyes. Besides, when a couple is careless with contraception, it always seems to be the woman's fault. I'd been the one who refused to go on the Pill because it made me nauseated. I'd been the one who made us rely on condoms. Condoms we ran out of one drunken night so took our chances instead.

I could see him falling out of love with me before my eyes. It was obvious from how distracted he was, and uncharacteristically short-tempered. He no longer raced home and made kissing me his first priority.

Instead, he was getting closer to a woman

who'd become his confidante.

"Who are you texting?" I asked one evening as I lay on the sofa watching a *Sopranos* box set with my swollen ankles propped up on the arm.

"Does it matter?"

"I was only interested," I muttered, then added: "Say hi from me."

He looked up. "What?"

"I said, say hi. To Georgina."

He ignored me and returned to his phone, to read another text. Whatever it said, it was enough to elicit his first smile of the whole evening.

She was increasingly in the area for work, and he'd go off to meet her for drinks. I was reluctantly invited, but usually declined. I couldn't bear sitting there with my swelling belly, sipping sparkling water and listening to them crying with laughter as they reminisced about something "you had to be there" to appreciate.

The only person to whom I articulated my fears was Becky. I couldn't tell my mum. She adored Adam, and I knew if I said anything, it'd ruin the excitement about becoming a grandmother for the first time.

Becky didn't think I should worry. "He's smitten with you. He just needs time to adjust to the pregnancy. Plus, the silk knickers phase might be on hold, but that doesn't mean he wants to sleep with his ex-girlfriend."

How wrong she turned out to be.

CHAPTER 17

I've packed a pair of white cutoffs on every holiday for the last eight years and never once had the guts to actually wear them.

But as I change before picking up Natasha from the airport late on Sunday afternoon, the sun has made a spectacular comeback, lighting up the hills and meadows as if to welcome her. And the cutoffs suddenly don't seem like a bad idea.

I've never been a shorts person. Even when I was twenty, I considered my legs not long enough, not firm enough, not Gisele Bündchen's enough. But, having been told by the GP to exercise as well as take my antidepressants, I've been sneaking away for a half hour Grit class on my lunch hour.

Part of me liked how punishing the class was, so tough that by rights, I should have glutes like steel. So when I saw the white shorts I thought, sod it. I was feeling quite

good about myself, all things considered —
until Adam appeared at our door, took one
look at me and exclaimed: "Nice shorts."

I grimaced. "Oh . . . be quiet."

"Sorry. But you used to go for a length
that was a bit more Victorian. Not that I'd
want to discourage you."

I attempted to hide the heat in my cheeks
and muttered: "Consider me discouraged."

Unfortunately, I didn't have time to
change. So, now I'm standing at the airport,
attracting glances and wishing I'd burned
the shorts and worn a kaftan instead.

Natasha emerges from arrivals looking like
Grace Kelly entering LAX — all dark
glasses, big handbag and perfect hair. She
waves and glides over before giving me a
hug so hard it must have shifted a few vital
organs.

"Oh my God, it's so good to see you." She
grins, then steps back and looks me up and
down. "Wow."

"What?" I ask.

"Nice shorts," she says, then qualifies:
"Nice *legs.*"

"Thanks," I reply, feeling a lot better hearing this from her. "How was the flight?"

"Lovely, except for my puffed-up feet.
Look at these — they could belong to a
hobbit." She thrusts one of her Michael

Kors wedges in front of me, and I laugh, even though she's exaggerating. "I can't complain though. Two hours and a G&T after takeoff, I was here."

"None of this sounds half as much fun as the relentless vomiting I had to endure."

She tuts. "Poor William." Then she stops and looks at me. "How's your mum? And how are you?"

"Mum's not great. But I'm fine. Honestly."

She narrows her eyes, but I head towards the parking machine before she presses me for more. I slide my ticket in, and she gently pushes me aside to pay. "So have you got used to being around Adam yet? Is he bearable?"

"I wouldn't have come here if I'd thought he wouldn't be. Even with you and Becky as backup."

"You deserve a medal. Most people would find it impossible to be in the same room as their ex," she says, as we head towards the multistory and wait for a lift to arrive. "I once saw Stuart in Sainsbury's and virtually commando crawled through the wine aisle so I didn't have to say hello."

I haven't dated many people seriously apart from Adam. There was Carl from uni, if you can count him, then a guy called

Toby, who I went out with for a year when William was six. He was nice by all accounts, and there really wasn't anything wrong with him. But, while I've never had to fall to the floor of my local supermarket to avoid him, I know what Natasha is saying. I wouldn't go out of my way to see him again. Unfortunately, with Adam, I don't have the luxury of steering clear.

"That is the problem when you have a child with someone," I tell her. "You might *want* to stay a million miles away from them, but you're stuck together forever. Whether you like it or not."

I met Natasha when I was nearly six months pregnant at a Christmas ball thrown by the chairman of Adam's company. I felt totally out of place at the party, which was held in a marquee in the grounds of a Cheshire mansion on a crisp, snowy evening. It was attended by the firm's biggest clients and key staff — a glitzy affair, all champagne cocktails and shoptalk. I was only drafted in to be there because someone on Adam's table had dropped out at the last minute.

Considering he hated his job, Adam obediently fell in with the other young hotshots, schmoozing with customers and senior managers until they were eating out of his hand. In fact, he was so good at it that it made his ill-concealed misery about staying put in the UK because of the baby even more frustrating. I, meanwhile, trailed around behind him, feeling thoroughly tired and fat and unable to contribute anything meaningful to the conversation beyond "how many months gone" I was.

I'd seen Natasha at the start of the evening, chatting to the chairman himself. She was model thin, in an elegant midnight blue silk gown with fine copper-colored hair piled loosely into a bun. Her blunt nose and straight eyebrows gave her a studious and single-minded air, until she heard something she considered funny, when her face would break into greedy, uninhibited peals of laughter.

After dinner, when people were mingling, she slid into the chair next to me.

"This must be mind-numbing for you," she whispered.

"Oh, not at all!" I protested politely.

"You're sure? Because I work for these people and actually enjoy talking about the global oil prices . . . but I'm aware that *normal* people don't share my passion."

I laughed.

"You must be Jess." She grinned, and we shook hands. She had a grip like a sergeant major. "I've heard loads about you from Adam. I can't believe he never mentioned you were having a baby though."

Natasha and I should have had nothing in common. Ambition and ability shone from her, while I was convinced the bump of my twenty-two-year-old belly gave the impression that I was either incapable or uninterested in a career.

When other people that evening had made an effort to talk to me, it felt as though they were humoring the pregnant lady when they'd rather be sucking up to clients. But Natasha wasn't like that at all. Natasha was warm, easy to be around and, frankly, hilarious.

We sat chatting at the table over everything from swimming — which she loved and I'd taken up recently — to the fact that she'd once dumped someone for eating Pringles in bed. "I'm not usually that shallow, but there's only so many times you can find a barbecue potato snack in your pants before you have to take action."

Then the DJ cranked up the music and she gestured to the dance floor. "Come on, I'm up for it if you are."

I glanced at Adam, but he was deep in conversation with the woman next to him. So we simply headed to the center of the room and danced like no one was watching, which I'm fairly sure Adam soon started wishing was the case.

Afterwards, Natasha and I ended up going swimming together three nights a week, all through the Christmas season and right until the day before I gave birth. Those evenings were bliss. Not just the feeling of weightlessness in my heavy limbs as I slipped through the water. But simply being around her. At a time when I was increasingly anxious about my relationship with Adam, having Natasha to talk to made everything feel about 500 percent easier.

Now, as she slides into the passenger seat of my car and I switch on the engine, one thing strikes me: I desperately hope she has the same effect here.

CHAPTER 18

The countryside is bathed in honeyed light as we arrive back at Château de Roussignol. We drop off Natasha's luggage at Les Écuries, then head straight to the pool, where a family barbecue evening is planned.

The unfeasibly large grill is commandeered by Ben (or Young Ben, as he's inexplicably known, despite being the same age as most of the staff around here). A small number of children, ranging from four years old to twelve, gather around the volleyball net, where Simone is organizing them into teams. On the stretch of adjacent grass, William finishes setting up an obstacle course with Adam, before heading over to join Simone's game.

"This place is incredible," Natasha says, clearly surprised. She'd seen the pictures and the website, of course, and read all the reviews, but up close the château is something else entirely.

"It's not Barbados though." I smile, as this is where she went last year, on a singles holiday.

"Bah, Barbados is overrated."

"Really?"

She sighs. "Well, no. Not really."

Natasha still works for the same company as when I met her — but these days she's their new business director and based in London, where she lives in a small, central apartment with designer taps and a cream carpet. When she first moved in, it looked like the kind of flat in a film adaptation of a spy novel, except Natasha never quite mastered the minimalist look, so she soon crammed every corner with books and travel knickknacks.

"Where's my favorite eight-year-old?" she asks.

"If you mean William, he's there playing volleyball. And he's ten."

She draws a sharp breath. "When did that happen?"

"March."

"Damn. I bet that means he's grown out of Bob the Builder?" She grins.

As we head to the pitch, Natasha waves to try to gain William's attention, oblivious to the fact that attention is the last thing a boy his age wants. When he doesn't respond, she steps onto the sand, just as the ball hurtles in her direction.

Without hesitating, she leaps up and smashes it out of sight as the other players, whose average age is seven, stand open-mouthed.

She looks almost as surprised as everyone else. "Huh. I've still got it." She chuckles. "High five, William!"

He gives her palm a limp slap, before slumping self-consciously so it looks as though he's trying to hide his own head in the gap between his rib cage. "Hi, Aunty Natasha." He smiles awkwardly as Simone walks over, looking cross.

"This is an under-twelves' match," she says stiffly.

"Sorry." Natasha grins, not looking at all sorry as she heads back to me.

"He's such a sweetheart, Jess. Now, how about some *vin blanc*? Or *vin rouge*. Or *vin* anything. I've been detoxing for a month and fell off the wagon during the flight, so I might as well continue."

William waits until Natasha is at the bar before jogging over to me. "Mum, can I do something with Dad tomorrow?"

"Has he said that's okay?"

"Yes, he said we could go rafting in the morning."

131

"Oh, okay. I'll see if Natasha fancies it. I'm sure she will — she likes that kind of thing. We can take a packed lunch."

But he shakes his head. "I meant just him and me. We want a *boys'* day." I clearly wasn't born with the correct appendage to join in this type of fun. "Is that okay? *Please, Mum.*"

I suddenly feel as though he's asking me to leave him in the care of Charlie Sheen. But the excitement in his eyes forces me to swallow my concerns. At least now Natasha's here I'll be able to distract myself from visions of him drowning while Adam's snuck off for a cigarette.

"It'll keep you off my iPad, I suppose." I smile.

"Yes! Thanks, Mum. I love you."

"Yes, you always do when you manage to get your own way." I smirk as he starts heading back to the game. "Oh, and where is my iPad, anyway?"

He frowns. "Er . . . I think I left it in Dad's office."

"You *think*?"

"I'm pretty sure. I'll get it after this game," he replies.

Natasha returns with a bottle of red and two glasses, and I can't help noticing that

Ben is looking over, concentrating more on my friend than on the burgers.

"You're getting some attention from there." I gesture over.

When she looks up, his face breaks into a shy smile, and there is a glimmer of recognition in her eyes. But it's momentary, a reflex action, before she lifts up the bottle and starts to pour. "Unquestionably gorgeous. But I'm actively avoiding hot young things at the moment."

I scrunch up my nose. "Why?"

"I've had too many flings in the last few years, Jess. I'm after something a bit more . . . meaningful."

"Oh . . . good."

"It's easier said than done though. And Tinder doesn't help."

"Really? Last time we spoke you were quite enthusiastic about it."

"That was before I started to get messages like this." She pulls out her phone and shows me her latest exchange.

Hi, Im very shy, but I don't mind saying Id like to bang you senseless right now. Your so HOT.

A laugh bursts from my lips as I scroll down to her response.

*You're. Thanks but go away.

"Natasha!" Adam is walking towards us, in combat shorts and a plain white T-shirt that clings to his chest. He bends down to give her a kiss. She looks initially pleased to see him, before stopping herself and straightening her mouth. Then she smiles again. It can't be easy when a man has given you a free holiday, but loyalty to me prevents her from being too enthusiastic about him. "Hello, Adam. How are you?"

"Really good," he replies. "It's great to have Jess and William here."

"Life's obviously been kind to you here, Adam. You look amazing." She catches herself and glances at me again. "Considering you're so much older now."

He laughs. "Yes, getting on a bit — thirty-three these days. Is work still keeping you busy?"

"Yes, but only in a good way. I'm looking forward to getting some sun though — and spending time with Jess and William. Which I believe you're keen to do too . . ."

"Definitely." He turns to me. "Has William asked if he can come rafting with me?"

"He has, and yes, that's fine. He's ridiculously excited about it."

"Good." He looks surprised and pleased.

134

"We went canyoning yesterday," he tells Natasha. "Jess is a massive fan."

"He's being funny," I drawl.

"To be absolutely fair to you, Jess, the weather was not ideal. Next time I take you I'll make sure it's sunny so your nose doesn't turn blue."

"In case it isn't completely clear, there won't be a next time."

Natasha laughs.

"Well, I was proud of you for having a go," Adam says.

The statement feels odd somehow; how can he be proud of me when I've nothing to do with him anymore?

I divert my gaze to William on the volleyball court, in time to see Simone looking over. Adam notices her too and responds by shifting a foot away from me, giving the ludicrous impression that he's trying to hide something.

"Have you had a look at your cottage?" he asks Natasha.

"Adam, it's gorgeous. Thanks for putting us in such a nice one."

"Natasha's used to luxury villas in the Maldives," I tell him. "It's a tough act to follow."

"Oh, Jess, stop it. I'm not some spoiled princess. Besides, if I get fed up of you two

135

I'm having one of those four-poster bedrooms in the château I saw on the Internet."

"I'll get a butler on standby for you," Adam says. "Right — I just wanted to say hello, but I've got a few things I need to do before I can sit down and relax. Oh, and Jess, I've left your iPad at reception — William's probably wondering where it is. He'd left it outside."

I tut. "Glad he's looking after it then."

He goes to leave. "It's *lovely* to have you here, Natasha."

When he disappears, she looks at me. "How does he do that?"

"What?"

"Make it impossible to hate him."

"I don't want people to *hate* Adam," I tell her. "He's William's dad. And yes, stuff happened between us, but that was a long time ago, and now we've all moved on."

Natasha glances up at Simone, who's looking over again. "I think somebody's certainly hoping so."

CHAPTER 19

William bounces into my room the following morning like it's Christmas Day.

"Mum, what time is it?"

I blearily look at my phone. "Ugh . . . seven," I croak as he disappears back into the kitchen.

I'm about to call after him and ask why he's up so early, before I remember all by myself. The rafting trip had almost slipped my mind until I went to tuck him in last night and discovered he'd gone to bed wearing his swimming trunks. His eyes flickered open briefly, and he explained that it'd save time in the morning if he got his kit on before he went to sleep.

I push back the cotton sheet and rub my eyes as I get out of bed to open the shutters, allowing light to filter onto the antique wardrobe and warm oak ceiling beams. It's a pleasant room to wake up in, with an unaffected simplicity to the tiled floor, pretty woven rug and sturdy wrought iron bed.

Sleepily, I tie up my hair with a band and follow William into the kitchen.

"What time did your dad say he was coming for you?" I ask. "I should have asked him for more details yesterday evening."

"At eight thirty, I think," he says.

"You *think*?" I go back into the bedroom to get my phone so I can text Adam, but as usual, there's no signal.

I have no idea what William is going to need for this trip, so I start packing two changes of clothes, a spare towel, trainers, factor 50 sun cream, insect repellent, flip-flops, a bottle of water and enough roast chicken crisps — to which he's developed a strange addiction — to feed a family of five.

"Do you think I'll get a chance to use these?" he asks, emerging from his room in a pair of flippers.

"I don't think so, sweetheart," I reply as he picks up my iPad and packs it in his rucksack. "And you can't take that either."

"But I want to make a video."

"Where are you going to keep it when you're on a raft?"

"Oh."

I check my phone again and find the glimmer of a signal. Trying to find one strong enough to send even a text has been a perpetual challenge since I got here. When the stars are in alignment and you're standing on one leg holding your phone three feet over the toaster seems to have worked best so far.

Do I need to make a packed lunch for this rafting trip or are you sorting it? And is it 8:30? He's beside himself with excitement :)

As soon as I've pressed send, I curse myself for adding the smiley face. Smiley faces and Adam are not an appropriate combination.

I watch as William sits outside at 8:20 a.m. to wait, while I pour a small cup of treacly coffee and follow him into the misty light of early sunshine. The courtyard is still and quiet; the only sound is that of the bees swarming around the bougainvillea and the birds circling above, their soft chirrups heralding the start of a new day. William says nothing but begins to tap his foot against the table.

I suspect that it's not the rafting itself that is the source of his excitement. This is about his dad. He just can't wait to be with him. I feel my throat tighten as my head rushes with unexpected emotion. I don't even know why this in particular has prompted it.

"What's the matter?" William asks.

I blink away the heat from my eyes. "Nothing. I think I might be allergic to something. The sun cream maybe."

But he's not really interested. He looks out towards the car park for Adam. "What time is it?"

I look at my watch. "It is 8:32 a.m."

"He should've been here two minutes ago."

"Be patient. I'm going to make some breakfast for myself. Have you had a drink this morning?"

"HERE HE IS!"

But I can see immediately that it's just a black car, similar to Adam's but a different make and model. "That's not him, sweetheart. But don't worry — he'll be here."

Fifteen minutes later, we are still outside. I've now told William not to worry approximately twelve times, so often that he appears not to be. Which is more than can be said for me. I glance at my phone, but there's no response to the message I sent. I briefly consider walking to the château to look for him, but unless we go along the road — which takes longer than the footpath

— he could already be on his way and we'll risk missing him. I try dialing his number, but it goes straight to voice mail.

"Can I have a quiz while we're waiting?" William asks.

"Hmm?"

"A quiz."

"Oh, okay." William is a big fan of quizzes; at least he is when he gets all the questions right. He's not old enough yet to have mastered his good loser face.

"What's the capital of Spain?"

"Madrid," he tuts. "You already knew I know that one."

I start pacing up and down. "What's the longest river in the world?"

"That's another geography one."

"So?"

"So you've just done a geography one. Can't we have something else?"

"Does this mean you don't know the answer?"

"No, it's the Amazon. Can I have another question now?"

I look at my watch and decide that if it gets to nine o'clock and he still hasn't shown up, I'll wake Natasha up to stay with William, and I'll go off looking for Adam.

"Mum?"

"Er. Okay. Spell *hydrochloric.*"

"Oh, *not spelling*," he groans. "What about movies?"

"Right," I sigh. "What was the name of Superman's father?"

"Jor-El."

"Well done."

Natasha appears at the door in an oversize T-shirt stretching languorously. "I'm glad you're up. Will you wait here with William in case Adam arrives?"

She rubs her eyes. "I'm not going anywhere. William and I will sit here and have a chat about . . . What would you like to chat about, William?"

"Can you give me a movie quiz?"

"Excellent idea!" Natasha says. "Right: name one of the lead actors in Hitchcock's 1963 version of *The Birds.*"

Chapter 20

I emerge from the woodland pathway and head straight to the château's grand doors. When I can't find Adam in any of the obvious places, I discover Ben on reception.

"He did mention that he'd taken the day off, Jess — and that he was going to the Vézère Valley."

My shoulders relax. "He's definitely going then. William seemed to think that he was being picked up forty-five minutes ago, and I can't get hold of him."

"Have you tried his cottage?"

Adam lives five minutes from the château, away from the guest accommodations, in a small cottage on the edge of the grounds. He tried to show me round a few days ago, but I only glanced in to be polite, uncomfortable with this level of insight into the life he lives these days.

His cottage is rougher around the edges than any for the guests, with a stone roof, a peeling blue door and weathered walls surrounded by swishing grasses and wild orchids. From what I saw, inside looked lived-in too, with overflowing bookshelves, stacks of letters, a well-stocked wine rack and old photographs fighting for space on an ancient-looking mantelpiece.

As I arrive at the front, my pulse is racing out of proportion to my levels of exertion. I hesitate before giving a sharp knock, only realizing as the door nudges open that it's unlocked.

"Adam? It's me." I push through and step in.

Then I shriek. Or possibly yelp. Either way, it's louder than I expected. But when you've walked in on a woman whose blouse is wide open, exposing a lacy, barely there bra, it's difficult to know what *is* the appropriate response.

Adam leaps away from Simone, as she turns away to button herself up. Then he starts blustering and puffing and demanding to know why I didn't knock.

"I *did* knock!" I protest, my cheeks glowing crimson. "You'd left the door open!" I hold my hand over my eyes, a reflex action that is hopelessly ineffective at unseeing a single thing I've just seen.

"That must have been me, sorry." Simone

smooths down her skirt and straightens her hair, acquiring an air of such angelic innocence you'd think I'd just walked in on her giving a Bible reading.

"It's . . . Look, it's fine," I say, backing out of the door, unable to look either of them in the eye. "Thank God I didn't send William though. I'd only come to see what time this rafting trip was taking place. The poor kid seems to think you should've been there nearly an hour ago."

"I can't take him rafting today," Adam replies. "I'm having a day off with Simone."

Simone folds her arms with a satisfied smile as I feel my chest stiffen.

"But you and I discussed this trip yesterday, Adam. You just can't say these things to a ten-year-old, then change your mind."

"I'll take him rafting at some point, but not today," he continues, breezily. "I can't today."

"But you *said* you could!" I argue.

"No, I didn't." He shakes his head as exasperation grips me by the throat.

"You *did,* Adam."

But he refuses to rise to an argument, despite the angry heat of Simone's glare. "You've got the wrong end of the stick, Jess. William came to ask me about this trip when I was fixing a leaky pipe in one of the

145

bedrooms. It was about to destroy a carpet I'd only recently paid through the nose for. I was distracted."

All I can think about is William, sitting on the step outside our cottage, clutching his backpack, tired but buzzing after a sleep fragmented from excitement. And how on earth I'm going to break this to him.

"So you're saying you *didn't* promise him you would take him today?"

"No, he did not," Simone interrupts tartly.

Adam's eyes dart sideways. "Well, you weren't there, Simone, to be fair." She goes to respond but decides to shut up.

"Look, Jess, I can't remember exactly what I said," he continues. "I did agree we could go rafting — which we can — but I wouldn't have told him we could do it today, because I'm busy. At the time, I just needed to get rid of him."

My incredulity starts to bubble into something far stronger. "What?"

"I didn't mean that."

"Whatever's been said, the fact is *he can't go,* Jess," Simone shrills.

"But Adam has *promised,* Simone," I say calmly, trying to reason with at least one of them.

"Well, he'll have to just get over it, won't

146

he?" she spits. "Besides, it wasn't a *promise.*"

"*Everything's* a promise when you tell a ten-year-old you'll do something with him," I fire back.

A *psthhwwhwh* sound is released from Simone's mouth, like she's got a puncture.

Adam glances between the two of us, then settles his eyes on me. "Jess. We did the canyoning only two days ago. I had it in my head that I could maybe take him at some point next week."

I think of William in his daft swimming trunks last night and feel a surge of fury. "So we've come all this way, and he only gets to spend proper time with you once a week?"

"You can't even book it at this short of notice," Adam continues, ignoring me. "I didn't realize he was talking about today. It was he who suggested 'about eight thirty,' and I thought he was talking . . . generally. Which was stupid, with hindsight, but like I say, I was distracted. I'm sorry, but I *will* take him." He glances sideways at Simone and adds: "Just not today."

I make one more attempt to reason with him. "Adam," I say quietly, my voice shaking. "It doesn't *even* need to be rafting. It can be anything. He just wants to be with

147

his dad. Whom he *loves*. That's why we're *here*."

Adam falters. For a moment, I'm convinced he's going to do the right thing.

"If you must know, Jess, we are booked into a Mr. and Mrs. Smith hotel," Simone announces. "It cost a fortune and takes ages to get a room there. So there's absolutely no way we can't go."

I stand there, my nails digging into my palms, as I process the news that Adam will be spending his day off in bed with his twenty-two-year-old girlfriend rather than being with William. I suddenly can't bear to be in the same room as the two of them.

I spin round and march away. Adam follows me to the door and calls out after me. "I'll sort something out to do with William as soon as I'm back. I promise."

I stop at the end of the path, my veins sizzling as I turn back. And I'm afraid I just can't help myself. "As I've discovered firsthand, Adam: your promises don't mean a thing."

CHAPTER 21

I can't pretend my own father was perfect. But he would have been if it weren't for one thing. By the time I was a teenager, I could no longer pretend to ignore Dad's drinking. In between the many times he was wonderful, there were others when he was an utter disaster. And alcohol was always involved.

There was the day he'd crashed the car into our front wall after convincing himself he was safe to drive to the off-license, or the night we'd found him slumped on the porch, unable to get his key into the door.

These things didn't happen all the time; there were long months between his blow-outs, not days. But I need to remind myself of them sometimes, when Adam pulls one of his stunts and I am consumed with fury on my son's behalf. There is a crucial difference though. My dad had his problems, but he *did* something about them. And he did it for Mum and me.

My parents had met shortly after he'd qualified as an accountant and got a job at Arthur Mitchell in Manchester, where she had been a secretary since leaving school at sixteen. My mother had always filled her spare time with baking, and every Friday, she'd bring a selection of whatever she'd made that week to work: gooey chocolate eclairs, coffee and walnut slices, zingy lemon-tons with crunchy sugar toppings.

"I finally asked her out over a Battenberg," Dad used to joke.

They went to the cinema on their first date, to see *The Evil Dead,* which was apparently Mum's idea, and were engaged four months later.

It's not a daughter's place to assess her parents' marriage, but there is no question that I assumed it to be happy when I was growing up. I sometimes look back and wonder how I concluded that. Because there were occasions when an objective observer would've called it anything but.

When I was sixteen, I won a part in the school play, an ambitious production of *Les Misérables.* It was a small role — as a tavern wench — with only one line, but I took it very seriously. And on the first night, I found myself anxiously waiting backstage to make my theatrical debut, when I overheard a group of sixth formers laughing.

"There's puke all over the boys' bogs. Mr. Jones slipped in it, nearly went arse over tit. Degsy reckons it was someone's dad, completely shit-faced."

Cold recognition seeped into me. I knew who they were talking about; when Mum had driven me to the performance an hour and a half before it started, Dad had already hit the bottle.

I stepped onstage with dread eating me up from inside and gazed across the packed assembly hall, as I sought out my parents' faces.

I had a single line to deliver, but when I saw my father, the words dried up in my mouth.

Dad was slumped three rows from the front, fast asleep, while Mum sat stiffly by his side, her face gaunt, her eyes glistening in the stage lights. I got the line out eventually, but by the time the play finished, I felt like the whole school knew what had happened.

That weekend, we barely spoke, and I couldn't look at him. I just lay in my room, listening to rain hiss on the windows, still simmering with fury. Mum tried to convince me nobody knew who it was, but it became evident on Monday, when it was the talk of the school canteen, that she was wrong.

When I emerged from my room for dinner that night, Dad looked at me nervously.

"Look, I'm sorry, okay," he said, as he placed the salt and pepper on the table and Mum walked over carrying a homemade lasagna straight from the oven. "But . . . I don't think what I did was *that* bad."

Mum froze, incredulity on her face.

My breath hovered in my mouth as I tried to anticipate what she was going to say. But for a moment she didn't say anything; you could just see this rage blistering up inside her, fighting its way out.

"YOU FUCKING IDIOT," she screamed.

Then she lifted the bubbling casserole dish and smashed it right across the kitchen. I heard Dad gasp and felt my own jaw drop as we gazed at the wreckage of glass and tomato sauce, hot and thick as it slipped down the wall.

For a moment, Mum glared at it, her hand trembling over her mouth, as if she simply couldn't believe what she'd just done. Then she ran out of the room.

I looked up at Dad, in the mild shock that puts your brain on autopilot. I stood up silently to go and get a pair of rubber gloves. He stooped down with a newspaper and started piecing shards of glass into it.

And that was when I became aware that he was crying.

"I'm sorry, Jess," he whispered, unable to look at me. "I'm so sorry."

But I wasn't ready to let him off the hook. "I'm sure you are, Dad. Just like all the other times. But this is just going to keep happening, isn't it? You'll hate yourself for doing this stuff *but you never change*. You just keep getting pissed, keep letting it ruin — everything."

His lips parted, his face wet with tears. He looked crushed by my words, but I wasn't going to let it go. "I am *devastated* by you sometimes, Dad. Mortified that you'd behave like this. All for a stupid drink. Don't you realize what you're doing to me and Mum?"

He went to his first AA meeting three days later.

My father's transition from dysfunctional alcoholic to recovering alcoholic was not easy, but then I don't suppose it ever is.

He stuck with the meetings, though don't let me give the impression that he simply signed up, sat in a circle and saw the light. He had a love-hate relationship with AA and never really clicked with the other members.

But he persevered, because he knew in his bones he couldn't get through without the meetings.

In the first year, there were times when he seemed to visibly teeter on the edge of slipping. At social events, Mum and I would hold our breath as we watched acquaintances urging him to have a drink, bewildered by why anyone would stick to lemonade at a party. In those days, the look in his eyes seemed to change when he even smelled booze, as if he was frightened of it.

It was hard to know how to support him sometimes. We didn't want to be in his face, constantly asking if he was all right. But there were times when I had to tell him how proud I was. That "one day at a time" had added up to something that once had felt impossible.

We played tennis together one summer evening about eighteen months after he'd had his last drink, and I remember him smashing the ball past me. I didn't mind losing to him; his rediscovered vitality made me happy.

"Who'd have thought you'd be this healthy a couple of years ago?" I said. "You're amazing, really."

"Give it a rest, Jess — I'm a middle-aged man with a squidge round my belly no amount of tennis will shift."

"You know what I mean."

And I must've looked slightly deflated, because his voice lowered a bit, and he said: "Of course I do. But *amazing* isn't the word. I'm just . . . determined not to go back to how I was. So you'll never need to worry about that. I promise."

And I never have. Because he's been there for all three of us every single day for seventeen years. Supporting us. Loving us. And doing it all completely sober.

CHAPTER 22

I dread telling William that today's rafting trip with his dad is off. But he doesn't kick up an enormous fuss, or complain or shout or any of the things he'd be within his rights to do. He simply listens in silence as I conjure up lies on Adam's behalf.

"He ended up having to step in and help a family who'd lost their passports," I say. "They wouldn't have been able to get home otherwise. He'll definitely do something with you soon though."

His bottom lip tightens as he lowers his head, and when I've finished, he leaps up and runs to his bedroom, closing the door behind him. I give him some space for ten minutes, before taking decisive action and organizing an alternative day out with him and Natasha.

We drive to Lac du Causse, near Brive, about an hour away, where there's a sandy beach, clear water suitable for swimming —

and pedalos.

"Fancy a go? This is what Grandma suggested," I tell him brightly.

"Hmm. Okay," he says with a shrug, but only because the iPad is out of battery.

He perks up as soon as we're on the water. Largely because there's something apparently hilarious about a grown woman pedaling for her life every time she comes within twenty feet of a windsurfer. By the time we've navigated around the lake, my knees are on fire and, nostalgic or not, I'm hugely relieved to be back on dry land.

As William messes about collecting sticks at the edge of the water, I spread out on a beach towel next to Natasha as she slips into the kind of deep sleep that eludes me these days. We laze in that position for a good couple of hours before returning to Château de Roussignol in the late afternoon.

It's as we're heading into the cottage that Natasha nudges me. "Someone's waving at you."

"Hi, Jess!" Charlie is outside his door, on the other side of the courtyard.

"Oh, hi!" I smile back, as I root round for my key.

"He fancies you," Natasha whispers, as I snap up my head to check William can't hear.

"Don't be silly," I hiss back. "How can you tell?"

"He's coming over, for a start."

I open the door and usher Natasha and William inside. He runs in immediately, but she decides she's going nowhere.

"How are you?" I ask Charlie, as he approaches.

"Glad the sun's made an appearance again after yesterday."

"Ha! Yes, hopefully that was a one-off. This is Natasha — she's just joined us."

"Pleased to meet you," Natasha says, looking him up and down as if she's in a car showroom assessing the paintwork on a new coupe.

"And you." He smiles before turning to me again. "Did you go to the family barbecue last night? We'd forgotten it was on and went out for dinner."

"It was nice," I reply. "Not sure it would have appealed to Chloe, but William enjoyed it."

His speckled green eyes settle on my features. "I wish I'd remembered — we'd have joined you if I had."

I become uncomfortably aware of Natasha's expectant grin.

"DAD!"

Charlie turns and looks in his daughter's

direction. "Ah. Sorry — the teenager beckons. Woe betide anyone who does not jump immediately. See you soon, I hope." And then he is gone, heading towards Chloe as I wonder if Natasha could be right about him liking me.

"He couldn't take his eyes off you," she declares, as we step inside.

"Oh, shush."

"It's true. Good job he didn't see you in those white shorts yesterday. He wouldn't have known what to do with himself."

We step inside to find William on the sofa, already on the iPad. "Did you have a nice time today, sweetheart?"

"It was fine," he says.

"Listen . . . I'm really sorry your dad let you down today."

His head snaps up. "He *didn't* let me down. He's the boss, so when he has to work, he can't avoid it."

I suppress a ripple of irritation. I know it was me who told William that Adam had to work, but listening to him leap to his father's defense requires a restraint I never knew I had. Nonetheless, I suppose it beats him knowing what his dad was really up to.

CHAPTER 23

The scent of the air changes by mid-afternoon each day. It happens when the sun is high and its penetrating warmth has infused every flower and plant, so that the sweet, herby perfume of summertime escapes into the breeze.

The day after our lake visit, William, Natasha and I stroll to the château for a cold drink. Some kids are gathering at the soccer pitch when one runs over. He was hanging out with William in the pool over the weekend, even though he looks a couple of years younger than my son, with hair the color of carrots and a large gap between his two front teeth.

"There's a big match starting in five minutes, and we need another player. Are you coming?"

"I'm not sure," William replies.

"Oh, go on, William, give it a go."

He thinks for a second and eventually

nods, looking a bit wan. He heads towards the pitch as I spot Ben tidying up some of the chairs by the pool. I wave to him, and he waves back before picking up another chair. Then he hesitates, puts it down and starts to come over.

"Enjoying your holiday?" he asks. He has a clutch of leather bracelets on his thick, tanned wrists and a vintage crew T-shirt with a faded slogan on the front. His face is burnished to the color of honey, injecting warmth into his brown eyes.

"Lovely, thanks, Ben. Shame you're stuck at work in this gorgeous weather," I say.

"There are worse jobs. And at least I'm not cleaning bathrooms today."

I realize I haven't done any introductions. "This is my friend Natasha."

"Pleased to meet you." Her eyes flicker up to his. "That sounds like a Cardiff accent."

His face breaks into a smile. "Well spotted."

"My grandmother was from there."

Seven kids of varying nationalities are now on the pitch, and they communicate mainly via the universal language of soccer. Unfortunately, this is not a language in which William is fluent. As the other children sprint across the pitch, my son seems to just . . . hover. In fact, you'd think he'd been told

161

that the primary aim of the game is to actively avoid the ball. Occasionally, he has a go, but short of someone introducing a new rule that involves solving a crossword, it's hopeless — and his face crumples in despair every time he misses the ball, cursing his own ineptitude. It makes my heart twist.

I continue to watch the game, my attention drifting only when Ben and Natasha begin to laugh, and I glance across to see him completely charmed. Eventually, she excuses herself to get ready for dinner, and he resumes tidying the chairs, with an almost visible spring in his step.

"Hi there." Adam appears next to me. I look up and catch sight of him in profile. I can't bear how handsome he's become over the years. It's as if all those things that once bewitched me — the smell of his skin, those pools of his eyes — exist now only to taunt me.

"Hello," I reply frostily.

We stand side by side silently, watching as our son slips as far into the corner as he can manage. We are the only spectators.

"Has he scored?" Adam asks.

"Not . . . yet."

"GO ON, WILLIAM!" Adam shouts. My son looks up, sees his father and his forehead creases with anxiety. But determination does not prove enough. He runs across the pitch like a fairy tiptoeing across a set of stepping-stones and is quite simply unable to get near the ball.

Adam has this strange look in his eyes, as if the worst kind of revelation has just been laid bare: his son is crap at soccer. "He's . . ."

"Do not say a word."

He turns to look at me. "But he's . . ."

"Yes, Adam, I know. He's rubbish. He's never going to score a goal. He's —"

"I was just going to say he's left his shoelace undone."

I snap back my head. "Oh. Argh. WILLIAM!"

I start waving at him, but he shoos me away, like he's trying to get rid of a mangy cat. "YOUR SHOELACE!"

It's too late by the time he comes to a dead stop and frowns at me. He's already been hit by one of the Dutch girls — entirely by accident — and is flying across the pitch, where he lands on his cheek and ends up with a mouthful of dust. Adam races over.

"I'm fine, Dad," he splutters, as Adam lifts him up.

"Are you sure? Why don't you come and

sit down?"

Heroically, he wants to join in again. Even more heroically, the kids on his team say they want him to. Adam and I slink back to the edge of the pitch.

"I thought you were about to complain that he was no good," I confess.

"I wasn't going to say anything."

"Sorry." There's an awkward pause.

"He is . . . astoundingly bad though."

I glance at him sideways and let out a spurt of laughter. "Oh, bless him. It's a good thing I love him."

Adam looks back at the pitch.

"*We* love him," he corrects me.

CHAPTER 24

My head is fizzing with objections to Adam's statement after the stunt he pulled yesterday. If he really loved William, he'd *act* like it. He'd do what love involves when you're a parent: putting your child first. Always.

"I'm sorry about yesterday," he says.

I can't look at him.

"Can I explain? It was Simone's birthday. She'd booked this hotel before you'd even confirmed you were coming out here. It was months ago. I should've mentioned it to you, but I'd assumed it'd be no big deal, because it was a single day in the five weeks you're here. I had no idea you'd want to spend every day off with me."

"*I* don't. But given that William hasn't seen you for months, whereas Simone has, can't you see that he should be your priority?"

He doesn't reply.

"You seem to think that because you've

taken him canyoning once, you've done your bit. You've played at being Good Dad, posted the pics on Facebook and can now go back to your normal life. A life in which William barely seems to exist."

"That's not true, Jess."

"But it is!"

"Look, we live a long way from each other; that's a fact of life. As it is, I have to make do with Skype and —"

"You hardly know him, Adam." He looks away, unable to answer. "To you, he's more like a . . . nephew you're fond of but don't see much of. You've never had to deal with the hard grind of parenthood. You've had the luxury of being absent. Of never having to grow up yourself."

His jaw tenses visibly. "What's going to happen in the future, Adam? I'm not just talking about when he's a child, but as he grows up. Who's going to be around to give him advice about buying a car, or moving into his first house? Do you just assume it's all going to be down to me?"

He looks bewildered, clearly wondering why I'm going on about a time that feels eons away.

"Jess. I don't want to fall out with you, I really don't. But sometimes you give the impression that you've forgotten it was *you* who wanted us to break up."

"Oh, don't get me started on *that,*" I say, because he hasn't got a leg to stand on. He knows I had no choice. I might have technically been the one to leave, but he was desperate to see the end of the relationship. He made that very clear in the months before and years afterwards.

He tries to meet my eye, but I refuse to indulge him. "Look, I'm sorry I can't be there all the time, can't do more to support both of you day to day. And I also apologize — again — about yesterday, but it was a misunderstanding, nothing more. I'm going to make it up to him."

I can feel my jaw clench as I glance over at William and remember the look on his face when I told him the trip was canceled.

"You need to man up and behave like a father, Adam," I whisper. At first, he doesn't answer. He simply feels the kick of my words in his stomach and lets them sink in.

"Can I say something?"

I brace myself for an onslaught, for the row I know I've started by uttering one inflammatory but completely fair and accurate sentence.

"I don't say it enough, but I want you to know how much I appreciate everything you do. You're a wonderful mum. And whatever happened between us, you're bringing up our son brilliantly. I know you're doing the hard work — I know that it isn't easy. And you're raising a kid who is amazing, whether he can play soccer or not."

I take a deep breath and feel myself growing dangerously emotional. I focus on the edge of the grass, trying to stop my lip from trembling.

"The other thing I want to say is . . . I don't know why, after all these years of trying to avoid me, you've suddenly decided to come here. But I'm glad."

I can't look at him as a swell of emotion fills my chest.

"It was Mum."

"What?"

"It was my mum who wanted us to come." The effort to keep from crying makes my head start throbbing. "Much as she hated what you did, Adam, she has a problem with the idea of you and William living separate lives. She's always felt like this. But since she moved into the home, she's become even more determined about it. She thinks family is important. No matter what's happened in the past." I look down at the ground. "On one level she's trying to be practical. She and Dad have basically brought William up with me. Given the circumstances, that's no longer possible. She worries about me doing this on my own."

"Do you want more money?" he asks.

"No, Adam. If I'm honest, when I asked to come to visit, I was just humoring her." He remains silent. "But, this is the truth: Since I got here, I've seen with my own eyes how much William *wants* you in his life. He idolizes you. And much as it pains me to say this, I think Mum is right. William *needs* you in his life. More than you are currently."

I glance down at my hands, before carrying on. "I know you'll never move back to the UK. I know your life is here but . . . maybe if you could think about coming back to visit more, or William coming to you or . . ."

"Of course. Of course."

As my temple throbs, I whisper a question that is bubbling at my lips. "Do you ever think you *would* move back to the UK? Just out of interest?"

He takes a second to reply. "I think you've already answered that question, Jess, haven't you?"

I sniff and smile cordially. "Just thought I'd ask." I straighten up and try to think of a way to lighten the mood. "Anyway, promise me you'll never pull a stunt like that with

William again, or else."

His eyes soften. "Are you threatening me, Jess?"

"Damn right. Step out of line again, and I'll review you on Trip-Advisor."

He laughs, then falls silent for a moment. "Are they any closer to finding out exactly what's wrong with your mum?"

My chest tightens. "It's a neurodegenerative condition."

"I know but . . . what, ALS or something?"

"They're not entirely sure," I say.

But I'm lying.

Because it still feels far too difficult to tell Adam the truth.

CHAPTER 25

When my mum's symptoms began, the changes weren't obvious to those around her. Because we weren't *looking* for them.

It was her mood that altered first. She went from being a woman who was usually even-tempered and happy-go-lucky to one capable of completely losing it, over the slightest thing. Not all the time, you understand; her rages were rare, but so volcanic that you couldn't miss them. And *anything* could spark them: My room not being tidy. The hem on her skirt coming undone. My dad trying to claim that vomiting in the school toilets before my school play wasn't a big deal.

I remember several incidents while I was at university whose significance looms even larger in hindsight.

Once when I was home for the spring break, I came down from my room one Sunday morning to find her in the kitchen surrounded by ingredients.

"What are you making?"

Amy Winehouse was singing on the radio, and cool rays of sunshine were streaming through the windows.

"An Easter cake," she said, inviting me to look at the picture in one of her glossy books. She'd made far more complex creations, but this was sweet — a single-tiered coconut cake, covered in grass green fondant, with a little white bunny popping out of the top.

"Very cute," I said, as I sat down at the table to flick through the paper and chat while she got to work.

But as I tried to tell her about one of my last classes before the break, I noticed that she kept stopping and reading the instructions, before glancing anxiously at the sugar paste. It was as if her brain was keeping her from working out how to marry the two. She'd start kneading a small piece, working it into the shape she wanted, before she'd stop again and mutter angrily to herself.

"Is everything all right, Mum?" I asked, closing the paper.

"Yes, I just had a late night," she snapped, blowing her fringe out of her face. "I'm not really in the mood for this. I'll do it tomorrow instead."

She slammed shut the book.

But the Easter cake was never finished.

Looking back, a mountain of evidence had started to develop before anyone did anything about it. Her fidgeting, her little twitches, odd but almost imperceptible movements — they all went on for ages before any of us thought too hard about all the signs.

I couldn't tell you if my mum was genuinely oblivious herself, or if she was deliberately ignoring them. Either way, there reached a point when I realized I had to make her go see a doctor.

The Christmas before William was born, she and I had decided to go to the Trafford Centre to finish our shopping. We were on our way home, the boot of her little red Corsa packed with presents and baby paraphernalia that she hadn't been able to resist.

"Do you think you've got enough sleep suits?" she asked, as we pulled up at the lights near the end of her road.

"I've got about forty, so I would hope so."

"Believe me, you can never have enough. If this baby is anything like you were, it'll be permanently covered in dribble."

The lights changed, so she put the car in gear and approached the end of her road.

But she sailed right past it.

"Mum, what are you doing?" I laughed.

She glanced at me but continued driving. "What do you mean?"

"You've just driven past your road," I said incredulously.

She flicked on her indicator and pulled in. Her face was devoid of color, her eyes full of panic.

"Mum, what's the matter?"

She shook her head. "Nothing. I just got distracted. I was thinking about the baby."

She waited until the traffic was clear and did a three-point turn. But as she gripped the steering wheel, I could see instantly something wasn't right. She couldn't remember how to get home. "Next left," I said.

"I know, I know," she replied crossly. But, without that simple instruction, I'm not sure she'd have ever found her way back to the house where she'd lived for fifteen years.

I made her swear she'd go to the GP afterwards. She told me she'd been sent for tests but that everyone was certain it was "nothing." She played down what was really going on, determined not to break her hideous news to me while I was pregnant, when she worried about what the stress would do to me and the baby.

Distracted by what was going on between Adam and me and focused heavily on the pregnancy, I accepted her reassurances. Because at that point, before I knew the truth, the really devastating effects of her condition were yet to come. I convinced myself that Mum was just one of those women who couldn't sit still and that I must've exaggerated my recollection of what'd happened in the car. It was easy to put it to the back of my mind.

I miss those days. When Huntington's disease was not part of our daily vocabulary. When I didn't know that what my mum had was fatal, hadn't heard it called the cruelest condition known to man. And certainly didn't know that I had a fifty-fifty chance of inheriting the faulty gene that causes it.

CHAPTER 26

Before I discovered that Mum had Huntington's, my attitude to my own body was the same as most people's.

We assume good health is our God-given right, to be taken for granted, as if we'll always feel this well. Serious illness is meant to be something that happens to other people. People in the newspapers or on Facebook, sharing noble stories and personal battles.

Only, overnight, we became the other people.

My mum and dad told me together about her HD diagnosis, a few weeks after Adam and I had split up.

They sat me down at the big pine table where I'd eaten dinners as a child. I remember their usually spotless kitchen showing unfamiliar signs of neglect. There were coffee cup rings left unwiped on the wood, a small stack of dishes at the sink, a floral tea towel screwed up in the corner by the washing machine, stained with angry splodges of food.

I was trying to feed William, but he wouldn't stop crying, his incessant fussing only abating when I stood pacing with him, rocking him back and forth.

"Here, let me take him," Mum said as she rose to her feet, and I placed him in her arms. He settled instantly. She looked into his eyes, holding my gorgeous boy, and looked so content that nobody could have predicted what she was about to tell me as she sank into her seat again and rocked him silently.

"The doctors have found out that I have a condition called Huntington's disease."

I narrowed my eyes, taking in her words. "What?"

"Have you heard of it?" she asked gently.

"I think so . . . I don't know."

"Okay. Well, I'm going to tell you everything I know."

When she explained that she had HD, what it was and that there was a 50 percent chance I'd inherit the faulty gene that produces it, it was in straightforward but unflinching terms.

She was forty-three at the time, too young, I thought, for anyone to have a fatal illness.

She was oddly calm when she spoke, serene almost. And although she was effectively telling me the most shocking, cruel joke I'd heard in my life, she didn't cry. She was saving her tears for later. The effects of the disease will kill my mum, probably sooner rather than later. She's a fighter by nature, but time is running out for her.

"There's a lot to take in, Jess," she said. "But I want you to know that . . . that no matter how tough things get, we're all going to be here, for one another."

I started sweating. I could feel my skin going clammy and my head getting fuzzy. I felt as though I was having an out-of-body experience, a feeling that, bizarrely, took days to wear off, after which I just cried. Big gulping sobs that wouldn't stop.

I spent that evening on the Internet and could probably still recite the first article I read about it, on the website of the Huntington's Disease Society of America.

Huntington's disease (HD) is a fatal genetic disorder that causes the progressive breakdown of nerve cells in the brain. It deteriorates a person's physical and mental abilities during their prime working years and has no cure. Every child of a parent with HD has a 50/50 chance of carrying the faulty gene.

Many describe the symptoms of HD as having ALS, Parkinson's and Alzheimer's — simultaneously.

Symptoms usually appear between the ages of 30 to 50, and worsen over a 10 to 25 year period. Over time, HD affects the individual's ability to reason, walk and speak.

Symptoms Include:

- Personality changes, mood swings & depression
- Forgetfulness & impaired judgment
- Unsteady gait & involuntary movements (chorea)
- Slurred speech, difficulty in swallowing & significant weight loss

Ultimately, the weakened individual succumbs to pneumonia, heart failure or other complications.

Only a handful of people know the full details of our situation, Becky and Natasha among them. For everyone else, I've avoided putting a name on what Mum's got, saying vaguely what I said to Adam: that it's simply a neurodegenerative condition, which everyone seems to conclude is ALS.

I don't like being secretive. I know this is

something that should be out in the open. My conscience tells me I should be helping to make more people aware of HD, or taking part in runs to raise money for research.

But until I've found the right time to tell William, this is how it has to be.

I've thought long and hard about when I should do it. Whether to drop it into conversation a few times, or sit him down and have a big talk. But it comes down to this: I can't bear the thought of him knowing about what — potentially — both my future and his may hold when he's only ten years old.

I want William to live as a child should — with excitement and optimism, where the only thing he has to worry about is not being able to master a decent kick in soccer.

CHAPTER 27

By the time William's team has conceded an 18–3 defeat, I've managed to have a long text exchange with Dad and undo four months of Grit classes by ordering a platter of calorific delights: *saucisson sec* served with tangy celeriac coleslaw and darkly crusted bread.

"I can't believe we lost," William says, sloping over despondently.

"Oh, never mind. Shall I get you a drink?"

I order an apple juice from Delphine, the young waitress on duty.

The sun is beginning to sink in the sky, the cascading orange light bathing over the cypress trees and soft hues of the château's stone walls. The pool is empty but for a lone swimmer doing laps, goggles tight across her face. The dying heat of the day has intensified the fragrance in the air, of cyclamen and thyme.

"Did Dad think I did well when he came

to watch the match?" William asks, as we wait for his drink.

"He thought you were fantastic."

"Did he see me nearly score that goal at the end?"

I can't imagine what he's talking about; as far as I could see, he couldn't have been further from scoring if he'd been standing in São Paulo.

"He couldn't have missed it, William. Well done," I say enthusiastically.

I look up and realize Natasha has arrived but has been sidetracked — she's talking to a guy seated farther along the terrace.

"You should have a kick around with your dad," I continue, as Delphine appears with the juice. "He used to be good at soccer. Maybe he can give you a few tips."

"Great," he says with a shrug, guzzling his drink as Natasha walks towards us, with the guy she was talking to next to her, glass of red in his hand.

"Jess, this is Joshua. He lives near me in Islington. We're virtually neighbors." Her eyes bore into mine meaningfully, and I realize via the power of female intuition — or possibly because she couldn't be less subtle if she'd thrown a brick at my head — that she sees potential in him.

"Oh, how lovely. Come and join us." I

smile and pull out a chair. "This is William."

"Great to meet you." Joshua has seaside blue eyes and a hard-earned tan that hides the faint bloom of rosy cheeks. He's slightly pudgy around the middle and a good five years older than Natasha. But he has a nice smile and the kind of thick, neat hair that would make my grandma consider him a dreamboat.

"I'll be on the swings," William announces, skipping off to join the other kids who are hanging about in the play area.

"I was just trying to persuade Natasha that she'd be right at home in my new flat when she gets back to London." Joshua grins.

I frown, wondering what I'm missing, but Natasha laughs.

"I dabble in property development," he explains, raising a smooth eyebrow.

"Ah."

"I'm afraid I'm very happy in my place," Natasha tells him. "And it took me so long to find it, I'm not going anywhere soon."

He twists his mouth to one side. "That *is* a pity. I'll just have to think of another excuse to see you again."

Over the next half hour, they seem to get on famously. This is despite, or perhaps because of, the fact that Natasha doesn't seem to notice that Joshua's favorite subject is very clearly . . . Joshua.

Eventually, when we've exhausted topics including his two cars, his house, the antiques business that brings him to the Dordogne, his golfing handicap and his snowboarding trip to Verbier earlier in the year, he looks at his watch.

"Well, I need to run. But I hope I see you very soon." She lifts up her hand and waves as he strides away.

"Do you think he likes me?" she whispers.

"Yes, I do." I take a sip of my drink. "Is the feeling mutual?"

"Well, he ticks all the boxes. Intelligent. Solvent. Well educated. Speaks five languages. *Lovely* hair. Oh, there's our neighbor again."

I glance up and spot Charlie, his eyes fixed on us. He seems momentarily unsettled by the fact that I've caught him looking, before his face breaks into a wide smile.

Natasha lowers her sunglasses. "You are definitely in there."

"So you keep telling me."

She grins. "So what did Adam have to say after the rafting shambles?"

I sigh. "He apologized, said he was grateful for everything I do as a mother, that he loves William and only went to that hotel because it was Simone's birthday and she'd booked it ages ago."

She purses her lips and lets out a small *hmm* sound. "Well, I hope you're not going to be sucked in by a word of it."

"Of course not. What sort of moron do you take me for?"

CHAPTER 28

In the days since Natasha arrived, we've developed a little routine that involves rolling out of bed later than William is used to, having a breakfast bigger than he can really stomach then going on a visit somewhere or relaxing by the pool.

I am there in body, if not entirely in spirit, for these simple pleasures. As soon as my eyes flutter open each morning, I start thinking about Mum, and the rush of thoughts that follow stay with me for the rest of the day, making it difficult to concentrate on anything else.

Still, I'm happy to see the arrival of Becky and her family — and if anything is going to drown out the noise crashing in my head, it's that lot.

"I might have to keep some of this plonk in your fridge if that's okay, Jess? I'm not sure there's enough room in ours," Becky tells me, as Seb staggers under the weight of a crate of beer. He has the same pale green eyes and playful grin he had at university, but time and three children have made his hair a bit greyer, his skin a bit sallower, his general demeanor more battle worn.

"What she means," Seb says, "is that we bought so much booze in the supermarket that the suspension on the car looks as though there's a kangaroo in the boot."

He thumps it down on the table and marches over to give me a bear hug.

"Oh, I've missed you two!" I squeeze him to me.

"When did I last see you, Jess?" he asks.

"New Year's Eve," I tell him. "Excellent party, by the way — though someone should tell your wife she should've grown out of waking up in the bath these days."

Becky and Seb's cottage is some way from where we're staying, in a workers' cottage close to the château that was renovated last year. It's a pretty little place, with old stone walls big enough to accommodate the five of them and smothered in creamy yellow honeysuckle. I peer into the back of their 4×4. It is piled high with pushchairs, toddler equipment, nappies and Barbie dolls. "Traveled as light as I did then?"

"We really needed a four-ton truck," Becky says, picking up two bottles of wine, shoving a baby-changing mat under her arm and grabbing a sports holdall. I take a suitcase and follow her.

Becky's hair was dyed auburn when we were at university together, and after a flirtation with sixteen or so shades, she's had a tangle of soft blond waves for the last year. She has gained a little weight, but the curves suit her and the peachy hues of her clear skin and hazel eyes. She's wearing faded jeans and a slouchy top the color of marsala, with dozens of silver bangles jangling against her arms.

Despite living in a respectable four-bedroom house in Hebden Bridge, Becky retains the air of someone who wasn't born to settle down. Maybe I'm basing this on the girl I once knew, who changed university courses twice, moved flats half a dozen times and whose only long-term relationship was with the Student Loans Company.

At university, Becky and Seb were friends with Adam and me long before they got together romantically. Seb, an economics student from Birmingham, was sweet, shy and, once you'd delved behind the quiet exterior, great fun with that unexpectedly dry brand of humor that makes you spit out your drink. He was beanpole tall, with thick blond hair that sometimes had a life of its own.

He'd been Adam's friend ever since they'd met in halls of residence. When I was introduced to him in second year, I quickly came to the conclusion that Seb was a sweetheart, and he still is: a loyal husband, great friend, all-round nice guy and the brother Adam never had.

My friends' initial failure to get together wasn't through lack of motivation on Seb's part. He adored Becky. Longing radiated from him every time she spoke, his eyes shone with admiration when she laughed and he'd blush when she flirted with him. Sadly, in those days she'd have flirted with a potato if she'd thought it had eyes for her.

But Seb wasn't Becky's type — her type being toxic time-wasters. It was when she was getting over the breakup from yet another beautiful shithead that one of us got tickets to see Oasis play at the City of Manchester Stadium.

That night, we got nicely stoned, and high on the music and a life we recklessly assumed would always be that easy and that good. Adam slid his arms around me in the dusky half-light, and as the uproarious guitar strings of "Champagne Supernova" throbbed through me, something caught my

189

eye. Seb had slipped his hand into Becky's. I could see him furtively checking to see if she was going to pull away.

But a faint look of surprise had appeared on her face. She must've realized before that moment what he felt for her. But his boldness seemed to place him in an entirely new light. As music filled our ears, the heady smells of summer in the city drifted around us, and two of my favorite people finally found each other.

"Becky, have you got a minute?" Seb calls from inside. She sighs and starts to stagger in faster with the wine, where we discover James and Rufus having a loud debate about who hit whom first, while Poppy has a tantrum on the floor.

"What's up with Poppy?" Becky asks over the din.

"There's no telly so she can't watch *Peppa Pig,*" Seb replies, rubbing his head.

Becky's shoulders deflate, before she squats down in front of her daughter. "Right, Poppy." Her voice is calm, authoritative and enough to scare even me. "If you carry on like that you'll go on the naughty step."

"It's a bungalow," Seb reminds her, before turning his attention sternly to the boys. "You two: *enough.*"

They don't even register his presence.

"BOYS. THAT'S ENOUGH!"

I've never heard Seb raise his voice before. "Look, you're *meant* to be on holiday. And that means getting along nicely with each other. Now, I want you to both tell me, quietly and calmly, what the problem is."

"*HEDIDITFIRST — NOHEDID — BUTHE-HITMEAND — I HATEHIMAND —*"

"STOP!" Becky interjects, pushing Seb out of the way, before telling both of them to go and sit on opposite sides of the room. They start arguing about which is the best side.

"It's been like this since we left home," Becky tells me.

"It's been like this since 2012," Seb corrects her.

Becky sighs. "Well, the place seems lovely. And Seb can't wait to see Adam."

Seb and Adam have stayed friends over the years, but not in the same way Becky and I have. We call and text each other all the time and make the effort to get together at least every few weeks. Seb and Adam have stayed in touch only in that way men do: by commenting on Facebook posts, going on stag dos and buying a pint for each other if life happens to lead them to the same general vicinity.

"Adam's in demand," I tell her. "He's got a new girlfriend."

"There's always a new girlfriend," she says dismissively. "Seb's been introduced to dozens over the years and couldn't tell you the name of a single one."

"Matilda," he interrupts.

"What?" she mutters.

"Matilda," he repeats. "I remember her."

"Was that the classical cellist with a figure like Jessica Rabbit?" Becky asks. "Can't imagine why she'd stick in your mind."

"You know how much I love Stravinsky." He grins.

CHAPTER 29

Given the journey Becky, Seb and the kids have endured, Natasha and I offer to host a barbecue for dinner. So we head to the nearest supermarket in the afternoon to stock up on burgers, sausages, a couple of steaks and another unidentifiable meat-based product that the lady at the counter was under the misapprehension we wanted. It felt too difficult to put her right.

The benefit of staying in the end cottage of Les Écuries is that we have more space to ourselves than the others do. When you step out and walk round the side, it over-looks a meadow that swishes with soft green grasses, and before that is a stony patch into which we can extend our sitting area. Adam brought over half a dozen folding chairs and a spare table earlier, and we've pooled the plates and cutlery from both our cottages.

The kids play tag on the grass, as the smoky heat from the grill rises into the sky.

Becky finishes topping up everyone's rioja before joining me at the barbecue.

"What *is* that?" she asks, as I pick up a pair of tongs.

"Meat. That's all I can tell you, I'm afraid."

"Seb'll eat it, don't worry. He's got a stomach like an industrial grinder." Poppy wriggles away from her and runs to her daddy, who scoops her up and tickles her neck, as she convulses with infectious laughter.

"It's lovely to see the boys getting along so well," Becky says. "William's such a calming influence. I hope it lasts."

The outburst between James and Rufus earlier was not an anomaly. I realize it's normal for all siblings to fight, but these two are sworn enemies who could've been born on two different planets: James is earnest, studious, a fan of One Direction, Barbie and *The Sound of Music.* Rufus is a rough-and-tumble five-year-old who loves WWE, rugby and being as loud as possible. They're both gorgeous children, until you put them together, when they turn into a couple of psychopaths.

"Are you sure you don't want me to take over?"

Adam is suddenly next to me, so close I

can smell the sunshine on his skin. I edge away and pick up my tongs.

"It's all under control," I tell him, turning over a steak.

He looks resolutely off duty tonight, in long shorts and an olive crew that skims his torso. I'd assumed he'd be bringing Simone to show off to Seb, but he tells us she's decided to have an early night and has gone back to the flat she rents with Ben in Sarlat. I can't deny this is a relief. I hope we've all moved on from the excruciating incident in Adam's cottage, but being in the company of old friends is easier, sweeter somehow, when you've got them all to yourself.

"I really wouldn't mind," he perseveres.

Becky bursts out laughing. "What *is* it with men and barbecues?" She nudges me. "Jess, you are clearly in what he considers his domain."

He grins at her. "Only offering to help. But now you mention it, I'm sure if you handed over those tongs to me —"

"Get lost," I laugh, flicking him away with a tea towel. "If you really want to help, you can do the salad."

"Oh, I see. So you get to stand at the barbecue turning rib eye steaks, and you're sending me inside to arrange a bowl of rocket. This could be the most emasculating thing you've ever said, Jess."

"You've clearly never heard what she says behind your back," Becky says.

"Fine. I'll make a salad. But just so you know, it'll be a *really* manly one."

Becky chuckles as he walks away, then stops abruptly. "Sorry," she whispers. "He's just funny. Still a tosser though. Definitely a tosser."

CHAPTER 30

As a starry night descends upon us, we drink wine and reminisce with the laughter of three tired but happy children ringing out across the meadow. It's nine thirty, and Poppy is fast asleep in her pajamas in her pushchair, cozy under a blanket. It's technically past bedtime for the other children too, but they're determined to stay up late, and nobody is in the mood to refuse them, even if it means Seb and Becky have to referee the odd argument. The adults sit around a table flickering with citronella candles, all of us full of food and booze and the sheer magnificence of being surrounded by people you love.

"Are we okay after what happened the other day?" Adam is leaning into me. I glance up with a start, before looking straight ahead, refusing to watch how the light from the candles illuminates his face and flickers in his dark eyes.

"Of course we're okay."

"If it means anything . . . I hear everything you're saying."

That aftershave is new. He used to wear a Hermès one I bought him for Christmas, even years after we were no longer together.

"Okay, good."

"And I will spend more time with him while you're here."

"That's great to hear. Thanks." I think about leaving the conversation there, but I can't. "So . . . when?"

He shifts in his chair, as if I've put him on the spot. "Well, I'll have a look at the diary."

I feel myself deflate. "Just do what you can, Adam. That's all I ask."

"Dad, will you come and play a game?" William appears next to us. He hasn't asked for even a moment of Adam's attention all night. And he hasn't got it either — Adam's been talking to Seb all evening.

"Good idea. How about gin rummy?" Adam produces a pack of cards from his back pocket.

"We were thinking maybe . . . cricket?" William says.

"It's too dark for cricket. Come on, sit down. James and Rufus: why don't you come and join in too?"

The kids plod over, more exhausted than intrigued, as he deals out the cards to all of us.

"So you're obviously *only* allowed to play for money," Adam tells them. "There's no point otherwise."

This, it turns out, is an entirely different prospect. The three boys' interest is suddenly piqued. "So, William, the question is this: how much have you got and how much are you prepared to bet?"

"I've got some pocket money Granddad gave me," he offers, standing up to go and look for it.

Adam puts his hand on his arm and gently pushes him down. "Just this once, I'll bankroll you." He pulls out a handful of coins.

We play for cents and, despite the dark air leaving a chill on our shoulders, part of me doesn't want it to end, which is saying something given that I'm repeatedly trounced by a five-year-old.

It's as Rufus is celebrating another triumph that I realize the light has gone on in Charlie's cottage opposite.

"Perhaps we need to keep the noise down," Natasha says, gesturing over in that direction.

"Shush, everyone," I urge them.

But as the game resumes, nobody is making the slightest bit of effort to keep the noise down, including Adam who celebrates one victory over the kids far too enthusiastically. "Wanker," I whisper in his ear, only a bit drunk and half joking.

He bursts out laughing. "Oh, come on. I let them win five rounds; I had to retain some dignity."

"I hate to break this to you, but you've failed."

"I'm just helping them grow up to be well-rounded individuals. Plus, I'm running out of money."

By now, Charlie is on his terrace, the light from the window illuminating the back of his body as he stands, absorbed in something on his phone. He lifts up his head, and I glance away as Natasha gives me a nudge. "Go and say hi from me."

I'm suddenly feeling brave. Or possibly tipsy.

"Excuse me a moment," I say self-consciously, pushing out my chair. But Adam is already dealing another hand of cards.

I stroll into our cottage, pause long enough to maintain my charade, then slip out to cross the courtyard to Charlie as he's finishing his call.

200

"I'm sorry about the noise. Are we keeping you and Chloe awake? We're going to put the kids to bed soon."

"Not at all, don't worry. Chloe's still up reading, and I never go to bed until after one in the morning anyway."

"Are those normal hours for a solicitor?" I ask.

"They're normal hours for an insomniac. I've got way too much to think about."

There's an odd but not uncomfortable silence between us as laughter clatters behind us. "Would you like to join us for a drink?" I offer.

"Oh, I wouldn't want to intrude. You've clearly got a lot to catch up on."

"Well, we have, but that doesn't stop anyone joining in."

He doesn't reply at first, and I feel silly for even asking. Then he smiles. "Okay. Just one. I'll let Chloe know where I am."

CHAPTER 31

I return to the table in time to hear William asking Adam for a quiz question. "Biology this time."

Adam thinks for a moment. "Okay, got one: which animal eats its mate immediately after they've, you know . . . *procreated*?"

I tut. "Only you would come up with something like that."

"What? It's a genuine question. The answer is a praying mantis. Or you could've had a black widow. Either way, it amounts to a very bad date."

"You didn't give me a chance to answer," William protests as I usher Charlie into the group and make some rudimentary introductions.

"Ah, you've been playing cards," Charlie says. "Who won?"

"Rufus has won loads, but I won the last one," William replies.

"I let him," Adam says, nudging his son.

"In your dreams, Dad." William grins, shaking his head.

Over the course of the next hour, we sit and talk and drink, and I get cold enough to need the jumper I'd packed but never thought I'd actually use. Although we're in a group, in our tête-à-tête, Charlie and I feel somehow separate, as he tells me about a full and genuinely fascinating life — about how he walked the Great Wall of China to raise money for Asthma UK after his brother died. That he's a keen tennis player who was once semiprofessional. That he turned forty-two this year. And that he's thinking of moving to Devon to be near Chloe, but is torn because his elderly father lives in Manchester and "if I'm honest, he needs me more."

It's gone midnight by the time everyone else has turned in. Yet Charlie lingers, helping me to clear up glasses as the cicadas buzz around us in the darkness.

"You don't have to do this," I tell him. "I didn't invite you over to do the washing up."

"Actually, I like washing up."

"Really?"

"Well, no, not really." He picks up another bottle. "It's a feeble excuse to stay a little longer."

Heat rushes to my cheeks, but if he notices, he doesn't let on.

"I wondered if you might be able to get someone to look after William, one lunchtime perhaps."

"Possibly. Why?" I ask, even though I already know what he's getting at. I want to be 100 percent clear that he wants to go on a date before I say yes to one.

"I hoped you'd be interested in going for a bite to eat."

I'm holding my breath as I walk to the barbecue and pick up the tongs. I've had no desire to contemplate anything like this for so long. I didn't think there would ever be room in my head again. And perhaps it's the wine, or the tingle of sunburn on my shoulders, but something is making me want to say yes.

"I'd love to," I reply, and the swoop in my stomach feels both strange and welcome.

"Great. How about a drive out somewhere for lunch on Saturday? I'll pick you up at about twelve."

CHAPTER 32

There was something about the way Charlie looked at me last night that reminded me how to feel desirable. I floated inside after we said good night, feeling light-headed as I crawled into bed in my underwear. I slept better than I have in months. Now, as the sun filters through the windows, I lie with my eyes closed, drifting in and out of thoughts as I try to remember what it would be like to have a man's hands on my skin again.

Then someone knocks on the window.

I tug the sheet up to my neck and blink at the glass, realizing that I left the shutters open. I blearily make out a figure outside, the outline of someone looking in as the sun shines fiercely behind, before he ducks down. "Argh!" I shriek, scrambling to slam the shutters closed. I grab a dressing gown, wrestle with it briefly, then abandon it and pull on a T-shirt and jeans before groggily

205

stumbling to the front door.

Adam is on the doorstep, looking maddeningly un-hungover.

"What are you doing here?"

"Good morning to you too." He steps inside, uninvited.

"Why were you looking into my window?" I demand.

"I wasn't *looking.* I'd knocked at the door three times and was about to give up when I saw the shutters were open and assumed you were up and about."

"I'd forgotten to close them last night, that's all."

"Well, I hadn't meant to impose on your privacy," he says.

"Good."

"Especially not when you were enjoying yourself so much."

I cross my arms over my T-shirt. "What do you *want,* Adam?"

He takes a deep breath. "I've decided to give Ben a temporary promotion and put him in charge this morning. Which means I have the morning off to do something with William."

"Oh. Well, he's asleep but —"

"I'M UP!" William enters the room in his pajamas, rubbing his eyes.

"Hello, buster," Adam says, as if he's

three. "Do you fancy going to a castle to-day?"

"He's already seen a castle with me. In fact, he's seen several. He should have a PhD in medieval architecture at this rate."

Adam refuses to be discouraged. "Yeah, but this is a really good one."

"That'd be great," William says enthusiastically. "Are you coming too, Mum?"

I briefly remember the conversation with Charlie last night. "Um . . . okay. Though there's no chance you could do this on Saturday instead, is there? Without me?"

"Why?" William asks.

"I might have something else on, that's all, so I thought you could have that boys' day out."

"What have you got on?"

"Just . . . I said I'd help Charlie out with something."

"Is Charlie that guy from last night?" William asks. "What are you helping him with?"

I feel myself redden. "Nothing . . . I . . . He's thinking of joining a Grit class, like the ones I go to, and I was going to tell him all about them."

"Does he want you to show him how you do the exercises?" William asks.

"No."

"Oh, that's good. You might want to spew

up again."

I'm about to protest when Adam speaks first. "I'll sort something out on Saturday too, if you like. I'll still have to be here, but William can help me out with some jobs."

For a bewildering moment, things feel awkward between us. It's stupid, really; it's not as though Adam's shy about his own love interests.

"So are you coming today, Mum?" William repeats.

"Does it involve any wet suits or waterfalls?"

"None at all," Adam reassures me. "It'll just be a nice family day out."

My lips part at the use of the phrase; I instinctively want to object to it. We're not a family. We are two fragments of a broken couple, superglued together by the most beautiful mistake we ever made.

We leave Natasha making plans to spend the day with Joshua and drive to Château de Beynac, which sits in austere splendor, high on the limestone rocks above the river Dordogne. It's a huge medieval fortification, the ultimate theatre of war, with a vast drawbridge and turreted ramparts. Inside, a labyrinth of cavernous dungeons weaves beneath secret spiral staircases, which we explore as William becomes increasingly fascinated by its gory history. We emerge into daylight at the top and are rewarded with a sweeping view across the valley, the glittering blue of the river snaking through lush green trees.

"Richard the Lionheart managed to conquer this castle," Adam tells William, gesturing to the sheer cliff ahead. "He climbed all the way up here."

William frowns uncertainly, trying to work out if Adam's pulling his leg. "No way."

"It's true."

"My favorite period in history was the Vikings," William continues. "Did you know that to stop the color coming out of their clothes, they used to wee on them?" William goes off on a gruesome trail of historical thought, firing bloodcurdling information at Adam, including the fact that you could toughen up a sword by leaving it in a dead person's stomach.

I follow the two of them round the outside of the castle, William's relentless chatter peppering the air as they shuffle through throngs of tourists.

"Hurry up, Mum!" He reaches the foot of a steep, winding staircase and starts heading up with Adam right behind.

"All right!" I laugh, as I grab the rail and

place my foot on the first narrow step, feeling the temperature drop in the dim light. My blood starts to pump the higher I climb up the cold, uneven surface and it's just as I reach the top that I lose my footing. I'm not sure how it happens; all I know is that one minute I'm trying to channel the words of my Grit instructor — *"Push into your glutes!"* — the next I'm clattering down five or six stairs, pain searing through my hands and knees before I come to a stop. I register a hand on my shoulder and glance up to see the blur of a young woman's face next to mine. "Are you all right?"

"I'm fine," I manage, shuffling onto my backside. "Thanks though."

"No problem." She smiles uncertainly. "Take it easy."

As I stand up, the back of my neck is prickling and my underarms are wet with a cold sweat. I look down at my hands and realize one of them is bleeding, and both knees are scuffed.

"Jess, are you all right?" Adam calls down, racing down after me. "What happened?"

He puts his hand on my back, and I look up sharply. His inky brown eyes are a few inches from mine, filled with concern. "I just fell, that's all. It's nothing. No broken bones," I insist, quickly stepping away, as

the lingering heat from his palm makes my
skin tingle.

CHAPTER 33

We take a walk along the grassy riverbank afterwards, heading out of the village into the endless countryside beyond, where birds swoop and dive above our heads, and the sun beats down on our shoulders. Adam and William stride ahead, my son's lanky legs skipping to keep up with his father's. Eventually, we reach a pool where the water stills, dragonflies dance on the surface and lily pads glisten in the bright light. A cyclist passes us along the pebbly path as an impossibly glamorous young couple sits picnicking on the hill.

We skim stones, long enough for William to master three or four hops and Adam to pretend to sulk when his repeatedly plop into the water and immediately sink under the surface.

Afterwards, he buys us lunch in a busy café in Beynac-et-Cazenac. We sit under a lipstick red canopy surrounded by diners devouring salads decorated with jewel-colored tomatoes, gooey Cabécou goat cheeses and strawberries with mimosa ice cream.

"I see everyone's giving the gizzards a miss," I point out to Adam.

"They'll regret it. What do you want to drink?"

"It's okay, I'll order." I turn to the waitress, determined my pronunciation will be perfect. *"L'eau, s'il vous plaît."*

"Pardon?" she replies.

"L'eau, s'il vous plaît." She looks at Adam and pulls a bemused expression as William sniggers.

"I said, *je voudrais* some *l'* . . . Coca-Cola."

"Ah oui!"

Adam orders the rest, as I sit back reluctantly, grumpily. Then the three of us linger under the soft shade as a brilliant blue sky stretches above us and the ancient village buzzes, as it has done for centuries before.

"What do you think of my team?" Adam asks.

"Lovely," I say. "Very professional. I particularly like Ben."

"Our in-house heartthrob? He's great, isn't he? He seems very keen on Natasha."

"She seems interested in that antiques

213

dealer guy, Josh, I'm afraid."

I glance at my guidebook, and when I look up again Adam is pulling out a pack of cigarette papers and some tobacco. I glare at him. When that fails to work, I give him a gentle kick under the table.

"Oww!" Then he realizes what's wrong. "Oh yeah, sorry. Still, William's a big boy, Jess. I'm sure he's sensible enough to know that some grown-ups do this without being sucked in by it himself."

"Do what you want," I say tartly. Adam hesitates before twisting the end of his cigarette and lighting it. He takes a long draw.

"Never, *ever* do that," I tell William firmly. "It will kill you. And before it does that, you'll have lungs like two shriveled-up kidney beans and a mouth like an ashtray."

"This is true." Adam shrugs. "Ashtray gob, that's me." He takes another puff.

"Why do you do it then?" William asks.

Adam lowers his cigarette. "I'm hooked. But it's not big, and it's not clever. That much is true."

"But . . . can't you *try* to stop? I don't want you to die."

Adam seems to hold his breath. He reaches over to the ashtray to stub the cigarette out silently, as a waitress arrives with our food.

William takes a bite of his croque monsieur. "I'm glad I was born in the twenty-first century," he says randomly. "That castle was brilliant, but I wouldn't like to have lived there."

"Me neither," I say. "Imagine having no flushing toilets or central heating or —"

"Or iPads," William finishes.

"Believe it or not, there were no iPads when your dad and I were your age."

"I know," he says. "And the televisions were in black and white and —"

"How old do you think we are?" I cough.

He giggles. "Anyway, you always said you had everything you ever wanted when you were a little girl."

"That's true," I reply.

He thinks for a minute. "What were your mum and dad like, Dad?"

Adam lowers his knife and fork. "They were a bit different from your grandma and granddad." And he isn't joking.

CHAPTER 34

I know I had a father who drank too much, but I still grew up feeling protected and loved and never anything less than happy. Adam did not have that luxury, something I only fully discovered about five months after we'd been together.

He'd already told me that he'd never known his father and that his mum had died in a car accident when he was nine. Beyond that, the details were sketchy, and I didn't push the issue because of the way his face shadowed with sadness when the subject was raised.

It was his aunt Julie who filled in the gaps, after she'd invited us to Sunday lunch once. Julie wasn't really his aunt. She was a distant older cousin who'd been close to his mother, Lisa, before she died and who'd taken Adam in afterwards, despite having three children of her own — Mike and Daniel, who were twelve-year-old twins, and

216

Stephanie, a year younger than Adam.

Aunt Julie was one of those women whose age was difficult to pinpoint. When I met her, she must've been in her early fifties, and although the lines on her face should've made her look older, she had an exuberance about her, a positivity that made her eyes shine.

"It feels quiet these days now you and Steph have moved out," she told Adam as she brought a humongous dish of roast potatoes to the table, where he was carving a hot, glistening chicken. Her terraced house in Leeds was small, but the fact that she was an assiduous housekeeper shone from the polished ornaments on the mantelpiece and the overpowering smell of forest pine that rose from the downstairs loo when it was flushed. "Do you remember what it was like when you first moved in, Adam? You, Mike and Danny all in the one bedroom. Absolute chaos."

Adam looked up. "But you made me feel at home."

She visibly melted. "Aw, thanks, love."

Afterwards, Adam went for a pint with Danny in the pub over the road while I hung back to help clear up, despite her protestations.

"So what was Adam's mum like?" I asked.

"He hardly ever talks about her."

She dipped her hands in a bowl of steaming hot water and glanced up. "Lisa was . . . hopeless and lovely all at the same time. She had terrible taste in men and was as mad as a bag of snakes. But she really was beautiful — inside and out."

Lisa had only been seventeen when she had Adam and, reading between the lines, had been a loving but dysfunctional mother. They were often hungry and cold, and Adam always wore coats with other kids' names sewn into the neckline. She was constantly not just letting him bunk off school, but actively encouraging it, just so they could go to the park to play, or snuggle up on the sofa and watch TV.

"When he was about six, she bought this camper van," Julie continued. "You should've seen the thing. It was a rust bucket. God knows where she got it. She picked him up from school one day with nothing but a map, some tins of food and a few clothes — and off they went on a bloody road trip around Britain. They were gone for four months, having the time of their lives," she laughed.

I raised my eyebrows. "Did nobody wonder why he wasn't in school?"

"You'd think so, wouldn't you? A woman

and her six-year-old son gallivanting halfway across Britain like Thelma and Louise. But no. They only came home when the van's suspension went and she couldn't afford to get it fixed."

I'd seen a handful of photos of Lisa, so I knew she had the same arresting looks as Adam: high cheekbones and a straight nose, Cupid's bow lips and dark, sleepy eyes.

"She tried her best to be a good mum," Julie said, and not for the first time. Then she told me about Warren, an insurance salesman Lisa had met about a year after their road trip.

"Lisa looked up to him. He was a professional man with a good job. At first, he treated her like a princess. She'd go on about how he cooked for her, brought her presents and couldn't keep his hands off her. But then he turned nasty."

"Violent?"

Julie nodded. "I could tell something was going on, but she was determined not to talk about it. Then Adam broke his arm, and they came up with some story about him climbing a tree . . . I knew it was rubbish. I told her I was going to go to the police, but she begged me not to. To be fair, Warren at least never touched *Adam* after that. She bore the brunt of it instead."

But Adam's young eyes continued to witness things that nobody should. "He turned into a different kid for a while. He'd always been loving and cheeky, full of fun. But he went so quiet. It was awful. I still can't understand why she didn't tell Warren to get lost. There was no excuse. I mean, you would, wouldn't you — with a little kid around?"

"Perhaps she was frightened of him."

"I'm sure she was."

Lisa died in a car accident when she was walking to school to pick up Adam. A witness said that she'd appeared to be daydreaming and stepped out from nowhere, slamming onto the bonnet of a 4×4.

"Lisa was in hospital, fighting for three weeks. Then her time came. Adam was sleeping on a camp bed upstairs here at the time. Overnight, the poor mite was motherless and homeless."

"So you took him in."

"Well, there was no way I was going to let him go into a home, although I had to fight for that. I've never regretted it once. He was an absolute joy to have around. I'm so proud of him, of everything he's done with himself."

Adam did well at school and earned a clutch of decent GCSEs, before moving to

Edinburgh to go to college.

"He just never stopped working," she said. "He'd wash dishes in a café during term time and gave up his summers to do jobs for a building firm in the Isles of Scilly."

I realized then that, by the time I'd met Adam, he'd lived half a dozen lifetimes.

"He barely talks about any of this," I said. "Apart from their trip with the camper van. I've heard him mention that a couple of times."

She didn't look surprised. "I think that's when Adam was probably at his happiest. When Lisa picked him up from school, sat him in the passenger seat of that daft thing and off they clattered on their mad adventure." She smiled at me. "I knew then somehow it'd be the first of a lifetime full of them for Adam."

CHAPTER 35

I've spoken to Dad a few times since I've been here, but trying to make a video call so I can see Mum too has been difficult. I'd have more luck reaching the International Space Station than getting enough Wi-Fi to keep a Skype connection for longer than ten seconds.

But on Friday, I get a text from Dad asking if I'm free to talk. There's something about the way he phrases it that makes the back of my neck prickle with panic — and it leaves me wanting to do more than simply phone and listen to his reassurances that they're both "fine." I want to see my mum with my own eyes.

I leave William and Natasha by the pool and head into the château, where I find Simone on the front desk.

"Hello, Jess." She's polite, bordering on curt.

"Hi, Simone. I wondered if Adam was in

the office?"

Her pinched smile wavers. "He is. Would you like to speak to him?"

"It's not him I'm after actually. I was hoping to Skype my dad, and Adam told me I could use the office, where I'd get a better broadband connection."

"Oh. Follow me then."

She leads me to the back of the hall and knocks on the heavy oak door, before pushing it open. Adam is at his computer, hammering at the keyboard.

"Jess's here." She sounds as though she's announcing the arrival of the nit nurse. He looks up.

"I wondered if I could take you up on your offer to Skype my dad here?"

"Of course, no problem. Everything all right?"

I glance at Simone. She takes the hint and backs out of the room. "I'm sure it'll be fine. Dad texted to see if I could talk and . . . well, I just want to make sure Mum's okay really."

He brushes his hand through his hair and starts clearing away papers. "Let me give you the password." He grabs a Post-it note and scrawls on it, before standing and handing it to me.

"I'll get out of your way. I can send these

emails in another room."

He picks up his laptop, stopping as we're shoulder to shoulder. Then he turns and briefly rubs my arm. It's a gesture of support, but it still makes me stiffen and leaves an odd kind of discomfort rippling under my skin.

"Thanks," I say.

"Give my love to your mum and dad, won't you?" he adds, slipping out of the room.

In the days before everything turned to shit, Adam got on well with my parents, particularly Dad. They were never short of something to talk about, be it soccer, or politics or how to replumb a washing machine (there was an inordinate amount of DIY talk, as I recall).

Mum loved him too, though that was before the stunt he pulled on the day her grandson was born, and my subsequent confession about how strained things had been in the run-up. He got a couple of firsthand experiences of the dragon lady she could turn into after that.

I turn on my iPad and watch it pick up the Wi-Fi, before typing in the password. I glance around the room as I'm waiting for it to connect. It's the only part of the building where there isn't a hint of styling, just

224

plain white walls, uninspiring office furniture and a dreary set of curtains on the high stone window.

This is a typical example of Adam's filing system, with stacks of papers piling up and an overflowing bin. I wouldn't say there's no order here whatsoever, but it's just enough to get him by, with one wall dominated by key hooks and a half-open filing cabinet, a precarious pile of tattered manila folders on top.

I click on the Skype icon, and as it starts twirling, my eyes are drawn to the corkboard in front of me, the one dotted with printed pictures, the kind most people haven't bothered with since the invention of Instagram.

The two or three of his mum must be the only ones that exist. Most are of William, as a baby, then a toddler and his first day at school, when he stood outside our front door, dimple cheeked and grinning through pearly milk teeth. I recognize lots of them as images I'd send to Adam every six months or so, making sure he couldn't forget about our existence entirely.

There are also a few selfies of him with William, a surprising number considering how little time they've actually spent in each other's company in the last ten years. In one of them, William looks about seven, and they're standing in the queue for the pirate ship at Alton Towers. In another, they're eating oversize ice creams in a pizza restaurant. Then there's one on Formby Beach, William hysterical as he buries Adam in the sand.

To look at the collection of images, you'd think that they'd been inseparable over the years. But really, these are a handful of occasions, a drop in the ocean — all a sharp contrast to the days I'm used to, the ones involving homework, piano practice, ferrying him to Scouts and shrieking the words, "SHOES!" and "TEETH!" as we try to get out of the house on time each morning.

Still, there's something reassuring about the photos, a sliver of a reminder that, although Adam is essentially clueless about the minutiae of parenthood, the potential is there, whether he realizes it or not.

I reach up and touch the photo of William in his uniform, accidentally dislodging the pin as three of the pictures tumble to the floor. I pick them up and put them back, when I spot a faded image concealed behind the others.

It's of Adam and me, in New York.

The trip was about a week after we'd graduated from Edinburgh, and we'd been planning it for ages, to stay with Steph — Aunt Julie's youngest — who'd won an apprenticeship to work as a chef for some smart new hotel on the Upper East Side. The flat she shared with a fellow trainee, a Bulgarian guy called Boyan, was so small that the only way to enter the bathroom was by turning sideways and breathing in.

But it was an unforgettable holiday. We took a boat to Ellis Island, explored Central Park, stood at the top of the Empire State Building as night fell, watching the city sparkle into life. The morning that picture was taken, we'd woken stupidly early, still jet-lagged and disorientated from the flight two days before. But this being the days before parenthood, all we had to worry about was ourselves, so we spent hours in that spare room while Steph was at work, sun streaming through the blinds as we stayed under the sheets, exploring every inch of each other.

He always said that was his favorite photo of us — a postsex snap of him, me and our mammoth breakfasts at a cool little place in the Meatpacking District. He said he had everything he'd ever wanted in life on that day. I asked if he was referring to me or the crispy bacon.

"Hello?" Dad's voice shatters my train of

thought, and I look up to find him in the entrance hall of Willow Bank Lodge, looking like a man in need of a good night's sleep.

CHAPTER 36

"Everything's *fine*," Dad tells me, which I've come to discover is what he'd say if he were on the *Titanic* surrounded by violinists. "We just had a bit of a fright this morning."

My heartbeat doubles in speed. "What do you mean?"

"There's no need to panic, but we've been to hospital today. It was a precaution, and we're back now. The point is she's okay."

Heat gathers around my neck as half a dozen questions flood my brain. "What happened? Why have you been to hospital? Where is she now?"

"Your mum choked on some of her breakfast." He glances up, but briefly, as if avoiding my reaction. "Raheem was here and managed to do his stuff and sort her out. They called me at work, and by the time I got to hospital it was all under control. She's absolutely fine, honestly. A bit down about

229

things but basically fine."

It's not the first time this has happened. Before we started mashing up Mum's food, I saw it with my own eyes. The sight of her face turning grey and lips blue while she struggled to catch a breath is not one I ever want to witness again. Her specialist, Dr. Gianopoulos, thinks she should've begun tube feeding, but she signed a document years ago — an Advance Decision to Refuse Treatment — which means that's never going to happen.

"*It's okay,* Jess," Dad says, filling the silence. "Just one of those things. We have to be careful from now on, that's all."

"I think I should come home," I decide instantly.

"No. Absolutely not." He shakes his head. "Everything's okay now. I wasn't even going to tell you, but I thought you'd hit the roof if I didn't."

"You thought right. I'm going to look at flights this afternoon."

Dad fixes a stern look on me. "What do you think your mum would say if she knew you were thinking of doing that?" he says gently. "She's had a bad enough day as it is."

I exhale, only then realizing I'd been holding my breath. "Is she there now?"

230

"Give me a minute." He walks through the corridor before pushing open the door to her room, where Mum is in her wheelchair, not watching the Australian soap on the television.

As Dad holds the iPad in front of her, I find myself conducting the usual assessment of the way she looks. Objectively speaking, she's probably no better or worse than when I left. But this is not saying much.

Her limbs are curled into uncomfortable-looking positions, her bottom lip drooping ever so slightly, as if pulled down by an invisible weight. Her skin clings limply to her bones, the sort of body that appears as though it shouldn't have enough energy even to move. Yet, she doesn't stop throwing her face up to the sky.

"Dad told me what happened, Mum. Are you okay?"

A second passes when she jerks repeatedly before she answers through a grunt. "Bloody toast."

I can't manage a smile.

"Porridge next time," she adds.

"Yes, good idea." I want to say a million things right now to my mum. That I love her, that my heart is breaking for her, that I'd do anything for her to be the happy, healthy woman she would be if it wasn't for this hideous disease.

But just thinking about these things makes my throat close up.

"It . . . nice there?" she asks. Every word requires effort, and even then it's unclear how the words are going to come out. Her jaw moves in a different way from how it used to, making awkward, hushed sounds.

I try to pull myself together. "Yes, it is, Mum. Adam's done a great job on the place, and William's really enjoying the time they're spending together."

She's silent for a moment, and my eyes divert to the ridges of her collarbone, which protrude above the top of her pale blue blouse. I bought that top from Oasis for her birthday more than a decade ago. I remember thinking at the time that a size 8 might be pushing my luck a bit. Now, she is swamped by it, her once-sumptuous cleavage replaced by a visible rib cage that twists into excruciating positions.

"William . . . there?"

"No, he's by the pool, but I can go and get him."

"No," she splutters. "Not today."

"Okay. Tomorrow then maybe."

But she doesn't respond. She simply writhes in her seat as facial muscles contort her features into something unrecognizable and exaggerated. It's a vision I know will return when I look in the bathroom mirror at my own face and I'm smothered by cold fear.

CHAPTER 37

I step out of the château after the Skype
call into an intense heat, the kind that burns
the soles of your feet and makes your skin
sticky. The pool is busy with splashing
children, while their parents look on, taking
refuge under the umbrellas.

Natasha is sitting at a table under a
canopy of tiny pink flowers and chatting to
Ben, who's standing next to her. He's either
unaware that he has a rival for her affection
in Joshua, or he doesn't care; from the way
he's looking at her now, he's a complete
goner.

William, James and Rufus are on the other
side of the table waiting for lunch to arrive.
I join them in the middle of a conversation
about the human esophagus.

"I saw it on an episode of *Operation
Ouch!*" William says earnestly. "It was brilliant. Some kid had bitten his toenail off
and swallowed it. Only, it was a really big

one and they had to give him an X-ray to check it hadn't punctured his lung or caused any major arterial bleeding."

Sunlight glitters on the pool as I pull up a chair and a waitress emerges from the château with a tray of food: salads drizzled with walnut oil, fragrant cheeses and salted meats, breads with fluffy insides and hard crusts that could dislodge a filling.

"I love your nail polish, Natasha," James pipes up.

She glances at her hands. "Oh, thank you, James. It's a new one."

"It suits you," he adds, and she flashes me a smile.

"Listen, I'll leave you to your lunch." Ben smiles and reluctantly heads back to work as Natasha's gaze follows him briefly.

"Where's Becky?" Natasha points to the pool.

She is attempting to do a few lengths, while Seb stands, stretching out his arms to catch Poppy each time she plunges in, sweeping her up to the surface as she blinks chlorine out of her eyes.

"AGAIN!" she giggles.

Then I realize Natasha is scrutinizing my face. "Everything all right?"

But before she can answer, Seb's voice echoes across the terrace. "Come on, sweetie! Daddy means it. POPPY!"

What prompted Poppy to do a runner isn't completely clear. All I know is that her little legs are racing around the perimeter as poor Seb frantically circles in the water, trying to coax her back.

"POPPY, STOP!"

She pauses for a heartbeat but darts off towards the trees. Seb and Becky both leap onto the side of the pool and hurtle towards their daughter as she giggles with mischief, refusing to look back. And, although they gain on her, the speed of those short legs is quite alarming.

Eventually, it takes James to save the day. "POPPY, YOU CAN HAVE MY SWEETS!"

She stops to contemplate whether she's been hasty, and Becky swoops in to pick her up. As she marches towards us with her daughter, stress is etched on our friend's face. She takes the seat next to me and starts toweling Poppy down as Seb appears a moment later.

"Was it not obvious that that was going to happen?" Becky asks furiously.

Seb frowns. "What?"

"That Poppy was going to run off if you put her on the side of the pool."

"No, it wasn't. She'd been jumping into

my arms repeatedly beforehand."

"You must've realized that if she'd raced off you'd be stuck in the pool and powerless to catch her."

"Not powerless."

"Yes, powerless! There's no point leaping out like the bloody bionic man if you're too far behind to catch her."

Defiance appears in a wrinkle above Seb's nose. "If you thought she was in such mortal danger, why didn't you say so when you saw her doing it the first time?"

"Because you'd have accused me of interfering!"

Seb lets out a long trail of breath before glancing at Natasha and me. "Can we discuss this later?"

"I'd rather not."

There is a visible pulse in Seb's neck as he stands, contemplating his next move, before finally taking the boys off for a game of Frisbee.

Becky pauses from drying off Poppy and looks at us from under her eyelashes. "Sorry. It's not always like that."

"Of course not," I reassure her.

"Kids do change you though, don't they?" Becky sighs.

"Yep," I agree. "I realized that the day you posted an inspirational quote on Facebook from Mummy Pig."

Becky snorts. "How was the chat with your mum and dad?"

I look towards the haze on the pool. "Mum ended up in hospital this morning."

Natasha lowers her glass. "Oh no. Is she all right?"

"She's okay now, but she'd choked on something." The sentence sounds matter-of-fact, but I can feel my nails digging into my palms.

"So is she out of hospital now? Do you need to go home?" Becky asks.

"Yes. And no. They don't want me to. They insist it's nothing to worry about."

Her eyes drop to my mouth, and I realize I'm chewing on my lip. "You don't look convinced."

And she's right. I'm not.

Chapter 38

I feel nervous about spending the afternoon with Charlie, though I can't work out whether that's a good, a bad or just a very strange thing. It doesn't help that our living room is a scene of devastation when he's due to pick me up in fifteen minutes.

"Hey, William, can you move your wet trunks from the middle of the floor?"

But he's on the sofa, ensconced in the iPad, so effective communication ceased some time ago. "William?"

"Just a minute, Mum," he mumbles. "I've nearly completed this level."

Meanwhile, I made the schoolgirl error of commenting on how lovely Natasha's skin looked, which prompted her to whip out her cosmetics box and subject me to "facial contouring" while I perch on the edge of the sofa. It's only when I glance in the mirror that I realize she's turned my face into a demented Picasso imitation, with two dark triangles under my eyes and bright pink circles on my cheeks.

"Are you joking?"

"I'm not done yet."

"Natasha, he'll be here soon." I look over to the sofa. "Come on, William — move these trunks before someone breaks their neck on them, please."

There's a knock on the front door, and it opens. My heart performs a loop the loop, until I realize it's only Adam. Who does a double take, as if he's missing the punch line of a joke. "I've got a red nose and pantaloons in the cottage if you want to complete the look."

"We're not finished," Natasha tells him, darting to the sink for some water. As she's on her way back, the toe of her sandal catches in William's trunks, and she stumbles, catching herself at the last second.

I frown at my son before striding over and taking the iPad from him decisively. He looks up in shock, then wrinkles his nose. "WHAT? What have I done?!"

"You're meant to have picked up the trunks." He blinks at me without a clue as to what I'm talking about. "Do it now or I'm confiscating the iPad."

You'd think I'd just told him I was planning to strangle his favorite puppy. "But I need to finish my level. I'm so close!"

"Now!"

"FINE!" he fires back, stomping over to the trunks.

I'm torn between not wanting him to get away with such cheek and desperately needing to get ready before Charlie arrives. I turn round to see Adam just standing there. Spectating.

"Perhaps you could have a word with him about this," I say.

Adam's eyes dart round the room as if he assumes I must be talking to someone else. "Me?"

"Yes."

He thinks for a moment, then shrugs. "Sure. Go and get ready, and I'll talk to him."

"Okay. Good. Thanks."

I head into the bedroom, where I begin wiping makeup from my cheeks. Natasha follows, wincing as I drag the tissue across my face. "Could you not just . . . blend?"

"There's no time for blending. Besides, what's wrong with foundation and a bit of blusher?"

When my face is presentable, I creep to the door and pry it open. Adam has his arm round our son, and while I can't overhear the exact conversation, I do catch several

241

sympathetic snippets that culminate in: "Never mind, mate."

"God, how annoying," I tut.

"What?" Natasha says.

"Adam."

"Don't worry about him. Your date is going to be here in —" She looks at her watch as the door clatters open. It's William.

"Charlie's here," he tells me.

My mouth goes dry. "Okay. Thank you."

He hovers at the door. "I'm sorry, Mum."

I feel my irritation dissolve. "That's okay. Come and give me a hug."

He puts his arms round me, then pulls back. "So you know you said you were going to talk to Charlie about your exercise classes . . . . Is that true?"

Natasha coughs.

"Why do you ask?" I say.

"I just thought it might be . . . a date."

I wonder how my ten-year-old became so perceptive.

CHAPTER 39

Charlie looks completely at home behind the wheel of his posh car. It could've been built for someone like him — an intelligent, professional guy, who's comfortable in his own skin and not worried about being a grown-up. Who has embraced his age and the Marks & Spencer shirts that go with it.

Pujols, the village Charlie chose for lunch, is over an hour south of Château de Roussignol. It's a smooth, undulating drive, and we arrive at a picture-postcard setting perched so high on a hill that it feels like the clouds have been lowered. We wander through narrow, meandering streets of limestone cottages with crumbling shutters and antique roses twisting round their doors, before finding a restaurant that overlooks the small square and its dusty, vanilla-colored buildings.

Charlie pulls out a chair for me and sits down opposite.

The waiter appears with menus. "What will you have to drink?" he asks.

"Badoit, s'il vous plaît," I say, conscious that he has to drive.

He looks surprised. "But you're on holiday. And I'm driving. Surely a glass of *something* is in order?"

"I thought I'd stick with water, for moral support. But when you put it like that . . ."

A little bit of wine seems to help the date along inordinately. Not that it was going badly in the first place. It's simply made me relax a bit, to appreciate all that Charlie has going for him: the fact that he's serious and intelligent, but without being even a tiny bit intimidating. Or perhaps he merely understands what it's like to have a child William's age. I find myself confessing that I'd lost my temper just before we left, and he assures me that he's been there.

"It's normal to have battles over stuff like that at his age. At least he's not on that iPad fifteen hours a day like some kids." I decide not to correct him. "Besides, nobody ever said being a parent would be easy sailing, especially on your own."

"It hasn't been that hard by myself," I insist. "I've had a lot of help from my mum and dad over the years."

He finishes a mouthful and ponders a

question. "So what's the deal with you and William's father? You still seem close."

"Do we?" The patch of skin below my ears reddens.

"Yes, you do. I thought that the other night when I came over for a drink."

I shake my head obstinately. "We're not close. We tolerate each other for William's sake."

"Maybe it's just the fact that you're *here*. Most people wouldn't dream of coming on holiday with their exes. I know I wouldn't."

"Don't you get on?" I'm glad to shift the emphasis away from me and Adam.

"Not exactly. She's a lunatic."

I look up. "Oh dear."

"Seriously. The most manipulative woman I know. She's absolutely horrible."

I'm not quite sure what to say about this and can only think to make a joke out of it. "It's easy to see why you married her then."

"We all make mistakes. I won't bore you with the sob story though. And anyway, why are we even talking about exes?"

"I'm sure you brought it up." I smile gently.

"I did, didn't I? Well, how about this instead: can we do this again sometime before the end of the holiday?"

I lower my knife and fork. "We haven't

245

even finished our main course yet. You might have gone off me by the time we get to the dessert."

He holds my gaze with an almost indecent intensity. "I seriously doubt that."

The date leaves me feeling surprisingly light on my feet afterwards. Not because, when we pull into the château grounds three hours later, I am overcome with lust. But because there is something spirit lifting about sitting opposite a man who fancies you. And he couldn't have been clearer that he does. It's not even a question of anything he *says* — it's more about the way he looks at me, with a hint of desire that stirs something in me.

It's only after we've strolled back to the car and driven through penetrating sunshine until we reach the gates of Château de Roussignol that something becomes obvious, to both of us. The opportunity for a kiss has already passed us by, floated away unnoticed, like the clouds on those hilltops. I realize he's thinking the same when the car slows and the conversation comes to a halt.

"I really enjoyed this afternoon." He is gripping the steering wheel, focusing on the road.

"Me too."

"Would you like me to drop you off here or back at the cottage?"

"Anywhere here's fine. I need to walk over to collect William."

He stops the car and pulls on the hand brake, adjusting his position so that he's looking directly at me. "Right, well. Thanks again. You really didn't have to pay for lunch, but it was extremely good of you and —" I babble.

"Jess." His hand slides onto my bare arm, the heat from his touch making goose pimples bloom on my skin.

"Yes?"

My pulse thunders in my ears as he leans towards me for a kiss. As his lips touch mine, I realize how much I don't want to mess this up. I want to be cool and seductive and for him to find me as attractive as he seems to think I am.

I also realize I'm thinking so hard about this that I risk slobbering all over him, so I make a conscious effort to relax my shoulders. To remember to enjoy the feel of his mouth against mine.

I'm concentrating on all this, when I become vaguely aware of the chatter of small voices somewhere outside. I don't give them a second thought at first, and even when the giggles start, the most I ever contemplate is the possibility that someone's enjoying a lively game of *boules.*

Then there's a knock on the window, and Charlie and I leap apart, registering half a dozen children clamoring to see into the car.

It's then that I hear another grown-up voice. It's vaguely familiar. "*Les enfants!* Children! Come away!"

As Simone bends down and we eyeball each other through the glass, it takes a second for me to register the change in her expression when she realizes it's me. The look on her face is not quite one of satisfaction but relief.

I know exactly what's behind that look. Because I've been there myself.

CHAPTER 40

When I was Adam's girlfriend, I was kept on my toes. It wasn't that he was constantly sleeping around; simply that, when your heart is hopelessly lost to someone, fear is an unfortunate side effect. Worry that one day all those girls who can't take their eyes off him, the ones prettier and probably funnier and cleverer than you, will finally turn his head.

In the early days, he'd made me feel great about myself; taller, slimmer, so witty and enchanting that I could be talking about grouting the bathroom tiles and he'd still be listening intently, gazing at me with those dark, infinite eyes.

How we went from there to the mess we became was complicated yet also straightforward: things change.

Although our troubles had started as soon as I found out I was pregnant, the thing that really changed us forever was the night of

William's birth. Before then, I remained convinced we'd work everything out between us. Afterwards, I knew we were doomed. I knew it the moment he walked through the door in the hospital and failed to answer my questions with any conviction.

"Where were you?"

Mum had excused herself to get a coffee from the hospital vending machine, and by this stage, I was beyond being nice.

"Okay. The thing is . . . I was with Jules." His colleague. "It turned into a late one. I lost my phone . . . and I only realized what had happened when I found it again."

"You weren't with Georgina?"

"Oh God, no," he said, as if the idea was ridiculous.

"So why are you covered in her lipstick?"

His hand shot to his neck. "That's not . . ." He drew breath but ran out of the energy to continue almost immediately. "Okay. We bumped into each other."

I looked at him incredulously. "Am I seriously expected to believe that? That of all the bars in Manchester, you and your exgirlfriend just happened to be there at the same time?"

He shifted about from foot to foot, his eyes darting anxiously, unable to meet my gaze. Of all Adam's talents, deception is not one; he is truly awful at it.

"Okay, fine," he said, sweat beading on his brow. "She'd been phoning me for days after she'd split up with that guy she'd been seeing, Johnny. So I arranged to meet her at the Bush Bar."

"Then why did you lie to me?"

"I didn't! Well . . . okay, I kind of did."

"So what about the lipstick?"

He swallowed. "I was giving her a . . . supportive hug."

I held my hand over William's tiny ear. "Did she give you a supportive blow job in return?"

"Jess, don't be like that," he spluttered.

"What do you expect when you turn your phone off for twelve hours when I'm giving birth to your firstborn son?"

He just kept banging on that I should trust him, believe him that Georgina went home alone — and he got sidetracked at his friend Jules's place. I might have been off my head on pethidine, but I hadn't totally lost my marbles. This was confirmed when I bumped into Jules's wife, Suzy, on my first trip to the supermarket after I'd left the hospital. She'd done the obligatory cooing over William, when I said casually: "So . . . did Jules have a late night at the team-building day? I know a few of them were out until the next morning."

She shook her head. "Jules is a lightweight, Jess. He got home at twelve thirty and was snoring away next to me within five minutes."

And so I knew for sure: Adam was lying about that too.

I'm not a churchgoer, but I've always believed in the power of forgiveness. I'm not the kind to bear grudges or refuse to let things go; I don't want them to eat me up from the inside out. But how *can* you forgive someone when the deception never stops? And it didn't, until Adam couldn't even be bothered lying about that night any longer. He just said I'd "got it wrong," refused to talk about it and that was supposed to be that.

We stayed together for two months and two weeks after William was born, and those days, when we were supposed to be bonding as a family, were among the most wretched of my life. That wasn't all Adam's fault.

I might have fallen head over heels in love with my new baby, but he was not an easy newborn. He was gorgeous but demanding, constantly unsettled, fussing and uninterested in feeding unless it was between the hours of midnight and five in the morning. It goes without saying that there were moments of pure happiness, when I'd wrap him up after his bath and snuggle him into me, or simply marvel at the velvet skin on his tiny hands. But there were also times when the lack of sleep and crushing exhaustion felt like it was never going to end. I blamed myself for the fact that William was not the gurgling, contented bundle of joy I'd assumed he would be. I was certain I must've been doing something wrong, despite having read every parenting manual going.

While Adam went back to work after a brief paternity leave, I stayed at home looking after William, pumping milk like a Friesian cow and stewing in my own despair. I was physically wrecked, riddled with mastitis and so far from the definition of a yummy mummy that I felt like burning my trendy baby sling.

I craved Adam's presence throughout the day but was irritated as soon as he strolled in through the door and I was reminded of what he'd done. A couple of friends asked me at the time if I had the baby blues, and maybe I did. But there was more to it than that, and worse was to come.

At the height of all this, Mum finally told

me that those funny symptoms she'd had for the last few years amounted to something distinctly big and unfunny. To say I was crushed doesn't come close to conveying its impact on me. I was devastated. I couldn't see straight. I was dizzy with the enormity of my feelings, the idea that my life was running away with itself, in a direction I couldn't possibly manage.

In this cauldron of stress and misery, my tolerance for Adam's bullshit was at rock bottom. So maybe I did have the baby blues, but I almost certainly had the mum blues and the Adam blues too, caused by the fact that I had started a family with a man I knew had done the dirty on me and wasn't capable of being the pillar of strength I needed.

Despite that, on the day I told him I wanted to split up with him, I'm not entirely sure I meant it. I don't even recall what prompted the particular row we had that day. But I do remember being gripped by a scalding fury, as if all my fears and resentment and anger at the way he'd behaved were suddenly concentrated into that moment.

"You don't deserve to be William's father," I told him. "You're just not up to this job. The longer time goes on, Adam, the more convinced I am: everyone would be better off if William and I just left."

I stood there, with those bleak words hanging between us in the very flat where we'd once shared so much intimacy and love. With hindsight, I'm fairly sure, naively, that I wanted him to man up and beg me to stay. I'm not sure why I thought I'd win that gamble, but I was too exhausted to think my actions through clearly.

He didn't even argue. "Okay," he said simply. "If that's what you want."

I packed a bag and went to Mum's house, feeling numb, gritting my teeth, grinding down my devastation. I cried all night as I lay, tossing and turning, in the same bedroom where my teenage posters had hung on the wall, with my baby fussing next to me in his travel cot.

By the morning, I'd spent hours torturing myself about whether I should phone him and take it all back. The reason I didn't wasn't because I was stubborn.

I just instinctively knew I had to stay strong. *He'd slept with someone else, for God's sake.* If there was any crawling back to be done, it had to be his.

I was in for a long wait.

Adam did not turn up at my doorstep with flowers or an engagement ring or make a

255

grand gesture that said: *I'm going to be the man you and William need. Who'll love you both through thick and thin. And yes, I had sex with Georgina and missed the birth of our son. But I'm going to change.*

He didn't say anything even close to it.

Instead, he slipped away quietly, leaving me helpless in his absence.

We did meet up once after the breakup — to see if we could "make a go of it." But I sat across from him weeping, while Adam numbly went through the motions. The gulf between us couldn't have been more obvious. I might've been the one who pushed, but he'd been edging towards the door, and he wasn't going to beg to come back now. In the absence of any begging, I stuck to my guns.

"After everything that's happened, how we can live with each other?" I said. I genuinely wanted him to give me a convincing answer, but he was silent. "If we can even hope to do the right thing by William, I think this is the only way, don't you?"

The words were coming out of my mouth like I was writing a script from a soap opera. I remember holding out my hand, offering it to him to shake and wishing he'd push it aside, sweep me into his arms and say, *No, I'm not going to let this happen, because you're the love of my life.*

Instead, he leaned in, gave me a brief kiss on the cheek, then turned and walked away.

I was consumed with regret in the following months. But as the years passed, I came to realize that I'd done the right thing. What I did was harder but braver. It ended our relationship, before our son knew any different. Before he had to go through the heartbreak of seeing his parents failing to make things work every day.

Adam and Georgina, meanwhile, got together officially less than a month after we'd split up.

He briefly moved in with her in London, and it was there that he got news that his mum's brother — Uncle Frank — had died of liver failure. He left his entire estate to Adam, and although this amounted to a modest three-bedroom house and a pension, it was enough for Adam to start thinking about making his dreams to live and work abroad a reality. He quickly started to plan to move to France, and while I don't know the details of why he split with Georgina, she was never part of that future.

I can't recall how often Adam saw William in the first year of his life before he went to France, because of the whirlwind of delight and despair I was going through. But I do remember feeling a bewilderment and fury that he clearly didn't see William as I saw him: our angel, the best thing in the world, ever.

It was soon after I recognized this that something snapped in me, and a defiance started building: if Adam wanted to stay out of the picture and leave bringing up William all to me, I was happy to oblige.

CHAPTER 41

The day after my trip to Pujols with Charlie, Adam turns up at the cottage.

"I believe your date went well?" He has an odd look on his face, and I can't work out if he's interested, amused or simply reluctant to miss the opportunity to wind me up. I try to look unfazed.

"It was nice. Yes. Thank you," I say, giving the air of someone who went for afternoon tea with the Countess of Grantham rather than a boozy lunch that resulted in a smooch in the front seat of a Range Rover.

He stares at me. "Good. I'm glad."

An unwelcome sensation starts to prickle under my skin; not disloyalty exactly — that would be ridiculous — but a whisper of something approaching it. Even if it hadn't been ten years since we split up, I'd feel like slapping myself on both cheeks, reminding myself of exactly what *he* did to *me* and that it's not long since I walked in on him and his girlfriend when she was in a state of semi-undress.

"What is it?" I ask, to fill the silence.

His lips twitch as if he's trying to disguise a smile. "Nothing. Talking about first dates just reminded me of . . . the Pear Tree."

The name of that pub makes a rush of memories fill my head, of a time at the very beginning of our relationship.

It was a balmy July night, and we whiled away an afternoon and most of the evening in an Edinburgh beer garden, under a canopy of gold light that warmed our shoulders.

We sat side by side on a bench, so close that our thighs brushed each time we moved. I watched the tilt of his head as he spoke and felt a dizzying warmth when he laughed.

I learned a lot about him that day: where he'd traveled, his passion for reading. I built up a picture of a man who was nice to bar staff, a generous tipper despite having little money himself. A man who went out of his way to befriend the guide dog whose owner sat at the next table and who didn't make a fuss when someone splashed their drink on his jeans.

Despite wrestling with anxiety in the run-up to the date, I don't recall a single gap in conversation. Talking to him felt oddly easy and natural. As the blanket of darkness fell upon us, I felt his hand reach out for mine. Then I looked up and felt myself drowning in those eyes, certain in the knowledge that I was losing myself completely to him.

"That was a good first date," I agree in the most perfunctory fashion I can manage.

He smiles briefly. Then our son appears at the door and begins a monologue about how William the Conqueror's stomach exploded at his own funeral.

Over the next few days, everything my mum ever wanted to occur between Adam and William starts to happen. They can't stay away from each other. I keep looking for an ulterior motive, a logical reason why Adam — who's been at best ambivalent about his responsibilities and at worst an absent father — can't seem to get enough of his son.

I realize that, technically, this is good. Not least because being able to report it back to Mum will give her a much-needed boost. But I keep wondering what the catch is. Can Adam really have finally fallen in love with William, just like that? Is he genuinely only now noticing that, although we screwed everything up between us, we still managed to make this gorgeous human being?

My only option is to stifle any cynicism and see what happens. Besides, I can't deny there's entertainment value in listening to conversations between the two of them. William trails round after Adam, offering to help with jobs — pretending he'd recognize one end of a screwdriver from the other — while giving his father long lectures about everything from a crocodile's inability to move its tongue and the fact that the ancient Romans vomited during dinner so they could make room for dessert. To Adam's credit, he just about manages not to fall into a coma.

I even heard him saying to Simone the other day: "Wait till William tells you about *Horrible Histories,*" before she was treated to a lesson about Egyptian mummification.

On Tuesday morning, William joins Adam on a series of errands in Bergerac, while Natasha spends the morning playing golf with Joshua; apparently, if it's good enough for Catherine Zeta Jones, she's prepared to give it a go. I had to stop myself from asking if she'd prefer to be playing golf with Ben, because I don't think she'd want to admit the answer to that. And there's no question that she's right about one thing — if she is looking to settle down, or at least have a more meaningful relationship, it's unlikely to happen with a twentysomething recently out of university. As gorgeous as Ben might be.

I think about wandering over to Becky's cottage but first pluck up the courage to knock on Charlie's door. Only, by the time I've made the decision to do it, his car has gone and nobody is answering the door. Realizing we're out of bread, I drive to the nearest village, Pravillac, where there's a small but well-stocked shop.

The door is open, and the second I step over the threshold, the air is filled with the sweet, hot scent of freshly baked croissants and floury baguettes. I pick one up, along with a newspaper from home, before finding myself in the wine aisle.

"Bit early for that, isn't it?"

Seb's tired but handsome eyes are smiling down at me, his blond hair ruffled, as if he's just rolled out of bed — which, given the time the kids wake up, I seriously doubt is the case. I spot Rufus behind him, browsing eagerly through the sweets.

"When you're on holiday, it never feels too early. I was only window-shopping though. I promise."

"I believe you," he laughs. "I think you've got a long way to go before you end up like

263

poor old Richard Potter."

It takes me a moment to recall that he's talking about a friend of his and Adam's from university. "What happened to Richard Potter?"

"Didn't you hear? He and Nicky split up about two months ago."

"I'm not really in touch with him, to be honest."

"Well, he's taken it badly, put it that way."

"Oh dear. I'm sorry to hear that," I say.

"He's just gone a bit off the rails, the way men do after a split," he says with a shrug. "Drinking too much. Sleeping with anyone who'll have him. You know the score."

"It's not only men who go off the rails," I remind him.

"True. Although women seem to be generally better at coping with that sort of thing, don't you think? It's the old cliché — they know how to talk about it, work out why it's happened, sing 'I Will Survive.' Men, on the other hand . . . do strange things." He shudders. "The thought horrifies me."

"Well, I don't think you've got anything to worry about." I make the statement before I've even got time to think about it. As soon as the sentence is out there, hanging in the air between us, I realize it feels both presumptive and not entirely accurate.

"Course not."

His jaw twitches, and I can't think how to respond other than to smile awkwardly.

"Things feel . . . tough at the moment though," he says, filling the silence.

"Of course they do. You've got three kids. Life's not easy when it's that busy, I know."

He glances anxiously at Rufus to check he's out of earshot. His younger son is filling a basket with so many sweets that he's staggering under its weight. "The thought of not having Becky around makes me feel sick to my stomach."

I'm momentarily stuck for how to answer this, worrying that I'm straying into an area I don't want to know about. But I feel compelled to ask: "Why would you say that, Seb? You're not concerned, are you?"

"No. Yes. I don't know." His chest rises before he speaks. "I just wish things were working right now. Does that make sense?"

I nod. "It does."

"DAD? Can we have this? I think it's what the Hulk drinks," asks Rufus, holding up a bottle of 110 proof absinthe.

"Just a minute, Ruf," he says, then turns back to me. "You won't mention this to her, will you?"

"Of course not," I reassure him, as he

gently guides his son by the shoulders towards something rather less green and toxic.

Chapter 42

The kids want to hang out at the château today, so Seb offers to take them on a grand expedition of the grounds, allowing Becky, Natasha and me an afternoon together.

After what I heard this morning, I can't help thinking that giving Becky a break is a good idea. So we jump into my car and, with Natasha in charge of the guidebook, head off for our own expedition that ends up in a little place called Sorges. Like so many of the Dordogne villages, its honey-colored houses and pretty square look as though they've wandered into the twenty-first century from another time.

"This is the truffle capital of the Dordogne," Natasha announces. "It even has a truffle museum."

"And to think, the kids had wanted to go to Disneyland," Becky murmurs.

I spend five minutes hovering outside a shop with her while Natasha browses inside, finally emerging with a jar of pear and truffle jam that cost more than I paid for my last handbag. We then wander around aimlessly, before stumbling upon a pretty auberge with a canopied terrace painted in cornflower blue, with crisp white tablecloths and a chalkboard menu.

Natasha orders coffees as I look at my phone and realize there's a new message. I pick it up in the vague hope that it's Adam updating me about William. It's not that I don't trust him, but confirmation that my son is alive and not currently plunging into another waterfall would be welcome. The text, however, is from Charlie.

I can't stop thinking about our kiss x

I tap my fingers on the table as I try to think of a response.

It was lovely, despite the abrupt ending! x

I lower my phone and realize Natasha is texting too, a private smile on her lips.

"Oh, look at you two all loved up," Becky groans, scanning her menu.

"I'm not loved up," I protest. "I'm just sending a text."

"And I'm only *receiving* one," Natasha says.

"Is it from Joshua?" Becky asks, and Natasha nods. "You know you're breaking Ben's heart every time he sees you together, don't you?"

"Don't be silly," Natasha replies, although I think we all know it's true.

"I long for the days when I'd get romantic texts," Becky sighs. "The last text Seb sent me was to ask where I'd left the athlete's foot powder." She looks at Natasha, who is now engrossed in her phone again.

"That text must be good, whatever it says," Becky adds.

"I'm looking at something else now, actually. I didn't seek it out, but there's an article on my Facebook feed called 'Cosmo's Ten Sex Tips You Should Try Tonight.' I can't imagine why the cookies thought I'd be interested in that."

Becky chuckles and takes the phone off her. " 'Give your man a massage without your hands. Try the reverse cowgirl position. Have your guy write a list of the top three moves that drive him crazy, and you do the same. Then swap lists.' Oh, that's an old one . . ."

Natasha and I exchange glances. "I haven't done it lately, mind you," Becky continues. "The only thing that drives me crazy these days is when he leaves the lid off the tooth-paste."

"You have a gorgeous husband," Natasha says.

"Yeah, but you try doing the 'reverse cowgirl' when one of three children is poised to burst in and demand to know why Daddy sounds like he's being tortured. Not that that happens often — we never get the time these days."

Natasha frowns. "You need to *make time.*"

"I enjoy it when we manage it, but the truth is . . . I haven't had an orgasm since before Poppy was born."

Natasha flashes me a disbelieving glance. "But she's nearly *three.*"

"It's not a big thing, in the scheme of things, Natasha. I've got other stuff to worry about."

Natasha looks unconvinced. As my phone beeps, Becky lowers her menu.

"Oh, come on, Jess. Let us in on what lover boy is saying."

"I couldn't possibly," I say coyly, then hold out the phone to show her.

I can't get the thought of your lips out of my head x

"Good man," Becky decides, focusing her

gaze on me. "I know everything is hard for you at the moment, Jess. But promise me you'll remember to enjoy this."

When we return to Château de Roussignol, I ask Becky to drop me off so I can go and find William. I spot him playing soccer with one of the Dutch boys.

"Hi, Mum," William shouts out, waving to me from the pitch.

"Had a nice day with your dad?"

"Brilliant. We had a kick-about when we got back — he showed me loads of tricks with the ball. Can I stay a bit longer to play with Finn?" he asks, walking towards me.

Finn looks alarmed. I suspect his tolerance is stretched to the limit given that my son couldn't shoot a ball in the right direction if his life depended on it. "Is okay. You go with mother. Is fine."

William frowns. "Okay — perhaps we can play again tomorrow?"

Finn gives him an unconvincing smile and disappears while he's got the chance. "Where's your dad now?" I ask.

"He had to make a phone call," he says, gesturing to the château, where Adam is on the terrace, speaking into his mobile.

He waves, and I return the gesture awkwardly. "Go and tell him we're heading to the cottage."

William disappears temporarily and returns to join me as we walk back to Les Écuries. After two and a half weeks of almost uninterrupted sunshine, the air is suddenly thick with moisture, thunderous black clouds billowing above us.

"Dad says it's going to bucket down," William tells me.

"I think he could be right," I mutter, stepping up my pace. "So what else did you do today?"

"I did some 'shadowing' when we went to Bergerac — that means I went with him when he had a meeting. When we came back, I helped Simone with some jobs too. She's really pretty, Simone, isn't she?"

"She is," I agree.

"I think she looks like Megan Fox."

"Megan Fox has brown hair."

"I know, but apart from that. I think she's really beautiful."

The growling thunder makes us quicken our step. "Come on — faster." I grab William's hand, and we break into a jog, until we finally reach our cottage. I'm scrambling with my key before the rain starts.

"I think this is a night to spend huddled up with the iPad," I tell him.

He looks shocked. "You mean you're actu-

272

ally going to let me use it?"

"Yes." I shrug.

"YESSS!"

I laugh. "Where did you put it after you used it this morning?"

His smile dissolves. He runs into his room, races back into the living room, gasps loudly and smacks his hand on his mouth.

"What?" I say in a low tone, but I already know exactly why he's behaving like this.

"I've just realized where I've left it."

CHAPTER 43

From the look of the sky, I don't have long to get to the château terrace, where William tells me he's left my iPad outside on a table. I wonder as I step outside how we managed to pack a popcorn maker and Super Soaker but no rain jackets.

I sprint past the car park, before I make it onto the path, mist rising off the dank green trees. I eventually emerge into the open to find the swimming pool abandoned, charcoal clouds reflecting on its surface. I step onto the terrace and look around, but there's no sign of the iPad.

It's when I head inside to join those taking refuge from the imminent storm that I spot the device — on a table under a lamp, presumably brought in by someone when the weather turned. I grab it and shield it under my sweater, as a crack of lightning illuminates the landscape and there's a whoop from the other guests.

After a moment of hesitation, I decide just to go for it, racing past the pool back in the direction of the woods. But I've only run a short distance when the sky opens and hard, heavy rain begins slamming my shoulders. My face is slicked with water as a deep groan of thunder fills my ears. It occurs to me that coming out in the open during this storm wasn't a good idea and not just because I'm already drenched. Then, a crack of electricity appears out of nowhere, blitzing the ground in front of me.

I gasp as someone yanks my hand.

"This way!"

Adam and I sprint across the grass towards a small stone outbuilding. He bustles me inside, as another bolt of lightning flashes in the sky.

"What are we doing in here?" I ask.

"Believe me, Jess, it's not a good idea being out there in the middle of a storm. We need to wait at least until the lightning's passed."

I squeeze up against a stack of wood and clasp my hands around my knees as Adam sits down next to me.

"What were you doing out there?"

A drop of water falls from my eyebrow. "William had left my iPad on the terrace. I needed to get it before it started pissing down."

He frowns, disapprovingly. "That lightning was close, you know. A few more feet and you'd have been toast."

I crane my neck to look at the sky and see another streak of lightning, but it's smaller than the last one. I realize I'm shivering. I also realize Adam is looking at me.

"What?" I ask.

He shakes his head and wrestles off the sweatshirt that was tied around his waist. "It's not completely dry but better than nothing."

"It's all right," I mutter, as my jaw quivers.

"Jess, just take it."

I go to put it on. But there's so little space that, as I attempt to wriggle into it, I fail to do anything except hit him in the face. He splutters with laughter. I find myself smiling and then kind of laughing too. I finally manage to get my arms through, followed by my head. I wipe the rain from my nose and glance up. His eyes soften, and he smiles at me.

It's a tiny gesture, but it provokes a rush of hot liquid happiness that makes my limbs feel weak.

"Thank you," I whisper.

But he doesn't reply. He just looks at me.

And I look at him too, for no other reason than I'm suddenly incapable of taking my eyes off him, studying how his features look in the shadows.

Everything that's happened between us — all the good and the bad — disintegrates, and my ears are filled with the sound of my racing heart, drowning out the thrum of the rain. I realize I want something I haven't wanted for years. I want something instinctive and animalistic and something that defies everything I've come to know, but I want it so badly that I'm close to grabbing him by the neck and just doing it. I want to kiss him. I am aching for it.

He cranes his neck to peer out the door.

"The storm's passing," he murmurs.

But I don't follow his gaze outside. I can only stare at him. Then the rain slows and I snap out of it. "I'd better get back."

He nods and leans back on the wall, but I can feel his eyes lingering on me, with an intensity that lays bare his own illicit thoughts.

I am drenched and disheveled but so fired up with heat that my cheeks are ablaze. I grab the iPad and shove it inside the sweatshirt. Then I crawl out of the woodshed,

this time refusing to turn back to him, too
scared of what might happen if I do.

CHAPTER 44

Natasha opens the door to the cottage when she sees me approaching. "Did you get caught in that?" she says, horrified. "I assumed you'd have stayed in the château until it died down."

"That would've been a better plan," I mutter, stepping in and shaking myself off like a wet Labrador.

"Did you get it?" William asks sheepishly, looking up from the sofa.

"Yes, I did," I reply, throwing him a purse-lipped glare. "I need to give it a good wipe down and make sure it's survived the experience before you get your mitts on it again though. But first I'm going to get out of these wet clothes."

I head to the bedroom, give the iPad a cursory wipe over, before laying it on the bed and peeling off my top, my skin raw with cold. I am still dizzy from what just happened as I grab a pair of jeans and a

T-shirt and start toweling my hair. I perch on the edge of the bed and return my attention to the tablet, turning it on and clicking on the Internet browser to give it a test run. Only instead of opening up a clean page, it loads the last thing I looked at online, having apparently forgotten to clear my browser history.

Huntington's disease genetic testing.

The breath catches in my throat as I reread the words.

They are among my most Googled on a subject that, for my own sanity, I shouldn't really be reading any more about.

"Oh God," I say under my breath, clicking on the link to remind myself exactly what the article says. Nausea rises in my chest as I scan the page, a blunt reminder of the singular issue that dominates my life these days.

A single abnormal gene produces Huntington's disease. The child of an HD patient needs only one copy of this from either parent to develop the illness.

A genetic test can make or confirm the diagnosis of HD. The children of someone with Huntington's disease can take this test after the age of 18 to see whether they have inherited the faulty gene.

If they have, they will develop Huntington's disease, but it is not possible to work out at what age.

Using a blood sample, DNA is analyzed for the HD mutation by counting the number of CAG repeats in the "huntingtin" gene. Individuals who do not have HD usually have 28 or fewer repeats. Individuals with HD usually have 40 or more repeats.

Deciding whether to be tested can be difficult. A negative result relieves worry and uncertainty. A positive test can help people to make decisions about their future.

Some people say they would rather not know because they want to enjoy their life before they start to display symptoms, which generally appear in mid-life.

Panic grabs me by the throat as I keep reading, sweat gathering under my arms. William might have seen this and worked everything out.

Then all I've hidden from him and almost everyone else I know for the last decade would be there for him to read in black and white. I throw down the iPad with a pounding heart and race to the door, prying it open as I peek out.

My son is on the sofa with his head in a book, stuffing roast chicken crisps into his mouth with his free hand. He starts chuckling at something, then turns a page. I tell myself to calm the fuck down.

He doesn't know. He can't know.

Even if he's seen what I've been reading, that doesn't mean he's made the connection, joined the dots to create the picture we've faced since the day my mother was diagnosed with HD.

I found out about the genetic test soon after her diagnosis, but in the early days I tried to convince myself it'd be better not to know. Most children of Huntington's disease patients decide against finding out, and it's little wonder when you think about it.

Yes, the idea that you might be declared HD negative is an enticing prospect. You'd be free from the relentless, twisting anxiety. Free to enjoy life and look forward to a long and healthy future. But a positive result is another thing altogether. There's no unknowing the news that you have inherited this beast; before the symptoms even appear, it ruins every glimmer of happiness you might have had.

Some people cope brilliantly without knowing whether they're gene positive or not and are able to get on with their lives. But as time went on, I became very bad at not knowing. I did try. I tried for years.

I never succeeded in putting this to the back of my mind; it was always there, like a noisy passenger opposite me on the train, whose voice I couldn't drown out.

And it got even louder after I got into my first relationship after Adam, even if it wasn't that serious.

I'd avoided getting involved with anyone for a long time. But when I met Toby a few years ago, he was so persistent, in the best kind of way. And he seemed such a lovely, straightforward guy that it was enough to convince me that my long martyrdom just wasn't necessary. So I told him very early on about my mum's HD and that I had a 50 percent chance of inheriting the faulty gene.

He was great; supportive, sympathetic and endlessly optimistic. At least, he was at first. The problem was, as his feelings for me grew, he began making noises about wanting to settle down and have his own family.

We went out for dinner one night at a little Italian restaurant in Didsbury, and he poured out his heart. "I love you, Jess. I want to make a life with you. I can totally see us as a family . . . you, me, a couple of little kids."

"And William," I pointed out.

"Yes, of course William." His hand slid across the table, and he clutched my fingers. "But we need to know where we are, don't we? With the HD, I mean."

The implication was clear: I was a contender to be his future wife and the mother of his children. But only if I took the genetic test and it came back with the right result.

I realized then that the problem wasn't just that my feelings for Toby weren't as strong as his were for me. The problem was that, whatever or whenever I decided about the test, that decision would have to be mine. Nobody else's.

So when he banged on about me taking it night after night, telling me he'd come with me, my drawbridge came up. I was not going to be marched to the clinic for a blood test — by a man who'd then decide whether to stay with me or go.

The more pressure he put on me, the less I wanted to do it.

So he left, and that was that. I was sad about it for a little while, but if I'm honest, it was a relief to be single again.

As the years passed though, the issue of

the test kept pushing its way back into my head. And as a bitter winter blew in at the beginning of this year, I would arrive at Willow Bank every day and feel the pain of my mum's worsening condition ever more intensely. I couldn't tell you if I was imagining the increasing pace of her decline, if the howling January wind intensified the hush of her speech and the gnarl of her hands.

All I know is that as I sat with her one afternoon nursing a cold cup of tea, I realized that what she was becoming was slowly ripping me up from inside.

I knew that the time had come to finally find out my own fate.

So I rolled the dice and took the test.

CHAPTER 45

Dad came with me to get the results of my blood test, four torturous weeks after it was taken. It was not the first time I'd met Dr. Inglis. She'd completed a basic neurological examination shortly after my first meeting with the genetic counselor and concluded after I'd successfully performed several tasks that I was displaying no symptoms of HD.

I knew that meant nothing in the scheme of things, but it still gave me hope.

My dad looked nice that day. He was wearing a smart navy jacket and new trousers; he was dressed for a happy occasion. As we sat in the waiting room, I felt an odd sense of weightlessness. I stopped myself from looking at the clock that ticked on the wall and instead concentrated on the receptionist's luminous manicure and the way the curtain fluttered above the radiator.

"I dug out my old *Frasier* DVD last

night," I told Dad. "I'd forgotten how good it was."

"Oh, which episode?"

"I watched three, back-to-back. Including that one where they throw Marty's chair out of the window."

"Ha! Brilliant," he exclaimed, but the laugh dried up in his throat. "Brilliant."

Neither of us had mentioned what we were actually here for since we'd left the house. I thought about saying something briefly but at the last minute moved on to the fact that my neighbor Graham's basset hound was pregnant.

Eventually, I found myself blurting out something I'd thought about for years. "You know when you and Mum first got together . . . . Do you think if you'd known . . . about her HD, I mean, would things have been different?"

"You mean would I still have married her?"

I shrug. "I guess so."

He looks disappointed that I've even had to ask. "Jess, when you love someone, something like this would never stop you from being with them."

I remember thinking, *Well, he would say that under the circumstances.*

But then he added something that sur-

287

prised me. "I love her more now than ever." I must've looked shocked. "It's true. I mean it. We've had plenty to test our mettle."

"Jessica Pendleton."

Dad and I followed Dr. Inglis down the corridor to her office. As we walked, he reached out and held my hand for the first time since I was eight. The arch of his palm against mine felt strong and smooth, exactly like it always had, and suddenly my heart was too big for my chest.

Once inside, I perched on the edge of my seat, and I could tell before she started talking what she was going to say. She didn't drag it out. She got straight to the point.

"It isn't the news we wanted, Jess," she began, and for a moment, before I actually took in the words, I remember feeling sorry for her, thinking what an awful job this must be.

It was only as Dad and I walked outside to the car park that I realized I was physically shaking, my entire arms trembling hard and the joints in my legs turning to mush.

We stood next to his car, and he pulled me into his chest and whispered into my hair, "It's okay, Jess. It's going to be okay."

That must've been the first time he'd lied to me since he'd been sober.

We didn't break it to Mum that day. The counselor had advised that it's not always a good idea, when emotion and shock are running so high and the decision is likely, in his words, to cause the parent "distress."

But we couldn't put it off forever, even though I knew what it'd do to her. Because I know what it feels like when there's only a *possibility* that you've passed a fatal gene on to your own child.

The force of maternal love fills you up from the first moment you feel the rolls and ripples of tiny limbs inside your belly. You breathe it in with their newborn smell when they are placed in your arms. It swells in you as they grow, when you clasp your fingers around his little hand on the first day of school, or kiss her bloodied knee when she falls.

And I know there are times when mothers are driven close to madness — from sleep deprivation or teenage tantrums or plain naughtiness and defiance. But you'll always love them, in ways that simply never existed before they did.

The worst day of my mother's life wasn't when she found out she had HD. It was on the bleak February day when she learned I was HD positive.

As for me, I couldn't even process what

was going on in my head at the time. Since then, there have been times in the past few months when I'm so scared I've barely been able to lift my head from my pillow in the morning.

This has left a question mark over the future of the person who means more to me than anyone else on earth, my son. As a minor, William can't have the test until he's eighteen. So I have at least eight years before I find out if I've passed it to him, and that's assuming he chooses to take the test.

I am thirty-three. My mum started getting symptoms when she was thirty-seven. I may not have long before things start happening to me that will one day affect my ability to be the person I want to be — the daughter, the friend, the colleague. And, most of all, the mother.

Someone who'll be smiling from the sidelines, as much when William becomes a man as I did when he was a little boy in mittens and a bobble hat.

I dream about him in middle age sometimes.

Occasionally, I can picture him vividly — sometimes he's a scientist, other times a historian; once or twice he's been a binman. I think about him finding love, having his heart broken, graduating, buying his first car, choosing a university, winning a dream job.

I find myself dwelling on which of those things I'll be there to support him through, if any.

But, oddly, it's the smaller things that I find myself thinking about most — like whether I'll still be around when his curly hair has thinned, or if I'll see flecks of grey appearing in a beard. I think about whether I'll miss hearing his voice thicken with age, and that Domino's habit creeping on his midriff.

The idea that I'll miss this future is impossible to accept.

Which brings me to our real motive for being here in France, the reason my mum was desperate for us to come. My son needs a dad, for a far more critical reason than I've let on; one that, in the light of my test result, I could no longer ignore. I'm praying that Adam will be able to step up to the mark and be the father William will need more than ever.

CHAPTER 46

A lustrous morning sun floods through my bedroom window. I lie on my back amid the soft white sheets, fixing my eyes on the ceiling, having spent all night convincing myself that William can't possibly have worked out anything about the HD — and attempting to interpret what happened in the woodshed.

The only conclusion I can reach is this: I have to pretend nothing happened. Because nothing *did* happen. I am simply what William would call "weirded out." Every time I think of the way Adam looked at me and the response it provoked in me, it doesn't feel entirely real. More of a curious dream sequence.

We spend most of the morning together as a group by the pool, before Natasha offers to prepare lunch for everyone. Becky and Seb have stopped bickering, but it strikes me that, even when they're not row-ing, communication between the two of them is often little more than functional: she asks him where the water wings are; he asks her if she brought any Sudocrem with her. They discuss eczema flare-ups, toilet training, electronic device usage and milk teeth, but none of the things they used to in the days when their eyes shimmered with desire for each other. And they're completely unable to relax. I take James and Rufus into the pool at one point myself — to organize a group game of water volleyball — but every time I look at the poolside, one of them is frantically trying to placate Poppy, while the other is rummaging around in a nappy bag.

They're the best and worst advert for parenthood I can imagine.

We gather our belongings and head back to the cottage for one thirty, when Natasha has promised a feast. As the others traipse across the dusty courtyard, Charlie emerges from his door and waves at me. I dump my towel and beach bag on a chair and head over.

"Been down at the pool?" he asks.

"We have, but it's busy there today. Everyone's trying to soak up the sun after yesterday."

"Listen, I wondered if you and William

293

wanted to come for a walk later with Chloe and me?"

"That'd be lovely. I'm sure he'd be up for that."

"Nowhere too strenuous," he says. "I picked up a trail map from the château, and there's a nice route by the lake."

"It's a date." A shot of heat fires up my neck. "Well, not a *date* as such. But we'll be there."

He laughs, glancing away only when his phone rings. "Excuse me, Jess." He reaches into his pocket to answer it. He's got nice hands — smooth and tanned, offset by a watch that even someone whose swankiest timepiece was a Swatch can recognize as expensive.

I stand there awkwardly, not knowing whether this is meant to be good-bye or not. "I'll see you later?" I mouth, as I back away.

He slides his hand over the phone. "About four o'clock?"

"Sure."

Charlie's nice. Exactly what the doctor ordered: not some big relationship that, given my circumstances, would throw up a dozen complicated and painful question marks over the future.

But a bright, friendly guy who lives near me. So we could go to restaurants together, or to the movies. We could have a bit of fun and maybe a kiss on a Saturday night. It'd be so *pleasant.* I can't emphasize how appealing the idea of pleasantness is at the moment. I've had my fill of high emotion and would love something as low-key as that.

My thoughts disintegrate the moment I step inside the cottage and hear Natasha's strangled voice. "Look, Becky, I'm *not* having a go at you!"

"Well, it sounds like it." Becky thrusts her bags down on the table.

"What's going on?" I ask, but it's already clear. And neither of them looks ready to back down.

CHAPTER 47

Natasha has the look of someone who is extremely worked up but is trying hard to control it. She's doing that deep breathing they teach in yoga classes, the kind that's easy when you're in a tranquil studio but less so when someone looks like they want to throttle you.

"You wanted to know why the lunch was late," Natasha tells Becky. "I was *simply* saying that it was because the little barbecue you and Seb borrowed the other night hadn't been cleaned — so I had to do it."

"Well, *I'm sorry.*" Becky doesn't sound very sorry. "*You* try dealing with three kids, two of whom are launching World War Three, one of whom has got the trots and another of whom has been up half the night in our bed because he's having nightmares after watching *Coraline.*"

Natasha frowns. "That's four."

"What?"

"That's four kids. You've only got three."

"I know how many bloody kids I've got!"

Natasha crosses her arms. "Becky, I'm sorry I mentioned it, honestly. But you asked."

"I only asked because I've got a toddler here who starts behaving like a gremlin that's been fed after midnight when she doesn't eat for hours. I didn't expect this reaction."

"There's no reaction," Natasha says gently. "I really didn't mean anything by it."

I touch Becky's arm. "Is everything all right?"

She rubs her forehead. "Let me do something else then, seeing as you cleaned the barbecue. What needs cooking?"

"You don't have to do anything else," Natasha continues, flashing me a glance. "Look. Relax. Please. Just go and sit down and lunch will be ten more minutes, that's all."

Becky nods and looks close to tears. "All right. Sorry," she mutters, before turning and heading back outside.

Natasha continues chopping a salad. "Are you okay?" I ask her.

She nods, then looks round anxiously. "Becky's been a nightmare lately."

"She's stressed."

"I know. But that doesn't mean the rest of us should have to get it in the neck constantly. *We're* meant to be on holiday too. God, look what you've got on your plate."

"I try not to."

She bites the side of her mouth. "How *are* you, Jess?"

I raise my eyebrows. "Purely in terms of my health, I'm absolutely fine — at least, for now. But I'm paranoid every time I drop a glass or trip down some steps. I went flying when I was at Château de Beynac with Adam and William the other day. I'm constantly worried that this is the start of it. And seeing the state Mum's in doesn't help."

"Poor her." Her eyes crease with concern. "Poor you."

I don't want Natasha's sympathy. In fact, I hate it. When I first told her and Becky, shortly after Mum broke the news to me all those years ago, the issue of my HD was all they wanted to talk about. Every time we got together for a drink, or a coffee, they were there, endlessly worried and full of questions.

I know they meant well, but I became completely sick of it. It's as if Mum and I were suddenly defined by it — *everything* became about the HD. Not my new baby.

Not my crumbling relationship. Not politics or *The Sopranos* or new Chanel nail polish colors or all the other things we used to talk about.

After a couple of months, I told them straight out: I don't want to talk about this anymore, not every time I see you. I am still *me,* not one of those "brave" disease-battling victims you read about in the papers, not least because I'm absolutely *not* brave. I'm the opposite of brave. So enough already. Please.

And although it all started again — inevitably — after I got the news that I was gene positive, I think they've finally got the message.

"Listen, don't take it personally about Becky," I reassure her.

She straightens up. "Oh, I'm not. I mean, I feel sorry for her. But I'm not prepared to be her whipping boy." I pick up a knife to start slicing a baguette as a notification beeps on her phone.

"The Wi-Fi's clearly decided to be nice to you today."

She picks it up and studies the screen. "Joshua's posted photos of us on Facebook. I think he might be keen."

She passes it over to show me a picture of them clinking champagne glasses, another posing with golf clubs.

"How did your round go?"

"Josh was brilliant, but I don't think it's my sport. I took so long on the sixth hole we gave up and went for a boozy session instead."

"So have you . . ." I raise my eyebrows.

"Slept with him? No, I'm holding out. I'm wondering if he might be relationship material."

I look at the phone again and flick through his profile. I really wish I'd warmed to Joshua more; I'm starting to think I might have become more judgmental than I used to be. His Facebook "Likes" — which include several ropy burlesque dancers and a site called Halt the Oppression of White Middle-Class Men — don't help though.

When I head back outside, I find Becky trying to muster the energy to read *The Book With No Pictures* to Poppy, while Seb instructs James and Rufus in the art of the pogo stick.

"You're a natural." I smile as he manages three jumps before tumbling into a trough of lavender.

I sit down next to Becky and offer Poppy some bread. "Fank you, Aunty Jess. You're a good girl."

"Listen, I had an idea," I tell Becky. "Why

don't you and Seb go on a night out somewhere and I'll babysit."

She looks at me, and her expression melts
into one of gratitude and disbelief. "Oh,
this is why I love you so much, Jess."

"So that's a yes?"

"Absolutely not. There's no way I'd leave
you with three kids, as well as William. But
you are an angel for offering."

"Becky, they'll be fine. I haven't lost my
touch," I argue.

"Of course you haven't. But Poppy would
just cry for us all night, James would deci-
mate your makeup collection and I'd spend
the evening worrying about what I'm putting you through."

"Well, you wouldn't need to."

"I'll think about it," she concludes, but I
can tell she's already decided it's not going
to happen. "There is one thing I do need to
do though." She looks up at the door and
sighs.

"What?"

"Go and make up with Natasha."

CHAPTER 48

It's clear that Chloe would rather be having her toenails surgically removed than be on a walk with us. Not that she's complaining, exactly. Complaining would involve talking, and she's barely said a thing as she trails behind Charlie and me. William, on the other hand, is determined to make conversation with her.

"Shall we have a chat?" he suggests eagerly.

She curls up one side of her top lip. "What about?"

"Hmm. How about the Black Death?"

I spin round and smile at her. "That's quite an offer, you must admit."

William scowls at my disloyalty. "Sorry, sweetheart," I say. "But Chloe probably doesn't —"

"What do you know about it, then?" Chloe asks.

He straightens his back. "Well, it started

in 1346 and was spread by rats and killed a third of the people in Europe."

"Did you know it made your spleen melt?" she offers.

He is beyond impressed. "Whoa."

Charlie and I exchange a smile. "So what should *we* talk about — smallpox, perhaps?" I suggest.

We've strayed away from the grounds of the château, into the neighboring meadow, where the grass is long and luxuriant, the air filled with the heady scent of wild orchids. We eventually arrive at a gate that separates two fields, and Charlie stands aside.

"Go on, kids, you two first." William and Chloe scramble across effortlessly, and Charlie invites me to go next.

I'm midway over when I realize he has a close-up view of my backside. But the hesitation proves to be my downfall, and I lose my footing, stumbling into a straddle with an accompanying "OOF!"

"Everything all right?"

I nod and smile speechlessly as the kids stride ahead. Eventually, we reach an open field laced with lush, green oak trees, and I become aware of Charlie leaning into me. When I look up he whispers, "You look gorgeous today."

"Stop it — you're making me blush," I reply, sticking to my lifelong instinct to diffuse all compliments with a joke.

"I'm serious," he perseveres, looking way too determined again, particularly given the proximity of our children.

I cough and try to change the subject. "Is Chloe enjoying the holiday?"

He takes the hint and straightens up. "She seems to be, when she's not complaining about being bored senseless."

"Oh dear."

"I think she'd prefer to be in Orlando, if the truth be told," he says.

"Orlando *is* brilliant."

"You've been?"

"Once. William and I went when he was six, with my ex, Toby. I hadn't expected to like it, but I was hooked instantly. I'm a sad Disney freak. Toby hated it. I don't think everyone feels at home in the sort of place where they break into song on every other corner, do they?"

"I must admit, I can relate to that. So why didn't it work out with him?"

"Aside from our differences over the Magic Kingdom, you mean?"

He awaits something less flippant.

"It fizzled out, mainly," I say. "We were never head over heels in love. It was all very amicable."

"Had William not minded you seeing someone who wasn't his dad?"

"No, I don't think so. Adam and I split up when William was very little, so he's never known any different. And Toby was never really a father figure to William. What about you and Chloe's mum?"

"Chloe *definitely* has a problem with the fact that we're not together."

"Ah."

"Unfortunately, there's absolutely nothing I can do about that." I don't say anything, but he continues talking. "Gina — that's Chloe's mum — works as a flight attendant. I'd trusted her 100 percent despite the rumors you hear about affairs among airline staff. One day my car battery went flat, and I had to borrow hers to get to work. I opened the boot and found an empty bottle of champagne. When I asked her about it, she said she'd had a lunch with the girls a week or so earlier and had brought it back with her."

"Sounds feasible."

"Then I discovered her second mobile."

"Oh no."

"I know, what a cliché."

He goes on to tell a tale of woe featuring a string of sordid revelations: a pilot who revealed she'd slept with half the airline, Jacuzzi parties in hotel stops and even, according to another member of the cabin crew, an incident in the cockpit that involved her playing with a set of controls that had nothing to do with the plane. She finally confessed to an affair after a friend who worked at his law firm spotted her in a pub in Chester, kissing another man.

"What hurt most was that she'd lied," he says. "I knew deep down that things were going on, but she continued to deny it, until the truth was overwhelming. She pushed me to my limits."

"Until you were left no choice but to end it." Then I glance away, deciding I don't want to explain that I've been there myself.

"Actually, I was prepared to forgive her."

"Really?"

"Yes, but she wanted to go anyway."

I suddenly want to say something to lighten the mood. I lean in and whisper, "She sounds like a complete cow."

He laughs. "Thank you. That makes me feel a lot better."

The slope of the ground begins to rise steeply, and my thighs burn as we march upwards. "We should reach the lake just over this hill. Come on, kids." Chloe and William have slipped behind and have stopped talking about airborne diseases to grumble about why we're putting them through this ordeal. The final strides up the hill make my legs burn. Charlie reaches down and grabs me by the hand, helping me up. "The view's tremendous," he says.

And it is: verdant rolling countryside, a glittering lake, water like glass until a bird swoops down to the surface, setting off a ripple of perfect circles. The air is hot and quiet, there is no breeze and the only movement is from the silent beat of a butterfly as it flutters past. I'm momentarily mesmerized by the creature, by its silky cerulean wings shimmering in the sunlight.

Then I register the figure at the jetty on the edge of the lake.

Adam is lying on his back, wearing only a pair of shorts, his head propped up on a T-shirt or sweatshirt, or something. His chest is bare, and he is reading a paperback.

The sight of him prompts a rush of memories that nearly sweep me off my feet: of the days when we'd cycle to the park together in the summer and lie under the shelter of the sky, reading side by side, pausing between chapters to wrap ourselves in each other, stealing kisses.

"Hey, it's Dad!" William shouts. "DAD!"

He skips down the hill towards Adam,

who pulls himself up and starts laughing at the sight of his son hurtling in his direction. William throws his arms round his father like he hasn't seen him for months, and Adam squeezes him back, before inviting him to sit down. I watch them for a few private moments, as my head rushes with senseless, unwelcome thoughts about what might have been.

CHAPTER 49

Nobody becomes a parent expecting to be thanked for it.

So when William produces a small, fragrant bouquet of lilacs for me the following day, I'm almost speechless.

"You bought me flowers?" I take them from him incredulously. "When did you get them?"

"When I was with Dad this morning. But they were paid for out of my own money," he adds hastily.

"But why?" I feel so touched by this that he almost looks worried.

"He said you'd like them. He said they were your favorites and that it'd be a good way of showing that I loved you."

"Oh, sweetheart, that's *so gorgeous.*" I can't resist throwing my arms round him and pulling his bony torso briefly into me. He rewards me with a perfunctory squeeze.

"Can I go now?"

"Go where?"

"Nowhere, you're just nearly strangling me."

I'm not sure where Adam got the idea these were my favorites — I haven't bought enough flowers to have anything as luxurious as a favorite, at least not recently. William shoots off to his bedroom as I go to the sink and find a blue-and-white enamel jug in the cupboard. I fill it with water and arrange the lilacs, before taking it to the table.

For all Adam's faults, he was forever giving gifts, small tokens of love and friendship that showed he was glad you were in his life. He didn't limit it to me either. I remember us being in London about a year after we'd started seeing each other. We stopped in to browse round Liberty in Soho, and he picked up one of their classic ties, in dark blue printed silk.

"This has got your dad's name written all over it," Adam decided. It was true that my dad loved a good tie. He's still got a huge collection that takes up far too much room in his wardrobe.

"Look at the price, Adam," I said. "I'll put it on his Christmas list."

"No, it's okay. I'll get this," he decided, and marched off to the cash desk before I could argue.

Sometimes this could be infuriating — I'd be losing sleep over how we were going to stop the gas being cut off, and he'd roll up with a new bracelet for me that he'd seen in some antique shop. And while part of me wanted to hit him over the head, the other part simply loved the bracelet and everything it represented.

Adam is hosting a barbecue at his cottage for us all tonight, except Natasha, who's gone out with Joshua. He arrived to pick her up half an hour ago, sweeping her out of the cottage in a cloud of overpowering cologne while he regaled her with a story about how he'd gallantly just corrected a former colleague's punctuation on Facebook, saving him further embarrassment.

I head to the bedroom to get ready, and though it shouldn't be hard, I can't find anything I want to wear. The prospect of sitting next to Simone in her hot pants doesn't help.

I settle on a flimsy floral cami, which I find still stuffed in my suitcase, and, failing to locate an iron in the cottage, I am forced to contemplate other ingenious ways to get the creases out of it. It's as I'm running Natasha's hair straighteners over the cotton fabric that there's a knock on the door.

I unplug them and open it to find Charlie on the step.

"Oh, hi! How are you?" I say, forcing myself not to look at my watch to check how long I've got before we're due at Adam's.

"I'm good." When I look up, his eyes are so heavy with desire that it makes me feel slightly on edge. It's as though he's been thinking of me and rushed straight over. Which I'm of course flattered by, but his gaze is so intense, it makes me shift away an inch.

"What are you up to?"

"Well, at the moment I'm trying to work out if I'd be able to iron my top with a pair of hair straighteners."

He is silent for a moment as his brow crinkles, genuinely perplexed. "Hair straighteners?"

"Just kidding," I mutter lamely.

He cranes his neck to look behind me, scanning the room. "Anyone else in?"

"Everyone."

His expression is sharp with disappointment. Then he leans in and touches my fingers, clasping them into his hand. "I can't stop thinking about you."

"READY!" William declares, bursting into the living room.

I snatch away my hand as Charlie fixes his

eyes on me. "Oh. You're going out."

"Only for a barbecue at Adam's place."

"Ah. I was hoping we could persuade William and Chloe to go and play soccer or something so you and I could have a drink."

"Oh, what a shame. We could do that another night," I suggest.

"I'd like that," William pipes up.

The pulse in Charlie's temple becomes more pronounced.

"Right. I'll leave you to it then. Have a good evening." And he forces a smile that fails entirely to hide his disappointment.

CHAPTER 50

The smoky scent of summer fills the air outside Adam's stone cottage, as old friends chat over blackberry-colored wine and the children play Frisbee for at least five minutes without wanting to kill one another. We sit around three mismatched wooden tables pushed together, some of us on benches, others on the kind of chairs you sink into, with curved backs and creamy canvas cushions.

William is stuck fast by his father's side, yapping away as Adam idly turns burgers. My eyes are drawn to the two of them in the soft amber light, and I find my imagination fast-forwarding ten, maybe twenty years. I picture them shooting the breeze, adult to adult, father and son — and for this to be the norm in their lives, not just what happens during one exceptional summer.

"There's a zip line park near Loussou we

could go to tomorrow," Seb says, passing me a guidebook.

I leaf through it as we try to determine how long it would take us to drive there, when I become aware of Adam behind me. He picks up my glass and starts topping it up.

"Just a small one for me."

"Why?" he asks, filling it to the brim.

"Oh, if you insist," I sigh, taking it from him as he sinks into the chair next to me.

He's wearing a pale cotton shirt that clings to his chest, sleeves rolled high up his tanned arms. My head swims with the memory of his hand on mine in the wood-shed, and an uncomfortable warmth spreads up my neck.

"Thanks for the flowers," I say, politely.

He smiles. "They were William's idea."

"Oh? He said they were yours."

"It was a joint effort."

"Well, it was a lovely thought. It's nice to feel appreciated."

Then he pauses, lowers his voice and says: "You look nice tonight."

"Thanks," I manage to reply, despite the fact that I am secretly sweating. Having to sit this close to him suddenly feels stifling. "It'll be the top I've just ironed with a pair of hair straighteners."

He bursts into laughter, and I feel so grateful that I join in too. "You always were resourceful."

"Hi, everyone!" We stop abruptly and turn to Simone. Her navy dress is dotted with tiny snowdrops and cut from a soft fabric that clings seductively to her breasts and skims her tanned thighs. Adam excuses himself to go and greet her. She stands on the tips of her pale ballet pumps, slides her arms around his neck and plants a languorous kiss on his lips. I fix my eyes on my wine.

As the sun sets, Adam brings plate after plate to the table: kebabs sprinkled with fragrant herbs, chicken marinated in garlic and lemon, thick sausages made of pork and duck. There are bowls of chips and colorful salads glistening with sharply scented vinaigrette, and platters of crusty bread.

We eat until we're past the point of feeling full and savor every mouthful.

Despite the heavenly setting, I feel strangely agitated around Simone. Guilty, almost. And I find myself making up for it by trying to involve her in the conversation, complimenting her on her dress, her shoes, how nice of her it is to randomly recommend another of the antiaging creams that her mother swears by.

Compared with the others, I haven't

drunk a great deal on this holiday — I rarely do. Growing up around Dad was the best anti-binge-drinking campaign I'd ever need. But tonight, my usual glass of wine turned into another and another, all of which amounted to quite a lot more than I'm used to. This becomes acutely apparent when I enthusiastically agree to the children's requests to join in a wheelbarrow race — and Becky and I find ourselves giggling, facedown on the grass with our respective ten- and seven-year-olds at the start line.

I can't claim there's any dignity in lolloping across a field with your child clutching your ankles and shrieking, "FASTER!" like you're some kind of geriatric donkey. But it *is* funny, the kind of distraction from real life — or at least my life — that's been missing lately.

We take it easy for an hour or so after that, picking at what's left of the feast, before the kids become restless again and decide they'd like more audience participation. Adam leaps up, requiring little encouragement. "I think it's time for a game of something. Cricket or *boules,* William? Your choice."

William doesn't hesitate. "*Boules.* Mum's brilliant at it."

I cough into my Bergerac. "I'm not sure

I'm *brilliant.*"

"I'm sure that's what you told me once," William protests. "That you were brilliant."

"I must've been using the term loosely."

"Come on, up you get," Adam instructs. He jokingly goes to take me by the arm, but I shake him off, afraid of how I'll feel with his hands on my skin. Then Rufus jumps up. All the adults seem to register at once that, with Adam, Simone and me, we have five people and only four sets of *boules,* the brightly colored plastic kind they sell in the supermarkets here.

"I'll sit it out," I offer gladly.

"NO!" protests William.

"Well, I don't mind," Adam says with a shrug.

"Oh, Dad, come *on.*"

Which only leaves two children and Simone. William and Rufus glare at her.

"Looks like it's me who's sitting it out then," she says through a pinched smile, before returning to her seat and crossing her legs tightly.

My eyes flicker up to Adam. "I *really* don't mind not taking part —"

"Just get on with it, Jess," Adam instructs. "Come on, show us what you're made of."

CHAPTER 51

I try to remember exactly why it was I said I was brilliant at *boules*. Dad always told the ten-year-old me I was a natural, but as I pick up a ball, I realize that I've drunk too much to have the razor-sharp focus required for the game. Or indeed for putting one foot in front of the other.

"Let's toss a coin to see who throws the jack," Adam decides, pulling out a handful of change from his pocket.

"Tails," William declares.

Adam flips up a euro and smacks it on the back of his hand. "Tails it is."

William takes the little white ball and, with intensity on his brow, throws it on the ground ahead of him. His first shot isn't bad, falling short by only a foot. Adam goes next and gets closer, before Rufus smashes that out of the way.

I step forward and cup the *boule* in my palm as I get into position, hotly aware of

Simone's eyes on me. This has a peculiarly fortifying effect on my adrenaline levels, and I become hyperaware of my movements as I lunge back and swing my arm, sending the *boule* flying off at a mad angle — and prompting a great deal of hilarity from our audience.

It turns out to be only the start. Over the next twenty minutes, I am repeatedly trounced by everyone, and it's the source of no end of amusement to Adam. "It's not *that* hard, Jess."

"I'm a bit rusty, that's all," I fire back. "Besides, don't go on about it, or I'll have to bring up the stone skimming."

He starts laughing and shakes his head. "I've got a good trick if you'd like me to show you?"

"I'll cope without a lesson."

"Suit yourself."

"You might learn something, Mum," William pipes up. Given that I've said this repeatedly to him over the years, this puts me in an awkward position.

"Fine. Come and show me where I'm going wrong."

Adam picks up a ball and walks towards me, grinning as he bounces it in his hand.

I am expecting him to simply demonstrate some daft hop, skip and jump maneuver, to which I'll respond by rolling my eyes and calling him a smart arse. Instead, before I have a chance to object, he is directly behind me, sliding his arm past my waist and clasping his hand under mine.

I freeze at his touch as my forehead throbs. I glance anxiously to check Simone isn't looking. But she's gone inside for something.

"Like this." I can feel his breath against my ear.

I consider pushing him away and genially making a joke about him being patronizing. But as his body presses against my back, I can't do it. Not without drawing attention to the effect he's having on me. So I remain still, my belly swooping with guilty pleasure as I try to slow my breaths.

I can feel the contours of his chest move against my back as, together, we swing the ball and release it. It trundles to the ground, miles away from the jack. It's the worst shot of the game.

He straightens up, and I glance backwards at him anxiously. His face looks too serious as he whispers: "Never mind."

"Fat lot of good you were," I reply.

I'm trying to lighten the mood with a joke, but it comes out sounding so flirtatious that my color deepens further.

"How about we try again?"

As he smiles his heart-stopping smile, we are interrupted by the shrill of Simone's voice. "Adam, I'm going home."

She crosses her arms tight against her chest, and I am stiff with shame.

"Simone, why don't you stay and take over from me," I leap in, stepping away from Adam. "I'm completely rubbish at this. Come on, I insist."

"Thanks, but I've got a migraine," she says flatly.

"Oh no. They're a nightmare," I reply, pretending I haven't noticed the tone in her voice. "Do you get them a lot?"

She glares at Adam. "I seem to lately. I'll see you all in the morning. Enjoy your evening," she says curtly, and walks off. I dig Adam in the ribs. "Go after her."

He looks genuinely confused by this suggestion. "Why? She's got a headache."

"She's pissed off with you, Adam."

"What have I done?"

But I can't answer that, because it would mean admitting what's changed between us. The change that's suddenly proving difficult to fight.

CHAPTER 52

Becky and Seb's children drift off to sleep on Adam's sofa like dominoes, first Poppy, then Rufus, then James. Adam and Seb carry the boys back to their cottage, deadweights over their shoulders, while Becky pushes Poppy in the pushchair, her little chubby fingers wrapped around Pink Bunny's ears.

William, meanwhile, sets out to prove that *Guardians of the Galaxy* never gets old, by curling up in Adam's spare room to watch it for the seventeenth time on my iPad while I offer to help clear up some dishes.

I pop my head round the door, and he looks up, surprised, then closes down the screen. "What are you looking at there? I hope it's not something inappropriate?" My head erupts with drunken, fragmented thoughts about the HD website I'd forgotten to close down on the day of the storm.

"No, no," he says, handing it over to prove

that he's been unsuccessfully attempting to watch a video entitled "Epic Fails."

"Is there swearing in this?"

"Not . . . much," he replies, as his jaw breaks into a greedy yawn. "I'm really tired."

"Come on, we need to head back, and you're too big for me to carry these days."

He groans and rolls over, pulling the sheet over his shoulders.

"He can sleep here tonight if he likes."

The heat from Adam's flesh next to mine makes me shiver, and I deliberately shift away.

"I'm sure he can manage to walk home, even at this hour."

"No, I want to stay here," William protests.

I glance between my son and his father.

"Fine, but take your shoes and socks off and at least get into bed. I'll come and collect you in the morning, okay?"

"Okay," he says eagerly, scrambling under the sheet, ripping off his socks and flinging them in my direction.

"Gee, thanks." I grimace as I catch them and walk over to kiss him. I let my cheek linger against his skin and, as I pull back, feel my heart twinge, overcome by one of those moments of pure gratitude that I have him.

"I love you," I whisper.

"I love you more."

"No, I love you the most."

"No way," he says as I laugh and back out of the room, expecting Adam to have left by now. Instead, he is watching us, his eyes blurring with unexpected emotion before he walks over and plants a lingering kiss on William's forehead.

As I head outside, the light from a high moon casts shadows across the grass, and constellations hang like celestial cobwebs above us. Adam begins to stack the chairs, and I pull my bag over my shoulder.

"I'd better head off," I say. "Are you sure you're all right with him?"

He stops and straightens his back. "Of course."

I nod and go to leave.

"Jess?"

"Yes?"

"Fancy a brew? I hate to boast about being able to get hold of illicit substances, but I've got Yorkshire Tea."

I smile automatically. "Who's your dealer?"

"She's called Maureen. She's sixty-six, comes here from Shropshire every year, and you wouldn't mess with her. Go on, I'll put the kettle on."

I sit on the faded bench outside his cottage and wait, as the lyrical rhythm of crickets breaks the silence.

When Adam appears with a pot of tea, the sight of his outline against the light behind the door makes my insides fizz. He brings it to the table and steps over the bench, sinking onto the wood so he's directly facing me. I glance away and study the knots in the surface.

He pours two mugs, then lifts his and clinks mine. "Cheers."

As the hot liquid slips down my throat, I find myself inhaling him, my head thick with memories. "What's that smell?"

He looks up and jokingly sniffs his armpits. "What smell?"

"It's not *unpleasant.* I just mean . . . your aftershave. I thought I recognized it."

A heartbeat passes. "It's Terre d'Hermès."

I swallow the cotton wool in my throat. "You always used to wear that."

He looks as if I've caught him out. "Well, not for years, but I saw some in Sarlat and remembered I liked it."

His dark eyes fix on mine, and I am flooded with a sensation so powerful it makes my fingers tremble. As I sit next to him, the man I've loved and hated, I find it suddenly impossible to remember why we're not together.

There is a vague logic whispering in the back of my mind, telling me that now's the time to leave. But the feeling that another person can turn you inside out just by looking at you is so exhilarating that I don't want it to stop.

Right now I ache for him. I cast my eyes to his lips and crave their taste. I want to run my fingertips along his jaw and see if it feels the same as it used to.

An intense pressure starts building in my belly, and I recognize a feeling I haven't had in years. A white-hot desire, gathering momentum as Adam refuses to remove his eyes from mine.

Above all else it reminds me of one thing. Whatever life might throw at me, right now, there's this: I'm *alive.*

I'm not sitting in a corner tormented by my future. I'm not torn apart by fear for my son, my mother and me. I'm living and breathing and feeling. He leans towards me.

When our lips touch, the kiss feels new and old all at the same time. He guides my leg over the bench, takes me by the hand and pulls me in, wrapping me around him, molding my body to his through my clothes as his mouth sinks deeper into mine.

"We shouldn't be doing this," I whisper,

arching my neck as his lips travel to the skin beneath my ear.

"We should," he says, sliding his hand through my hair, kissing my mouth, my temples, my neck, as I consider a vague thought that I'm drunk, that this is why I've allowed things to go this far.

But that's not it.

I might be full of wine, but I want this.

I want it when he takes my hand and stands, inviting me to do the same. I want it as he leads me into the cottage, past the door where we left William, stopping only to check that he's asleep under his sheets. I want it as we walk along the corridor to the other side of his cottage and I enter his bedroom, where he clicks shut the door, kissing me again as his hand slides up my spine.

We undress each other slowly, savoring every moment of new, bare skin.

I'd forgotten how beautiful Adam is naked. I am torn between whether to touch him or look at him, the agonizing perfection of his body. I don't get to choose. As the weight of him sinks into me, I grip the small of his back with my fingers and feel my blood pulsate. Then he stops and puts his hand on my chin.

"Do you know how beautiful you are to

me? Do you know how beautiful you've *always* been to me?"

His words make tears prick into my eyes. But I don't want to talk. I only want the heat of him inside me, and that soaring, obliterating feeling, just like it was in the beginning.

CHAPTER 53

The sound of a crowing cockerel grates in my ears until I'm jolted awake, lifting up my head from Adam's chest. My eyes skitter around the light-filled room, taking in my surroundings, the shutters we left open, particles of dust reflected in the sunlight, the clothes strewn across the floor, like evidence in a crime scene.

I turn to Adam and feel my stomach lurch at the sight of his parted lips, his bare neck, the skin on his shoulders.

Then my head explodes.

There are so many things wrong here, my head throbs with the insanity of what happened last night.

Top of the list is William. Who was *right there,* on the other side of the cottage, when this happened! I know he was fast asleep and that parents all over the world have sex in the same house as their kids, but not when the parents in question are meant to have split up a decade earlier.

He's had his whole life to come to terms with the fact that Adam and I are not together and are never going to be together, so what this would do to his poor prepubescent head doesn't bear thinking about.

He wouldn't just be confused by it; it'd be worse than that. He'd be *hopeful*. Left under the terrible, misguided impression that this can *mean something.*

I'd be completely unable to reassure him with a viable explanation, because there isn't one, other than that it was a drunken mistake. He'd be bound to read more into it than there is. It's not like I've had a huge amount of casual sex in my life. The most promiscuous thing I've ever done involved imagining I was ruffling Jamie Dornan's hair when I was sleeping with Toby.

My only option would be to look William in the eye and tell him that this was what it was: a one-night stand, with his father.

Which brings me to the other unpalatable part of this sorry affair — the fact that I am the *other woman.* Me. I've spent so long feeling wronged that the shock of self-loathing about what I've done to Simone is like a punch in the gut. I don't care that I hardly know her, or that she may be nothing more than Adam's latest flame. At this moment in time, he's meant to be hers.

And yes, there've been dozens like her, before the next one kicks her off her pedestal. But I don't want to be *the next one*. How the hell did I become *the next one*?

That thought makes me leap up as if the sheets are on fire. Adam stirs. I wince and glare at him as he adjusts his position, his eyes still closed.

I silently bend down and grab my top, edging off the bed as I begin to creep round the room, collecting my clothes. I pull them on, my heart pounding as I pray I'm not going to open the door and find William in the hall looking for somewhere to plug in the iPad charger.

When I'm almost done, I perch on the edge of the bed and slip on my sandal. I pick up the other one, when a hand grabs my wrist and I gasp. I'm expecting Adam to say something flippant, until I see the look on his face.

"Don't regret this."

At first, I'm lost for a response, so I simply shake him off and stand up. Then I spin round and scowl. "Well, Adam: I *do.*"

"Why?"

"Do I really need to spell it out to you? What about Simone?"

He pulls this infuriating expression, dismissive, almost, as if the small matter of his having a girlfriend is irrelevant.

"Jess . . . there's no comparison. What you and I had —"

"*Had* is the operative word."

A bang outside the door silences us both.

"He can *never* know about this," I whisper.

Adam swallows. "No. I mean, yes. You're probably right."

I sit back on the bed anxiously and start biting my nails as I listen for movement outside the door. "Shit, what if he's up?"

"That was the bathroom door — it blows closed if the window's left open sometimes. I'm sure he's still asleep at this hour." I look at the clock. It reads 7:15 a.m., about an hour earlier than he's generally been rising since we got here.

"I'm going then."

"I suppose a good-bye kiss is out of the question?"

I tut. "What do you think?"

I walk to the door, pry it open and peek out. The coast is clear. "Remember — not a word."

"Yes. Okay."

The floorboards creak under every step, even when I find myself on my tiptoes, against the wall, edging along it like a poor impersonation of a cat burglar dodging lasers in the Louvre.

I silently pass the bathroom and, with my heart thumping in my throat, eventually make it to the front door. My hand is inches from the handle . . . when the sodding cockerel crows again, and I nearly jump out of my skin.

"Mum?"

I look up and realize that unless I let out some breath, I might keel over. "William! Did you sleep well? I thought I'd pop over early to get you. Have you just woken?"

"No, that rooster woke me up ages ago. I've been watching *Guardians of the Galaxy*. Then I heard you and thought Dad must've been up."

"Hmm . . . no, he must still be in bed. I've only *just* arrived, so I couldn't say for sure."

"You've only just got here?"

"Yes!"

"How did you get in?"

"I . . . picked the lock." The reason I plump for this explanation — rather than something simple like, *the door was unlocked* — is anyone's guess.

His eyes expand to *mind-blown* proportions. "You can pick locks?"

"Hmm. Actually, it was kind of open. In

334

fact, it *was* open. Ha!"

He rubs his eyes.

"So are you ready to go?" I ask.

"I'm not dressed yet."

"Well, be quick about it. Lots to do. Come on, spit spot." I have never said "spit spot" before in my life.

At that, the door to Adam's bedroom opens and he walks out, yawning and stretching in nothing but a pair of Paul Smith trunks. I blush to my roots. He grins. In fact, you'd think he'd just had a lottery win.

"Morning, sunshine," he says, ruffling his son's head, pulling him towards him into a hug. I bite my hand, panicking that Adam must smell of sex. "Spectacular day, isn't it?"

"Morning, Dad." William beams up at him. "You're in a good mood."

"Just glad to be alive, son," he says, holding my gaze.

I roll my eyes.

"So," says Adam, prying him away, "how about some bacon sandwiches for breakfast?"

"We need to get back," I say quickly.

Adam opens his mouth to protest, then decides against it. "Fair enough. But you can stay over again whenever you like, both of you."

Oh, I want to throttle him. *"You stayed over?"* William turns to me.

"Only on the floor." Adam grins, clearly thinking he is doing me a favor. "Hope it was okay for you, Jess? I'd have put some nicer sheets on the blow-up bed if I'd known in advance."

Adam seriously needs to give up lying. He's unbelievably bad at it.

"You said you'd just got here," William says, with an accusing tone in his voice.

"Just go and get your clothes on."

He looks between the two of us. "What's going on?"

"Nothing!" Adam and I say in unison.

He turns into his room and gets himself dressed while I wait outside, thrumming my fingers against the table and completely unable or unwilling to engage Adam in conversation.

Then William and I head back to our cottage in last night's clothes, as a morning mist gives way to blistering sun and families emerge onto their steps looking bright-eyed, fresh and ready for the day ahead.

It strikes me that I must be the first woman in history who's done the walk of shame with her ten-year-old son by her side.

CHAPTER 54

Becky responds to the news that I've slept with Adam in a predictably low-key manner.

"You've done what?" she splutters into her coffee. We are outside her cottage, as her two eldest children try to think of unique ways to break each other's legs.

I'm about to respond when Seb calls out from inside the cottage. "BECKY? THIS IS AN EMERGENCY."

Her chest rises. "He means Poppy's got a dirty nappy and he's run out of wipes," she drawls, darting inside.

She emerges three minutes later to separate Rufus and James, before rejoining me. "Why is it that men change nappies like they're performing open-heart surgery? You've got to be on hand with all the correct implements to hand over, while the master is at work. Anyway . . . Adam. Christ on a bike."

"Don't tell a soul, will you?"

"Who am I going to tell?"

"Seb, for a start."

"We barely have time to have a conversation about whose turn it is to make the coffee these days. *Bloody hell,* Jess." A smile creeps to her lips. "How was it?"

"Terrible."

Her face drops. "Seriously?"

"I mean it was terrible that I did it. What was I thinking? I wasn't even that drunk."

"I beg to differ. When you were playing *boules* you nearly decapitated Seb with the jack at one point. Seriously — *was* it awful?"

I bite the side of my cheek. "What do you think?"

Enlightenment spreads across her face. "It was awesome, wasn't it? I bet you had half a dozen orgasms. I bet you were screaming from the rafters and swinging from the chandeliers and —"

"Yes, all right, it was good," I hiss. "Fantastic, in fact. Possibly in the top ten experiences of my life."

"Oh God. You swam with a dolphin once, didn't you?"

"I know," I sob.

"Ha! Brilliant!"

A low groan escapes from my lips.

"Why are you worried about this, Jess? Compared with everything else you've got to think about . . . how can mind-blowing sex cause any harm?" I open my mouth to answer, but she continues. "I'd give anything to feel like that again. Not that Seb isn't good in bed; he is. His technique hasn't changed, but now when he goes down on me I end up wishing he'd get on with it because I've got so much ironing to do. I'm sure he feels the same."

"Actually, I doubt that, Becky. Are you sure everything's okay between you two?"

"Oh yeah," she says dismissively, taking a sip of coffee as her eyes blur. "Actually, I don't know."

She places down her cup. "I'd thought a holiday would make all the difference. But everything's just the same. The kids are still fighting, and Poppy, gorgeous as she is, never lets up. Seb and I are exhausted by it and . . . I think we're taking it out on each other." When her eyes meet mine, they are pink around the rims. "I sometimes feel like I'm not very good at being married with three kids. At heart, I still feel the same as I did when I was twenty-two, but everything's changed around me. It's as if I don't know how this has all happened to me."

"Becky, lots of people feel that way. We all

love our kids, but who wouldn't find the idea of being young and free from all those commitments appealing? They were great times. And you actually got a lie-in every weekend."

"I'm not saying it to sound dramatic, Jess. But there have been moments when I've wondered if . . . if Seb and I will end up splitting up."

I'll admit it: I'm shocked. "Is that what you want?"

She frowns. "No, of course I don't *want* it. But I don't want to feel like I do either. I used to be good company. I was fun to be around; people liked me. Now, look at me. I'm a physical wreck, I spend my whole life shouting at the kids, I even gave Natasha hell the other day when she didn't deserve it. I love my family more than anything. But sometimes I don't . . . *enjoy* all this." She closes her eyes and sniffs. "I feel like a total failure and a complete bitch, for even saying this. What kind of mother am I?"

"A tired one," I reply, reaching over to squeeze her hand. "Becky. You're *allowed* to feel worn out and fed up sometimes. It's okay to feel as though it's all getting on top of you on occasions. You're human."

She draws breath and nods.

"But the first thing you need to do is accept some help. Let Natasha and me babysit," I continue.

She groans. "We've been through this — this is your holiday too."

"They're no trouble."

She snorts. "I adore those kids, but that's one thing that could never be said for them."

"Well, I don't care," I insist. "Let us do it. No arguments."

She hesitates again and looks up at me uncertainly. "Okay. If you're really, truly serious. I just hope you're speaking to me afterwards."

I smile, satisfied, and reach out to pick up my cup of coffee. But instead of grasping the handle, my hand slips and tips it over, spilling hot liquid on the table. I leap up and start mopping with some of the tissues in my bag, while Becky runs inside for a tea towel. When she returns, she lays it on the surface, soaking up the mess, as I slump back in my chair and hold up my trembling hand, unable to take my eyes off it as despair rushes through me.

I sometimes feel as though, if I look hard enough, I'll be able to envisage what's going on underneath the skin on my knuckles. To see with my own eyes if something is already happening inside my body, if the HD is quietly taking hold of me.

"You okay?" Becky whispers.

I nod. "Yeah, fine."

But I continue turning over my hand, studying it, searching for the answer to a familiar question: was that the kind of accident everyone makes, or was it something more?

I glance at the pile of tissues, engorged with cold coffee, then realize Becky is looking at me. "It was just an accident, Jess. It was nothing."

I nod stiffly, blinking away the tears I'm determined not to cry, grinding my teeth and swallowing the emotion swelling up inside me. She could be right, of course. It's not as though I never knocked stuff over before. Anyone can be clumsy.

I've experienced dozens of odd feelings over the last couple of years: tingling in my face, my legs feeling woolly, as though they don't belong to me. A few weeks ago, I parked the car in Tesco, did a shop and when I came out had absolutely no recollection of where I'd left it. It took me five minutes to locate it, during which time I walked around the car park clicking my key fob, trying to give the impression to passersby that I was taking a casual stroll in the teeming rain, for the hell of it.

I was convinced after that: this is IT. This

was exactly the kind of thing that happened to my mum in the early days, and that the HD patients on the forums report as their first symptoms.

Then Becky insisted she'd done the same thing repeatedly over the last five years, including once when she actually phoned Seb up to come and rescue her, convinced her car had been stolen. He drove past their Ford Focus on the way in, where she'd left it by the recycling skips.

Dr. Inglis says that, at present, she believes these incidents are nothing more than anxiety. She says I'm displaying no clinical signs of HD; my last MRI was consistent with that and, mutant gene or no mutant gene, I'm healthy. For the moment.

The problem is when your future involves what my mother has had to endure, it's not easy to put it to the back of your mind. So I can't help asking the same question over and over again: when will this disease crawl under my skin and take away everything there is that defines me? The way I think. The way I move. The way I look. All the things that make me who I am.

CHAPTER 55

I get to talk to Mum on Skype later that morning. As the picture flickers on, I make the usual assessment of her physical state and feel a swoop of ill-placed optimism when she is still. Then I realize the screen is frozen. As it springs to life, her shoulder yanks upwards, and my stomach twists with a familiar agony.

I smile. "Hi, Mum! How are things?"

My dad is holding the iPad for her. There's a moment when she tries to answer, but she can't get her words out properly.

"It's been a busy morning," Dad says eventually. "Gemma popped in for an hour or so." Her friendship with Mum goes back to when they were teenagers. They were inseparable. In some ways, they still are. "Plus they had a visit from some local schoolchildren, and we're seeing Dr. Gianopoulos later."

"Oh right, good." Dr. Gianopoulos has

been Mum's consultant since the beginning, and she's fond of him, mostly because he's clever and supportive, but also, she once said, because he reminded her of Rob Lowe.

"So . . . William's playing soccer, Mum. Sorry, I should've waited till he finished and brought him over. He's really enjoying the game these days. I'm not sure he'll ever give Ronaldo a run for his money, but he's at least getting stuck in."

She doesn't answer. Her eyes seem vacant today, unable to meet my gaze through the screen, as her thin shirt hangs off her shoulders. Dad leans in, takes a tissue from his pocket and wipes away a droplet of moisture from the side of her mouth.

"So what did the schoolchildren come for?" I ask her.

She pauses for a long time, searching for the right word. Eventually, she says: "Singing."

"Oh, lovely."

"Tuneless," she corrects me, and I manage to laugh.

"So William's spending every spare minute with Adam lately. He's having a great time. I had my doubts about all this at the beginning, as you know, but I've got to hand it to you — they're getting on like a house on fire."

She grunts. Then I make out: "Nice."

"I thought you'd be pleased. I'm happy too."

"No, you. Pretty today."

"Oh. Really? Thanks."

After another long pause she adds: "Happy."

I have no doubt that the bloom in my cheeks and air of well-being can be attributed to sleeping with Adam, but this is not information I'm inclined to share. "I've been . . . eating lots of fresh fruit," I mumble.

Once upon a time I'd have told her about the feelings I've been having about Adam. I know relationship talk is a step too far for some mums and daughters, but it always felt natural for us.

I described the intense happiness I had when I first met him, and my internal meltdown when we came to an end. It was at that point, in the months after we'd broken up, that I realized how reliant I was on her. She was strong. She could see reason, when I couldn't think straight. And she taught me, rightly, that no matter how broken I was, I'd rise from the ashes and manage without him.

One evening soon after I'd moved back in with my parents, before I knew what she was going through herself, she gave me what I can only describe as a good talking to.

"Jess, you are tough and clever, and you're going to be a brilliant mother. Things haven't worked out with you and Adam, but you've got so much ahead of you to look forward to. You can get through this."

That was her attitude about everything in life: don't moan, don't dwell, just get on with it and make the best of what you've got. She never wavered from it.

In William's last year of preschool, he performed in the nativity play, and I took Mum and Dad along to see it. This was in her pre-wheelchair days, but the chorea — her involuntary movements — was by then so pronounced that it was enough to cause a hush in the room when she stepped in with stiff, jerking strides.

"Come on, Mum. There's a seat over here," I said, nodding hello to a couple of other parents and the head of the PTA.

"Jess, can I sell you a raffle ticket?" Diana, the mother of William's friend Oliver, appeared, waving a booklet. "There are fantastic prizes up for grabs — three bottles of Buck's Fizz, a mixed meat platter and an electric foot spa. Don't be put off by the shop-soiled packaging. It's brand-new, I

347

promise!"

"Yes, of course," I replied, taking out my purse as her eyes darted to the stranger at my side. I handed over the money and realized that she wasn't looking at me any longer. Instead, her gaze kept diverting to my mum, the way her face twisted into crooked grimaces. To those who didn't know about her condition, she was probably a monstrous sight. Diana's reaction was a common one, and I never got used to it. And although I was sure I'd vaguely mentioned to Diana once that my mum wasn't well, it was clear she wasn't prepared for this. She hadn't had time to settle her features into a "relaxed" look.

"Thanks, lovely," she replied awkwardly, as I decoded a spectrum of emotion behind her eyes: bewilderment, alarm, disgust.

Dad took Mum's arm, and we headed for three seats near the back, trying to squeeze past the milling crowd.

"Out of the way," whispered one woman, as she pulled her young daughter towards her, clearly afraid after she'd seen my mum that she was drunk. Or, as one other child later asked William, "Did your nana come from the loony bin?"

The play started, and despite our tucked-away chairs, the inhuman noises that escaped from Mum's mouth remained audible as I prayed for her sake that they'd start another rousing song to drown her out. Afterwards, mince pies and mulled wine were served in the canteen. I'd wanted to go straight home, but William was desperate to stay.

"No, let's head back, sweetheart."

"It's fine," Mum interrupted. "We can hang on for a little while."

We'd only been there a minute before Mum spilled a drink over William's new form teacher, who'd been handing out half-full plastic cups of wine.

Miss Harrison was sweet, kind and clearly stunned by how one minute she'd been chatting to parents about King Herod's enthusiastic performance and the next she had hot crimson liquid steaming off her chiffon blouse.

Mum dealt with it with typically phlegmatic humor. "I'm sorry, love, my co-ordination is terrible."

"Oh, it's quite all right," Miss Harrison insisted, reddening.

"I'll happily pay for your dry-cleaning," Mum added. "I'm their most loyal customer these days."

I snap out of my thoughts and glance back to the Skype screen.

"Well, Mum. I'd better go."

My mother looks at me, her head continuing to jerk as she tries to focus. Then her face twists again into what may or may not be a smile. I leave the room choosing to believe that it is. That in the dark mess that her brain has become, sometimes it's still possible to turn on a light.

CHAPTER 56

I head to the soccer pitch after I've finished my call, to find Natasha watching William and the boys.

"Very good call of yours to suggest we babysit," she tells me. "I'm looking forward to it. I've been thinking about activities for this afternoon."

"We don't need to put too much thought into it. They've got games there. We can just play with them."

"I managed to download a copy of *Toddler Taming* earlier," she continues. "I've only had a flick through, but it's useful. Are you okay? You seem distracted."

I focus on William as he attempts to tackle a German boy half his size and who looks as though a strong sneeze would blow him over. My son never gets anywhere near the ball, instead managing to trip over his own feet, stumble towards the ground and pull himself up at the last minute.

"Something happened last night." The fewer people who know about this the better, but it is against the laws of friendship for me to tell Becky and not Natasha. "Something that shouldn't have."

She blinks at me and says: "You and Adam?"

"Who told you?"

"No one. I predicted this ages ago. I didn't say anything, but I *knew* this would happen."

I can't decide if what I feel is disbelief or indignation. Either way, we're interrupted.

"Hello, ladies." Sunlight glistens on the blond strands of Simone's hair. Her smooth, plump skin is radiant and free of makeup. She smiles directly at me, and my cheeks prickle with warmth. "William's getting much better at soccer, Jess. He's come on leaps and bounds."

"Oh . . . that's nice of you to say, Simone." I smile uneasily, fixing my eyes on my son as he approaches the goal. The space between him and the back of the net is completely clear, but he still manages to welly the ball into the corner.

"Oh, he was so close then!" Simone exclaims. Anxiety bubbles up inside me, and I desperately try to think of an excuse to leave. Natasha registers this and steps in to make conversation.

"Simone, we were just debating where to visit tomorrow. Have you got any recommendations?"

"Have you been to La Roque-Gageac yet? There are some botanic gardens. Adam took me for the most romantic picnic there once."

She talks at animated length both about notable local landmarks and the endless gestures of devotion that Adam has made while there. I, meanwhile, attempt not to die on the spot, of shame, guilt, regret.

The only positive thing to say about all this is that it's clear that she is oblivious to what Adam and I got up to last night. Any suspicions that might have been aroused while we were playing *boules* have dissolved entirely, which is bizarre, because I feel as though I am wearing my betrayal like a big flashing sign on my chest.

"Don't you think, Jess? *Jess?*"

I realize Natasha has asked me a question.

"Um . . . that sounds wonderful," I reply enthusiastically.

"I was complaining about the maggots I saw by the recycling bins on the road this morning."

"Oh. Sorry. In my own world."

"I've been like that myself lately," Simone

continues happily. "My mind's not really on the job now I know I'm leaving."

My head snaps up to find her blue eyes piercing into me, her soft lips pinched into a half smile. "You're leaving?"

"Not until the end of the season. We've been keeping it hush-hush, but it's been on the cards for a while."

"Where are you going?" I ask, trying to process this news. I suppose it would've been a record if she'd lasted as Adam's girlfriend beyond the end of the season.

"Around the world. Some of it, anyway. I'm in the process of planning it all at the moment."

"Gosh. Wow, lucky you. What a brilliant thing to do." Adrenaline is streaming through my chest. "Which countries are you visiting?"

"First stop is Southeast Asia. Adam knows someone in Thailand who he used to work with, so he's putting us up for a week. Then we're heading to Vietnam, which is supposed to be brilliant, although I did see a menu with roasted field mice on it online last week. Not sure I fancy that." She giggles. As she babbles on, I feel as though the breath is being sucked out of me as I take in what she's saying, trying to process it. Eventually, it's Natasha who asks the million-dollar question.

"Sorry . . . did you say *Adam* is going with you?"

"Yes!" She grins, clearly enjoying the moment.

Then her eyes widen theatrically. "Oh God, *sorry,* Jess! He probably wanted to tell you himself, what with William and everything. Though it's not as though he sees much of him under normal circumstances, is it? It won't even make that much of a difference — he'll see him after a year, rather than every six months."

"But what about this place?" Natasha asks. "Who'd run it?"

"The Blanchards."

"The couple he bought this place from?"

"Yep. It's a temporary arrangement, but they know the place inside out, Adam trusts them completely and they can't wait to be at the helm given that the château has been in their family for generations. Adam will be checking in while we're on the road."

The strength seems to leave my legs.

"Sorry, Jess." Her eyes are glinting, her beautiful face beaming. "But you had to know sooner or later. And you're probably not even surprised. If there's one thing we all know about Adam it's that he hates being tied down."

CHAPTER 57

I can barely comprehend the news that Adam is buggering off around the world with Simone. The fact that he was re-acquainting himself with the stretch marks on my inner thighs a few hours ago is only part of the problem.

In the dozens upon dozens of conversations we've had since we arrived — about our son, about him, about where to buy the best ice creams in Domme or how to get the lid off a bottle of beer without an opener — he apparently didn't once think this was worth mentioning.

Fundamentally though, what's killing me is this: the entire reason I'm here is basically for nothing. I am going to have to return to England and break it to my mum that I've failed. That Adam hasn't changed. In fact, nothing's changed.

I'd been deluding myself in thinking he'd turned over a new leaf and suddenly become a devoted father to the son he's neglected for years. But apparently, he's doing nothing of the sort. He's simply spent a few enjoyable weeks with us, made William idolize him and is now going to disappear out of his life for a second time. Only now, William isn't a baby who can't comprehend what's happening.

This time, he's ten years old and adores Adam. Moreover, William needs him, far more than either of them realize.

The enormity of this punches me in the chest until I have to walk away before Simone sees my reaction. Natasha senses my anguish and tells me she'll watch William while I go and do . . . whatever.

I don't even know what *whatever* is, beyond the fact that it involves striding into the château and seeking temporary refuge in the bathroom, away from everyone else. I eventually emerge with a head full of anger and an overwhelming urge to go home to England right this second.

The feeling doesn't subside, as William and I head back towards the cottage, the sweet scent of herbs and grasses under our feet completely at odds with my mood.

"I saved a goal, Mum," he tells me, excitedly.

"Seriously?"

"YES!" he laughs. "I wish you'd been there to see it. It was amazing!"

"That's brilliant, sweetheart," I mumble. "Did you score any?"

His face darkens. "Well, no," he mutters, before launching into a detailed explanation of why scoring goals is overrated.

"I'm so proud of you," I say, sliding my arm around his shoulders. "How did you get so good?"

"Dad," he says simply. "He's a brilliant teacher."

I feel the muscles in my back stiffen. "He's so amazing at tackling, Mum," he continues. "He's really strong, isn't he?"

"I suppose he is."

"And he's a really fast runner."

"Is he?" I murmur, as a Technicolor flashback of Adam kissing my neck crashes into my head.

"Mum?"

"Yes."

"Are you having a funny turn? You look like Mrs. Garrett at school. She's always having funny turns. She said that's what happens when you turn fifty."

"I'm not having a funny turn. And I'm a long way from fifty. Now, can we talk about something else?"

"Okay, what?"

"Anything you like."

He thinks for a minute as we arrive at the little car park behind Les Écuries. "How about the Jurassic period?"

Charlie is strapping a surfboard on the top of his car. I know we're not exactly an item, but the fact that I have slept with someone else — never mind that that someone else is Adam — is so embarrassing I can barely bring myself to look at him, let alone acknowledge him.

"Hi, Charlie," I say awkwardly.

He looks up, finishes tightening a buckle and heads over. "How are you?"

"I'm good, thanks," I reply.

"Did you enjoy the barbecue? Chloe said she saw you coming in this morning." He scans my face, as if looking for an explanation.

"Um . . . yes, we had a . . . *yes.*"

His face tautens into an uncomfortable smile. "A 'yes'?"

I nod. "We . . . stayed over at Adam's."

A heartbeat passes as Charlie attempts to decode this sentence. "William fell asleep, so I slept in the spare room," I lie.

I suddenly wish I could rewind the clock to a few days ago, when I was having a holiday romance — something that might not have led anywhere beyond the end of this summer but *could* have resulted in a few trips to the cinema or some nice dinners.

"Would you like to go to dinner again?" I blurt out. I instantly realize that this is a feeble attempt at punishing Adam, at proving to myself, and him, that last night meant nothing to me. It's an adolescent approach, I know, but right now, it's all I've got.

Charlie is visibly taken aback. "Really?"

"Yes."

"I was getting the impression that there was something going on between you and . . ." But his voice trails off as he glances at William. "Sorry." He smiles. "I'd love to."

CHAPTER 58

As I march across the château's grounds in search of Adam, my anger builds with each moment I fail to find him. Eventually, I head to reception and find Ben at the desk. He smiles with those sweet brown eyes, and the smattering of new freckles across his tanned nose seems to exaggerate his youth.

"No William today, Jess?"

"Um . . . not today. Have you seen Adam? He's not answering his mobile, and I've been to the cottage but can't find him."

"Last time I saw him he was on the way to the shed to look for a saw. Can I help at all?"

I'm touched by the concern on his face. "I don't think so. But thank you."

I find Adam at the front of the shed, bent over a bench as he pumps a saw back and forth, the bare skin on his arms glistening with moisture. He looks up as I approach, his face breaking into a smile. Then he registers my expression.

He places the saw down carefully and walks towards me, wiping his hands on a cloth. He swigs a mouthful of bottled water before he speaks. "I came to look for you earlier."

Longing shines in his eyes, but I am numb to it, crushed by Simone's revelations. He reaches out his hand, and I push it away. "I wonder if you could explain something."

"Sure, what's up? Do you want to go and get something to drink?"

"No." Words clamor for room inside my head until I finally manage to get something out. "I saw Simone earlier."

He runs his hand anxiously through his hair. "That must've been awkward for you. I'm sorry, Jess. I'm going to speak to her today."

"Adam, she told me you're going around the world with her," I snap. "That you'd made some arrangement for the Blanchards to look after this place for a year and then you're just . . . going. Is that true? Are you planning some big trip with her?"

I can tell instantly from the look on his face that he is. "Right. This is compli-cated . . ."

"No, Adam. It's simple. Is it true? Have you booked the flights, planned to take the whole year, like she said? Or is she a liar?"

He winces, before the confession begins to crawl out of him. "She's not a liar. But that was before —"

"Before what? It wasn't before you knew you had a son who wouldn't see you for over a year because you were off behaving like you're still eighteen. Someone with no commitments. No cares in the world."

What a nag I sound. What a party pooper. For a moment I wonder if I'm jealous that Adam gets to do something I don't have the luxury of dreaming about.

"I was going to tell you when you first got here."

"So why didn't you?"

"Because I changed my mind."

"Oh well, that's nice. So you were going to be honest and then you thought you'd just lie to us instead."

"That's not what I mean. I changed my mind about going."

I'm about to continue, when I register his words. "What?"

"I changed my mind about being away for so long. And about . . . everything."

"Er, seriously, Adam?" I say sarcastically. "I'm supposed to believe you're not going but you haven't broken this news to Simone?"

He wrinkles his forehead. "I've been putting it off. I wanted to wait until after her birthday and see how things went with you and William here."

"So you were hedging your bets?"

Now he stands square in front of me and crosses his arms. "Of course not. Jess, I realize I haven't seen enough of William in the past, that I haven't been the father I should've been."

"Quite right."

"But you've had a part to play in that too."

"Me?" Adrenaline is firing through my body now, and I can tell he wants to take the words back. But it's too late. "How the hell can you say that, Adam?"

He closes his eyes briefly and inhales. "Jess, I'd always been certain I'd be a crap parent. But what I *should've* done — I now realize — is just got on with it anyway. Like parents do, whether they feel qualified or not."

I know what's coming next.

"I am not *blaming* you, Jess. But you did make it absolutely clear that you wanted me out of your life — and out of William's life. You told me he'd be better off without me. I've never mentioned that since, because . . . well, because I was already convinced you were right."

I swallow, my breaths getting shallower.

"I should've fought harder," he continues. "Tried to prove to you and to myself that I could be a better parent than the ones *I'd* had. Instead, I went along with the idea."

I'm lost for words as he continues talking. "There was always a bit of me that hoped things could be different though. I had no idea how, but I thought a lot about him spending holidays with me over here, just like this one."

Adam had asked me once if I'd visit with William when he was a toddler. I can't remember exactly what I'd told him, but I'm fairly certain it was a polite version of "sod off." I feel smothered by this conversation.

He wipes sweat from his brow with one hand and sits down on a log. "When you emailed me out of the blue saying you were coming over here, I was over the moon. I mean that. Then as the whole thing went on, the more time I spent with him, something started gnawing at me. I knew I couldn't go off round the world with Simone. I didn't *want* to go off round the world with her. But Simone is a good person. A nice person. And I've been a shit to her. I've slept with you, for a start."

My eyes flicker to the ground.

"So I was trying to pick my moment to tell her that I can't go. But you're right. It's now. In fact, it was weeks ago."

I close my eyes and take everything in, how the sizzling fury I felt only minutes ago has dissolved, replaced by something completely different. Salty tears gather in the rims of my eyes, and I try to blink them away before Adam can see.

"I need to get this over with," he says.

"Oh God, well now I feel like I'm colluding with you," I sniff.

He stands up and reaches out to touch my hand. Then he pulls me in towards him and puts his arms around me, as I wrestle with the ache in my chest. I gently push him away.

"I have to go," I whisper, but he reaches out for my hand again.

"I want to tell you something first."

"What?"

"Jess . . . last night. It really meant something for me."

I look at the floor. "Don't, Adam."

"Why not? It might've been some drunken mistake for you, and if that's the case, then . . . Christ, I can't argue with you. But I need you to know that it wasn't for me. You mean more to me than —"

"Stop," I whisper and pull away my hand.

"Please, just . . . don't." And then I turn away and run towards the dark woodland, grass scratching my ankles as I trip over my own feet, and I wish I could run all the way home to Manchester.

CHAPTER 59

The question of whether I could or should engineer an early departure from France dominates my thoughts for the rest of the day. Even with the distraction of a cottage full of kids to babysit.

"So, Poppy," Natasha begins, perching on the sofa, "how about a story?"

Poppy looks up. "I hungry."

"Oh. Okay, would you like a banana?" She grabs one from the bowl.

"I like sum sweets."

"Oh dear, we haven't got any. How about this instead? Mmm . . . yummy." Natasha kneels down and peels the banana, before handing it over. Poppy looks at it as if it's been scraped off the bottom of her shoe.

"NOOOOOO!" She thrusts it back at Natasha. "Put it back!"

"Put what back?"

"BACK BACK BACK!" Poppy flings herself on the floor.

"What does she want?" Natasha asks, bewildered, as James looks up from the picture he's coloring in.

"She wants you to put the banana back in its skin."

It's ten minutes before Poppy has calmed down, and Natasha pours a glass of wine for each of us.

"Can I ask you something?" I begin, as she hands it to me and sits down.

"That sounds serious." She smiles, but I can't bring myself to return it.

"How would you feel if William and I went home early?"

She inhales sharply, then releases it as if she's not *completely* surprised.

"I feel awful because it was me who persuaded you to come out here," I continue, "but you'd still have Becky and Seb, and you could get it on with Joshua without us cramping your style. The last thing I want to do is leave you in the lurch, but . . ."

She starts shaking her head. "You wouldn't be leaving me in the lurch, Jess — I'm a big girl. Are you worried about what's going on with Adam? Or is it that you want to be back with your mum?"

"Both. I know my mum has Dad with her, but still. Plus, yes: I can't believe what I did with Adam, drunk or not. Everything feels

369

so complicated here."

She glances at the kids to check that they can't hear, before leaning into me. "I understand why you're worried, Jess. Adam goes through women like I go through knickers, and you're worried that the same thing would happen to you, which would be horrible for William. But . . ."

"But what?" I whisper.

"You're not just *some woman.*"

"Technically, I am."

"I mean, you'll always be more to him than that." I wonder where this is heading. "What if it worked between the two of you?" she continues. "What if you managed to sort out the differences that drove you apart in the first place —"

"It wasn't differences that drove us apart, Natasha. It was the contents of Adam's trousers. Besides, it really wouldn't work. It's ridiculous even thinking about it."

She sits back defiantly. "Why?"

"Where do I start? The fact that we didn't manage to stick it out the first time round. The fact that Adam and me mucking about together would mess with William's head."

"Yes, but —"

"And more than all that put together — times a million," I continue fiercely, "is . . .

that I am facing a future with a fatal disease."

She slumps back in her seat.

And instead of being able to protest, to try to convince me to jump in with both feet because I've got nothing to lose, she realizes she can't do that with me. Other friends, yes. Not me. I can almost see her head peppering with thoughts of what the next decade and beyond is going to hold for me.

"It's not something I could even contemplate, Natasha," I continue gently. The urge to cry seems to rush up inside her, hard and fast. "That's why I think it'd just be best for everyone if I go home."

She turns to the wall and silently takes a mouthful of wine, swallowing it hard. "It's just not fucking fair, Jess."

I reach over and squeeze her fingers, still cold from the touch of the glass. "No, it's not. But that's the hand I've been dealt."

I glance over at the kids, and she sniffs away tears, pulling herself together before they become aware of any of this.

"Okay, I get it," she continues. "But don't run away, Jess. You'll just end up at home, alone, without me and Becky here to support you. And we want to do that, you know. That's why we came." I look down at the light sparkling against the rim of my glass. "Besides, William would be devastated."

I smile at her briefly. "Cheap shot."

"But it's true," she argues.

"You're right, but he'd get over it."

We both turn to look at William, who is currently playing with Poppy, teaching her how to spell *cat*.

"B-C-T-R-P-E-D-G," she declares.

"Oh, well done!" he says.

Natasha and I both chuckle, before falling silent. Then she says something that makes my heart tighten.

"You're still in love with Adam, aren't you?"

I open my mouth, but then don't say a word.

Because both of us already know the answer.

CHAPTER 60

I have one question for Becky the following day.

"Why did you come home so early?"

"Well," she squirms, "I was just worried about what was going on back at the ranch."

"Nothing was going on! It was a doddle. The kids were great."

"There were really no tantrums?"

"Not unless you count Natasha when she couldn't find the corkscrew. Look, the idea was that you and Seb really relaxed and had a nice time."

"We did, kind of," she protests, though I'm far from convinced. "Though I wish I hadn't had that massive dessert. I'm going on a diet tomorrow."

"You don't need to. You're exactly right as you are," Seb replies, appearing at the door.

"Thanks, but my old jeans would beg to differ."

I laugh as we hear a piercing shriek from

outside, followed by a cry of "MUMM-MMM!"

Becky wearily looks at Seb, who sighs and says, "I'll go."

"I meant to tell you, I bumped into Adam earlier," Becky says. "He looked . . . a bit odd."

"What do you mean?"

"Kind of intense. Speak of the devil." Adam is walking towards us. I feel my shoulders tense.

"Hi, Becky. Good night out?"

"Lovely, thanks," she replies as Poppy toddles in. He smiles, and I find my eyes drawn to his mouth. "Right, I've got to go to the supermarket to feed this lot or there'll be hell to pay. Come on, Poppy, let's get your raisins and go for the shopping. Catch you both later." She glares at me unsubtly, before grabbing her keys.

"Fancy a walk?" Adam suggests.

"William will be heading back to the cottage after his soccer match, and I want to be there when he arrives."

"How about we go over there, then?"

I nod tightly. "Fine."

We head to the woodland and make our way along the path, where speckled sunlight casts patterns on the carpet of dark ferns. As I gaze at the ground, he tells me he's

broken it to Simone that he can't go
ing.

"I said I didn't want to leave William
that long. And . . . that I had feelings
someone else."

I force myself to look straight ahead. "Did
she ask who?"

I feel his eyes dart to me. "I don't think I
needed to spell that out."

I swallow. "So, how did she take it?"

"She quit her job and told me she was
leaving to catch a flight home to her parents
this afternoon. Then she told me to expect
her father's lawyer to be in touch about su-
ing me for intolerable working conditions."

I draw breath. "That went well then."

As we approach the cottage and sit on the
chairs outside, I have a knot in my gut. I lift
my chin, closing my eyes silently to feel the
red heat of the sun on my eyelids as I
fantasize for a tiny moment that I could
make this work somehow. That I could
mend the broken fragments of our family
and put the jigsaw pieces of us together
again.

Maybe that's why I feel the need to say
something that's probably woefully late in
coming.

"I'm sorry."

He looks bewildered. "What for? You were

right about Simone and the

. . . I've been thinking about
...i. About me letting you think
...b good at being William's dad.
...y I said he'd be better off without
...hat was really wrong."

I register the emotion in Adam's face as I continue. "It also . . . wasn't true, as you've proved since we got here." My eyes search his face. "He loves you, Adam, he really does. And since we've been here, I think you've earned his love. You deserve it."

He squeezes his eyes together, embarrassed at his reaction. "Jess," he says urgently. "We can make a go of things, you know. We absolutely can. My feelings for you . . . they've changed. No, actually, they've simply become crystal clear."

Adam keeps talking, arguing as if he's taking part in a sixth form debate that it makes sense for us to be together, to try again.

But I really can't focus on his words. All I can focus on is what I haven't yet told him. On what I've hidden from him for a decade.

"Why are you crying?" As he turns to me, the look in his eyes makes my heart twist.

"It wouldn't work, Adam. We can't be together."

I realize I've got to tell him everything. I

owe it to him. I should've done it years ago.

"The thing is . . ."

But my voice seizes up, unwilling to be a party to this revelation. How *do* you tell a man who's never fully vacated your heart something like this? When you know it'll change everything he's ever thought about you? When you know he'll never be able to look at you again and see a woman he desires — only a woman he pities? I open my mouth to try, but he speaks first.

"It's that guy next door, isn't it?"

I splutter with shocked laughter. *"What?"*

"That Charlie guy. He's clearly mad about you."

I shake my head in disbelief.

"It's not him." He crosses his arms defensively. "Adam. I never even fancied him. He's just *some guy* I've met on holiday."

His eyes burn. "I understand."

"No, you don't!"

I want to fill my lungs and shout across the meadow: *It's not that Charlie guy. How could it be him when there's still you? Lighting me up every time I'm anywhere near you. Filling me up with an unbearable longing every time I inhale the smell of your skin.*

Only that wouldn't help matters. So instead, I say flippantly: "Adam, the guy wears cardigans. With a collar. I assure you,

377

it's not him."

I look up and see Charlie glaring straight at me, having heard every word. His eyes flicker away momentarily, before he turns and strides to his cottage, shutting the door behind him.

CHAPTER 61

An hour later, I'm curled up on the sofa, too ashamed to emerge into daylight in case Charlie's out there. Wondering if I should go over to explain, or apologize. William, meanwhile, is moping about, saying very little and lost in his thoughts.

"Why did you come back early from soccer?" I ask.

He shrugs, refusing to answer.

"Did you fall over again?"

He looks up and glares at me, appalled by the idea that he'd perform to anything less than Real Madrid standard these days. "No, I scored."

"Oh!" I possibly sound a bit too shocked about this. "Gosh, that's brilliant, William. So why so sad?" He shakes his head and frowns. "Come on, spit it out."

"The other kids called James gay. I told them to leave him alone, so they said I was gay too. But I'm not."

"Oh, William," I sigh, feeling annoyed and proud all at the same time. "Well done for sticking up for him. Though . . . even if you were, that would be okay, you know. Just for the record."

One side of his lip rises as if I've failed to grasp this situation entirely. "I just didn't want them to be mean to James."

"Yes, I know. Where was Seb when all this happened?"

"He was reading a newspaper by the pitch, too far away to hear what was going on."

"Sweetheart, you did the right thing." I walk over and put my arm round his bony shoulders, attempting to squeeze him into me, but he shakes me off.

"Now I've got nobody to play soccer with. Just when I got good too." He stands up and heads into his room.

I let him go, until the urge to follow him becomes irresistible. I walk to his door and push it open, where I find him lying face-down on the top bunk.

"William," I say softly. If he were on his bed at home, I'd sit on the end of it and rub his back supportively, until he was so annoyed by the gesture that he'd be forced to talk to me.

I put my foot on the bottom step of the

ladder and go to climb up. It's only as I'm on the third rung that I realize how unstable this whole thing is; it possibly wasn't designed for two people, one of whom is a grown woman who has eaten so much cheese in the last three weeks that she's considering burning her jeans. Still, I get to the top and try to hoist myself onto the mattress.

"What are you doing?" William asks, turning over and sitting up as he scrunches up his nose.

"Just coming to join you," I reply, having finally scaled the bunk bed and crossed my legs, as though I've joined him for a sleepover. "Is something *else* the matter?"

He responds with one of those preteen looks, the ones that are supposed to indicate that he's confused, but only because I've asked a silly question. "No."

"Well, listen . . . I think I might have a solution to the fact that soccer isn't really working out," I tell him.

"What?"

"I've been having a think." He looks up, as if this sounds horribly dangerous. "I reckon it'd be a good idea if we go home early. Perhaps tomorrow. I've had a quick look at the ferry schedule, and it'd only cost a little bit more to change the one we're booked on. That way you'd be able to see your friends at home and play *Garden Warfare* with Jake and —"

"*What?*"

"I'm just saying . . . I thought we could perhaps leave. Tomorrow."

"NO!" he protests, so violently that I sit up in shock.

"Look . . . just think about it."

He crosses his arms hard against his chest. "I've thought about it, and I don't want to go." His face has blanched white. He's gone from being sulky to enraged in the space of ten seconds. He's nearly shaking with it.

"I know you've been having a lovely time with your dad, but he's very busy with the business, and wouldn't it be nice to be back with your friends?" I persevere.

He glares at me, grinding his teeth. "Is this because you can't get on with Dad?"

I don't know whether to cry or laugh with relief that he hasn't worked out what happened the other night. "Well, no — it's not that."

"It is, isn't it?" he says furiously. "You *hate* him. You can't even stick it out here *for my sake.* Just when we've become really good mates and he's teaching me how to get better at soccer and —"

"It's not that, William," I interrupt. "Your

dad's got lots on at work, but he's already said he's keen to organize a trip home to see you." How do I tell him it's not William I want to keep away from Adam, but me? I don't realize how scared I am by the prospect of staying until he forces the matter.

"Well, I'm not going anywhere," he declares. "You can do what you like."

I blink incredulously at this new, unwelcome tone in his voice. "I beg your *pardon*?"

"I said I'm not going."

I don't know what it is about the way he says it, growls it, almost, but I am suddenly overwhelmed by how out of control this all feels. How wrong. I want to scream.

"I think you'll find I'm *your mum,*" I say, forcefully enough to hide how shaken I am. "So . . . so if I say you're going, you're going. And do NOT speak to me like that again. You're ten, not twenty-five. And even if you were twenty-five, you shouldn't be speaking to me like that. Or indeed anyone."

"Like WHAT?" he shrieks. "I can't believe *I'm* being told off, and I haven't even done anything. You're the one who's going back on all the plans and ruining everything. Deliberately."

There is something about the whinging, martyred tone in his voice that flips a switch in me. I suddenly don't give a toss about everything I've read in the *Supernanny* books about how when you shout at a child they've won. I don't care about trying to be reasonable. I can't take any more of what life is throwing at me, and this has tipped me over the edge.

"Right, that's it, William!" I yell. "You have literally NO idea what I have to deal with. You haven't a bloody clue. Because if you did, you'd give me a break and just roll with me on this one. And you certainly wouldn't go around speaking to me like I'm a piece of crap on the sole of your shoe, not the woman who's brought you up single-handedly."

"You only brought me up because you wouldn't let Dad come anywhere near me!"

I can feel the enamel on my teeth biting into the flesh inside my mouth. "That is not true, William. It isn't."

"Whatever. I'm *not* going home."

"Two things: First — speak to me like that again, and I am not letting you near that iPad until you're in your seventies. *And second,* we ARE going home tomorrow. So if you don't like it, tough. Life sucks sometimes, William. Get used to it."

At that, he pushes back the sheet and flips his legs over the bunk bed, vaulting down to the floor. Then he steps out of the door

384

and slams it behind him, leaving a sickly dread in my chest.

I've never had an argument with him like that before.

Part of me doesn't know what came over me. Part of me is still furious with him for being so insolent. Either way, guilt envelops me like a blanket, and I want to rewind and stop the last seven minutes from happening.

I wearily begin to renegotiate the ladder, but it's been a long time since I've been on one of these, and there is no vaulting involved on my part. Instead, I make the mistake of trying to go front first, realizing as I clatter down it with my pelvis in the air and my knees like a pre-basted turkey that this isn't going to work. So I edge back up again, turn around and go the other way. I pause to gather my thoughts, before following William into the living room.

Only he's not there.

"Where did William go?" I ask.

Natasha looks up from the sink. "Just outside, I assume. Are you all right? That sounded bad."

"It was."

I walk to the door and open it, looking out into the courtyard. It's empty but for a couple of nightingales hopping along the edge of the wall, bees swarming around the bougainvillea. "Didn't he say where he was going?" I ask.

"No. Sorry. Is everything okay?"

I rub my forehead with the ball of my hand. "Actually, I don't know."

CHAPTER 62

Natasha and I split up to look for William. We agree that I'll try the château, while she heads to Adam's place — and whatever happens we'll meet back at the cottage in twenty minutes, because trying to communicate by phone is so unreliable.

My feet pound along the woodland path as I call William's name, but I'm rewarded only with silence and the erratic beat of my racing pulse. As I emerge from the trees and sprint to the château, Adam appears at the double doors and can instantly see that something's wrong. "What's going on?"

"It's William. We had a row, and he stormed off somewhere. Christ knows where he's gone."

He pauses to process this information. "Look, don't worry, he's a sensible kid. I'll come and look for him too. I'll jump in the golf cart."

Adam starts on the opposite side of the

grounds, while I take the other path, calling William's name over and over again, stopping everyone I meet en route to ask if they've seen him.

It's only when I get back to the cottage and see Natasha standing outside that I hear myself whimper. I break into a faster run, desperate for news. "Don't panic, Jess," is all she can offer. "I'm certain he won't be far."

Next we try the woodshed, Becky and Seb's place and the other buildings near them. We eventually find ourselves back at Les Écuries, as I pace up and down, feeling the sweat cool on my back. A minute later, Adam has still not appeared. So we sit tight, feigning calm as I try to convince myself that he'll drive round the corner with my son sitting next to him in the golf cart and all will be okay. Natasha looks up, and I follow her gaze to see Adam. Alone. I race towards him as he steps out.

"No luck." It's not even a question.

He shakes his head, and the expression on his face frightens me. He looks worried too. "I've looked everywhere I can in this thing. But he *can't* have gone far."

"I hope to God he hasn't done something stupid," I say.

"He *won't* have," Natasha insists.

"You didn't see how angry he was."

"Look, Natasha's right," Adam says convincingly. "He'll have stormed off somewhere and gone to clear his head. I'm going to head to the château to get Ben to help look for him." He turns to me, his eyes searching mine. "Please, don't worry." Then he reaches out, squeezes my fingers and for a small moment, things feel a tiny percentage better.

"Right, let's go. Why don't you two try the woods over to the east that way — I'll go in the opposite direction. I'll meet you back here in thirty minutes."

"What if we haven't found him by then?"

Adam's jaw clenches. "We'll cross that bridge when we come to it."

Natasha is fitter than I am. I know this because she also does Grit classes but actually enjoys them. As far as I'm concerned, each class is like giving birth — so ugly and painful that it's only when it's over that you gradually forget how bad it was and consider repeating the experience.

Despite this, she can barely keep up with me as we sprint through the woods, shouting William's name.

Eventually, she shrieks, "Jess!" and I spin round to find her bent double, her elbows on her thighs as she catches her breath. "Jess . . . we need . . . to get back."

I look at my watch and realize it's time to check in with Adam and his search party. As we head back, I register that we're slower this time, *I'm* slower, restrained by a wave of negativity. I'm not sure I can bear walking through the opening in that road and seeing Adam outside our front door with no William.

We return before anyone else.

"This could be a good sign." I'm unsure of Natasha's logic but nod to stop my jaw from trembling.

Then Adam walks round the corner with another figure, and my stomach swoops. "He's got him."

"Oh, thank Christ."

My head rushes with muddled prayers, thanks to God and promises that I'll be a better person, before I look up and my hopes implode. The person Adam is with is wearing trousers, where William was wearing shorts. He's too tall, too old, too . . .

He's with Ben. It's not William at all.

CHAPTER 63

An hour and a half after William disappeared, I want to phone the police. As much as I'd like to believe that Adam's right — he'll be hiding somewhere in a sulk — this is completely unprecedented.

Still, the fact that Adam is absolutely convinced William will be fine does help.

I crave his certainty, asking him to repeat over and over again that this will turn out okay, that he'll be back here as soon as his iPad withdrawal kicks in. But eventually even he agrees that we should decamp to the château to use a landline and make the call no parent wants to make.

He has his hand on the door of his office, when Julien, one of the kitchen staff, walks past and says hi. *"Est-ce que tout va bien?"*

Adam opens the door and goes to sit down at his desk. *"Nous ne pouvons pas trouver William,"* he says distractedly, as he begins hammering numbers into the phone.

"William?" says Julien, turning to me. "I saw him by the lake just now. I went fishing before I started at work."

"What? *My* William?"

"Yes, he was talking to a guy."

Adam slams down the handset. "Let's go look."

We take the golf cart as far as we can before the terrain becomes too much for it. Then we abandon it and all three of us run — me, Natasha and Adam. I can't remember how long it took us to walk to the lake with Charlie and Chloe that day, but I do know it was a good thirty minutes or more. This time, it seems to take forever.

By the time we reach the bottom of the hill, I am nearly sick with fatigue. I gallop up the grassy slope, but not as fast as Adam, his legs and arms pumping like pistons until he's there. I scramble next to him a couple of seconds later.

And alone next to the lake is a small figure, skimming stones.

I don't call out his name; I'm panting too hard, and I feel mute anyway. Instead, Adam starts to stride down the hill. William looks back when we're halfway down, sees us and turns to face the water again.

When I finally reach him, I touch his shoulder, spinning him round and pressing

392

him into me, squeezing his ribs against my chest.

My head pounds with the blistering reminder that I would do *anything* for this boy.

"What the hell are you playing at, William?" I can barely get the words out. "Your dad and I have been worried sick. I thought you'd run away. Or . . . or drowned or any number of terrible possibilities. Who was the man you were talking to?"

He looks at me from under his eyelashes. "Just Charlie. He'd come for a walk with Chloe."

My chest contracts, and I force my shoulders to relax. My lip trembles as a tear slips fast down his cheek, then he looks away defiantly. *"Sorry,"* he fires at me, swiping it away.

"*Promise me* you won't ever do something like this again, okay?" I implore. "Never." He ignores me, so I turn his chin to face me. "William, promise me."

"Okay!"

My lungs feel as though they might explode. "William, I'm serious."

"I know!" he shrieks.

"Well . . . well, you don't *sound* like you know. You sound . . . completely unrepentant."

He goes to march away, but Adam touches his hand and stops him. Then I watch him put his big arms around our son, leaving me with the helpless feeling of being an outsider. William begins to cry into Adam's chest while he strokes the soft tendrils of his hair. "It's okay," he whispers, kissing him on the head. "Nothing to worry about. We're all going to be fine."

Then William looks up at me, his eyes blazing. "No, we're not, are we, Mum? We're *not* going to be fine."

I swallow the sandpaper in my mouth. "If this is about going home . . ."

"It's not about going home." He scowls. "It's about *you* not being honest. You always said to be truthful. And talk about your problems. But you haven't told anyone. And *I* know . . . I know."

CHAPTER 64

Silently, I try to decipher the meaning behind William's words. Could I have successfully hidden this secret from so many people except the one I *really* wanted to conceal it from?

"Listen, we all need to calm down here," Adam intervenes, turning to William. "Why don't you and Natasha head back for a game of Ping-Pong or something while your mum and I have a chat? And no running off, okay?"

He shakes his head. Natasha smiles tentatively. "I bet you'd be brilliant at Ping-Pong, William. I warn you though, I kick ass myself."

"If Ben's still around, see if he'll give you some tips, William. He's the champion around here. Nobody's beaten him since the start of the season."

He hesitates before trudging up the hill with her, clearly deciding that being around

Natasha beats hanging out with me right now. Adam sits down and looks towards the lake. I sink onto the ground next to him as a white stork soars to the water, before swooping away. The air smells hot and sweet, the sky richly blue under a high sun and the grass soft as it tickles the back of my legs.

"That was terrifying," Adam says.

Then, after a moment's hesitation, he puts one arm round my shoulder, pulling me into his side. I let him do it because I can't bring myself to stop him. It feels too good to be held, too safe and comforting. Nobody has had the ability to comfort me lately, and it's an unfamiliar and wondrous feeling.

I become aware that he's looking at me, and I return his gaze, refusing to object when he leans in to kiss me, the touch of his lips so soft that it takes all my might to pull away.

"Don't tell me to stop again," he says.

"Well, you need to."

And the kisses do stop, but his eyes continue to burn into me. "I've fallen for you, Jess. Again. I don't ever want to stop kissing you."

I shiver and focus on the mirrored surface of the lake. "You make it sound simple."

"Isn't it?"

"No."

Then he leans back on his hands and narrows his eyes. "So what's this big secret William was going on about?"

Again, I try to tell him. I know it's the right thing to do, despite the fact that I don't think either of us is ready for it. I open my mouth to speak as a warm breeze whispers through my hair and my skin tingles with the feel of the sunshine.

And I can come up with a million excuses, but really it's about this: in this beautiful place and time, I don't want to talk about Huntington's disease with Adam. I want to kiss him and pretend everything's okay.

So I lean in and press my lips against his, luxuriating in the heat from his body as my breasts brush against his warm chest. He sinks into my mouth, greedily returning the kiss, before pulling away. "Okay," he whispers, brushing hair from my face. "Then if you're not going to tell me, I return to my original point."

"What original point?"

"That I've fallen for you."

A trail of breath escapes from my lips. "That's very lovely, Adam," I say flippantly, pulling back. "But you're forgetting a few things. Such as the fact that you've 'fallen for' every living, breathing woman who's crossed your path in the last ten years."

"Not true."

"And that, even if, for argument's sake, I had feelings for you too — and I'm not saying that this is the case, you understand —"

"Of course not."

"Then I'd be mad to just say, 'Whoopee! Adam and I can get back together.' The same Adam who was happy to skip off and enjoy himself when I was struggling with incontinence and cracked nipples." He winces. "The same Adam who was busy shagging Georgina while I was in agony giving birth."

"I did not skip off to enjoy myself. And I didn't shag Georgina. I've told you that."

"You moved in with her!" I protest.

"I *mean* I didn't sleep with her that night."

I don't even argue with him. We've gone over this conversation too many times to go there again. He pulls away and sighs. "This is still a big thing for you, isn't it? The fact that I wasn't there for the birth."

"Of course, Adam. It always will be."

"It was a big thing for me too," he insists. "A massive thing. You know I wanted to be there, but —"

"But you were busy with Georgina."

"I was not with Georgina. Well, I mean, I was. I saw her that night, but I didn't sleep with her or anyone else. I wish you could've just *trusted* me, Jess. Believed me when I said I was in the Northern Tap all night and tried to get back in time, but —"

"Hang on," I interrupt. *"The Northern Tap?"*

"What's the matter?"

"You said it was the Bush Bar. You said you were there all night."

He holds his breath, his shoulders stiff with realization. "Did I?"

"Yes, Adam. You did."

"Well . . . why does it even *matter* where I was? The point is I said I wasn't sleeping with another woman, and that's the truth. Why can't you believe me?"

"Because it's completely obvious that you're lying."

"Not about that."

"Hmm."

He looks away and runs his fingers through his hair, thinking hard. "I can't win this one."

He's right.

"Look, it doesn't even matter," I continue. "It was a long time ago, water under the bridge. But the point is this: It would be a really bad idea for you and me to get tangled up with each other again, Adam.

For a multitude of reasons, not least William."

"William would love it."

For a moment, I almost tell him the rest. The big reason. The killer reason. The reason that would take any argument he tried to throw at me and stamp on it until it was a bloody pulp. But again, the words stick in my mouth. "At the moment his life is simple. He has a mum and a dad, who aren't together but who both love him. Why would we selfishly put him back on a roller coaster that could make him the happiest boy alive for a time, and then destroy him if we split up again?"

His eyes don't falter. "I'd make sure we wouldn't."

"But Adam," I argue, "I don't think that's a guarantee either of us could make."

CHAPTER 65

I spend the rest of the evening trying to work out what's going on behind William's young eyes, or if his cryptic words just meant something innocuous.

Finally, I ask him directly as I'm standing on the bottom rung of his bunk, tucking him into bed and steeling myself to have the talk I've been dreading since the day my own mother told me about Huntington's disease. "You said something earlier about me not being honest. What did you mean?"

He doesn't look up, instead fixing his gaze on his dog-eared copy of *The Maze Runner.* "Nothing, Mum. I said it because I was angry. I'm really sorry about running away."

"I know, you've said. I'm sorry as well. I hate arguing with you. I don't ever want that to happen again."

"Me neither."

Given that he'll be a teenager in three years, I silently question the odds of this

401

and smile to myself.

"So are we still going home tomorrow?" he asks, pulling the sheet up to his chin.

I hesitate. "No."

His eyes shine. "*Not* because you pulled a stunt like you did. I just decided we should stick it out until we were meant to leave."

He grins.

"The thing is . . . you and I do need to talk at some point though," I say.

"What about?" When he looks up at me, the expression on his face makes me stop in my tracks. I ask myself if now, *really,* is the right time — when he's got nearly two weeks left of his holiday to enjoy? Am I really going to raise the prospect of my son ending up like his grandma, when he was meant to spend the next seven days relaxing and swimming in the sunshine? I feel as though I've had enough drama on this holiday already.

"I wondered if you had any more questions from your facts-of-life book?" I ask, improvising.

He develops a studious look on his face. "Not at the moment."

Thank God for that. "So did you win at Ping-Pong when you played with Natasha?"

"Yeah, we got Ben to join in like Dad suggested. He's amazing at it."

"Really?"

"Yes, but he kept letting Aunty Natasha win, for some reason. I think they like each other. She should be his girlfriend."

"Oh, you think so?"

"Yep." He nods, clearly quite proud of his powers of perception. "Or is that other guy — the old one — her boyfriend these days?"

"Joshua is not that old."

"Isn't he? Ben's more fun anyway."

"All right, Cupid. Time to get some sleep." He snuggles into bed. "I love you," I say.

"I love you more."

Then I close the door and promise myself: as soon as we get back, I'll tell him.

My room is filled with a hazy light the following morning, as I lie listening to the soft whir of the ceiling fan. The end of the holiday is both hurtling towards me and feels forever away.

Being around Adam is agonizingly bittersweet, my longing for him alloyed with the knowledge that I could have him only under a false pretense. He thinks I'm the same woman I was when we were first together, young, bright-eyed, with a long, healthy future ahead.

I tell myself that I'm staying until the end for William's sake. And, despite everything, the fact that he is so dazzled by his father can only be a good thing. I really believe that now. Even if I have a tiny, niggling worry that Adam might return to his old ways at the end of the holiday. He still behaves more like a buddy than a parent.

I become aware of voices outside and sit up, trying to work out if it's Charlie and Chloe.

I leap up to brush my teeth, wash my face and throw on a beach dress.

Rehearsing fragments of a speech under my breath, I open the door and step out into the courtyard, full of determination. I follow the voices to the parking area behind Les Écuries, and as soon as I register the absence of Charlie's car, I realize that all I've heard is the couple opposite who checked into one of the cottages yesterday with their toddler.

I deflate, partly relieved, partly disappointed that I can't get this talk over with until later today. I return to the courtyard, when I realize that Chloe's red pool float, the one that was always propped up against the wall, melting in the sun, is gone. The flip-flops next to the door aren't there. There are no beach towels draped over chairs or citronella candle from the night before.

I slowly approach the building and press my hands against the glass, peering inside. The living area is empty. The cottage has been vacated, its guests gone.

CHAPTER 66

After all the drama, lying flat on my back and feeling the sun's rays soak into my legs is a release. The sound of Becky and Seb's boys bickering is the only impediment to complete peace until, in a bid to separate them, I suggest that William take Rufus to see if they can persuade any other kids to play a game of soccer. James stays behind to flick through Natasha's copy of *Glamour.*

I am about to top up my sun cream when the two boys trudge back. I try gently to quiz William to see if he's being given a hard time again, but he shrugs and tells me his dad said he'd be coming out to have a dip with him soon. Adam arrives ten minutes later, and I deliberately avert my eyes as he strips off by the pool.

"I wonder when *Poldark* is coming back on TV?" Natasha muses, pushing down her sunglasses to scrutinize Adam's physique.

Becky chuckles and pauses from wrestling

a sun hat onto Poppy. "Whatever made you think of that?" she says, nudging me. "No wonder you had a nice time with him the other night, Jess."

I sink down into the sun lounger to focus on my paperback again, trying to stop myself from glancing above the pages.

Then I wonder why I'm bothering. Why don't I just allow myself to look at Adam, William and everything else in front of me? I lower my book and let my eyes drift to the ribbons of light sparkling on the pool. The damp-haired children in floaties, licking fluorescent ice lollies and pouring chlorinated water into teacups before presenting them to their mums. The sound of my son's helpless laughter as Adam splashes him and William responds by dunking him under. A surreal sense of calm overcomes me, a feeling — no, a reminder — of how much good there is in my life; how much beauty and sunlight and laughter.

"Aunty Natasha," James pipes up, "you look really brown."

Natasha looks at her arms and leans in. "It's fake tan, sweetheart, but don't tell anyone."

"Can I have some?"

"No," Becky laughs.

James frowns. "Did you have it when you

407

were a little girl, Aunty Natasha?"

"No, sweetheart. It hadn't been invented when I was little."

He flicks over another page of her magazine. "What else didn't they have in the olden days?"

Natasha chokes on her Diet Coke.

"Well, hello!" Josh is standing above us with a lighthouse grin, his polo shirt pulled tight across his belly.

Natasha looks up and smiles. "Pull up a chair." She pats the seat next to her, and he sinks in, spreading his knees as widely as possible.

"You all look fabulous today," he declares, and Becky widens her eyes at me.

As Josh leans in to Natasha and they start talking, I notice Ben on the other side of the pool, cleaning the barbecue and looking over. The disappointment on his handsome face makes me glance at Joshua, wondering what it is that Natasha is trying to convince herself she sees in him.

Becky leans in to me. "He can't stop looking," she whispers, popping a walnut into her mouth.

"Ben? I know."

"Not Ben. *Adam,*" she mumbles.

My head snaps to the pool, where he's standing, his eyes on us. I glance away.

"You know . . . you two were really good together once."

I fix a stern gaze upon her. "Becky, stop it."

I turn to Natasha and Joshua to try to join in on their conversation instead. "I know it's all the rage these days, but why in public?" Joshua appears to be talking about breast-feeding. "I can't stand all these do-gooders who argue that it's a 'normal human function.' So is having a crap, but you don't see me squatting down and doing that in front of everyone."

Becky pulls a face. "That's hardly comparable with *feeding* a baby. Giving them a meal, you know."

"What's wrong with bottles?" he argues. "Or at least going into a toilet cubicle to do it."

A debate ensues between Becky and Joshua, in which it's clear he's not going to back down until his views have been rammed so far down everyone's throats they're almost gagging. And it's equally clear that Natasha wishes with all of her heart that he would shut his trap.

"Sorry to interrupt," I say, "but I'm going to head back."

Becky leaps on the opportunity. "Oh, I'll come too." Then she looks to the pool, where Seb is playing with Poppy and Rufus. "Seb, I'm making a move to have a shower before dinner. I'll take the kids with me so you can have a swim if you like?"

"No, it's okay," he replies. "I'll bring these two back when they're ready."

William stays with Adam, while Becky holds James's hand and the three of us meander towards the woodland.

"Interesting conversation with Joshua," I murmur.

She rolls her eyes. "That's one way of describing it. He's awful."

Then she glances back at Seb, as he throws Poppy up in the air and she howls with infectious laughter that makes both of us chuckle.

I realize as we start walking again that Becky is smiling to herself.

"What's up?" I ask.

She shrugs. "I picked a good one there, didn't I?"

I shake my head and laugh.

"What?" she asks, bemused.

"I went to all the trouble of babysitting to try and reignite your passion for your husband, when all it really needed was five minutes in Joshua's company."

She laughs.

"Surely you didn't need to compare Seb

to him to work out how fantastic your husband is?"

"Don't be silly," she tuts, then flashes me a sideways grin. "It did help though."

CHAPTER 67

The following day, William and I pack a rucksack full of sandwiches, roast chicken crisps and Day-Glo sweets before driving to the Vézère Valley for a hike with a tour group. Going with an official guide felt like a good way to get some exercise, without the risk that I'd get us both lost up a mountain. He's lukewarm about the idea until we get there, when his newfound sense of adventure quickly gets the better of him. Soon, he's scrambling into dank, glistening caves and crunching along stony mountain pathways where birdsong fills our ears and wildflowers peek out of the rocks.

We take a rest at the top of a slope, perching on the crags in the hazy heat to rehydrate and give our legs a break. William finishes his apple and hands me the core. "Am I still going to be your personal walking bin when you're twenty-one?" I rummage in my rucksack for a plastic bag.

"Better than throwing litter." He grins sheepishly.

I wrap up the apple core and stuff it in the bag. "I was thinking: why don't I come along to watch you play soccer tonight?"

His expression is not filled with unbridled joy at this idea. "Then they'd just think I needed my mum to defend me."

"Okay, then I wouldn't *say* anything. If I was simply there to *watch,* you know, with my badass face on . . . I bet things would be different."

He looks unsettled by my choice of language. "I'm not even that good at soccer anyway."

"Oh, come off it. You've become brilliant this holiday," I argue, which I admit is pushing the point slightly.

"Can we talk about something else?"

I finish my chocolate and take out a tissue to wipe my hands. "Okay, what?"

He thinks for a moment. "How about politics?"

And so we embark on another conversation that's so like a piece of Channel 4 News reportage that I feel ill-equipped to take part until I've got a proper 4G reception and Google to help.

"I've decided what I want to be when I grow up," he concludes, as we start heading down the mountain.

"Oh, what?"

"I'm going to work in refugee camps, to help people there. I might be a doctor."

I put my arm round his shoulders. "That would make me incredibly proud. But I'd be proud of you whatever you do."

"Yeah, of course. It might not happen anyway. I might become a model instead."

I start coughing, until he flashes me an indignant look and I thump my chest as if a piece of undigested apple is responsible. "Right."

"Dad says I'm good-looking enough," he continues. "He said he wasn't as handsome as me when he was my age, so I'd definitely be able to do it."

When we arrive back at the cottage an hour or so later, William's first instinct as we walk through the door is to pick up the iPad. He's stayed away since our blowout, presumably not wanting to draw attention to the threat of my six-decade-long ban.

"Don't go on that," I tell him. "We're eating at Becky's tonight, so you need a shower before we head over."

"Okay, Mum. Just a minute."

I'm about to challenge him, when the door opens and Natasha walks in.

"Hi there. Have you been out with Josh today?"

She flashes me a glance. "No. I'm kind of avoiding him."

"Oh. You've gone off him then?"

She nods despondently. "He ticked all the boxes apart from the one that said: 'Must not act like an arsehole.'"

"Sorry, Natasha."

"Oh, don't be," she says, dismissively. "He's going home tomorrow, and London's big enough for me to never see him again. At the end of the day, he was just some bloke who fancied himself rather too much."

"Why are my ears burning?" We look up and see Adam at the door.

"Not you," Natasha laughs. "Right, I'm going to grab my sweater and head to Becky's. You coming?"

"William needs a shower first. Don't you, William?" I say pointedly.

"Yes. Coming," he mumbles, failing to move.

As Natasha goes to the bedroom for her sweater, I realize Adam is looking at me. "Did Becky mention I can't come tonight because I've got to drive over for a dinner meeting in Montignac?"

"She did."

I glance over at our son. *William,"* I say,

through gritted teeth. He doesn't answer. "WILLIAM!"

"Just a minute, Mum."

I consider myself to be a reasonable person, but this is ridiculous. "I've already given you a minute. In fact, I've given you a lot more than a minute." I march over, remove the iPad from his hand and switch it off.

"Noooo!" he yells, reaching out his hand like Kate Winslet on that raft in the closing scenes of *Titanic*.

"I've asked you at least five times. Don't ruin the lovely day we've had."

"Okay! I've lost now," he mutters.

He stands up and goes to head to his bedroom.

"William. Hang on a minute." Adam's voice is definitely Adam's voice, but I can't say I recognize it. William spins round. "Don't talk to your mum like that."

My son's cheeks bloom with red blotches, his eyes frozen with shock.

"Nobody should have to ask you to do something that many times," Adam continues. There's the hint of unease in his voice, as if he's not entirely sure he's doing this right. "How would you feel about it if the rest of us did that with you?"

William shrugs stiffly.

"So don't do it, okay?"

A cornucopia of emotions fight for space on William's face: first defiance, embarrassment, then quiet mortification and regret. "I'm sorry, Mum."

I nod. "Okay. Now go and jump in that shower."

Then I add, "Thank you," as Adam leaves the room.

Natasha touches my elbow before he can respond. "See you over there. Will you be long?"

"Ten minutes," I reply, and she heads to the door and shuts it behind her as I realize that Adam looks agitated.

"Can we go outside for a minute?"

"Sure."

We step out as the sun is low on the horizon, casting a golden glow on the ribbons of wildflowers in the field beyond. He sits down first, and I deliberately choose a chair that's not next to his, for the simple reason that being in close proximity to him these days is too exquisite and unbearable.

"I've been thinking a lot about the future of this place. And, I don't want to make any promises yet to William because I haven't boxed everything off . . . plus there would be a lot to do before I could make it happen . . ."

"Adam, what are you trying to say?"

"I want to come back and live in the UK." He fixes his dark eyes on me, awaiting my reaction. But I'm too stunned to reply, so he continues. "I think there's a way I can make it happen. It won't be straightforward, and it won't be immediate, but it's a solution."

I let the words sink in before my head bubbles with questions. "What about this place? And what would you do for a living?"

A small laugh escapes from his lips, as if he doesn't need reminding about these monumental issues. "I mentioned I've had someone interested in buying this place for some time now, but I've always said no. The business is successful, but I'm still in debt after all the work that's been done over the years, and now was supposed to be the time when I started making some of that money back . . ." His voice trails off. "The point is, I started looking into it seriously, and the numbers sort of add up. Just. Or, kind of anyway. And even if they don't, it doesn't matter, because at least if I got a job back in Manchester again, I'd be near William and be able to help you. To do this together. Be a parent, I mean."

Thoughts begin colliding in my head, but I can't turn them into words.

"I'm not saying I expect anything from you, Jess," he continues, his eyes flickering to the ground. "I respect what you've said about not wanting to be involved with me again . . . at least on that level." Then he looks up, certainty etched on his expression. "But I want to be in William's life. I want to go to the parents' evenings and take him to his school clubs. And I'll do anything I can to make that happen."

I realize how unfeasible this once would've felt.

When I arrived in France, I was perpetually pissed off with Adam, challenging him to be a better father without ever believing he'd succeed. I wanted to do as Mum asked simply so I could tell her I'd done as she wished. I was going through the motions, convinced without saying as much that he'd fail. Only he hasn't failed. He's surpassed expectations. But I'm afraid he still doesn't have a clue that he's taking on a lot more than the school run.

CHAPTER 68

Reassured that the sky didn't cave in last time, Becky again agrees to hand over her children to Natasha and me the following day.

"Are Mum and Dad going on another date?" James asks.

"Actually, they're going to have a sleep," Natasha replies.

"Why would they want to do that? Sleep's boring."

"They've both been awake since 5:45 a.m., so I think they'd disagree," I tell him.

Poppy protested her parents' disappearance with a forceful burst of tears, which ceased the second they disappeared. Now, she sits with William and has completed four jigsaws, read two stories and hiccoughed with laughter at an episode of *The Simpsons* on the iPad, as if she has the faintest idea what's going on.

The older two boys are also in good form,

though there's some confusion when Rufus tries to fill us in on details of their visit to Domme yesterday.

"Mummy had a crap," he tells us earnestly.

"No, she didn't," James snorts.

"She did! She had a really big one and said she enjoyed it so much she wanted another one straightaway."

"You're a liar," James mutters.

"I'm not! You had one too — with strawberry ice cream on it."

"Do you mean . . . a *crepe*?" Natasha deduces.

"Yes. A crap. It was yummy."

After an hour, the brilliant blue of the sky and high sun tempts us to the pool. The heat is less oppressive than yesterday, the air crisper and clearer, and filled with the scent of the little lemon-colored flowers that tumble from the pots against the château walls.

William, wearing permanently steamed-up goggles, plays in the water with Rufus and James. They amuse themselves by throwing in dive sticks, then scrambling after them.

Natasha, meanwhile, lies on her front in a halter-neck bikini, her crimson-painted toes hanging over the sun lounger, as she has a tea party with Poppy with a mini watering can and a couple of tumblers.

When Ben appears to clear away the glasses on our table, she looks up and smiles. They look almost shy in each other's presence. It's sweet and excruciating to watch: they're both dying to say something. Thankfully, William jumps out of the water, splatters towards them and puts them out of their misery by breaking the silence.

"Did you know that a parrot can see behind itself without even moving its head?"

They both laugh. "I *did* know that," Ben tells him.

"You did a veterinary science degree, didn't you?" I ask.

"That's right. I don't remember knowing that sort of stuff at your age though, William."

"William's very clever," Natasha tells him. "He's on a brilliant and talented list for maths."

"Gifted and talented," I correct her, but neither of them is listening, and William is already plodding back to the pool. I pick up a teacup and ask Poppy if she could fill it up for me, leaving Natasha free to talk to Ben.

"What are you up to for the rest of the week?" he asks.

"We're kind of out of ideas," Natasha replies, tucking her legs underneath herself.

"What do you do on your days off — anything you'd recommend?"

"I usually drive over to Lac du Causse. You can water-ski there."

"Oh, I love waterskiing. I learned in the Caribbean a couple of years ago but haven't done any since. I'm probably rusty now."

"I learned in South Wales. Far more glamorous."

They make small talk until it fizzles out and Ben simply looks at her and declares, "If you're interested, I could take you there tomorrow. It's my day off."

For a moment I'm convinced she's going to say no, for all the reasons she gave me when we first got here. Because he's too young, because he lives in France, because this simply *can't* lead to the meaningful chapter in her life she's looking for.

But as the golden light of the sun rains down on his skin and a breeze twirls the smells of summer all around us, there's too much magic in this place to listen to reason. "That'd be lovely."

His smile illuminates his entire face.

"Great. I'll pick you up at ten."

As he walks away, she sighs. "I'm my own worst enemy."

"I wouldn't worry about it," I reply.

"Well, I am. He's lovely — but I'm hardly

going to end up choosing Habitat crockery with him."

"When it's your time to fall in love, you'll find your Habitat crockery guy, Natasha. But you just can't force these things. In the meantime, if I were you, I'd just enjoy waterskiing."

"Mummy!" Poppy exclaims, and we look up to see Becky and Seb heading towards us, his fingers threaded through hers.

"I feel like a new woman." Becky grins, bending down to give Poppy a kiss. "I had forgotten the sheer luxury of an afternoon nap."

"*Really* appreciate that, you two. It was a real treat. We were shattered," Seb adds, as he pulls off his top to jump into the pool with the boys.

As Becky's features leak into a yawn, she lazily pulls up a lounger and has barely smothered her skin in her almond sun cream before she's in such a deep sleep that her eyelids are twitching and fluttering with dreams.

Natasha taps me on the thigh and leans in to whisper to me. "Becky's out cold — do you think they might be lying that they spent that time having a nap?"

I suppress a smile and whisper back: "I hope so."

CHAPTER 69

My dad's smile seems fainter every time I look at him these days.

It used to fill his face when he laughed, which he did often. I miss that sound almost as much as my mother's voice, a voice that once sang lullabies to me when I was a little girl, and soothed my son if he tripped and cut his knee.

I am in Adam's office, surrounded by papers, and talking on Skype to my dad, who is trying to reassure me that he's keeping his chin up. Natasha is water-skiing, and William is off on a fishing trip to the lake with Seb and the other boys.

"Gaynor came round earlier, so that was nice," Dad says. Gaynor's one of Mum's oldest friends. They went to school together, and although she lives in Peterborough these days, she still makes the effort to visit every couple of months.

"Oh, how is she?"

"Very good. She and Barry have just come back from Kenya — they did a big safari with the whole family. They said it was wonderful."

"How fantastic."

His eyes drift for a moment, and I know what he's thinking. Mum would've loved something like that.

"I think Gaynor was shocked," he says.

"About . . . how Mum is these days?"

Dad doesn't answer at first but eventually manages to nod.

Because he's with her daily, the changes in Mum are nearly imperceptible to him. They're so slow and creeping, it's like watching a dying flower; you can't see a thing happening when your eyes are fixed on it. It's only when you step away and return that you can see the withered bloom in its place. And with Mum, there is nothing more unsettling than the devastated faces of friends who haven't been around her in a while.

I watch in bleak silence as Dad covers his mouth with a trembling hand, failing to hide his emotion from me, his determination to stay strong wilting under the pressure of all-consuming sadness.

And it takes this to remind me that he's not just my dad, and she's not just my mum.

They're two people who've held each other up for thirty-five years. The glow of their love has shone through the bad times, the beautiful times and the times that would've broken other couples.

Mum's decline has been long and drawn out. And, while I know she's showing no signs of leaving us yet, when it does happen, it will be sooner than any of us are ready to handle. I genuinely don't know what he'll do without her.

"I'm going to come home, Dad," I decide. "It'd only mean us missing the last week." I'm saying it not just for her but for him. He can't do this by himself. As one of the nurses walks past, distracting him, I change the subject before he tries to talk me out of my decision. "Oh, and Adam wants to come back to the UK."

Dad looks startled, straightening himself into shape. "Really?"

"Yes, he wants to spend more time with William."

My dad's fondness for Adam appears in the creases at the side of his eyes. This is about more than just making Mum happy; when the rest of us were furious with Adam, Dad never seemed capable of it.

"Well, that's great, Jess. It can only be a good thing, for you and William."

"Yes. Though the proof will be in the pudding."

Dad's expression falls slightly. "Are you saying you don't think Adam will be interested when he gets back?"

"No, I'm not saying that . . ." But as my voice trails off, I'm still trying to work out what I *do* mean.

Then I realize what it is. I'm holding back. I don't want to believe that Adam is going to transform into Super Dad until I see it happen in real life. Not when we're here just on an extended holiday.

"William and I have been let down enough over the years by Adam to know that it might happen again. I hope it won't, but I've got to be realistic."

"He won't let you down, Jess."

I smile at him curiously. "I know you've always liked him, Dad, but it's not as though he's been reliable. Proving yourself as a parent is about more than a few weeks in the sun. He's still the man who left me in the lurch to sleep with an ex-girlfriend when William was born."

Dad sits back. "You thought he was sleeping with an ex-girlfriend?"

"I *know* he was sleeping with an ex-girlfriend."

Dad swallows. "Your mum said that too,

428

but I'd thought that was just her jumping to conclusions."

"Not at all. It was unforgivable."

"But . . . I thought you'd liked having your mum there when William was born." I can't help bristling at this conversation.

"Well, I did, but I'd have preferred both of them," I say, exasperated. "Adam was the father, after all!"

He nods, his eyes flitting away. "I just . . . Things were different when you were a baby. Nobody batted an eyelid if the dad wasn't there."

Then he lifts his chin, his chest tight as he stares at me, his mouth twitching anxiously.

"What's the matter, Dad?"

"Jess, I need to tell you something."

CHAPTER 70

The door next to my dad opens, and one of the nursing staff pops round her head. She's about fifty and is wearing a name tag I can't read, and given the fact that I don't recognize her, I can only presume she's new.

"Your wife's finished her bath now," she tells Dad.

"Oh. Right, okay." He puts down his tablet to open the door. I am soon watching the blurred screen as Mum's wheelchair is pushed to her room and two nurses proceed to get her onto the bed.

By the time she's settled and Dad's holding up the screen so she can see me, her position doesn't look even slightly comfortable; she's stiff and twisted, her limbs like the gnarled branches of a tree.

"I've got Jess on the line, love," he tells her. "Did you want a chat?"

She replies with the familiar sound that I know means yes. Aside from the fact that she's lying down, she looks exactly the same as last time I saw her. Of course, *the same as last time* isn't all that good.

"How are you, Mum?"

She rolls her head, not answering. "I'm . . ." But her voice trails off before she's even started the sentence. I wait for a moment to see if she's going to say something else, but she doesn't.

"Mum, I'm coming home early. Things have gone well with Adam and William, and . . . it just feels like I've been away too long," I say. "I would've been home earlier, but William wanted to stay, so really, it was him who persuaded me. But I'm just going to have to speak to him again. I mean, he's ten years old, and it's not his decision. I needed to be home ages ago, and —"

"No." I stop talking as Mum twitches. "Don't."

"Don't what? Come back early? But I want to, Mum."

She is silent for a moment, her head dropping, her mouth stretched open. My chest contracts as she tries to speak. But at first there is nothing but silence as my stomach twists helplessly and her mouth refuses to follow her wishes.

Then she finally speaks, and it's as hoarse and quiet as it always is these days, but I can make it out as clear as day.

"Remember."

"What, Mum?"

"Wha . . . I said."

Dad reaches out and rubs her arm with his hands, the pads of his fingers tenderly reassuring her. "What do you mean, love?"

But memories are already bubbling up inside me. I know what she's talking about. She doesn't need to say another word.

We celebrated Mum's forty-eighth birthday on the Venice-Simplon Orient Express. It was only a day trip, but even that nearly bankrupted me — I could never have made it all the way to Venice short of a lottery win.

It was worth every penny to see her in her favorite silk polka-dot dress as she stepped inside the glamorous vintage interior of that train. The experience was everything I'd hoped it would be: unforgettably luxurious, in surroundings that were the epitome of elegance; crisp damask curtains, opulent oak panels, tablecloths whiter than icing sugar. As the train sliced through the English countryside, we dined on finely dressed lobster and sipped champagne.

Yes, her legs wobbled as she climbed up the steps, as if unable to hold her own weight. Yes, she twitched and lurched, and people stared as I transferred champagne from the vintage crystal flute into her plastic toddler cup.

By then, she was already in the fierce grip of the disease — but that day, it didn't matter.

The staff was superb. I'd called before we left to let them know about her condition, and they did everything they could to make her day as special as possible.

She loved every second. The train, the food, being with me.

Yet there was a moment near the end when she had something she wanted to say, something she wanted me to always remember.

"Make as many moments like this as you can for yourself, Jess," she told me. "When life is tough, as it will be for all of us, you have a duty to yourself. To live without regrets."

Emotion rose in my chest, but she didn't want me to say anything. Just listen. "You might think I should be full of regrets, Jess, but I don't have any. I married a man I love, and I have a child and grandchild I adore, and I'm lucky enough to have spent many healthy years with all of them." She reached over and clasped my hand. "I am *not* dying of Huntington's disease."

I snapped up my head. "What do you mean?"

"I'm living with it," she said. "There's a difference. I'm living life as though every day is my last. And until things get really tough, that's what I intend to do. Think about all the good around me and not what lies ahead. Do all the things I enjoy, just for the hell of it. I'm going to swim in the sea. Bake cakes. Do more dancing."

She hesitated. "But you've got to remember today and what I'm telling you now. No matter how bad things get for me — no matter what happens to you — you've still got plenty of life to live. Remember that, Jess. If you want something, go and get it. Just do it."

Now, as I look through the screen, tears slip down my cheeks in hot, thick tracks, and I nod. "I remember, Mum."

I wait for her to smile, greedy for another moment of connection. But her head turns away, her eyes empty again, as my dad brushes the soft wisps of her hair away from her face and tenderly kisses her cheek.

CHAPTER 71

I am reeling when I step out of the château and grip the edge of the wrought iron door, its heat burning into my palm. It's not only my mum's words that force me to focus on what's important right now, but something else too: what Dad said about Adam and the night of William's birth.

The bits I'd remembered — the hours that passed, the lipstick and booze on Adam's shirt — I'm sure they all happened. But I'd filled in the gaps with my own version of events, imagining a hotel room, Adam's hands in Georgina's silken hair, long, drunken limbs entwining, while I was abandoned and vulnerable.

I could think of only one explanation. Except now an alternative suspicion is growing inside me as I start running, breaking into a sprint across the grounds. I spot Madame Blanchard picking flowers by the edge of the woods and ask her breathlessly if she knows where Adam is. "Back to his cottage, Jess. But you must be quick — he goes to Bergerac soon."

By the time I arrive at the cottage, my heart is pounding. When Adam opens the door, he looks so concerned that it takes a moment to compose myself.

"What's happened? Not William again?"

I shake my head. "No," I pant, snatching breaths. "He's fine."

"Do you need to sit down? You look like you're about to keel over."

"I'm fine."

"Listen, I've got to be at a meeting in Bergerac in an hour, so I need to get going." He grabs a stack of papers from his dining table. "I'm really sorry, Jess, but can we make this quick?"

He turns round to stuff the papers into his bag.

"What *really* happened on the night of William's birth?"

He freezes momentarily, before continuing to organize the sheets, buying himself time. "We've had this conversation two dozen times, Jess. Why would you want to have it again now?"

"You were with Dad, weren't you?"

He doesn't look up. "I need to get going. But we'll have a chat later," he says, step-

436

ping out of the door and inviting me outside before he closes it and clicks his car lock.

"You were out in Manchester and you met Dad and something happened," I continue. "That's why you couldn't get there in time." But he refuses to engage with me, simply opening the car door.

"Adam, I want the truth. I can deal with it. And it's not fair . . . all these years if you've been carrying the burden of all this when —"

"Stop, Jess," he says firmly, holding up his hand. "I'll talk to you about this, happily. But I *have* to go to Bergerac. I'm already late."

He steps into the car as my frustration tightens. I'm not going to stand here help-lessly as he drives off and avoids an issue I've waited ten years to get to the bottom of. I open the car door and climb in. "I'll come with you. You can tell me on the way."

"Don't be ridiculous. Who's looking after William, anyway?"

"Seb. They've gone fishing."

He turns the ignition. "Please get out, Jess."

I pull the seat belt across me. "Not until you tell me what happened."

He looks at the windscreen as a bright blue petal drifts onto the glass. It skips away, dancing into the sunlight as he sighs and turns off the key. "Your dad would never forgive me."

"He would," I reassure him. "In fact, he will — I promise. He nearly told me what happened himself until we were interrupted."

He shakes his head, a bead of sweat appearing above his brow. "This is not right. It'd be a betrayal."

"Adam, you're not betraying anyone but yourself unless you tell me the truth."

His chest rises as he fills his lungs with air, closing his eyes before he eventually lets it go. Then he begins speaking, unraveling what really happened the night that for so long was central to everything that broke us.

CHAPTER 72

Adam *had* been in Manchester that night, finishing off his team-building day in the Bush Bar. And so had Georgina.

"I hadn't told you I'd arranged to meet her, because I knew you thought there was something going on between us," he says. "And with her being newly single . . . I didn't think you'd have understood. But this is the truth. She was a mess after she broke up with Johnny. It wasn't just breakup blues; it was more than that. She was seriously depressed . . . on the edge."

"I thought you'd said she was better off without him?"

"Oh, she was, but she couldn't see it at the time. He'd cheated on her at least twice and fleeced half her savings. For some unfathomable reason she wanted him back."

Adam tells me that Georgina phoned him that day, upset and determined to beg her ex-boyfriend to take her back. He persuaded her instead to meet him for a drink at the Bush Bar, where he knew he'd be with his colleagues from work. By ten o'clock, she still hadn't turned up, and he was desperate to get home, but he hung around for her sake, coldly sober and surrounded by friends six pints ahead of him.

He texted me to check all was okay, and I told him I was off to bed. In our last communications, we exchanged simple *good night* and *I love you* messages, which I'd interpreted for years afterwards as us going through the motions.

"When Georgina finally showed up, she was falling-down drunk," he continues. "She had these two girls in tow, friends of hers I'd never met before. They were determined to drag her round the Northern Quarter to drink away her sorrows and throw herself at any bloke who stood in her path."

She was bawdy, tearful and reckless enough for him to conclude that his friend's fragile soul was in trouble. So he didn't recoil in horror when she draped her arms around him, telling him she *just wanted to be held*.

"I just kind of . . . . froze. Only she started kissing my neck, and I had to pry her away. There was no way to be subtle about it."

He swallows a lump in his throat. "She was mortified."

Georgina ran into the night, burning with shame and not nearly drunk enough to pretend it hadn't happened. One of her girlfriends chased after her, and he watched at the door of the bar as they stumbled into a cab. He slipped away after that, wrung out from the evening and craving the warmth of his bed. He describes how he strode through rain-drenched streets, his clothes soaked with grimy water as he stepped up his pace to the car park. He was nearly there when he saw the figure of a man being bustled out of the Northern Tap.

"I dodged out of the way at first," Adam says. "He was in a seriously bad way."

"Drunk?"

He nods.

I picture a man that could've been any old pisshead: aggressive but vulnerable, righteously indignant about being manhandled.

"Then he kind of dropped to the ground and started making these awful noises. I couldn't just leave him there. So I bent down to try and help him. I thought about phoning an ambulance, so I tried to roll him over, and it was then that I realized . . . I knew the coat."

My heart turns over as I reinterpret this sentence. "You mean, you knew the man."

It takes a moment before he nods, confirming what I already knew. That the old drunk rolling around in the rain was my dad.

Who hadn't touched a drink for years and whose sobriety had been — for me and Mum — the source of so much pride and relief.

"I tried to wake him up, but he started thrashing out at me. He didn't know it was me. He was . . . disoriented."

Adam is choosing his words carefully, but it's hardly necessary. I can picture every detail.

"I remembered all the stories you told me about what he was like when you were little. But this blew my mind. I'd never seen your dad like this."

It turns out that Dad had been heaved out of the pub because he'd thrown up on the bar. More worryingly, he'd fallen on top of his arm; Adam was convinced he'd broken a bone.

He was sweating panic, his mind racing, but there was no way he was going to phone his heavily pregnant girlfriend, who was tucked up in bed with his child still inside her belly.

So he ran back into the Bush Bar and grabbed Chris, the only other vaguely sober colleague left. "We managed to bundle your dad into the back seat of my car so I could drive him to hospital. He was in such a bad way . . . I was pleading with him to stay awake, shouting at him to try and get him to respond. I thought he was . . ."

"You thought he had alcohol poisoning?"

He nods.

The ER staff were wearily professional. They'd seen it all, every Saturday night.

When Dad eventually came round, he was terrified, frenzied almost, clutching at Adam's hand, begging him not to go. "And it was slap-bang in the middle of all this that I realized my phone had run out of juice," he tells me numbly. "I forced myself to stay calm. I kept thinking, if there was *any* chance of Jess going into labor, she'd have said something in her last text. I thought about using your dad's mobile, but that would have involved explaining why we were together. I'd already worked out that Martin wouldn't want a soul to know about this. And . . . more to the point, I couldn't even contemplate what it'd do to you if you'd found out about it."

He knew it would've broken my heart; that's what it would do.

"Your dad's arm turned out to be badly bruised but not broken. When we finally got out of hospital hours later, what he needed more than anything was somewhere to shower. So I drove to Chris's house — I couldn't have taken him home to your mum in that state, not without getting him sorted. When we were in the car, your dad was . . . He was upset. He was sobbing. I kept saying to him, 'You're going to be okay, Martin. You'll feel like shit, but you'll survive.' "

But this was about more than feeling like shit, and both of them knew it.

"As we pulled up outside Chris's house, he grabbed me by the arm. And he made me swear I'd never tell you about it. Not you, not anyone. I promised him I wouldn't. I told him he'd never need to worry — that this would always be between him and me."

It was nearly seven in the morning by the time he bundled Dad into the shower. Then he walked into Chris's kitchen and plugged in his phone. And it sprang to life for the first time since ten o'clock the previous evening.

CHAPTER 73

Just seeing the desolation in Adam's eyes lets me know that it's true. It makes sense in the worst and best way, and although I don't really need Dad to confirm Adam's story, I know he will when we finally get round to talking about it. Not just about the night itself, but about *why* he fell off the wagon. It was when Mum was having the tests for HD — before her diagnosis but certainly when they knew what might be coming.

"I couldn't betray your dad," Adam says. "Despite how pissed he was, he was right to ask me to keep quiet. He didn't do it for his own sake; he did it for *yours*. For your mum's. It would've destroyed you."

"But Adam, that changed everything. That was the reason . . ."

"The reason you left?" He raises an eyebrow. "No, it wasn't, Jess. Let's be honest.

There were dozens of reasons, and that was one."

"A big one," I argue.

Adam looks through the windscreen at the hazy sunlight, unable to meet my eye as he speaks. "I hadn't wanted to be a father, because I was scared and immature and unwilling to admit any of those things. I should've stepped up to the mark when you got pregnant. But I didn't. And I compounded all that after William was born by staying away."

I bite the flesh inside my mouth. "I didn't exactly make you welcome."

"You didn't say anything I wasn't convinced of all by myself, Jess. Even your mum thought I should fuck off and disappear from the face of the planet. I knew things must've been bad if it'd come to that."

I frown. "What makes you say Mum thought that?"

His jaw tightens. "I turned up out of the blue once to see you and William. She completely lost it with me. She terrified the life out of me, if I'm honest. I'd got on so well with her before, and she'd always been the kind of woman who'd make you feel welcome the second you stepped through the door. When I saw how much she hated me . . ."

"She didn't hate you, Adam. She didn't *like* you after that night, admittedly. But those rages . . . they were part of her condition. It wasn't the real her."

He looks ahead, scraping the bottom of the steering wheel with his thumb. "Whatever it was, it became one of the things that made me think you and I just weren't meant to be. That I had to get away from you and William and do something else with my life. I was an idiot."

"I've got my regrets too, I promise you."

I am suddenly lost for words at the thought that Adam has carried this secret for so long, while I've harbored a completely unwarranted grudge all that time.

"Listen, Jess. I really do need to go. I'm already twenty minutes late." He turns the key to start up the engine and waits for me to get out.

But I don't want to.

Instead, I reach over and touch his arm. Then I unstrap my seat belt and lean across with both hands, taking his face in them. His eyes look young again, shining with emotion. I kiss him gently at first, brushing the tender skin on his lips, before he opens his mouth and allows me to sink into him. I unclick his seat belt.

"What's going on?"

I kiss him again, more deeply, before speaking, his lips an inch from mine. "Why? Are you complaining?"

"No," he croaks. "Absolutely not. In fact, carry on." He pulls back and glances at his watch. "Although . . . possibly after my meeting."

I kiss him harder now, and he responds instantly, pulling me towards him. Then he stops, looks at me, his chest rising as he goes to object.

"Okay," he says urgently. "Screw the meeting. I'll text and tell him I've got a flat tire."

I burst out laughing as he yanks the keys out and clicks open the car door. I follow suit. We emerge onto the grass outside his cottage, straightening our clothes.

We stumble inside, and the door slams behind us. I press my back against the wood as he threads his fingers through mine and plants a trail of kisses on my face and neck. His lips feel hot on my skin, silent and feverish. I unclasp my hands and run them up his shirt, tracing the contours of his ribs as my desire builds in waves. I reach up to his shirt, but I'm not fast enough for him, and instead he opens the first two buttons and tugs it over his head.

The sight of his body makes me throb with longing. The salty dampness of his skin. The athletic curves of his muscles. The dark hair that brushes his collarbone.

I start kissing his chest, but he gently lifts up my head and begins undoing my blouse, slipping it off my shoulders with eyes heavy as they linger on me. Our clothes pile up on the floor until he takes me by the hand and leads me to the bedroom.

I couldn't tell you the reasons why sex with Adam has always been better than with anyone else. Maybe he's just particularly good at it. But there's a magical alchemy when the two of us are together, one that's never been replicated.

As a fierce sun streams through the windows, Adam makes love to me in the same way he always did it: like it is the first time and the last. As if every moment is as precious as the ability to live itself.

CHAPTER 74

Afterwards, I lie with my head on his chest, as he strokes the skin along the line of my jaw, his touch making me shiver. He is unusually quiet.

"Is everything okay?"

"Yes," he replies. Then: "No."

I lift up my head. "Go on, spit it out."

He props himself up on his elbow and takes a moment before speaking. "Are you going to tell me you regret this again?"

A bittersweet smile creeps to my lips. "No." I push myself up and kiss him briefly on the lips. "No, I don't regret it. Why would I after two orgasms?"

I'm being deliberately flippant — I don't think we need any more high drama. Although he laughs, he doesn't seem placated.

"You don't need to look so proud of yourself," I say, trying harder.

"Why, were you hoping for three?" He then looks down at his hands, his eyes serious. "Look, I'm glad you had two orgasms. But I want it to be about more than that."

My shoulders soften. "It was, Adam. It definitely was about more than that."

"Right then, I'm going to ask you something." He pushes away my hand and kneels up in front of me, strategically holding up a pillow to cover his modesty.

"Jess. I love you."

My heart almost stops. Allowing myself to believe these words feels like way too much recklessness for one day. "The thing is, Adam —"

"I haven't finished. I want to marry you."

I can feel my jaw lower. "Adam, calm down, for God's sake."

"I know it probably feels sudden," he argues, "but it's not really. I was in love with you right from the beginning."

"You never even noticed me right from the beginning."

"You're splitting hairs — the point is this: I love you. I loved you every moment we were together, whatever you think is the case, and I've spent ten years trying to get over you. Dating women I've hoped will come close to matching you, then realizing within months, weeks, that none of them could."

Emotions battle for space in my head. I'm

451

lost for words.

"I realize this is the crappiest proposal ever. I haven't got a ring, I haven't prepared a speech, I haven't done it right. But there's one thing it's got going for it, and that's that I *mean* it. Every word."

He seems to not be joking.

"Will you marry me, Jess?" he repeats. "I'll get down on one knee if it makes it any better."

"That won't be necessary, Adam. Not when your balls are on show."

He gives a spurt of laughter, which dies down as he starts rubbing his forehead. "You haven't answered me."

The urge to cry swells up in me, rising in my throat. "No, I haven't. I've got something to tell you, Adam. I should've told you a long time ago. But I've hardly told anyone. I've not been honest with you about the person I am. Why I *couldn't* marry you. And why you really wouldn't want to anyway."

He frowns, clearly lost. "*Is* there someone else? I know you said it wasn't Charlie, but is there another man?"

I shake my head, wishing that it were that simple. That all I had to worry about were the small distractions of romance and relationships that concern everyone else.

I pull the sheet over my chest and sit up, running my hands through my hair.

I'm not going to start crying.

I'm not.

"This isn't just about you and me, Adam. This is about you, me, everything."

"What do you mean?"

"The thing that Mum has is called Huntington's disease."

He narrows his eyes, trying to work out why I'm bringing this up now.

"It's a brain condition that affects her nerves and is fatal. There's no cure, and there's no way of even slowing it down."

"I've heard of it. I don't know much about it, but it rings a bell."

"Okay." I take a breath that's supposed to be fortifying but isn't. "Well, the thing about it is . . . it's not just what it's done to my mum, turned her into this wreck of a human being who can't think straight and can't eat properly or talk or . . ." I glance up, trying to find the courage to say the words that have haunted me for so long.

"It's an inherited condition. And I carry the faulty gene that causes it too." I grind my teeth together, buying myself a moment before I have to carry on. "Which means I am going to be exactly like Mum, Adam. It is going to do terrible things to me, physically and mentally. And then it's going to kill me."

I wonder for a moment if the calm understatement with which I've told him has meant he's failed to grasp what I'm saying. He simply looks at me, or looks through me, trying to comprehend what I've said.

"And as I have the mutant gene, there's a 50 percent chance William will as well."

I sit back and let Adam take everything in, watching as the lower half of his face softens until his lips part. The look in his eyes goes beyond shock. It's not yet anger, or fear, or pity, but there's a whisper of all those things. It's disbelief so smothering that he's yet to let out a breath.

"There's a test you can have to find out if you're going to develop it," I continue. "I took it, so that's how I know I'm going to get it. William isn't eligible for it until he's eighteen."

"But it might be wrong, surely?"

"It's not wrong, Adam. The test is definitive. I am going to get Huntington's disease. I can't escape it."

His head is clearly ablaze with questions, but he starts with one. "So . . . are you sick — now, I mean?"

"No. My consultant says I have no symptoms, although I've learned from experience that you can convince yourself they're there if you look hard enough. Every time I trip over something, I think there's a problem with my coordination. Every time I forget a shopping list, or get annoyed with someone, I think, *This is it.* But my doctor says it's just anxiety."

"Okay." I can see how his mind is working as he thinks about how to respond. I was just the same when Mum told me about hers. He wants to come up with a solution. He will quickly recognize that this particular problem is unsolvable.

"You say there's no cure, but are they working on one? Medical advances are happening all the time, so surely you might never get to the stage your mum's at?"

It's the single hope I cling to, one I read about constantly. But the science that might one day end all this remains elusive. "It's possible. There's work being done all over the world. I read about breakthroughs all the time."

Still, I realize I can't leave him on this hopeful note. "At the moment though, Adam, there isn't even a drug out there that can slow it down. Only drugs that can manage the *symptoms.* Not the disease itself."

There will be dozens of questions, I know, but for the moment, the only thing left in

Adam's eyes is a desire to comfort me, to touch me and hug me, to make it all as much better as he can. But now is the time to be straight with him about everything. "This was why we came here, Adam."

"What do you mean?"

"My mum has always wanted you and William to have more of a relationship, but when I tested positive a few months ago, it became a practical matter, as well as an emotional one."

He swallows silently.

"My mum's symptoms started only a few years from the age I am now, Adam. And, although this is a long disease — it lasts ten, sometimes twenty years — there will inevitably be a stage when I can't be the parent I want to be to William."

It's at this point that the tears start coming for the first time, making the rims of my eyes hot, stinging my skin. "And if that happens, he will need you."

To my endless relief, Adam doesn't cry. His face is simply gaunt with devastation. Then he takes my hand and gently rubs his fingers back and forth over my knuckles. "He's got me, Jess. I promise. Whatever happens, he's got me."

CHAPTER 75

I've spent so long thinking about how I'd tell Adam about the HD that now it's happened, I almost don't know what to do with myself.

Still, I feel lighter on my feet in our final few days in France, as if the burden of my secret is no longer making me stagger under its weight. I can finally get on with injecting a sliver of certainty into my uncertain future.

It helps that he's forgiven me for not being open about it until now, and that I finally know the truth about what happened on the night of William's birth. But most of all, it helps that we both understand the need to be grown-up about what happened this summer. Between the two of us, I mean.

The knowledge that it can't continue won't stop me reliving every sweet bit of it. The way my skin tingled when I watched him laugh. The way I felt on fire from his touch. The way he did beautiful, bittersweet things to me and, for the first time in as long as I can remember, made me stop thinking of my body as my enemy.

But the fairy tale stops there. It has become one more thing that HD has taken from me. Adam and I cannot be together, and any ideas that we can have been stopped dead in their tracks. Because there is quite simply no happy ending that involves *both* of us.

Not one where Adam and I grow old together, salsa dancing our way into our nineties and going on the kind of world cruises where they have onboard yoga teachers.

I fell in love with Adam again this summer. And it must have been real love, because what I feel for him is also unselfish enough to want him to still have all those things with someone. Not Simone — I wouldn't go that far — but *someone.*

I still smile every time I think about his proposal though.

It reminded me of everything that's good about Adam. It was funny and unorthodox, sweet and passionate. All of which was possible before bitter reality set in.

In Adam's case, that reality is still setting in. Sometimes I catch him looking into space, tormented as to how all of this happened. It's as if he's spent the last few weeks hurtling towards something bigger and better in life, only for all of that to disappear overnight.

Still, the way we withdraw from each other is quietly decisive.

The kissing is over. The flirting is over. The double-orgasm sex is over.

The summer of second chances is drawing to a close in the best way someone with my future could expect, knowing that, whatever happens to me, William will be loved and protected by his father. He's a better man than I ever gave him credit for.

I am optimistic that Adam and I will end up being something wondrous: parents who are also friends. I think we could be bloody good at that, a winning team, until I can't win any longer.

When that point comes, I at least have this: I know William will be looked after. Not just when he's little, but beyond that. And although Adam's advice to our grown son may not ever be the same as mine would've been, I know he's in the hands of a man who loves him and will do his best. No parent is perfect. Mine weren't, and I'm not.

But if a father loves his child with every

bit of himself, that's all anyone can ask.

Of course, there are dozens of practicalities to discuss, which we do repeatedly over coffee, but I know we'll get there. We discuss Adam moving back to Manchester in October and him looking to rent somewhere in Castlefield initially, not far from us. We discuss William staying overnight at his place on Wednesdays and Saturdays, an arrangement that both of us are happy can be flexible. We decide Adam's welcome to pop over for a cup of tea sometimes, and we have an open invitation to Sunday lunch every week at his place.

He keeps saying things like, "I'm looking forward to it, Jess. Life's going to be good," and it comes out with such conviction that I believe him. Almost.

Whatever happens, I can't wait to get home. I've been away from Mum too long, and suddenly, all I can think about is returning to her. Natasha, however, does not seem to share my enthusiasm for our imminent departure.

"I thought you'd be looking forward to getting back to work." To anyone else, this would sound sarcastic, but I actually mean it with her.

"Well, I am, but . . ." I wait for her to finish, but she squirms, embarrassed to be confessing something. "I really like Ben."

"I'm not surprised; he's gorgeous."

"Yes, but you're not meant to get over-emotional about holiday romances at my age. The last time I did that I was fourteen years old."

"Have you two talked about keeping in touch?"

"We've deliberately avoided the issue, though we did become Facebook friends. All that seemed to do was expose the massive age gap."

"Nobody would flinch at nine years if it were the other way round," I argue. "Besides, you don't look like you're in your late thirties."

"Thanks, Jess. It's all down to yoga."

"Really?"

"Well, that and the Botox."

CHAPTER 76

Natasha, William and I head to the games area to meet up with the others and watch the kids play soccer. The sun is setting on the sandy pitch as we find a spot that's a safe distance from stray balls. Natasha pulls up a chair and sits down, stretching out her legs under a pair of pale shorts, her slim, bronzed feet peeping out from leather sandals.

I notice quickly that William is hanging round at the side of the pitch, looking shifty as their numbers swell.

"Come on, you lot. It's like herding cats!" Becky and her clan emerge from the woodland in the same way they always do when they travel as a group: loudly, haphazardly — with one child ahead and a couple behind as both parents attempt to keep them moving vaguely in the same direction. Poppy spots us and, with a surge of energy, runs into my arms and plops onto my knee.

William taps me on the shoulder. "I might go for a swim instead."

I groan. "We've walked all the way over here now, and you've left your swimming kit back at the cottage."

"Okay, then I might just have a go of my iPad and —"

"But James and Rufus have come to play too. You're not going to sit here with your . . . *my* iPad for the next hour."

He starts chewing his lip as James appears next to him. "I don't want to play soccer either."

The penny drops. "Is it those mean boys again? I can come over and say something to them if you'd like."

"NO!" they reply, so appalled you'd think I'd threatened to distract them by streaking across the pitch. They reluctantly slink off towards the other kids, muttering that they can handle it, before joining in the game. The rest of us edge forward to make our imposing presence clear by fixing our stern-est parental gaze on them.

"Not with Ben today?" Becky asks Natasha.

"Not until after he's finished work. Then he's decided he wants to cook for me, so we're —"

A huge cheer erupts, and when I look at

the pitch, William is running round, his arms aloft in the kind of Messiah pose you might reserve for scoring at the last minute in a World Cup final.

"What a brilliant goal!" Seb grins.

I stand up and glare over, wishing I had a rewind button. "Was that *William*?"

He chuckles. "Don't tell me you missed it."

"Did you *see* that, Mum?" My son's face is a vision of unmitigated happiness.

I leap to my feet, clapping my hands so hard my palms sting. "AMAZING, son. Brilliant!"

Then I sink back into my seat as Becky smirks at me. "Never apply for Equity membership with acting skills like that."

"Don't say that. I might get away with it," I reply from the side of my mouth.

"What on earth's going on now?" My eyes dart to the pitch in case I miss another miraculous example of sporting excellence from my son. Only her focus is not on William. It's on one of the bigger boys, who appears to be saying something to James that's upsetting him.

"Oh God . . . I wonder if that's the kid who was being horrible to them the other day? I thought it'd all blown over."

"It doesn't look that way." Fury simmers

in Becky as she rises to her feet. But she can't get there quick enough. Before she's even close, someone else has stepped in.

"DON'T BE MEAN TO MY BROTHER OR ELSE." Rufus's threat might be fairly nonspecific, but what it lacks in definition it makes up in force. Which is nearly coming out of his ears. Unfortunately, Rufus is about a foot shorter and two stones lighter than his adversary.

He responds by pushing Rufus in the chest with both hands, so hard that he stumbles back and ends up thumping on the ground on his bum.

"RUFUS!" Becky shouts.

But Rufus is quickly back on his feet, retaliating with a swipe to the kid's stomach that makes his eyes bulge.

"Arrgh, don't fight! This isn't the Wild West!" Becky shrieks, and she tears Rufus back as the boy hobbles off and runs away. She grabs her son by the hand and marches him back to us.

"What on *earth* was that?" Becky asks him.

"They were being nasty to James, and I told them to shut up."

James appears beside us, nodding breath-lessly. "He did, Mum. He was just sticking up for me. Don't tell him off."

Becky glances between the two of them.

"Look, Rufus, well done for defending your brother. But next time, don't hit, okay?"

Then they both run off to reclaim the soccer pitch as Becky returns to Seb. "It's at times like this I think our kids might actually turn out okay."

"Course they will. Remember that when they start fighting again in ten minutes though."

She slides her hand into his, lifting it to kiss the skin on his knuckles.

He glances at her. "What was that for?"

"Just blotting my lipstick."

"You're not wearing any."

She looks up at him and smiles. "Must be because I love you then."

CHAPTER 77

On our second-to-last evening in France, William kicks his feet along the dusty road next to his father, as we approach a vineyard covered in plump purple grapes.

"Did you know that if you ate the liver of a polar bear you would die of a vitamin A overdose?" William says.

"Everybody knows that." Adam smirks.

William's mouth opens.

"I'm kidding. What other facts do you know?"

"Hmm. I know where snot comes from."

I groan.

"Okay, what facts do *you* know?" William grins at me.

The sky has delivered a luminescent curtain call tonight, the horizon bathed in pink and orange swirls of light, with whispers of white in between. "Shakespeare's parents were illiterate," I tell him. "Caracas is the capital of Venezuela. Um . . . and I know how to do a split."

"Go on then," William suggests.

"I don't think so. We're here now, and I don't want to put anyone off their starters."

We arrive on the edge of the tiny hamlet and follow Adam to the bistro. He's booked a table outside that overlooks a stony court-yard flanked by a Byzantine church and pretty houses overflowing with honeysuckle. The restaurant is busy already. Adam pulls out the chair for me, and I edge into the seat.

"Why did you do that?" William asks.

"That's what you're meant to do for a lady," Adam replies.

William looks momentarily perplexed, as if it'd never occurred to him that I might be one of those. A waiter comes and takes our wine and food order from the menu, before inquiring if we'd like anything else.

"Je voudrais L'EAU, s'il vous plaît."

He nods and writes it down on his note-pad, just like that, as I look at Adam in amazement. "I can leave a happy woman now."

"You're almost fluent."

William excuses himself to go to the toilet, and I'm left temporarily alone in Adam's presence. I feel awkward, as though we're faltering for conversation, unsure of what to say. Partly because we've only got a minute until William returns, partly because neither of us wants to discuss anything too difficult right now. Both of us have had enough with *difficult.*

"Well, Natasha's certainly going to miss it around here when she leaves," I say.

"It takes everyone a while to reacclimatize to the British weather and food —"

"And in Natasha's case, Ben," I add.

His eyes crease at the sides as he smiles, slightly more than they used to. "I'm sure he'll show her a good time back in London."

"What do you mean?"

"I assume they're going to see each other back home?" he asks.

"But Ben's staying here."

"His contract runs out in October, so he's going home to try and get a proper job," Adam says.

I frown. "I don't think he's mentioned this to Natasha."

"Strange. Maybe he's gone cool on her. It does happen, even to the best."

When William appears again and sits down, Adam nudges him in the side, ruffling his hair as his son ducks away, giggling. "I'm going to miss you, you know."

William looks up anxiously. "You *are* still moving to Manchester, aren't you?"

"Yep. I'll be home in three months, then there'll be no stopping me. You'll be fed up with me by Christmas."

"Does that mean you can spend Christmas with us?"

We'd never got this far in the practicalities discussion. "We'll talk about that closer to the time, eh?" Adam says.

"But I'm sure we'll do something together," I reassure him. "And with Grandma and Granddad too, of course."

He looks down at the tablecloth. "Will Grandma still be alive by then?"

The question makes the hairs on the back of my neck prickle. "Of course she will. Grandma's sick, but she's not going to be . . . going anywhere by Christmas." I finish the sentence with a half laugh as if the very thought is preposterous.

"Okay," he says quietly. "But the thing she's got *will* kill her, won't it?"

"I hope that Grandma will be with us for a good while," I tell him lamely.

He doesn't answer at first. "It's Huntings disease, isn't it? That's what Grandma's got." He looks at me starkly, his eyes blinking as he waits for an answer, and my heart starts thumping through my chest.

"Huntington's," I correct him numbly. "How did you know that?"

470

"It was on your search history on the iPad. I know that's why you've been so upset lately. I Googled it."

I feel the color drain from my face. This was exactly what I feared, but I'd convinced myself I'd got away with it and he was still none the wiser. I can't actually believe that after all the heinous stuff I've worried about him seeing on the Internet over the years, the worst thing he's found was probably on the *New Scientist* website.

Adam looks as unprepared for this conversation as I am. And at least he's got an excuse: he only found out about it this week. I've had ten years to prepare a speech for William and have completely failed to do so.

"Have you got it too, Mum?"

My mouth goes numb as I try to form the words. "I haven't got it, sweetheart, no. At the moment, I'm completely fine."

"Okay."

"But . . . I have got the faulty gene that causes it," I add. "So one day, yes, I will have it."

I scan his face for every nuance of his reaction. "I might have it too, mightn't I?"

I swallow, trying to force my mouth to start working again properly. "The faulty gene? Yes, you might. But you might not.

471

And even if you do, the likelihood is that you wouldn't develop HD for many, many years."

"I know. The average age is, like, forty. *Really* old." I chew the side of my mouth as he continues. "I don't think I've got it anyway."

I nod, feeling tears prick at the back of my eyes. "Why's that?"

He shrugs. "Optimism."

My chest tightens, but I refuse to let the tears out. I refuse to do anything but hold myself together. *Keep the floodgates shut, Jess. Don't let them open.*

"I *really* don't think you need to worry, Mum," William continues, so brightly that I'm not sure I can bear to look at his shining eyes and the soft, young skin on his cheeks. "Scientists are working on a cure. They're bound to find something soon. There's been research in San Diego and in London where they've tested drugs on mice. That must really suck if you're a mouse, obviously. But in some cases they've made the sick animals better. So if that ends up working in humans too, it'll be worth it." I'm unable to release the air from my lungs, so I just nod. "I might become a scientist when I'm older so I can find a cure for it, if they haven't already."

472

"That would be great, William."

"I might still want to be a model though," he adds, as if to say, *So don't get your hopes up.*

Adam catches my eye.

"I'm not scared, Mum," William continues. I don't know if he instinctively knows what I need to hear, but he does.

"Good. I'm not either," I reply, so forcefully that for the small moment before the waiter appears with our meals, I actually believe it. "But what I am is absolutely starving."

I pick up my knife and fork and start cutting into my duck breast, concentrating on the contents of my plate, rather than Adam. I know he's silently imploding as he listens to this, his son and me, discussing our curse in the starkest terms. My fate is already sealed. Between us, we can only pray it's kinder to William.

"Anyway, Dad," he continues. "You didn't tell us what facts you know."

Adam snaps out of his trance. "Oh. Oh yeah, you're right. Okay." He thinks for a moment. "I know that the line 'I have a bad feeling about this' is said in every *Star Wars* movie."

William looks impressed. "I know that puffins mate for life." He scrunches up his

473

nose, now less impressed.

"And I know . . ." Adam falters, then looks up at me. "I know that you and your mum are the two best people in the world."

CHAPTER 78

"MUMUMMMMMYMMUMMY!"

I step outside the cottage to see Becky hobbling towards us, Poppy clutching her leg and sobbing. Eventually, Becky pauses and picks her up to carry her, wrapping her daughter's little legs round her waist.

"It's Pink Bunny," Becky explains, kissing Poppy on the forehead but entirely failing to quell her distress. "I was starting to actually feel relaxed on this holiday, but losing Pink Bunny is a catastrophe I hadn't prepared for. Did we leave it here?"

"I don't think so," I say sympathetically, which prompts Poppy to start wailing. Becky sits her down on a chair, before marching round the side of the cottage, then back again. She looks under the bench, inside the door, under the cushions of our sofa, then back outside behind the door.

"Somebody looking for this?" Natasha appears at the threshold, holding Poppy's beloved toy.

"BUNNY!" Poppy scrambles off the chair and dives towards her.

"You left her at the table over breakfast. I was going to bring her over to you."

Tension visibly drains away from Becky, and she wipes her forehead with the back of her hand. "I'm *forever* indebted."

"No problem. She was just on a little holiday, wasn't she, Poppy?"

"You're a good girl, Aunty Natasha," Poppy declares, and Natasha looks surprisingly chuffed with this praise.

"Hi, everyone."

We look up as Ben crunches across the courtyard, sun glistening in his salty hair, the smell of citrus clinging to him as he approaches. "I wondered if you fancied a walk, Natasha?"

"That'd be lovely." She smiles.

Natasha and Ben head towards the woodland looking like two shy teenagers as Becky's eyes follow. "It's a shame those two are a nonstarter."

"Hmm. He's apparently moving back to London but didn't tell her."

"Really?" She looks as surprised as I was.

I nod. "I can't really work that one out, can you? I kept thinking about it after I found out."

I glance at the table and realize a text has arrived on my phone.

"Oh God," I groan, opening it up. "It's from Charlie."

"What does it say?" Becky asks.

I scan the words and smile as I hand it over to show her.

Sorry I didn't say good-bye, but we made an impromptu decision to go and stay with friends in Carcassonne for a few days before heading home. I enjoyed meeting you, Jess. Enjoy the rest of your stay, Charlie x (p.s. I've ditched my cardigan!)

She passes it back to me, her hand over her mouth, while I simply cringe.

Later that evening, William skips ahead as Natasha and I walk through the woods towards Becky and Seb's place. He's carrying a large bag of sweets, while I have a bottle of champagne I picked up earlier in the supermarket. I've even dressed up slightly for our final night, but only because Natasha spotted my pretty yellow dress on top of my luggage and insisted I wear it.

Since then, she hasn't stopped talking.

"Ben had been worried about telling me he's moving to London," she beams, unable to hide her delight. "He'd been avoiding the issue because he was actually concerned that I'd think he was some kind of stalker, that I'd think he'd decided to follow me after our fling."

"From what Adam says, he'd always been planning to move there after the end of the season. I take it you've arranged to get together when you get back?"

"We're meeting for a drink, yes." A quiet smile spreads across her face. "Oh, I still think he's too young —"

"But you like him, and he likes you."

"Well, yes," she says tentatively.

"Natasha, I know you're looking for Habitat Crockery Man, but you and Ben have chemistry, age gap or not. And you never know . . . maybe one day you *will* be buying plates together."

"One step at a time, Jess."

I suppress a smile. "I'm sure that's meant to be my line."

We're having a barbecue for our final evening. It feels like a fitting end to the summer, a low-key dinner, like so many of those we've had for the last few weeks. One in which the kids play Frisbee, the adults play cards and we can all relax in the company of good friends. Friends who are loyal, funny, who might squabble, but whom I love regardless.

We arrive to find the air filled with the smoky scent of the barbecue, its glowing embers radiating heat onto Seb's face as he chats with Ben.

"Oh damn, I forgot the sausages," I realize, slapping my forehead.

Becky grabs me by the arm before I can turn back. "You don't need sausages."

"But they're *artisan*," I protest.

"It doesn't matter."

"It does — they cost a bomb. I'm convinced they're from the most privileged pigs in France."

Natasha scoops her arm through my elbow. "You don't need sausages, or supermarket champagne, or anything else. Not where you're going."

"What do you mean?" I frown.

"You're leaving," she replies.

"I'm not."

"I'm afraid you are."

Then suddenly Adam is in front of me, car keys in his hand. He is dressed in a black shirt, top button open, with slim charcoal trousers that sit low on his hips, his hair still slightly tousled from the shower. He's the kind of handsome that makes your breath hover in your throat.

"What is going on? Is this some sort of a

479

conspiracy?"

"Yes!" William exclaims, and I realize I really don't stand a chance.

As I sit in the passenger seat of Adam's car, I'm not really contemplating where we're going or why. I can only think about how he'll always have the ability to dazzle me, surprise me, set my heart alight.

"I give in: where are you taking me?"

He glances across. "We're going caving."

"I hope you are sodding joking," I reply.

His face breaks into a luminescent smile. "I *am* sodding joking."

I laugh. "Good."

As Adam's car sweeps through the countryside, I turn off the air-conditioning and open the window, closing my eyes as the breeze caresses my skin.

"You okay?" Adam asks. He goes to touch my hand, then stops and withdraws.

"I'm fine. Thank you."

"We're here now," he replies, as he turns the car down a sweeping driveway.

CHAPTER 79

A neat signpost reading "Château La Pra-
doux" greets us, along with the voluptuous
scent of thyme and wisteria.

We creep along the graveled drive towards
two high iron gates, as a rosy sky glows
through their swirling filigree patterns.
Beyond them, the château rises from the
green hills, perched high upon a smooth
terraced lawn.

Adam steps out of the car to open the
door for me and walks round as I'm fum-
bling with my handbag. "Isn't this place
your competition?" I ask.

"More like our inspiration. Though there
are no kids here, and they've got a Michelin
star. As good as Ben's burgers are when he's
on barbecue duty, I think we're some way
from that."

"So why are we here?"

"I thought it'd be good to talk about stuff.
There's obviously a lot to discuss, and —"

"Adam, let's not. I don't want to talk about that anymore."

His shoulders relax. "Good, because I was lying. I just wanted an amazing dinner on our final evening. And I've heard they do a mean lamb shank."

He offers me his arm. I link it, smiling to myself at the thought that we look straight out of *Downton Abbey.*

A waiter greets Adam by name and shows us inside. Every element of the Renaissance architecture has been masterfully and lavishly preserved. We step across a polished floor, through a sumptuous reception room with tall crystal vases of blousy peonies and blossoming lilies. We're led up a stone staircase towards a restaurant that is candlelit and quiet, with only a smattering of diners. When we reach the door to the terrace, Adam takes me by the hand, threading his fingers through mine.

We're shown to a table on the edge of the terrace, overlooking the clipped gardens and rambling vines, the perfect spot to watch the sun sinking beneath the hills.

"I've got to hand it to you, Adam: you know all the best places."

He allows a flicker of a smile as the waiter reappears with a wine list. I watch as Adam scans it, his eyes intense as they read downwards, then he catches me looking at him. The corner of his mouth turns up, and I glance away.

The prices on the menu are notable for their absence, a sure sign that this is the stuff of a second mortgage. Adam translates, and I'm happy to let him order as the light in the sky starts to fade to a blackberry hue.

"You look absolutely beautiful," Adam says, taking me by surprise. "Sorry. I had to let you know."

I take a sip of wine to hide the warmth in my cheeks and remind myself to thank Natasha for insisting on the yellow dress later.

The food is sublime, and although we don't drink a lot, I feel drunk on the night — on the surroundings, the reminiscing, being here with him. And the strange and lovely feeling of security; the certain knowledge that I can rely on this man when it comes to William.

And we have some serious laughs. About the neighbor who lived below us in Manchester who used to dry his underpants out of the bedroom window. About the time we came in from a night out and he — romantically — tried to carry me up the stairs but banged my head on the ceiling and nearly gave me a concussion.

"Do you remember the first time I told

you I loved you?" he asks.

I stiffen at the question, reminding me that we were once so much more than we can be now. "It was after Patrick Goldsmith's party," he says, as I twist the napkin under the table.

"Yeah, I remember."

"We'd got caught in the rain on the way home and had to make a run for it. By the time we got back you had mascara down to your chin, your hair was plastered on your face and your nose was blue."

"I'm glad you remember all the best details."

He laughs. "I do. Because I remember still thinking you were gorgeous. And I just had to say it. That I loved you."

I squirm. "You don't need to remind me of that, Adam. I'll be okay, you know. I'll cope with all this," I tell him, because if I say it enough, perhaps I'll eventually believe it.

"I know that. That wasn't what I was talking about."

I swallow. "What were you talking about?"

He inhales and then starts talking. "When I knelt, semi-naked on the bed, and asked you to marry me —"

"You were *naked*," I correct him. "Not semi-naked. *Naked*."

"Whatever. It was a crap proposal. I knew even as I was saying it that you deserved better. I had to tell you how I felt. And the point I'm trying to make is this: the fact that you'll one day have Huntington's disease doesn't change anything."

My chest tightens.

"Not a single thing," he continues. "I'd love you if you lived a long and healthy life or a shorter, more challenging one. You're still going to be the same woman I fell for years ago."

My head rushes with blood until I realize that Adam is speaking and all of a sudden he's on one knee and the bloke behind us has almost choked on his *filet de rouget.*

"Jess. Will you marry me?"

I cannot speak.

"Oh. Forgot something," he continues, reaching into his pocket, pulling out his hand, then starting to pat both sides down as a look of panic engulfs him. The couple on the next table is enraptured. Even the pianist is faltering, missing the odd key.

"Oh my God, I've lost it!" he mutters.

Then he pauses as if he's remembered something and reaches into the top pocket of his shirt. I can feel my heart thrumming against my breastbone. "I put it there so I wouldn't forget where it was."

"That worked."

I'm quipping because I can't think of any words. Real words. Only he holds it out: a diamond ring, radiant in the candlelight. It's gorgeous. I try not to look at it too much, because I know I can't let myself get swept along with all this because of *the ring* . . . But for the record, it's incredible. I'm not talking big, or flashy, just beautiful — platinum, I think, with a single diamond cut into the shape of an almond.

But this is not about the ring. It's not about the tremble in his hand and the luster on his inky brown eyes. It's not even about the fact that I want to say yes. It's about something bigger.

"Adam . . . we can't do this," I say.

Both of us become uncomfortably aware that the whole restaurant is looking. "Why don't you get up?"

He glances around self-consciously and edges back into his seat.

He looks mortified.

I hate myself for that, but I also know I've got no choice.

CHAPTER 80

"Adam, you don't realize what you're asking."

He waits for me to elaborate.

"If you'd seen the state my mum was in these days, you couldn't possibly sit here . . . kneel here . . . and ask me to marry you." I feel my teeth clenching hard, before I find the strength to continue. "She can't speak properly, Adam. She can't walk, she can't eat, she can't go to the toilet anymore. She can't even sit most of the time — she's mainly in bed these days. And my poor dad has to watch this, powerless to do anything to stop her deterioration. Being unable to live the life either of them imagined for themselves."

He looks down at a napkin, twisting it around his fingers before he answers. "Tell me this, Jess: why do you think your dad is still around?"

"What do you mean? Why hasn't he left

my mum, you mean?"

"Yeah. Because some relationships wouldn't survive it, would they?"

I don't answer him. I've never even thought about it before; I've just assumed my dad would always be there. "Do you think it's because he feels sorry for her?" I wince at the idea. "Or because he feels it's his duty? Or is it for *your* sake — because you'd be upset if they split up?"

My face starts tingling with rising tears. "Probably all of those things."

"Bullshit, Jess. He's there every day, by her side, *because he loves her.*"

I swallow silently.

"He might hate the disease. He might hate what it's done to her. But he loves your mum. To him, she's worth everything he's going through. And I happen to feel the same about you."

My hands are trembling as I touch the edge of the tablecloth.

"Jess, listen to me. I've spent every spare minute since you told me reading about it, watching videos of people who have it, including the ones in the very late stages. I've read the reports, the Huntington's Disease Association guidelines, the blogs and forums. I know *exactly* what it does to people. I didn't ask you to marry me without knowing." He pauses before continuing. "And here's the thing, Jess: I realize things are going to be very, very difficult for you. For us. But you're not there yet. You're nowhere near there. You're healthy. Right at this moment, as you sit here in this restaurant looking like the most beautiful woman I have ever set eyes on, *you don't have Huntington's disease.* So you need to stop worrying about your future and *live.* Preferably with me as your husband."

I shake my head, sniffing back tears as I manage to meet his eyes. "But Adam . . . how could anyone want this?"

"I'm not anyone."

"No, I know, but —"

"When you get married, it's meant to be in sickness and in health. Most people never have to think about that bit at the beginning, but I have. A lot. And *I'm in.*"

I'm faltering, stumbling over what to say. Until a smile creeps to my face, and I realize I don't really need to say anything.

"Well, now we've established that — and the pianist has started up again — I'm going to try for a second time," he says.

I let out a spurt of laughter and wipe away my tears.

He lifts up the ring and holds it up, sparkling under the lights. "You're not going to make me get down on one knee again, are you? I mean, once in one evening is acceptable; twice just looks desperate."

I laugh. "No, don't."

He falters. "Okay. I won't embarrass you. But I *will* ask you again, Jess. Will you marry me?"

I stop smiling and look into the eyes of the only man I've ever loved.

We were never perfect, but we were made for each other. It's taken ten years, a baby, a terminal illness and a roller coaster of emotion in between to work that out.

So I suppose there's only one answer.

"Okay, Adam."

He frowns. "Is that a yes?"

"Yes. Yes, it's a yes."

His face breaks into a greedy grin. "Christ, that was hard work," he says as he leaps across the table to fling his arms around me and the guy with the *filet de rouget* bursts into rapturous applause.

CHAPTER 81

I drift in and out of sleep in Adam's arms that night, stirring only to feel the gentle rise and fall of his chest underneath my fingers. A high moon shimmers through the gap in the shutters, casting mysterious shadows across the room.

I can't sleep because I'm high on excitement, on whatever unexpected and glorious thing it is fizzing inside me. For the first time in years, I'm thinking about the future with optimism and an almost supernatural certainty that everything's going to be okay, no matter what life throws at me.

A smile creeps to my lips as Adam sleepily pulls me closer into him and, almost unconsciously, leans in to kiss me, pressing his mouth against mine, his eyes still closed.

"You're awake," I whisper.

"Only just. What time is it?"

"Oh, I don't know . . . six o'clock or something."

His hand travels down the skin on my back, and I press myself against him, brushing my lips across the rough part of his chin. Then my phone starts to ring.

It takes a second for me to register it, and we both freeze at the same time. I scramble away from Adam, out of bed and across the room to the phone I'd left on top of my bag underneath the window. I fumble with it, my fingers not functioning as fast as I need them to, before I finally hit the answer button.

"Dad?" I say urgently.

When my father speaks, it's very clear from the tremble in his voice that this is the call I've been dreading for the last ten years.

"Jess. I'm phoning about your mum."

CHAPTER 82

I barely remember the clamor to return home. All I know is that I managed to catch a flight later that day, alone, leaving William and everyone else in France, along with my car and most of my worldly belongings.

I do remember looking bleakly out of the window onto the tops of the clouds and thinking how peaceful and blue and perfect it all looked up there, knowing that as soon as the plane dipped below them, I'd be plunged back into a world that was far darker.

Five days later, the "when, not if" that Dad and I have talked about over the last ten years is imminent. And it's only now that I realize how unprepared for it I was. I don't think anything could've prepared me for this.

My mum is dying a wretched, ugly death, one it feels impossible to believe is really happening. The choking that had worsened in the last few months was what finally did this to her.

The doctors think that she inhaled some food, and it went on to cause the pneumonia that her body was already too weak to fight. Since then, she's been pumped full of antibiotics, but her lungs are so ravaged, so tired, that they stand no chance.

It's not that people aren't trying to make it better, because they are. Everyone's doing their best. But their best isn't helping. And the sight of my mum right now is one that will haunt me forever. Even when she's sedated, she never looks comfortable. She looks tortured.

Dad and I have taken turns by her bedside, stroking her knuckles, watching as she moves underneath her thin cotton nightie, her skin draped across her bones.

My father's heart is being slowly crushed with every cry that escapes her lips. And I am so overwhelmed by the sheer awfulness of this that on some days it takes all my might to look out of the window and not despise every last person going about his business. I've cried so much in the last few days that the skin on my cheeks is raw.

Adam drove William to Manchester in my car shortly after I left, and is currently staying at our house with him. My son keeps saying he wants to see his grandma, but I haven't let him. I blamed the medical team, saying they wouldn't allow it. I might have promised him honesty while we were in France, but absolutely no good could come out of him witnessing this: his grandma slowly being suffocated by her own body.

"You should go home and get some sleep, love," Dad says to me for the fourth time today.

But the decision to go always involves a gamble. I want to be here when she dies. I'd thought it was going to happen days ago, when she was still trying to communicate as best she could.

I've repeatedly braced myself that *this is it,* convinced that someone couldn't possibly keep fighting when her body was in this state.

Yet here she is, clutching onto life. Part of me hates myself for wishing it were over. But she no longer looks like my mum, or smells like my mum, or sounds like her.

"I will soon, Dad."

But I don't move. Instead, I allow my eyes to drift across the room, to the windowsill, the pictures Dad had brought from the care home, small trinkets for her to focus on, in the days when she could focus on anything.

There's one of their wedding day, a balmy

September Saturday that they both always said must've been the hottest day of the year. At nineteen, Mum was an impossibly young-looking bride. Her dress was high necked, with lace that caressed the length of her arms, and she wore a hat — a jaunty, wide-brimmed kind of thing, with a veil that went right down her back.

I was tickled by that hat when I was a little girl; I used to try it on and dance in front of her bedroom mirror, swirling the tulle around me like a gymnast. My mother's radiance shines through in the picture, my dad looking dapper, beaming like the cat that got the cream, as they stood side by side ready to embark on their adventure together.

There are five or six other framed pictures, of people, places and — in the case of our old dog, Lady — animals she loved. The one that catches my eye is the photo of the two of us together, on my sixth birthday, standing behind the fairy-tale castle cake she'd made.

People always said we looked alike, but it's in that photo that it's most striking. I've got the same full mouth, pale coloring, smattering of freckles across the nose. My only hope is that, when it's my turn, I will have the same amount of fight.

The most recent addition is one I had printed in a little booth in the supermarket when I went to buy Dad and me some sandwiches a couple of days ago. It's the picture I took on my phone, of Adam and William laughing by the lake that day. I don't know if she ever registered it, but I hope so. That and the engagement ring I showed her and Dad, as he clutched her hand and smiled for the one and only time since I've been home.

For no other reason than to stretch my legs, I decide to stand and fix the curtain that's been crumpled in one corner since the nurse opened it this morning. I brush against Mum's hand as I stand up and re-alize it feels cold.

My heart starts racing, and I panic that it's already happened. Then a sound escapes from the back of her throat.

"Jess," Dad whispers, but his eyes aren't on me; they are fixed on the face of a woman he's loved for his entire adult life. He clutches her as she rasps intermittently, her breathing becoming quiet, before it starts again. I am rooted to the seat, until the stop-start of her lungs changes.

When life leaves my mum's body, it is quicker than I'd imagined.

The expression on her face softens. There

are no more movements, no more twitching, no more of the sounds or grunts we'd all become used to. And, between our tears and shock and overwhelming sadness, the room is filled with something that comes before grief.

The room is filled with peace.

CHAPTER 83

Twelve months later,
summer 2017

Adam turns the ignition on the VW camper van, and as it springs to life, William and I let out a cheer. I'd never seen the appeal before, but having bought this one last year and spending the next three months doing it up on weekends with William, Adam is completely smitten. I've never seen him so happy as when he slips into that driver's seat — you'd think he was in a Lamborghini.

It's sage green and white on the outside, with a retro interior that features leather seats, new Shaker cupboards and gingham curtains tied back with yellow ribbons. We've called her Lisa, after Adam's mum, and his favorite photograph of the two of them, in front of their own camper van all those years ago, is pinned on the sunshade at the front.

Of course, the problem with driving something built in 1962 is that it's not hugely compatible with hilly terrain, particularly if you're hoping to travel faster than the average lawn mower. This meant that our drive all the way from Manchester across the French countryside took longer than we'd imagined — and that's saying something given how pessimistic I was.

Still, eventually, we near our destination, even if my heart has almost stopped every time we've had to negotiate some of these treacherous mountain roads.

"Why do you look so nervous, Mum?" William asks.

"Oh, I don't know — something to do with the cliff below, perhaps?"

"That's a *hill.*" Adam smirks and puts the van into second gear.

"If you say so," I reply, distinctly relieved as the road widens and we pull up to the spot where we've arranged to meet Enzo, the guide who took us canyoning last summer.

As I step out of the car and look out across the sweeping valley, I'm reminded of the singular but monumental lesson I've learned in the past year.

Everyone's future is uncertain.

500

Most of us don't think about the fact that we could be run over by a bus tomorrow. We plod through life, taking everything for granted.

I, on the other hand, take nothing for granted. Not a single thing. I savor every kiss from my son, every bite of chocolate, every leaf that falls from an autumn tree and every burst of laughter with my friends.

I have a good life.

An amazing life.

I no longer walk through it terrified about the future, because that would be a waste of my limited time. I live my wonderful, rich life with the courage I never had until recently. Sometimes it takes darkness to see how we shine.

That's not to say that the last year has been easy, although this week, with the anniversary of my mum's death looming, that feeling is probably magnified. Being back in France for a holiday has helped all of us, including Dad, who flew in to meet us a few days ago. Nevertheless, the ache of loss is permanently inked on his broken heart. He misses her desperately. We all do.

I miss her smile. I miss her wisdom. I miss her cakes. And I miss her breezy humor, the one that never faltered no matter what life threw at her.

There is no doubt that it has been a difficult twelve months.

And sometimes my instincts get the better of me. Every time I drop a glass or feel short-tempered or forget the name of our new neighbor, the familiar rush of panic returns.

I've come to the conclusion that to live any other way would be impossible, given what I've seen and what I know. But I refuse to let the fear rule me. If there's one thing my mum taught me it's to go down fighting. I won't waste time on sadness.

It helps that we've had some nice things too. Moving house, for one thing. Once the sale of the château was finalized and Adam was back in the UK full-time, it became clear that having the three of us under one another's feet in one tiny terrace house wasn't going to work, especially now we have a son who's almost as tall as me and seems to fill the entire sofa every time he slumps down on it.

So we looked into trading up to somewhere bigger. I'll be honest: it was so much fun spending weekends nosing round other people's houses that I was almost sorry when we actually found somewhere.

We now live in a four-bedroom redbrick house in Didsbury, which we moved into three months ago. And I love it. I love the way its high windows allow brilliant light in every room, how the big old staircase looks as though it's been there since the dawn of time, and that every twist and knot of nature is ingrained in patterns on the heavy pine doors. And William's over the moon with his new bedroom, which is a shrine to *Match of the Day* — a taste-free zone with pictures of soccer balls and players on every available surface.

There's also the wedding to look forward to, the nature of which has been the source of some discussion, shall we say. I'd been thinking of something low-key, a hotel or posh pub with only a handful of us. Adam had been thinking something on the scale of the opening of the Rio Olympic Games.

We met somewhere in the middle and are planning a Christmas wedding, with fifty or so friends and family; not too small, but enough of an unabashed celebration to shout from the rooftops that we've found each other again.

It made sense on every level, because spending any more than we are on a wedding was out of the question. We're not broke, but the proceeds of the château sale are mainly being plowed into Adam's new business venture. He is setting himself up as a property developer and has found a beautiful but crumbling house last used as a nursing home. It's not as big as Château de Roussignol but has all the same issues it did when he first bought that — possibly more. There's nothing like a leaking roof and dry rot to really get my future husband going.

His plan is to renovate it, turn it into swish apartments and then either sell it on or rent them out himself, before looking for his next project. So there hasn't been much time for holidays, until now, when we've spent the last three weeks exploring France, ending up back here in the Dordogne. We spent last night in Château de Roussignol, as guests of the new owners.

It's lovely to be back and experience the nostalgic pang of all the sights and sounds of last year: the climbing flowers rampaging across the walls, the nightingales and the butterflies, the scented air and warm breeze.

As we follow the same waterfall trail that Enzo brought us on last year, I'm reminded how gorgeous it all is, flanked by damp, sweet-smelling grass and a necklace of ferns along its craggy rock side.

I'm also reminded about how ridiculously scary it was.

Not that you'd think it to look at William

as he plunges into the turquoise pools and is carried on his back by the undulating slipstream. I follow along dutifully at first, scrambling tentatively down the banks after them, squealing under my own breath every time my foot slips.

But although I've got goose bumps, I no longer feel cold. I am too busy splashing with my son, laughing with my fiancé, feeling the icy water against my hot cheeks, sunshine burning it away as soon as it touches my skin.

"Okay, you were right," I say to Adam. "This is quite good."

He glances at me. "*Quite* good? It's brilliant. You just need to get into it."

I'm about to reply when William comes wading up to me, running so fast through the water he almost falls flat on his face. "Mum! It's the big one next. Are you jumping in? Come *on.*"

"Your mum has absolutely nothing to prove," Adam tells him, then turns to me. "You really haven't."

I stride to the edge of the rock and look down, as water rushes past my feet, adrenaline racing inside the pit of my belly. I clamp my teeth together and inhale.

"We could do it together." William slips his hand in mine.

Adam clutches my other hand, and I lift my chin up until my eyes focus on the brilliant blue of the sky.

I have William on one side. I have Adam on the other. All we have to do is step off. As they start counting down to the moment when we plunge into the crashing water below, their hot fingers squeezing mine, I remind myself of one other thing I've learned in the last year.

When you are surrounded by love, you have nothing to fear.

AUTHOR'S NOTE

In December 2017, following several decades of research, scientists announced a major breakthrough in their work on Huntington's disease.

A human trial of a new "huntingtin-lowering" drug successfully and safely reduced levels of the harmful protein that causes HD. The research team at University College London says there is now real hope that the disease can be slowed or prevented altogether.

At the time of writing, vital long-term data is still needed, and the next wave of trials will set out to show whether lowering levels of huntingtin will change the course of the disease.

To learn more about Huntington's disease, or find out how you can help, visit the Huntington's Disease Association in the UK (www.hda.org.uk) or Huntington's Disease Society of America (www.hdsa.org).

ACKNOWLEDGMENTS

It's hard to know where to begin in thanking all those who've championed this book. But Sheila Crowley at Curtis Brown is a very good start. Without Sheila's ambition, energy and vision, *You Me Everything* would not exist, let alone have propelled my writing career in such an unexpected and wonderful direction.

Thanks also to Rebecca Ritchie for her enthusiastic support and all-round loveliness. And to Anne Bihan, whose hard work and passion for this novel is the reason it's being translated into so many languages.

One of the most frequently asked questions of any author is: "Would you like your book to become a movie?" I'd hardly allowed myself to fantasize about such a lofty ambition, until Luke Speed at Curtis Brown delivered the news that *You Me Everything* had been optioned for a film by Temple Hill's John Fischer. Huge thanks to both.

Thank you to my American editor, Pamela Dorman at Viking Penguin, with whom it's been an honor and pleasure to work. I'm grateful, not just for the opportunity to write for readers in the U.S., but also for the care she's lavished on this book and the immense amount I've learned from her during the editing process.

It has been a joy to work on the new direction of my writing with my long-standing publishers, Simon & Schuster UK. Thank you to Suzanne Baboneau, Jo Dickinson and Sara-Jade Virtue — for their commitment, unstinting hard work and, in S-J's case, gin. Thanks also to Clare Hey for her enthusiasm and direction on the first draft.

I'm indebted to the Huntington's Disease Association for their assistance when I was researching this book. It felt daunting until I came across Bill Crowder. His guidance and willingness to answer my endless questions was invaluable, as was the time generously given by Cath Stanley, who was kind enough to read through the final draft.

Thanks to the Huntington's Disease Society of America for allowing me to reproduce the section from their website featured in chapter 26.

Thank you to Frederique Polet, my editor from Presses de la Cité, for polishing up the

French dialogue, significantly improving my own efforts, which stemmed from a rather rusty A level.

Finally, thanks to my lovely family: Mark, Otis, Lucas, Isaac and my mum and dad. Also to Uncle Colin for the number crunching and to my brother, Stephen, for using his best lighting on my author photos.

ABOUT THE AUTHOR

You Me Everything is **Catherine Isaac**'s American debut. She lives in Liverpool, England.

The employees of Thorndike Press hope you have enjoyed this Large Print book. All our Thorndike, Wheeler, and Kennebec Large Print titles are designed for easy reading, and all our books are made to last. Other Thorndike Press Large Print books are available at your library, through selected bookstores, or directly from us.

For information about titles, please call:
(800) 223-1244

or visit our website at:
gale.com/thorndike

To share your comments, please write:
Publisher
Thorndike Press
10 Water St., Suite 310
Waterville, ME 04901